Praise for

"Sharfeddin has captured the family-like entanglements in a small community—by showing us what happens when those relationships begin to come apart."
—*Philadelphia Inquirer*

"A good old-fashioned cowboy tale that's as gritty as they come...a nice piece of emotional storytelling."
—*Chicago Tribune*

"An accomplished western...Authentic descriptions of the stark, isolated landscape, rustic conditions, and the bitter winter form a backdrop to the characters' turmoil, suggesting a timelessness that is only occasionally broken with touches of modernity....Impressive."
—*Publishers Weekly*

"Superbly crafted...Characters are wonderfully drawn.... Explores a wide range of themes related to sin and guilt, personal integrity, and the destructive power of prejudice. Essentially, however, this is a story about the miracle of love blossoming in unlikely places. Highly recommended." —*Library Journal* (starred review)

"Comparisons will be made to Kent Haruf....Sharfeddin's...eye for detail...and her unsentimental compassion for her characters...will entrance readers. The stark terrain is beautifully rendered."
—*Kirkus Reviews* (starred review)

"Striking . . . A deceptively simple contemporary western about two loners who have learned from their mistakes and flaws, but not overcome them."

—*Portsmouth (NH) Herald*, in selecting *Blackbelly* as one of the five top novels of 2005

"Juicy reading [with] some powerful themes: faith versus religion, sin and forgiveness."

—*San Diego Union-Tribune*

# MINERAL SPIRITS

"A thoughtful blend of crime (high-country style) and social commentary."          —*Seattle Times*

"Sharfeddin's writing is sharp, the characters real and the setting grittily recognizable to anyone who has driven a stretch of I-90 between Spokane and Missoula. There is no mistaking this place for any other, from the particular sound of the semis on the highway to the lonely geography and the decided chill in the air."          —*Oregonian*

"Sharfeddin has a masterly way of telling a hushed story. . . . *Mineral Spirits* is enjoyable not because we want to know who did it, but because we want to linger just a little more in the depth and complexity of the people who live in the steely blue cold winter of Montana. It's hard to let them go."          —*South Florida Sun-Sentinel*

"Sharfeddin's empathy for her characters and sense of place keep the reader engrossed. . . . A spellbinding, high-country thriller."          —*Kirkus Reviews* (starred review)

"A first-rate page-turner from start to finish."

—*Denver Post*

"A sharp, perceptive blend of crime and contemporary life issues...Tight and emotionally satisfying, this impressive novel should gain the author new readers."
—*Publishers Weekly*

"Exquisite use of language and detail...Neither a typical mystery nor a standard western, [*Mineral Spirits*] examines themes of love, hope, and aloneness-versus-loneliness....With its strong characters...as well as its good story line, the book will appeal to a wide variety of readers."
—*ForeWord*

"Masterly...Transcend[s] the conventions of a simple whodunit and plunge[s] the reader into a fully realized world populated by believable, complex and fascinating characters...*Mineral Spirits* explores important issues: poverty, longing, loss, sorrow and the consolations and discontents of life in a small town....[The novel is distinguished by the author's] sensitive and knowledgeable portrayal of Montana, her skillful storytelling and well-woven plot."
—*South Florida Sun-Sentinel*

"[Sharfeddin's] intimate understanding of the land and characters of the West comes across smoothly in her writing....Sharfeddin's writing is clear, precise and full of true-to-life details that bring the story to life. Her dialogue captures the wary tone heard throughout the remote West, imparting a sense of tension that keeps the reader hooked."
—*Lewiston (ID) Tribune*

"A hybrid modern-western-murder-mystery: taut, gritty and layered with enough subplots to keep the arc steady... One hopes for more explorations from Sharfeddin of the psyche of a modern West which still retains some vibrancy while struggling to maintain identity."
—*Booklist*

Also by Heather Sharfeddin

BLACKBELLY
MINERAL SPIRITS

# Windless Summer

## Heather Sharfeddin

DELTA TRADE PAPERBACKS

*Windless Summer* is a work of fiction. Names, characters, places and incidents either are the product of the author's imagination or are used fictitiously. Any resemblance to actual persons. living or dead, events, or locales is entirely coincidental.

A Delta Trade Paperback Original

Copyright © 2009 by Heather Sharfeddin

Published in the United States by Delta, an imprint of The Random House Publishing Group, a division of Random House, Inc., New York.

DELTA is a registered trademark of Random House, Inc., and the colophon is a trademark of Random House, Inc.

Library of Congress Cataloging-in-Publication Data

Sharfeddin, Heather.
Windless summer / Heather Sharfeddin.
p.   cm.
ISBN 978-0-385-34187-5 (trade pbk.) 978-0-440-33840-6 (ebook)
1. Hotelkeepers—Fiction. 2. City and town life—Fiction.
3. Washington (State)—Fiction. 4. Miracles—Fiction. I. Title.
PS3619.H35635W56 2009
813'.6—dc22                    2008028463

Printed in the United States of America

www.bantamdell.com

BVG 9 8 7 6 5 4 3 2 1

Book design by Catherine Leonardo

For Bobby. Thank you for believing.

1

BY THE TIME THE BEDS had been made, the toilets scrubbed, the carpets vacuumed but still stinking of cigarette smoke and french fries, dusk had painted his motel in dingy purple. Tom Jemmett stood at the edge of the swimming pool, inside the chain-link fence. The giant neon arrow was popping and buzzing to life above him. A hot breeze brought his hair up on its short ends and gave him a whiff of his own sweaty armpits. He stared down into the murky pool water at a fuzzy, disintegrating turd left there by those kids in room eight. He hadn't even found time to skim the bugs off the water in the last five days. The pool had always given Tom trouble. He'd have to drain the damn thing now.

He left it as it was, turning the *Pool Closed* sign to face the nearly empty parking lot and padlocking the gate. It was July, 104 degrees that afternoon on the bluffs overlooking the Columbia River in eastern Washington State. His guests, the few he could expect, would demand refunds.

In the office Tom's twelve-year-old daughter, Sienna, was wedged into a tight corner between the wall and the battered metal file cabinet. An electric fan blew the heat around the tiny room in slow, side-to-side repetition. He glanced at her and snapped the fan off.

"You can come out now," he said, dropping onto the stool and looking across the counter at the lobby. The plastic tree in the corner needed dusting, and he could smell this morning's now stale doughnuts, which were drawing flies to the half-round table along the wall.

Sienna emerged from the corner, pointing at the television. "Six," she said.

Tom looked at the photo on the news. A woman, bandaged, her face scratched and battered.

"Six," Sienna repeated.

He looked more closely and finally recalled the woman on TV. She'd splattered him with her complimentary morning coffee a few days back because it wasn't hot enough. He leaned over and turned the volume up to hear that she'd been mugged while visiting her sister in Portland.

"Yup, that's the woman," Tom said. Sienna's memory was extraordinary. She could point out a guest from a year ago and remember the exact room assignment. He wondered, though, if all people were nothing more than numbers to her. Did she remember their hair? The color of their eyes? Whether they smiled? "Serves her right. She was a vile woman," he said.

Sienna didn't seem to hear him. She picked up the glass paperweight on the counter and began running the tip of her finger around its circumference, tracing the vibrant colors beneath its surface. Tom imagined she'd wear a groove in the smooth glass for the time she spent enamored with it. He opened the daily ledger and checked off the rooms he'd rented the previous night as having been cleaned and made ready once again. As he jotted notes about broken lamps and leaky faucets, a tall, neatly dressed man lumbered in trailed by a squeaky-wheeled suitcase.

"Evening," Tom said, pushing the ledger aside.

"Got a room?"

"Twenty-six, actually."

"Twenty-six," Sienna echoed without looking up from the paperweight.

The man grinned with coffee-stained teeth. "I only need one."

"Pool is closed." Tom didn't want to be cleaning a room that he'd given a refund on.

"No problem. I haven't got time for swimming, anyway." He scrawled his name on the registration card that Tom slid toward him. Cologne wafted from the man, musky and thick. When he finished, he paid cash for the room, all the time smiling at Sienna, who acted as though he didn't exist. "Pretty girl you got there."

Tom grabbed the first key that caught his finger, glanced at it, and thought, *What a coincidence*. He handed it to his guest. "Room six. Just down the end of the parking lot in the corner." The man was still trying to catch his daughter's eye. Tom had recently become more aware of how people, men mostly, looked at Sienna. She was tall for her age and slender. She had her late mother's Latina complexion with eyes so dark they appeared black.

"She's quiet. Won't say hello," Tom said.

With a polite nod, the man was out the door and on his way, his wheeled suitcase skipping behind him on the cracked sidewalk.

Tom read the man's name on the registration card: Carl Warren of McCall, Idaho. From the looks of him, his tie and pressed trousers, Tom concluded he was a salesman. He turned to Sienna. Wanted to suggest that she say hello when people address her, but why would she start now?

Tom had checked in two more guests when Lauren Kent showed up shortly after eight o'clock and dropped a bucket of fried chicken on the counter.

"That smells good," he said, accepting a rushed peck on the lips. Lauren, a compact woman with the strength of a man, smelled like antiseptic soap. "I wasn't sure if we'd see you again. It's been...what...a week? Ten days?"

"I didn't think you'd be in the mood to cook." She brushed wisps of red hair off her sweaty face and her flat green eyes met his. "Not in this heat."

"I'm never in the mood to cook. Heat or otherwise. It's nice to see you again, though."

Lauren studied Tom, giving him her full attention and a warm, engaging grin. "If you weren't so damn good-looking I might be able to stay away for good."

"Is that your goal? To stay away?" He didn't know why he was making an issue of her long absence. He rather liked their loose relationship. So far Lauren hadn't demanded he consider marriage, an idea too remote and raw to imagine. But still, he needed a little more from a girlfriend than dropping by unannounced every seven to ten days. A little more regularity, consistency. He needed the female company to help him remember the important things in life.

"Hardly. But you do need an air conditioner. At least turn on the fan." Lauren didn't wait for Tom to do it, but rounded the counter and clicked it on with a jab of her finger.

Sienna froze as the air rushed over her bare shoulders.

Tom turned it off again. "You know she doesn't like the fan." He began placing napkins on the counter.

Lauren watched Tom without commenting, then her eyes drifted to Sienna. "Do we have to eat out here?" She gestured at the lobby and the large windows facing the parking lot and the highway beyond. The dimly lit units opposite the pool stood silent like ever-present spectators. "Can we take this back to the apartment where there's a little privacy?"

"It's a mess back there," he warned. "Spend all day cleaning other people's shit and I can't get to my own place."

"Shit," Sienna said, pulling the lid off the bucket of chicken.

Lauren scooped it away from her before the child could grab a piece.

Tom halted in the middle of restacking the napkins and looked at his daughter. He turned to Lauren. "She always tricks me into thinking she's not paying attention." He looked at Sienna again. "That's not polite and I shouldn't have said it. Don't use that word."

Sienna's gaze passed right through him.

"How are the dogs?" he asked Lauren as he set the night bell on the counter. She was right; eating in the lobby afforded them no privacy. He started for his apartment through the door at the back of the lobby.

"Cats today; it's Wednesday. Dogs on Mondays, Tuesdays, and Fridays."

"How are the cats, then?"

"Missing all their little testicles. That's how."

"You ever get tired of taking care of people's animals?" Tom found a sour sponge in the sink full of dishes and wiped the stickiness off the dinette table in his cramped kitchen.

"Sure," Lauren said. "Although, today we had a cat with a perforated diaphragm. That was interesting. Was shaken by a dog; lucky to survive."

Tom didn't say what was on his mind straight off. She scared him a little, Lauren. Ever since she kicked his ass at pool the night they met. He was a master with a cue stick and used to being the victor, but she'd surprised him. They'd bet a beer and when he paid up, she swallowed it down within two minutes and ordered another one on his tab. It was a miracle he'd even met Lauren; he got away from his motel so infrequently. They'd been through the topic of living arrangements before. But the last time was months back. He opened the fridge and handed her a Henry's beer.

"Could move in together," he said. He wasn't sure he really wanted that, but he knew she wouldn't agree to it, anyway.

"How do you figure?" Lauren splayed her fingers, sweeping her hand widely at the single-bedroom apartment crammed with odd piles of paper and scraps of plastic. Buttons littered every surface, tiny shirt buttons, large coat buttons, yellow buttons, brown buttons, green buttons. Some were stacked in neat rows along the edges of the furniture, some displayed in geometric patterns, all sorted by color and size. There was a red nylon sleeping bag flung across the sofa where Sienna slept when she finally got tired of whatever had gripped her attention during the day.

"Sienna's a bit of pack rat, I know. But we could make it work. This button phase will pass." He turned to his daughter, who was cramming a drumstick into her mouth, grease oozing over her chin like a toddler. "You'd pick up your stuff, wouldn't you, Sienna?"

The child said nothing, and Lauren nodded as if she'd made her point.

"I'd suggest my place, but that wouldn't be practical with trying to run a motel seven miles away. Besides, Rocket is too crowded for a guy like you."

Tom believed Lauren was grasping for excuses now. Rocket was an eight-block stretch along Highway 14, with a school, a post office that doubled as the newspaper office for *The Rocket Rocket,* an IGA, and three bars. He imagined Lauren's reluctance had a little to do with her snobbish sense of style and design, evident in her carefully renovated bungalow, a place that set him on edge because he was afraid to touch anything, and a lot to do with his daughter. Lauren had been solicitous of Sienna in the beginning, but over the months her interaction with the child had turned to curt little statements spoken loudly, as if Sienna were deaf. They'd only been dating about eight months, but Tom had hoped that having a woman around might be good for Sienna. Lauren and Sienna's relationship had been more disappointing to him than he'd been willing to admit, and perhaps that was why he was pushing the issue. Some misguided hope that it would get better if they spent more time together. Wiping Sienna's chin with a napkin, he wondered if he even liked Lauren anymore. Maybe he shouldn't be seeing other people. Being tied to a business like his wasn't exactly conducive to meeting women or having a rich and varied love life.

"How long have we been dating?" he asked against his own better judgment.

Lauren sighed. "Can we talk about this later?"

"Later, when?"

"Just later."

☀

Tom awoke well after sunup, alone in bed. He stared at the ceiling. A note lay on the pillow next to him, but he didn't pick it up. He'd dreamed of Maria again. Dreamed she was still alive, still lying next to him in this bed. He'd reached an arm around her shoulder and cupped her small breast in his hand, where he held it like some glorious treasure. The memory caused an ache in the center of his chest. Had it been Lauren's breast he'd caressed in the night, believing it was his dead wife's?

Tom became suddenly aware of the low rumble of a man's voice. He flew from bed, turning a circle in the tiny bedroom as he searched for his pants. Dressing in haste, he whisked up the note and rushed out into the living room, where he found the door between his apartment and the lobby standing open.

His salesman guest, Carl Warren, was talking to someone. Tom searched for his daughter, but her sleeping bag was in a crumple on the floor.

In the lobby, Tom found the coffee made, the doughnuts set out for his three guests. "Sienna?" he called. "Sienna?"

"She's right here," Carl Warren said, pointing at the stool behind the counter. Tom's daughter was carefully perusing the pages of a large book with bright pictures. "She's reading about Africa. I sell educational books for early readers." He pulled out a business card and handed it to Tom. "National Foundation for Literacy," Carl said. "Mostly I visit rural areas that don't have access to what urban kids have."

Tom let his breath out, aware for the first time that he'd been holding it. He took the business card, but didn't read it. Instead, he opened the now-crumpled note from Lauren.

*Sleep in, baby. I'll take care of the*
*coffee & doughnuts today. Luv, L.*

He blinked at the words. Her gesture stung, only because he'd believed in that split second that Sienna had done the coffee. A silly idea.

"Is it okay if she keeps it?" Carl asked.

"Huh?"

"The book. Can she keep it? No charge."

"Oh." Tom watched Sienna a moment. "It would... she doesn't..."

"Hey, it's okay if she just wants to look at the pictures. It's a children's book, has lots of pictures. It's okay."

Tom's stomach sank. Rare as these moments of understanding from complete strangers were, they still happened often enough that Tom believed he should know how to handle them. Should be used to them. But he never got accustomed to the unexpected urge to break down and cry. And he resented that a stranger's kindness could make him feel that way.

"She's a special girl. I don't mean any harm. I just want to share the world with her," Carl Warren said quietly. The man mercifully didn't look Tom in the eye, but kept his gaze on Sienna, who seemed enchanted with the book.

"Thank you," Tom croaked.

2

### When Will the Wind Return?

Hap Mitsui blotted the fresh ink of his front-page headline in *The Rocket*. "When indeed?" he said with a mix of satisfaction at pinpointing the issue on everyone's mind, a not-so-difficult feat for a weekly paper in a town where the economy is driven by the weather, and frustration at the drop in ad sales *because* of the weather.

"That's a dumb question." Charlene, the postmistress, was looking over his shoulder. "Unless you have an answer." She stepped back and squinted at him suspiciously. "And I'm sure you don't."

"It's rhetorical."

"It's dumb."

"Don't you have mail to sort or something?" Hap heaved a bundle of papers onto his shoulder and carried them out to his Econoline van in the post office parking lot. The city leased him half the building for his newspaper, but the space didn't include walls. So he and Charlene shared the giant mail-sorting room in the back. When he returned, Charlene was slipping folded newspapers into the honeycomb of mailboxes that took up the west wall. He paused to watch her. She was too pretty and young, barely twenty-nine, to be stuck in Rocket, sorting mail. She was wasting her youth windsurfing and carousing with out-of-town boys when she should've been at university studying to be something. She'd let her hair down today and the streaks of blonde against her tan arms repeatedly drew Hap's eyes to her figure. He wished he wasn't well past twice her age. He'd like to take her out for dinner somewhere nice. Show her how a gentleman behaves, not like these yahoos with their sailboards and pot pipes. Here today, gone tomorrow, and more than happy to whisper sweet nothings in Charlene's lonely ear. But he guessed that with her history, loneliness was a condition she was condemned to, and nothing would ever change that.

Anyway, Hap was just glad to have her company during the day. The last postman he'd shared this room with was a mean old dog who wouldn't give Hap the time of day. Hap had first thought it was his Japanese surname, but over the years Hap had come to understand that the old man he shared his office with was an equal-opportunity grinch.

"When *is* the wind going to return?" Charlene said when she finished depositing the newspapers he'd given her into each of the mailboxes along the wall. "This sucks, all this calm and quiet. I haven't been on the water in three weeks, except that Sunday up in Hood River. Even then, it was just a breeze. Nothing to get your sails up. The place is a friggin ghost town."

"Hood River?"

"No. Here." She gestured past the small entryway at the quiet street beyond, which should have been teeming with windsurfers this time of year. "Hood River still has *charm*." She made exaggerated quote marks in the air.

"It's a nice place."

"It's a friggin yuppie haven. A *lovely day* for rich people from Portland."

"I wish you'd quit using that word." Hap hoisted a second stack of papers onto his shoulder.

"What? *Friggin?*"

He grimaced as he passed.

"I only use that word because you don't like it when I say *fucking*."

"Thank you," he called over his shoulder. "Thank you for that!"

☀

Hap eased his van along the side streets of Rocket— Chemeketa, Chemawa, Siletz, Chinook, Grand Ronde. Named after Indian tribes severely dwindling or now vanished altogether from the Pacific Northwest landscape. He drove down the left side, pausing at each mailbox and sliding in a paper. A few residents sat on porches, trying to escape the heat inside their tiny, poorly ventilated houses. Some waved, but no one ran down to their box in excited anticipation of the latest *Rocket*. Rocket sat far to the east of the confluence of the Klickitat and Columbia rivers. It was once a rail stop, though not any longer. It had never been a prime spot, even when the logging industry was at its peak. The town had been built in the 1920s, and its dwellings were proof of its legacy. Asbestos shingle siding, one or two bedrooms, a single bath retrofitted with a shower. Tacked-on additions ruined what little style they might've possessed.

Rocket had enjoyed a quiet revitalization after thrill-seeking young men discovered that the wind was a commodity rather than a liability. But even with that, the first house over two thousand square feet ever built in Rocket was only ten years old and wasn't really in Rocket. It sat atop a tall bluff above town, a mansion of six thousand square feet with a sweeping southwesterly view of the Oregon side of the river, Mount Hood, and the constantly changing colors of the Columbia Gorge. Hap had run a story on it when it was built. Its mysterious owners declined to be interviewed, and a decade later no one knew anything more about them than that their last name was Tibble.

On the north side of Main Street, Hap delivered papers to Rocket's elite, the veterinarian and the handful of professional folks who called the place home. Their dwellings were modest by Portland standards, but well kept in their muted colors and freshly stained fences. They faced the city park and the neighborhood stretched about three blocks before abruptly ending in the industrial section with its wrecking yard and taxidermy outfit. Hap parked on the main strip in downtown and walked along the shops and storefronts, delivering papers. The brick buildings along that short bit of Main Street were charmingly decorated with colorful windsocks and whirligigs, but all hung limply in the windless heat. Mike Petrich sat behind his counter in the kite shop, eating a French dip sandwich as he waited for tourists who were nowhere in sight.

"Afternoon, Mike," Hap hollered on his way past.

Mike waved, but didn't get up.

Hap walked past the Rocket Antiques store without looking in. He enjoyed relics and oddities from the past, but found Dillard Meek a hard man to abide. Dillard talked exhaustively about his own breadth of knowledge, his unmatched skill, his professional equipment. The man never did anything halfway. Or so he liked people to believe. It was all BS, in Hap's opinion, propped up by a handful of technical details that Dillard had gleaned from others here and there or surfing the Internet. When he took up rockhounding, he bought expensive cutters and polishers and books, and bored everyone senseless with long, dry geological history lectures about the Columbia Gorge. As if the rest of Rocket's residents had been living under one of the very rocks Dillard hacked out of the earth. Everyone knew the cliffs were basalt. Everyone knew they were formed by volcanic eruptions millions of years ago. Everyone knew that the gorge had been blasted out by Ice Age floods from Lake Missoula. And because of that, Dillard Meek instinctively pissed Hap off before the man could even open his mouth.

At the Windy Point Diner, Hap filled the paper box in the entryway near the hostess stand, then walked to the counter and waited for Linda Hendricks to show up with coffee. The place was empty except for a table of elderly people, their Bibles laid out in front of them, their dishes smeared with the remnants of pie and shoved to the center. Hap had nodded on his way past, but they were deep in discussion and didn't notice him. He took a stool and studied, not for the first time, the diner's décor. It had been built in the seventies with drab wood paneling and orange vinyl booths, and no one had bothered to modernize it during the intervening years. It had changed hands at least six times since Hap first arrived in Rocket. He didn't often patronize the place, except for a cup of coffee on his weekly news drop. It depressed him with its dated bleakness. Especially because it sat atop an overlook where diners ought to have been entertained by windsurfers as they supped, but the architect or the builder or someone had not bothered to consider the possibilities when positioning the building, and its big windows looked out on the back side of the wrecking yard and Highway 14 beyond. But Hap liked Linda, the diner's newest proprietor. She was an honest, hardworking woman who'd moved here with her two young sons after losing her husband in a car accident in Bothel. She was as open with her personal life as she was adept at balancing dinner plates, and she'd only been in town a few days before the entire population of Rocket knew she'd spent every last cent of her husband's life insurance to purchase the place.

"Afternoon, Hap." Linda grabbed a mug from under the counter and filled it with black coffee. She always insisted on pouring him a cup and never charged for it. "What's the news today?"

"Same as yesterday and the day before."

"I'm about ready to call up the guy who sold me this place and demand a refund. Where are my windsurfers?" She swept a hand out at the nearly empty dining room.

"In South America, or Hawaii, or some other marvelously windy place."

"Guthry was in here last night, he comes every Wednesday for the chicken fried steak special, and he said his auto shop is suffering bad."

"Yeah, I'd say we're all in this together."

"Guthry thinks it's global warming. Says it's why they're getting snow in Los Angeles and polar bears are going extinct." She set the coffeepot down and placed a menu on the counter next to Hap. She never did that, and today it made him feel obligated to order something. He turned and looked at the Bible study table.

"Was that cherry pie you served them?"

She grinned.

"Looks good. I'll have a slice, if you've got any left."

Linda disappeared into the kitchen as Hap rubbed his large belly. He'd sworn off sweets in an attempt at losing a few pounds, but he reasoned it was for a good cause.

Linda returned and set down an enormous wedge of cherry pie smothered in vanilla ice cream.

"Are you managing to make ends meet?" Hap asked as he took a bite. The cherries were just right, a little tart, making the glands in his throat seize up in that painfully delicious way.

She sighed and leaned against the counter. "I'll get by."

Hap could hear the doubt in her voice, and he wished he could help. He hated the idea of Linda losing her business, and Rocket losing another resident.

☼

After delivering his papers in town, Hap headed east on Highway 14 along the windswept bluffs above the river. The grassy plateau had paled to the color of bone under the punishing sun, the black basalt cliffs standing in high relief to his left. The Columbia glimmered, its surface flat, save for the wake of a solitary barge headed for Portland. Hap missed the windsurfers for the way their colorful sails danced across the water. Even if they were mostly just a bunch of beach bums, he made a general habit of stopping along the highway to enjoy their acrobatics as dozens, sometimes hundreds, zigzagged across the water. The thrill of watching them fly off the waves and flip over in an airborne loop still made his palms tingle. Their absence this year was like spring without blossoms.

At the Jemmett Motel, Hap pulled up in front of the lobby and grabbed a stack of papers. A couple of kids shrieked and splashed in the pool as their overweight mother lounged in her bikini. Tom emerged from one of the rooms with a green spray bottle in his hand. He waved at Hap and followed him into the lobby.

"How's business?" Hap said, dropping the papers on the small table by the door.

Tom gave him a baleful look. "Take a wild guess."

"Bad. But at least you're not alone." He made a mental note to stop asking people that asinine question.

"Glad to hear I won't be the only one in the poorhouse this fall. I'll have my fellow Rocketeers to keep me company."

Hap smiled at Sienna, but she was studying the pages of a huge book. "What's that you've got?"

She didn't respond.

Tom turned the fan on in the lobby, which caused her head to snap up, a look of anguish on her face. "Go back to the apartment, sweetie," he said to Sienna. "It's too hot not to have the fan on."

When she didn't respond to Tom, he reached down and lifted her chin, repeating himself. Sienna watched his mouth intently, as if reading his lips, then obeyed without a word or a glance in Hap's direction.

"You hear about that guy who won the lottery?" Tom asked as he disappeared into the apartment. When he emerged a moment later with pale-green bottles of Henry's, he was grinning. He thrust one at Hap.

This was the last stop on Hap's delivery route and the one he most looked forward to. Tom always had a beer and a few minutes to spare. The two had forged a solid friendship through these weekly paper drops.

"Ninety-eight million bucks!" Tom whistled.

Hap squeezed the twist top and dropped the cap on the counter. The first sip was like dipping into heaven, cool and sharp.

"That was Carl Warren from McCall, Idaho," Tom went on. "He stayed here about a week back. Nice guy. He gave Sienna that book she was looking at."

"I'd like to win the lottery."

Tom nodded. "What would you do with the money?"

"I don't know. Maybe persuade Charlene to run off with me. I think the money would be a powerful entice-ment for her. She'd forget I'm an old man."

"Charlene's practically a kid."

"She's working on thirty." Working on thirty, but lived enough life for sixty, Hap thought. Then he wondered if Tom knew about Charlene's past. No one ever talked about it. "You know . . . you might want to get on that."

"What?"

"A guy like you . . ." Hap pointed his beer bottle at Tom's chest.

"Naw. What would she want with a forty-five-year-old man chained to a fleabag motel? Besides, I've got a girlfriend. Most of the time, anyway."

"What's that mean?"

"Nothing."

Hap thought about Lauren Kent, but he couldn't grasp what Tom saw in her. The town veterinarian and owner of the Rocket Pet Clinic, tough and stout, she was no-nonsense to the point of brutal. A woman of hard edges, Lauren was. Hap conceded that he was a little envious of Tom for his standing with the local women. He'd overheard plenty of post office conversations about Tom, usually instigated by Charlene. The women all commented on his impressive height, his flaxen hair, his well-toned physique. They speculated about his wounded soul, a poor widower left to care for a girl child alone. Yet, Tom chose to date Lauren Kent. Why?

"That pool looks awfully nice today," Hap said, choosing a new subject. "How do you keep from spending all day in it?"

"Shoulda seen it a few days ago. Barf city!" Tom leaned on the counter and sipped his beer. "I thought that pool was an amenity when I bought the place."

Hap nodded.

"Not! It's a money pit. And the liability insurance, Lord Almighty! I'm thinking about having it filled in."

They talked awhile about the latest news. Tom didn't hide the fact that he didn't read *The Rocket*. He claimed he didn't have time. So Hap usually caught him up on the doings around town: who'd been arrested for what, and new businesses like Yolanda's Used Books, which had just opened. Sometimes he included the most interesting classified ads, the '95 Ford 4×4 Steve Wittenberg listed for $6,000, or the antique Victorian parlor set that Roberta Frink was asking $12,000 for.

Tom shook his head in disbelief. "Who's gonna pay that kind of money for used furniture?"

"It's antique," Hap said with a wry smile as he finished his beer. "She probably consulted Dillard Meek about it."

Tom rolled his eyes.

"Well, I better get back to town."

"Wish Yolanda good luck for me, whoever she is." Tom scooped up the empty bottles and set them on the floor next to the trash can. "Wonder who she's planning to sell books to, anyway. I went in to pick up my mail the other day and the place was a ghost town. Never seen it so deserted, not even in January. Couldn't have been more than three cars parked on Main."

Hap thought that was an exaggeration. There probably wasn't anywhere near that many.

"I guess I better get back to work, too. Though at the rate I'm renting rooms I could leave them dirty until the end of the summer and still not run out."

Hap paused in the doorway and looked back at Tom. "Why don't you come into town sometime? Have a beer down at the tavern, shoot some pool. I could use the company."

Tom glanced over his shoulder at the open door to the apartment, then back at Hap. "Maybe... sometime."

Hap understood without Tom having to say. "Maybe that girlfriend of yours could be persuaded to stay with Sienna once in a while. Everybody needs a break now and then."

Tom scowled.

"Just a thought." Hap stepped out into the smothering heat, dreading the temperature awaiting him inside the van. As he pulled out of the gravel parking lot and back onto Highway 14, the steering wheel scalding his hands, he struggled between regretting his comment and a sense of satisfaction for having pointed out that Lauren Kent wasn't exactly stepmother material, at least not what he knew of her, and especially not for a girl like Sienna.

☼

"Sienna? Sienna, look at me." Tom waited for his daughter to hear him and obey, but ended up reaching across the dinette table and gently lifting her chin out of the book. "Look at Daddy."

She squirmed away from his touch.

"I want you to wash the dishes. Do you understand me?" He used an assertive but patient tone.

Sienna stared across the supper dishes at his chin. The setting sun streamed through the dirty kitchen window, lighting her hair in rich auburn.

"Sienna, answer me. Do you understand what I just asked you to do?" He waited, but she said nothing. The smell of spaghetti grease and garlic wafted off the plates. "Sienna, what do you say?"

She looked at the ceiling.

"Sienna?"

Finally, she locked in on his face, but didn't quite make eye contact. "Wash dishes."

"Yes," he praised. "Very good. That's great. Wash the dishes."

Sienna stood off her chair and began running water into the sink.

"I love you," he said. "Do you love me?" He watched her add too much soap to the water, wishing that just once she would say that she did.

The bell rang in the lobby and Tom got to his feet. "That's a good girl. Wash the dishes while I go see who that is."

At the front desk, Tom found a stern-faced woman who appeared to be sniffing the corners of the room.

"Can I help you?"

She rounded on him, her tiny eyes boring into his chest. "How many stars is this place?"

Tom looked out at the neon motel sign with its aqua bowling-style stars. "The sign has three, but I think that's a holdover from when the place was new back in the sixties."

"Very funny." She ran her finger down the Formica countertop between them and pulled the tip up to her nose to inspect.

Tom pondered whether he could afford to tell off a potential guest. He needed the money badly, and that made him want to tell her off all the more. "The place is old, but it's clean. You'll find the beds comfortable, but the bedspreads and artwork out of style. The pool was drained and refilled less than a week ago, and the highway doesn't get much traffic after dark. Rooms are fifty-nine a night, and it includes coffee and doughnuts in the morning."

She tilted her round head to the side and listened to Tom's description skeptically. Her mousy hair fell limply to her shoulders, where dandruff speckled her navy blouse. He looked past her at the twenty-year-old station wagon in the turnaround and wondered where she got the nerve to be concerned about how many stars his motel rated.

"I don't know," she said, looking around the lobby again. "Is there another place to stay around here?"

Tom smiled. "No. And I guess that means you've got a long drive ahead of you, so you better get going now." To hell with her, he thought.

She gaped at him. "Are you suggesting that you won't rent me a room?"

"Look, what you see is what you get. You want a room or not?"

The woman huffed indignantly. "I guess I have no choice but to take it."

"Fine," he said, handing her a registration card.

"I want a ground-floor room, though. Something convenient to the parking lot. I'm not dragging my stuff up a flight of stairs. And quiet, too."

"Yes, ma'am." He reached for a key. "This one's on the ground floor, down at the end." He pointed out the window at the unit in the far corner.

☀

As Tom finished with his paperwork he glimpsed his newest guest, Helen Simpson, lugging her suitcase out of her car and into room six. *Witch,* he thought. But he became suddenly aware of the sound of running water. His stomach dropped and he darted back into the apartment, slipped on the sopping linoleum, and landed hard on his back. Water soaked into his jeans and shirt, and as he struggled to his feet he saw dead bugs floating across the kitchen floor, dislodged from their hidden graves in the crevices under the cabinets.

Sienna sat at the table, her face inches above her book while the kitchen faucet poured on relentlessly.

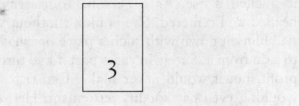

3

LAUREN KENT STOOD in the brightly lit waiting area of the clinic and opened a thank-you card from a patient whose dog she had saved from heartworms. Belinda, her new receptionist, was late and it was only her third day. Lauren had had reservations about the woman, round as a bowling ball and well over fifty, when she hired her. She had to remind herself during the interview that to not give Belinda a chance would amount to age discrimination. Let her prove out, she'd told herself. Besides, Belinda was the only applicant she had to choose from at the time.

Lauren had considered referring Belinda to Tom. He needed help worse than she did. But he wouldn't hire anyone in this economy and she knew it. She understood that it wasn't just Tom being cheap, though she suspected that was part of it. His business was much more affected by the lack of wind than hers, but she hadn't been immune, with families moving away and people putting off less urgent care for their pets.

Lauren contemplated Tom's motel, not for the first time. It wasn't even a *ho*tel. The place looked like every seedy, nasty, fourth-rate dive she'd ever driven past in any lonely little town or desolate stretch of highway. And it smelled worse. As a person, Tom seemed so level-headed and centered. She couldn't fathom why he had tied himself down with such a place or what he'd hoped to gain from it. Surely in years past it had turned a decent profit, but it would never make Tom rich. It probably wouldn't even pay for his retirement. He had so much more potential. She hated that motel as much as she believed she loved Tom. A man devoted to his dead wife and broken daughter the way fairy-tale fathers are devoted to their underdog children. Fiercely.

"Good morning." Belinda bustled in from the front parking lot reserved for customers, clanging the bell over the door.

"Morning," Lauren said.

"Sorry I'm late."

Lauren looked down at the letter in her hand, wondering if she should say something now, or wait until she could do it gently. She'd alienated enough friends and employees through the years by saying what was on her mind to second-guess her judgment in situations like this. But then again, she thought . . .

"This is only your third day." Lauren didn't look up as she said it, but tried to sound polite.

"I know and I'm really sorry. Roger is off today and I just got carried away chatting over breakfast."

"Well, I need you here at eight. Please try harder to watch the time."

"I will. I promise," Belinda said as she sank into the seat behind the reception desk, causing the chair to pop and squeak under the strain, and booted up the computer. "I'll pull the files for today's appointments right away."

"Thanks," Lauren said, heading down the long hallway toward the exam and operating rooms. She paused and turned. "Oh, and I'd appreciate it if you'd park behind the building. You can use the back door. That's where the staff comes in."

Belinda nodded, frowning down at her hands as she smoothed the wrinkles from her skirt.

☼

Tom wiped his towel across the steamy bathroom mirror and examined the large purple crescent on his left hip. Twisting to either side sent sharp stabbing pains through his back, and his elbow was tender and stiff. He eased into his clothes, skipping his morning shave, and made his way out to the lobby. It was too early for the sun, and his electric motel sign stood radiant against a lavender sky. As he made the morning coffee he remembered that he was supposed to call the bakery yesterday and renew his order. It irked him that Petra Osterlundt, the bakery owner, expected him to confirm his daily doughnut order on the fifteenth of each month. It must be a German thing, he thought. Why wouldn't I want doughnuts every day? I'm running a motel here.

"Customer service is a lost institution," he said aloud. "She should deliver my doughnuts unless I call and cancel them, not the other way around." He paused and looked behind him to make sure no one stood watching as he talked to himself. Nobody eats them anyway, he thought. Just as that comforting idea flitted through his mind, Helen Simpson emerged from room six and loaded her suitcase into her station wagon. Tom groaned.

The woman came into the lobby like a hurricane, slapping the door against the plastic tree in the corner. "This place is a dump," she announced. "The room stunk like cigarette smoke and the carpet is stained. Don't you clean?"

Tom said nothing, but pulled his ledger out to review his to-do list for the day.

She glanced around, immediately recognizing the absence of morning confections. "I thought you said there were doughnuts. Is this some kind of game you play? Tell people they get doughnuts so you can sell them a room, then conveniently run out?"

"I didn't run out, ma'am. The bakery didn't deliver them this morning."

She stared at Tom a long while, as if expecting him to do something. He turned his attention back to the ledger. The only saving grace about not having very many guests was that he'd have the rooms cleaned within an hour and could move on to some of the bigger maintenance tasks. Last summer during the windsurfing festival it took him all day to clean the twenty-six-room motel. Windsurfers were mostly young, free spirits. Too free to worry about the cost of the broken bedsprings they left behind, the towels they took with them, or the expense of steam-cleaning various forms of goo out of the carpets.

"Aren't you going to refund my money?" Ms. Simpson finally said.

He looked up, astonished. "Because I don't have doughnuts?"

"It wasn't just that, obviously. The room was awful. I want a refund." She set her purse down on the counter with a thud.

"I'm sorry about the doughnuts, ma'am. I strive to provide my guests with the best possible service. Sometimes my vendors don't have the same goal in mind."

"I already told you it's not just the doughnuts."

Tom stood. "Look, lady, I'm not giving you a refund. You slept the whole night in that room and I didn't hear a word of complaint from you until you found out there were no doughnuts."

"I didn't have time to complain."

"You had all night."

The woman tensed and looked out the lobby door at her car parked in the turnaround. "You promised coffee and doughnuts. It was part of the room price."

"You don't *need* any doughnuts," Tom whispered under his breath.

"What did you say?"

Tom could think of plenty more to say, but didn't dare open his mouth, amazed by the sudden depth of his fury.

"What are you implying?" she growled.

Tom rounded the counter into the lobby. He walked straight to the coffeepot, filled a Styrofoam cup, handed it to Helen Simpson, and guided her by the elbow out the front door to her waiting car.

"Bye now," he said and pulled the door shut behind him.

She stood on the sidewalk stunned. She spun a circle, her face turning shades of violet and plum to match her terry-cloth pantsuit. She looked back at Tom, speechless.

He dropped back onto his stool and returned to his list, his hands shaking with anger. He didn't look up again until he heard the crash. Remembering it later, the sound of skidding tires whining across the asphalt is what stood out, then the *pop* and *crunch* of Helen Simpson's station wagon being flattened like a beer can. A semi carrying Hermiston watermelons had skidded into the ditch and flipped over, releasing its cargo of green-striped fruit. Tom stared out at the mangle of metal and bouncing fruit in disbelief. The cloud of hot smoking rubber was burning his nostrils before he found the phone to call 911.

☀

Tom stood by as the ambulance drove away with Helen Simpson sheathed in the back on a stretcher. The driver wasn't in any particular hurry. Tom had to look away when they finally freed her bloody corpse from the car. Police cruisers now jammed his parking lot, abandoned at odd angles, their radios squawking information as the officers paced the accident site, circled scraps of metal with fluorescent pink paint, and interrogated the truck driver until the man broke down and cried. The sweet aroma of watermelon drifted up from hundreds of broken rinds scattered across the highway. An occasional passerby edged his car along the far shoulder, further pulverizing the fruit.

"She pulled right out in front of me," the truck driver kept insisting. He was in his early sixties and had about three days' growth on a gray and red beard. His pale eyes watered, and his forehead had turned black and purple in the time since he'd climbed from the wreckage. "How could she have missed me? I was right there," he kept asking, gesturing with his hand. "I tried to stop, but she was so close. I couldn't even swerve out of the way."

Tom swallowed a hard lump. Had he caused this? Had he rushed her out of his lobby and into oncoming traffic just because of a stupid doughnut?

Hap Mitsui pulled in and parked next to the swimming pool. He slid out of the van wearing gray sweatpants and a tank top. He walked over to Tom with a notepad in his hand. "Tom, I heard on the scanner there was a wreck. What happened?"

"I just heard it. Didn't see it." The same explanation Tom had given the police, six times.

"The driver injured?"

It seemed a bizarre question to Tom, standing there in front of the mangled station wagon. He nodded, then shook his head, then nodded again. He felt queasy.

Hap's eyebrows went up as he interpreted Tom's response. "Dead?"

Tom didn't answer. Had he caused this? "I gotta go check on Sienna," he said.

Hap interviewed Sheriff Turnbull, took photos of the smashed car, the highway painted pink with melons, and the upended semi. He gathered names, assuring Turnbull that the next edition of *The Rocket* wasn't due out for another few days, giving the police plenty of time to notify next of kin. He interviewed the trucker, a man named Will Barton from Spokane. Hap had recently run a story on depression, and among those he'd interviewed was a man who'd accidentally backed over a child, killing her. The tragedy had happened more than two decades ago but, looking into the subject's haunted eyes, Hap had understood that time can't dull the pain and guilt of a memory like that. And he detected the seeds of similar despair in Will Barton's eyes now.

He closed his notepad and placed a hand on Barton's shoulder. "It wasn't your fault."

Will Barton brushed away tears as he shook his head and stared at the ground, his jaw working.

"You can't let this eat you up," Hap said, more forcefully than he intended. "This isn't your fault."

The man didn't answer.

"Can I give you a lift somewhere?"

"No. I've a got a wrecker coming for the truck," the man said quietly.

Hap fished in his pocket for a business card and held it out to the trucker. It seemed crass, a newspaper editor's card. As if he were only looking for a juicy story. "I'm going to write that it wasn't your fault. I'm going to tell the truth."

Will Barton took the card and slipped it into his breast pocket without looking at it. He turned, and Hap watched the man walk away with his head bowed and his hands in his pockets.

Inside the lobby of the Jemmett Motel, Hap found Tom

dazed and staring out the window. "May I have some of that coffee?" he asked as the sharp aroma hit him.

"Help yourself." Tom perched on his stool, his elbows on the counter, his chin resting in his hands.

"How long was this woman a guest of yours?"

"One night."

Hap nodded and blew steam off his coffee. It was bitter and burned his tongue, but he was glad to have the caffeine. He could feel a headache spawning behind his eyes. "Can you say anything about her? For the article. Anything at all?"

Tom stared out the window at the highway. The sun was well up now, and the smell of baking watermelon seeped into the lobby.

Hap waited.

Tom shifted on his stool. "She ... liked doughnuts."

☀

The two rooms Tom had rented the night before Helen Simpson died remained dirty, though his guests had long checked out. He sat in the lobby most of the morning, watching Sienna snap and unsnap the clasp on her change-purse one hundred times, then fall onto the yellow sofa and study each page of her book. He hadn't eaten, and he hadn't fed his daughter, either. The book's spine was broken now, and the cover scuffed. He saw that she preferred the animals, studying photos of zebras and rat snakes far longer than pictures of people or maps.

"Sienna, what do you like about that book?" he asked.

She continued to finger a picture of a porcupine.

"Sienna, I asked you a question. What do you say?" He waited. "Sienna?"

Nothing.

"*Sienna!*" he erupted, standing off the stool. "Answer me!"

Her head snapped up, eyes round.

"Answer me when I talk to you, damn it. I'm talking to you. Answer me."

She stared at him. He'd frightened her, he could see that. He ran his hands over his head and then pressed his palms against his eyes, feeling like a jerk. She doesn't understand, he told himself. Don't take it out on her. He rubbed fiercely, until his eyes leaked at the corners. When he took his hands away his vision was blurred. Sienna was still watching him.

"Try to answer me when I talk to you, Sienna," he said. "What do you like about that book?"

She looked at the book, then back at him, then at the book again. "Colors. Animal colors."

Tom sat down again, exhausted and ashamed. He hadn't raised his voice to her in nearly three months. Not since he'd started seeing Dr. Taglione at the Hood River Mental Health Clinic. He'd always known yelling at Sienna didn't yield the behavior he wanted. Worse, it made her retreat deeper into her silent world. He'd counseled his wife on this very fact so many times before her death, cautioning her not to yell at the child. But today he just couldn't help himself. He gave Sienna a weak smile. "Which animals do you like best?"

She looked again at the book, as if confounded by the question.

"Do you like lions and cheetahs, or antelope? Do you have a favorite?"

"Cheetahs," she said, still focused on the book.

He imagined she was only parroting the word, maybe because it was unusual. She wasn't answering his question. Her limited vocabulary didn't include cheetahs.

"I'll buy you a cheetah someday, sweetie."

She smiled, a response so rare he could probably count the number of times he'd seen it. Tom wanted to hug her, hold her so tight. Never let her go. But he couldn't do that, either. She'd squirm away, screeching. He had never held his little girl, not in the way a parent yearns to. The only touch they shared was the weekly catfight to bathe her. He looked down at his arm and the purpled outline of her teeth, uppers and lowers, in an arching circle on his forearm. The scratches and bite marks drew curious stares from strangers. People in town simply pretended not to see them. Now that Sienna was bigger, Tom took her in the shower with him. The previous morning he'd pinned her arms to her sides while shampooing her hair with his free hand. She'd screamed so loud he was certain his few guests had heard, even though they were on the opposite end of the building. It wasn't until he soaped up the washcloth and did the thing no upstanding father wants to do to his twelve-year-old daughter that she bit him. As he scrubbed her crotch in a frenzy to get it over with, her teeth sank deep into his flesh. So deep he nearly relented. But he'd never get the soap rinsed off if he let go. He had only recently begun wearing his swim trunks into the shower because she'd grabbed hold of his testicles a month before and nearly caused him to pass out.

He looked at her now, studying the picture of an electric-pink flamingo, and wondered what events she remembered. Did she think about their bath routine? Did she have memories of her mother? Was she capable of looking back with any sort of recognition or understanding? For all his dreams and wishes, this, he hoped, she could not do.

☀

Hap crafted his story for *The Rocket* as Charlene greeted every postal patron with the news about Helen

Simpson. He listened with half an ear to the story as it grew and took on new details that he had not shared nor were they true.

"The life flight helicopter was dispatched, but it was too late," she told Patrick, an elderly man who lived on the edge of town in a ramshackle house and a yard full of chickens.

When Patrick left, Hap asked, "Where did you hear about the helicopter?"

Charlene turned to him, her face pink from the excitement of having something interesting to talk about. "Julia told me."

"Julia?"

"Yeah." She stared at Hap. "Remember Julia Guthry? They own the auto body?" Charlene pointed across the street at the brick garage with *Guthry's* emblazoned across the front.

"I know who she is." Hap turned away, exasperated. "It would be nice if you all would give me a chance to print the news before you spread it all over town."

"Hey, can I help it if you're slow?" Charlene picked up a stack of parcel notices, small pink squares of paper, and started sliding them into assorted mailboxes. "You wanna be the bearer of news, you gotta get out there."

Hap scowled. Out where? "Julia say anything else?"

"Said her mom was down for the weekend. I guess that heart attack wasn't too serious if the woman is coming down alone for a visit. Or maybe she's just trying to escape her husband. Julia doesn't paint a very rosy picture of family get-togethers with her dad. Drinks too much."

Hap read the opening paragraph of his story and cut a few unnecessary words. Honed it down to the bare essentials.

"Julia once said she could've written that Christmas

song that goes . . . like . . . *Please, Daddy, don't get drunk this Christmas.*" Charlene sang it out in such a clear, bright tone that it startled Hap. He halted to listen to her perfect pitch.

"You have a beautiful voice. Did you know that?"

"I sang in choral all the way through school."

Hap wondered what else he didn't know about Charlene. He knew enough that he was afraid to talk about her family the way she talked about others' like Julia Guthry's. He realized that knowing the sordid details of a person's worst moments could somehow give the false sense of understanding everything about them. He suddenly wondered what she said about him.

"She also said the kite shop is closing."

Hap looked out at the street.

"When is the fucking wind coming back?" Charlene said, mostly to herself.

☼

Late afternoon, as Tom heated up leftover spaghetti sauce, Lauren called.

"Hi, baby," she said. "Heard you had some excitement today. Why didn't you call me?"

"You talk to Hap?"

"Robbie Schafer was in today with her ferret and told me what happened. Everybody in Rocket is talking about it. What happened? Did you see it? She was a guest, right?"

"I didn't see it." He scraped congealed noodles into a rubber bowl and put them in the microwave. "There isn't really anything to tell."

"I heard there were watermelons scattered for two hundred yards. Was she killed instantly? I can't imagine getting run over by a semi. People joke about that kind of stuff all the time, but geez . . ."

Tom's stomach lurched and he walked away from the bubbling sauce. Fifty-nine dollars, he thought. For fifty-nine stinking dollars he could've saved Helen Simpson's life. "I don't really want to talk about it. Okay?"

Lauren sighed heavily into the phone. "Fine. I just thought, since you saw it and all ..."

"I didn't see it. I only heard it."

"What did it sound like?"

He shook his head and peered into his empty lobby. "I gotta go, there's a guest waiting."

"I'll come out, spend the night."

"No." Tom said the word so fast it surprised him. "I'm kind of tired tonight. It's been a long day. How about tomorrow?"

There was a long pause on Lauren's end. "I'll see if I'm available," she said and hung up without saying good-bye.

☼

Tom lay in bed, staring at the water-stained ceiling, asking himself if he had caused Helen Simpson's death. If he hadn't rushed her out the door angry, she'd have looked where she was going. If he had refunded her money, she'd be alive today. If he had just called the bakery and ordered the damn doughnuts!

As he thought about it, Sienna appeared in the doorway.

"Six," she said.

A chill ripped up Tom's spine. "What?"

"Six. On TV." She pointed into the living room, where she routinely fell asleep in front of the television.

Tom got up and followed her. A news anchor was talking about the accident. A small photo of Helen Simpson was displayed in the upper left corner of the screen. He looked at Sienna. How had she known that

Helen Simpson stayed in room six? Had he told her? Did she overhear him telling someone else? His skin prickled. He stared down at his daughter, who had begun sorting the buttons that were laid out across the windowsill.

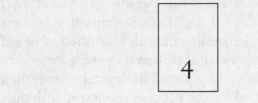

**4**

"SO? WHAT DID TOM say about the accident?"

Lauren paused from shaving the front leg of a cat in preparation for an IV needle. "Nothing. Said he didn't see it."

"It happened right in front of his motel." Dr. Mercer, the physician who worked in Rocket on Tuesdays and Thursdays, scrubbed her hands at the sink. "How could he not see it?"

"I don't know." Lauren focused on the cat, which had been sedated. It was a brown tabby with gray around its muzzle. She regretted hanging up on Tom the night before. Being grilled by Ellie Mercer about the accident made Lauren realize how she must have sounded to Tom.

Lauren inserted the needle and taped it down, then watched as liquid antibiotics dripped into the tube from a bag above the table. "This cat is too old to spay. Look at it, it's already gray."

"It's not too old to have kittens," Ellie said as they inventoried the surgical instruments. "It belongs to my neighbor, and it's had four litters since I moved in. I can't stand to see all those homeless kittens get run over one by one. It makes me sick."

Ellie Mercer was the only person in Rocket that Lauren truly considered a friend. Perhaps it was their shared medical backgrounds, though Ellie often came off a little superior because she worked on people instead of animals, a much less complicated biological system than the seven Lauren had had to become proficient with during veterinary school. She finished shaving the cat's belly, then turned on the overhead operating light. It made the bright white surgical room seem bigger than it was. "Do you want me to turn the temp down in here?"

"Sure." Ellie waited as Lauren scrubbed up for the procedure, then anesthetized the animal. "Do you think you and Tom will ever tie the knot?" Ellie stood ready to hand Lauren a scalpel. "You two have been dating forever."

"It hasn't even been a year." It felt to Lauren as if she and Tom were stuck. They couldn't seem to move forward, nor could they break it off. She'd thought about moving on, especially lately. But Tom was different from other men she'd dated. She couldn't conceive of a bond with her father like Tom and Sienna had and she envied the child, even as she was a little repulsed by the situation. Lauren felt that Tom's devotion was out of proportion to his daughter's handicap. Sienna wasn't helpless, though she seemed to have Tom convinced that she was.

Ellie, a woman who by her own admission would never date a man with less education than herself, seemed overly interested in what Tom was doing, how things were going between them, and what plans they had for the future. Ellie was divorced. Her marriage hadn't survived medical school and now she was almost forty and worried she'd never have children of her own. Lauren wondered if her doctor friend was a little jealous, and that made her smile.

Several minutes passed as the two concentrated on the procedure, a welcome diversion from Tom.

"How's his daughter doing? Any progress?"

"Nope." Lauren swiftly removed the cat's reproductive organs. "Sooner or later he's going to have to face the fact that Sienna is too much for him to raise alone."

"What do you mean?" Ellie asked as she stepped in and began stitching the incision closed.

"She needs something that Tom can't give her. She needs a home for kids like her ... or something." Lauren's eyes followed each stitch, comparing it to her own. Ellie's were long and clumsy because she didn't do surgery. She spent her days looking at tonsils and pressing on people's abdomens, then writing prescriptions for antibiotics or referrals to specialists. To Lauren it seemed like Ellie was handing over the most interesting work to others who were more qualified, and she knew she would never enjoy that kind of practice. No wonder Ellie was always bringing strays in to neuter or spay. As long as she was willing to pay for Lauren's time, Lauren was happy to let her stitch up the incisions.

Ellie looked up and the intense light made the wrinkles around her eyes seem deeper. She looked older than her years. She didn't say anything, and Lauren felt the sting of judgment. She rarely spoke her true feelings about Sienna, even to Ellie, because people always jumped to the conclusion that she was callous or mean. What did they know? They didn't see Tom struggle with the simplest things, like getting the girl dressed in the morning.

"I care about Sienna," Lauren said.

Ellie nodded, but Lauren wasn't convinced it was a genuine acknowledgement.

"Tom refuses to give her any meds. Says she's the way nature intended."

Ellie shrugged. They'd had the debate before about whether to medicate or not. Ellie came down cleanly on the side of the parents. It was Tom's right to decide, she felt. But Lauren believed he was making things worse for Sienna by not helping her with her attention problems.

"She's almost a teenager. She needs a lot more structure than he can give her while trying to run a motel. Either that or he needs to sell that damn place."

Ellie's eyes came up again, but only briefly as she knotted the last stitch.

"Maybe that's it. Maybe I can't stomach the idea of living my life out there on the highway, helping Tom run that crappy motel."

Ellie nodded more purposefully. "Yeah, I know what you mean."

Lauren felt better for having pinned it down. She could count on Ellie's understanding that no self-respecting professional woman would jump at the chance to be Tom's unpaid desk clerk. But recognizing it didn't bring her any closer to giving him up. Her gut pulled when she thought about letting him go. He could be so kind, and early on he'd had a great sense of humor, though she hadn't seen it in a long while. She wished Tom would show her the devotion he showed his daughter. She was certain he would, if his circumstances were different.

She decided she'd pick up his mail for him on her lunch break, then take it out after work. She'd apologize for grilling him about the accident. Maybe talk to him about finding help for Sienna, a day care or ... maybe something more permanent. Sooner or later he had to see that he needed help.

☀

Hap handed Charlene the typeset story of Helen Simpson's accidental death. "Read it over for typos, would you?"

Charlene cast him a sideways glance before homing in on the printed words.

Hap knew Charlene was no proofreader. She'd once

1

tried to convince him *angerment* was a real word, as in *you need to work on your angerment*. Still, he wanted to impress her with this story. It was among the best he'd ever written. Carefully and cleverly absolving the truck driver of all responsibility.

He watched the back of her head as she read. "Well?"

"Give me a minute, geez. I'm not a speed-reader."

Hap realized he sounded a little needy and sat down at his computer, pretending to busy himself with the classified ads. The smell of stamps overtook the place on hot afternoons when the tiny wall-mounted air conditioner could no longer make an impact on the temperature. He wondered if it was the chemicals in stamp glue that made postal workers flip out and shoot each other. It was such a quietly insidious smell.

"It's good, but you spelled Jemmett wrong. It only has one *t*." She thrust the article back at him.

"Thanks, but it has two *t*'s." Hap swallowed back disappointment that she had nothing more to say than that.

"No it doesn't." Charlene crossed the room to the honeycomb of postal boxes and ran her finger over the label below slot 892. "J-E-M-M-E-T."

Hap shook his head. "Who made that label?"

"I did."

"Uh-huh. I rest my case."

"Fine, see if I proofread another friggin story for you." Charlene pulled her hair back into a ponytail and began sorting the outgoing envelopes into stacks by size. "No one told me that I'd have to be a newspaper assistant just because we share the same building."

"You hungry? I'm going over to Petra's. Want me to pick you up something?" Hap fished his wallet out of his pocket and counted his cash.

"No, I hate that bitch," Charlene said. Her forehead was dotted with tiny beads of sweat.

He rolled his eyes. Charlene's *let it rip* style wore on him most in the heat. When she first began sharing the office, he thought it was refreshing. She said whatever came into her head, uncensored. She didn't mean half of what came out of her mouth, though she'd put off plenty of postal patrons with her swearing and insults. No one was above being called a freak or an asshole by Charlene. The difference was that she only said those things to the victim's face. She never spoke mean words about people who weren't present to hear them. Although, he realized, Petra Osterlundt, owner of the Rocket Bakery, seemed to be the exception to that.

"I can't wait for the wind to come back," Hap said.

Charlene looked at him. "Why? You don't surf."

"Because I'm about to the end of my rope with your foul mood."

"Screw you."

"And you think that'll get someone to buy you lunch?" He stalked out of the back room and into the post office lobby.

Room eighteen checked out at three minutes to noon, forcing Tom to wait for them before placing a note on the lobby door that he'd be back by three o'clock. He locked the motel up and loaded Sienna into his sweltering pickup. She whined persistently, but refused to roll down the window. He had needed to get away from the place. Even if all he did was sit in the parking lot of the local burger joint and drink a milk shake with his daughter, he'd go out of his mind if he didn't find a moment's reprieve from that damned motel. The truck's air conditioner finally kicked in a few miles outside Rocket, but by then Tom could smell both of their sweaty bodies. All the vents were turned toward him, and he cranked the fan to high, trying to cool himself.

He looked over at Sienna and the ring of dirt around her lips. She needed a bath worse than ever, but it was only Thursday and he couldn't stomach two battles in one week. He felt a pang of resentment toward Maria. She died and left him to struggle through this alone.

He came into the thirty-five-mile-per-hour speed zone where the highway narrowed and traffic, when there were tourists, came to a near standstill. He pulled his foot off the accelerator and coasted into town. *Going out of Business Sale* signs plastered the front windows of the kite shop. Windsocks in the shape of fish and dolphins hung like noodles from poles in the sidewalk. A large butterfly kite adorned the building above the door, as if it had alighted there of its own volition. There was no risk of it being swept away by the still air. Sienna stared at it, her eyes glued to the fluorescent yellow, green, and orange of its broad wings, her head twisting like an owl's, refusing to release it from her sight.

"I love you," he said. "Do you love Daddy?"

She said nothing.

"Want a milk shake?"

Sienna nodded without looking at him. Her head tipped from side to side as she watched objects fly past her dusty window at close range. She was in a quiet, subdued mood today, Tom noticed. She got that way, just as she sometimes got hyper and agitated without apparent provocation. And though he knew he'd never unravel the mystery of her, the vagaries pestered him like a toothache.

"Okay, one milk shake coming up, right after the post office." Tom pulled in to the parking lot and glanced again at Sienna. Taking her with him would turn a five-minute trip into an ordeal, but on a day like today he couldn't let her roast in the truck. He decided to leave the engine running with the air conditioner on while he went inside to collect his mail. He'd only be a second.

Charlene greeted him at the window with a big smile. "We were just talking about you, Tom."

"We?" He glanced around at the empty lobby.

"Lauren was here a minute ago." Charlene's tone went markedly flat at the mention of Lauren's name. "She insisted on picking up your mail. Hope that's okay."

"Well, since you asked...no. I'd really rather you didn't give my mail to other people."

"I'm sorry, I was just trying—"

"I know you were helping out. I appreciate that. But I'll let you know if I want someone else to pick it up. Okay?"

Charlene looked down at her hands, stung. "I'm really sorry, Tom."

"It's okay. Don't worry about it. Just...next time don't do it."

"I'm a lousy postal clerk."

"No you're not." He wished he hadn't mentioned it. He hadn't meant to hurt her. Maria was right. He could be stupidly insensitive. He remembered how she used to tease him about it and felt himself flushing.

"I hate this job, anyway. If there was anything else to do in this shit-hole of a town, I'd take it. Anything! I'd scrub toilets even." Charlene slumped heavily on the counter. "I suck at this job."

"Be careful what you wish for. I've got twenty-six toilets. Too bad only two need to be scrubbed."

Charlene grinned brightly at the idea. "Do you need help? I can do that. It would be kind of fun."

Tom laughed. Help? Boy, did he need the help. He just couldn't afford it. "This is a way better job, Charlene. You don't wanna give up a well-paying career to be a motel housekeeper, even if you are sick of sorting mail. Trust me on that."

"Don't overestimate this job." She nodded at the wall

of mailboxes. "There's a reason people go postal, you know. We don't all start out as friggin psychopaths."

Tom laughed. He knew Charlene pretty well, but not because she sorted his mail. He knew her because his was the only motel for fifty miles and in more prosperous summers, a steady parade of buff young windsurfers brought her out there. She had probably stayed in every one of Tom's rooms at one time or another.

"Really, I do want to give this up," Charlene insisted.

"Tell you what, if you still wanna be a housekeeper when business picks up, you're on. But don't blame me when you realize what a huge mistake you've made in giving up the post office. Okay?"

"Well, I guess that could be never, with the way things are going around here." She leaned against the counter and pulled her hair back.

Tom noticed small beads of sweat on her neck. A few strands of hair clung to her smooth skin, snaking along her collarbone. It was a lovely collarbone, and he flushed again as he realized how badly he wanted to run his finger along it and down into her shirt.

"How's Sienna?" Charlene asked.

"She's growing up. About this high now." He held his hand up to his biceps. Tom smiled. Charlene always gave him the sense that she really wanted to know and wasn't just asking to be polite—or worse, gathering tidbits for the ladies' gossip hour. "She's gonna be tall."

"Like father like daughter," Charlene said. She paused and looked Tom straight in the eye, making his head unexpectedly swim. "Tell her I said hi. Maybe one of these days I'll take her with me to Hood River. That is . . . if we ever get some wind. I bet she'd like watching all those sails and kites with their pretty colors. Sometimes I like to just sit on the beach and watch."

Tom didn't know what to say. Sienna would love that,

he knew it. But how could Charlene manage Sienna, and at the river no less? He thought of the danger. She might run away from Charlene, throw a tantrum, fall in the water, run into traffic, wet her pants and then take her clothes off in front of all those boys. He banished the idea.

"Well, I better go get my mail from the pet clinic," he said, heading out the door.

"I'm really sorry about that, Tom," she called after him. "I'll be a better housekeeper."

In the pickup Sienna had disemboweled the glove box. Papers were scattered all over the floor, the seat, and in her lap.

"Sienna, no." Tom scooped them up and jammed them back in, crumpling his registration documents along with napkins and old notes with phone numbers. "Leave that stuff alone. I need those papers."

"Hot," she whined. "I want out." She pulled at the door latch, but he'd rigged the lock to stay engaged until the door was opened from the outside. "I want out!"

"Honey, sit still. If you want a milk shake you have to be good for Daddy."

"Want out want out want out," she chanted, pulling the latch with every syllable.

Tom ignored her and drove down the street to the pet clinic. If he could get away for a little longer than a couple hours he could take Sienna to the river himself. But if there was enough wind to bring out the surfers, there would be business enough to keep him from taking her. It was a nice idea, though.

Turning to Sienna, he said, "Stay here and don't open the glove box. I'll be right back."

"Want out want out want out want out," she continued, but louder.

Tom sprinted inside, the chilled air hitting his face. It felt refreshing for an instant, until he realized it smelled like dog piss. "Is Lauren around?" he asked the receptionist.

"I'm afraid she's in surgery right now. Unless you have an appointment to be neutered, you're out of luck." The large woman laughed boisterously.

Tom didn't find her comment funny. For some reason it felt uncomfortably close to the truth. Lauren was certainly capable of emasculating a man, but that was part of what made her intriguing, in a freakishly dangerous sort of way. He tried to place this woman, but she wasn't familiar. The pet clinic seemed to go through receptionists like he went through motel guests. Still, he wondered where these people came from. Rocket was too small to have an endless supply of receptionists. He'd had a heck of a time finding and keeping desk clerks in summers past. Usually he ended up with surfers who needed just enough work to support their passion. They stayed a few weeks—barely long enough for him to get them up to speed and for them to give away free rooms to their destitute friends—then they were gone.

"Tell her Tom came by for his mail."

"I'll—"

Before she could finish, there was a loud crash outside. Tom spun around to find his pickup in the middle of the street, the back fender smashed in and a smoking Honda Civic dripping fluids from its crumpled front end.

"Shit." He darted out, frantically searching for Sienna. Images of Helen Simpson's mangled body flashing through his mind.

By the time he reached the truck, the driver of the Civic was standing in front of it shouting.

"What the hell is your problem? Can't you look before you back out?"

Sienna's head emerged from beneath the driver's side dash. She looked through the windshield at him, bewildered.

"Are you okay?" Tom shouted at her.

The other driver thought Tom was asking him. "Yeah, I'm okay. Good thing I wasn't going that fast. Hope that stupid broad has insurance."

Tom opened the pickup door and grabbed Sienna. He tried to hug her, but she shrieked and fought her way out of his grip, then cowered under the dash again. He turned to the driver, who continued to rant about the damage to his car. "That *stupid broad* is my daughter."

5

"SHE DOESN'T WANT to be a motel maid, Tom. She wants to be *your* motel maid." Lauren gave Tom a pointed look across his tiny dinette table.

He suppressed a smile. Even if that were true, a man could do worse than have Charlene Anderson wanting to scrub his toilets. "We call them housekeepers, not maids."

"Oh, is that an industry term?"

"Yes, as a matter of fact, it is. It gives the position a little more dignity, and since I happen to be the one doing the housekeeping most of the time, I concur."

Lauren paused from her cheeseburger to study Tom. Flies buzzed the overhead light, and Sienna made a racket of blowing bubbles in her soda next to him. It was late to be eating dinner, almost ten o'clock.

"Don't tell me you're considering hiring her," Lauren said.

"Of course not. She's got a good job. It would be crazy for her to give it up for this." He gestured at his apartment.

"She's half your age!"

"I wasn't even thinking like *that*. Get your mind out of the gutter." But Tom wondered how Lauren knew he was in fact thinking exactly like that. Ever since that un-expected eye lock this afternoon, Charlene had been swimming and bobbing through his head like a sea otter. And she wasn't half his age, either.

Lauren jabbed a french fry into a spot of ketchup and shoved it into her mouth. "She's just after your knob, and I don't want her around."

Tom wished he hadn't shared the conversation with Lauren in the first place, though he did find her jealousy a little flattering. It also made him wonder if he really cared for Lauren or if she was just filling the adult void in his life. He didn't have wayward thoughts about other women when Maria was alive. That woman had occu-pied every last cell in his brain from the moment he saw her until ... well ... for long after she'd been laid to rest. There was nothing about her, from the way she smiled to the way she cleaned the oven, that didn't elicit a deep car-nal urge from him. Having experienced a connection as deep as his and Maria's had only made its absence more profound.

He'd brought the conversation with Charlene up to deflect Lauren's obsessive rehashing of Sienna's little wreck that afternoon, a wreck that struck too close to his heart after Helen Simpson's death. Thank God the truck didn't get much more than a dent and the other driver didn't make a big deal about him leaving his daughter alone in the truck with the engine running. Once the man had gotten Tom's insurance information and figured out that something wasn't right about Sienna, he called for a tow and wandered into the Red Tail Tavern.

"Yeah, well, that might be kind of nice," Tom said, "now that you point it out. Having a woman around who just wants to get ahold of my knob."

Sienna stopped blowing bubbles and peered at her fa-ther as if she'd been following the conversation all along and was now keen to know what he would say next. Tom poured more fries onto her paper plate and she immediately began stuffing them into her mouth.

"How are things at work?" he asked Lauren. He didn't really care to hear the sordid details of her day, and she was quick to dive into the most gruesome topics, like what heartworms do to dogs, or the sort of skin lesions cats with flea allergies were prone to suffer, but Tom needed a new topic.

"Slow."

He nodded. "Sounds familiar."

"Yeah, but people still have pets. I mean, it's not like tourists bring their pets with them, at least not most."

"Maybe people are just being more selective about what they spend their money on. Vaccinations for your dog would probably fall pretty low on the list if your business is going under."

Lauren nodded dismissively, her face pressed hard, her lips thin white lines. Tom had noticed that she didn't accept his opinions and ideas when it related to her business, as if running a motel versus a veterinary practice were so different that his input had no value to her.

"Are you going to get your truck fixed?" she asked, turning the conversation back to the wreck again. But the look she gave him told Tom the conversation about Charlene was not over.

"No, it's just a dent in the fender."

Lauren picked the tomato out of her burger and laid it on the side of her plate. "I told them no tomatoes. I hate tomatoes."

Sienna abruptly stopped chewing and stared at Lauren's tomato, then at Lauren.

The bell chimed in the lobby and Tom rose, leaving his half-eaten burger on the table. As he left the room he could hear Lauren reprimanding Sienna for something, but his lobby was suddenly packed with people and he had no time to worry about what was happening in the apartment.

"Can I help you?"

"We got a flat!" someone hollered.

A man stepped out of the crowd. He wore a uniform with *Independent Living* embroidered on his chest. "We got a flat tire after leaving Maryhill Museum and we're running behind. We turned back, thinking we'd stay here tonight, if you've got enough rooms, then drive back to Portland in the morning."

"I've got rooms. How many are we talking about?"

"He's got rooms," another person said, and the room hummed with acknowledgement.

The driver turned and looked at the group. "I have thirty-eight people."

"Yup, there's thirty-eight of us," someone piped.

Tom looked the crowd over. The man standing next to the driver was wearing his belt just below his armpits and his pants were several inches too short. A woman near him wore a fuzzy orange hat pulled over a hooded sweatshirt. Another picked his nose and examined his finger. Tom realized the people in his lobby were mentally retarded adults. "I've got twenty-two available rooms, you want 'em all?"

The driver turned again and looked at the crowd, who stared back. They watched their leader with palpable anticipation.

"We'll double up where we need to," the bus driver decided. "That okay?" he asked the group.

They suddenly erupted with loud confirmation and began shouting out names of who they wanted to bunk with, until Tom could no longer hear the driver over the excitement.

One woman near the door stamped her feet and insisted that she not be put in a room with a boy. "I know what boys do. You can't put boys and girls in the same room."

Tom was instantly reminded of Helen Simpson. A flash of anxiety shot through him, but as he surveyed the small crowd he smiled. At least these were people capable of being pleased. He handed a registration card to the driver. "Fill out this card and list everyone in the party on the back, then the two of us will write down which room each person is in and hand out keys."

The bus driver exhaled loudly and beamed at Tom. "I had two chaperones when I started out, but I stupidly agreed to let them drive in a separate car. They're probably home drinking beer right now without a care in the world. You know, people like that should go to prison. Leaving a poor man to handle a group this size alone."

"We can manage it," Tom said.

"Thanks, mister." The bus driver thrust his hand forward. "I'm Art."

They shook hands and proceeded to assign rooms and hand out keys. Tom made eye contact with the recipient of each key as he pointed out the room to be sure each knew where to go, while Art gave strict instructions about lights out and the next day's early departure. At last, Tom and Art were standing alone in the lobby, having watched as the last two people found their rooms.

"You're in room six. It's in the corner there." He pointed out the lobby window. "Easy to see what's happening in the other units from there."

"Thanks for your help. You went above and beyond the call of duty, you know."

"It's no problem."

"I mean it. I half expected you to throw me out when you realized I had three dozen retarded people and no chaperones."

Tom shrugged.

Before he returned to the apartment, Tom called the

Rocket Bakery. He ordered three dozen more doughnuts for morning.

In the kitchen, Lauren was sitting sideways in her chair, her back to Sienna. The burger Tom had left behind was smashed and bits of bun were ground into the table, which was crisscrossed with mustard trails.

"I tried to stop her," Lauren said. She put her hands up in irritated surrender.

Tom smiled. "I just rented every single room. Can you believe that?"

"I thought it was awfully noisy out there," she said.

"A whole busload."

"*A whole busload,*" Sienna parroted.

"That's right, sweetie. Daddy just rented the *whole* motel to a *whole* busload of people."

"The *whole motel* to a *whole busload of people,*" Sienna sang, tipping her chin up and peering at her father through a tangle of hair.

Tom grinned. She could be so cute. "Go see what's on TV."

Sienna scrambled off the stool, dropping her empty soda cup on the floor. The lid burst open and ice cubes scattered at her feet. Tom pulled Lauren to a stand. "Now, about this knob-jumping thing . . ."

"You think I'm that easy, do you?" Lauren kissed Tom softly, apologetically.

Tom kissed her with force. He was a ravenous man suddenly. The busload of retarded people had served to remind him that life was only as difficult as he made it.

❋

Hap Mitsui unlocked the office he shared with Charlene and flipped on the light. She didn't usually come in until eight-thirty, and he had a full hour to write up the clip about Sienna Jemmett attempting to take her daddy's pickup for a joyride. Hap had seen the truck blocking traffic when he came out of the bakery, so he pulled his camera and notepad from his van and wandered over. He took pictures, and laughed with Tom about the mess. Tom wasn't all that jovial, but he usually tried to be a good sport where his daughter was concerned. News of the incident would be all over town before *The Rocket* came out, but Hap could at least add a little humor to ease Tom's embarrassment. Hap called it a day after that, dreading the hot afternoon sharing a room with Charlene, whose mood had darkened steadily as the day wore on. She'd seen Tom, which usually put her in good spirits, but yesterday she went on about how inept she was as a postal clerk. Hap had to remind himself at times that she had suffered hardships that most people could never imagine. Her mood swings were, he guessed, the logical by-product of her past, and he made a point of steering clear when she was unhappy.

He dropped his keys on his desk and paused a moment to look at the Hershey's chocolate bar sitting neatly on his story about Helen Simpson. He nodded, satisfied. Charlene had apologized the only way she ever did, without words. He balanced the chocolate bar on his dictionary for later. He'd share it with her, but she probably knew that when she left it there.

☀

Tom waved to the bus full of cheerful faces as it pulled out of his parking lot. The group was ecstatic about the doughnuts, repeatedly asking if it was okay to eat them, then thanking him again and again. But Art had forbidden any of his charges to drink the coffee because of the caffeine. Tom held his breath as the bus groaned onto the highway, transported back to that moment when Helen Simpson encountered the semi. But nothing had happened.

Only one guest still remained, and Tom knew he had

a lot of work ahead of him. In summers past, cleaning a twenty-six-room motel was all in a day's work. He and Maria could do it in their sleep. And after her death the turnover in housekeepers kept him well acquainted with the ins and outs of bathroom scrubbing, spot removing, and bed changing. His mother would have been proud of his crisp and efficient hospital corners if she had lived to see them. Even still, he felt a little intimidated by the number of dirtied rooms ahead of him today.

"Charlene, where are you when I need you?"

"Excuse me?"

Tom turned to find Lauren standing in the doorway between the lobby and his apartment. He felt his face redden. "I've got a lot of toilets to scrub today. That's all."

She turned on her heel and disappeared.

Tom knew he'd blown it. He cursed himself for opening his mouth. He had plenty of unsuitable thoughts that he managed to keep in his head: Why did he have to go and blurt that one out? Especially today, when things seemed like they were improving between the two of them. The sex last night had been great, like it was in the beginning. She'd pretended to be a prude at first, scolding him for touching her breasts. But once they were alone in his room the gloves came off and she took over, rough and hard.

"I need a housekeeper," he said, following her into the apartment. "That's all I meant."

Lauren came out of his bedroom with her shoes in her hand and they almost collided.

"You're the one who does it for me, babe." He grinned, trying to cajole her.

"I have to go to work," she said, sweeping her hair up in a ponytail. "I'm already late and I talked to my receptionist about coming in late the other day."

"But you're the boss."

"I know, so I should set a good example."

"Come out tonight. I think I owe you a spanking for your behavior last night."

Lauren paused to look at Tom. She wasn't in the mood, he could see that, but she at least seemed to be considering it. When he stopped to think about it, it was odd for him to say things like that to a woman like her. A veterinarian. She had eight times the education he did, and at least three times the income. He and Maria had come from similar backgrounds. He'd been able to offer her a familiar lifestyle of hard and unending physical work, but at least it carried the hope of financial payoff because the motel was theirs. What did Lauren see in him? That was the bigger question that he didn't have an answer to.

"I'll see." She gave him a quick peck on the lips and was gone, leaving him standing in the dimly lit apartment. The smashed burger drew flies to the table and gave off a smell of old grease.

Tom peered over the back of the sofa at Sienna. She was sleeping with her hair wound around her face so he couldn't see her features. He walked around and knelt beside her. Her breath snapped in and out quietly. He brushed her hair away and ran the back of his fingers over her cheek. She made a face and rolled over with her back to him. He stayed there, just watching. Would it always be like this? He'd hoped—they'd always hoped, he and Maria—that Sienna would someday be normal, or at least close. They used to imagine that Sienna would grow out of her odd behavior, mature into someone who could at least manage. But instead she destroyed his papers and dented his truck, putting herself in danger, too. Sometimes he imagined that if she would just see him—connect with him somehow—he could manage the rest. But he hadn't planned for Sienna's future, for his own future. Maria's death had thrust him headfirst into the relentlessness of caring for a handicapped child as a single parent, a responsibility not twice as difficult as it had been when Maria was there to help, but ten times as difficult. Maria died when Sienna was just three. They knew by then that Sienna had problems. They'd been counseled by numerous specialists in those early years, some as far away as Seattle and Salt Lake City. At first they both focused on chasing that glimmer of hope—hope that it wasn't as bad as the doctors suspected. They wanted to believe that Sienna was a special case, different somehow from those other kids with autistic tendencies. Certainly not worse. But somewhere on that journey they had become realists. The mounting expense of their fantasy, coupled with the shattering disappointment that each new physician ultimately delivered, finally brought them to a new approach: allow Sienna to be who she is and to hell with labels and behavior modification plans. Tom didn't believe in miracles; Maria had been the religious one. But after Maria's death, as time marched on and Sienna stayed the same, Tom was coming to see that a miracle was what they needed.

☼

"I got a brand-new pool table," Dillard said from the doorway of his antiques shop as Hap passed by on his way back from the bakery.

Hap threw a hand up in acknowledgement, but didn't slow. "That's great."

Dillard followed after him. "It's full-size. Slate with walnut trim."

Hap nodded, retreating quickly up the street.

"It's the best model professionals can buy," Dillard called.

Hap paused, knowing he would regret it, but unable to let that go. If the man knew anything about professional pool tables, he'd know he couldn't afford one. He turned to Dillard, who was right on his heels, forcing Hap to step back.

"I didn't know you were a professional pool player, Dillard. You've been keeping secrets from us."

Dillard smiled but, seeing Hap's face, shifted his weight from one foot to the other, as if he were considering retracting his statement. "I've been practicing and I'm pretty good."

Hap knew there was nothing Dillard wanted more than for him to run some sort of feature story about him in *The Rocket*. "I could write a story about that."

Dillard's eyes lit up. "Yeah?"

"Oh, people would love that. A real live pool shark right here in Rocket. Who knew?"

"I don't know about *pool shark*." Dillard laughed, his voice trembling a little.

"Ah, you're just being modest," Hap said.

Dillard smiled at his feet.

"Course you know that everybody in town will want to come over and see you shoot. I couldn't run the story unless you were willing to kind of show off a little. We could use a good special-interest story like this to get our minds off the weather. Know what I mean?"

Dillard seemed to imagine it as Hap thought about Dillard. The antiques dealer wasn't an unattractive man, a little over six feet tall, a full head of hair. Physically fit for a man almost fifty. But there was something pathetic about him. An urgency, a too-loud begging for acceptance in everything he did and said, that only made people want to run for cover. Dillard was needy. Hap recognized that now. It was neediness, and that annoyed Hap even more.

"You could show 'em some fancy shots. Maybe make some money, too. Do you know any trick shots? People love trick shots."

Dillard's face went dark. "I don't want a bunch of

yahoos pounding on my door wanting to use my pool table. They've got tables over at the tavern for that."

Hap could see the internal struggle going on behind Dillard's creased forehead. Fame or ridicule? Hap guessed Dillard had been down this road enough times to understand that it would certainly end in the latter. "I don't blame you, I wouldn't want that, either," Hap said. "I prize my solitude."

Dillard smiled as if the two men understood each other, shared a characteristic that set them apart. "Thanks for offering, Hap. Maybe another time."

Hap turned and crossed Main. *Crackpot,* he thought.

☀

Tom emerged from room one, the last on his long list to clean. Sweat dripped from his temples and his tee shirt was sopping. No one had checked in for the night and it was already past five. He turned on the spigot and guzzled water straight from the hose, glancing at the thermometer under the eaves. One hundred and five degrees. He groaned and held the hose over his head, letting the lukewarm water cascade down his shoulders and soak into his jeans and shoes.

On the back porch of his apartment, he stripped down to his boxer shorts and draped his wet clothes over the railing. The television blared through the screen door, and he wondered if he should look for some sort of day camp for Sienna. It wasn't good for her to spend the entire summer alone, watching garbage on TV. Last summer he'd paid an elderly woman to come out and look after his daughter, but instead of doing things with her, the woman merely joined Sienna in front of the tube. He'd paid her a nice salary to sit on her ass and eat all his food. Maybe he could pay someone to pick Sienna up and drop her off at a day program in Hood River. That was always the tough part; he just couldn't afford the time away from the motel. He had to be here to check people in, fix problems, make sure parents didn't let their kids swim unattended, strip beds, make coffee ... the list went on and on.

As he cycled through all the people he knew who might possibly be willing to drive Sienna, an animal-like screech rippled from the kitchen. "Sienna?" he called. Water dripped from his shorts as he made his way through the apartment. "Sienna!"

When he reached her, she was slapping a kitten on the head and shouting, "Bad! Bad!"

"What are you doing?" Tom wrenched the cat away from her, its claws gouging deep into the flesh of her hands, drawing blood.

Sienna screamed and tried to hit the cat again.

"Where did you get this kitten?" Tom looked at the tiny orange cat. Its tail was kinked and blackened. It smelled singed. It struggled weakly to get free, but Tom could see it was badly injured. "Sienna, answer me. Where did you find this cat?"

Sienna examined her wounds. The cat had scratched her face and arms. "Bad," she said angrily. "Bad."

The kitten's mewing suddenly ceased and Tom cradled it in his hands. Its breathing was labored and it closed its eyes. He stroked the soft fur, realizing he'd either have to take it to the clinic or put it out of its misery. He looked at his daughter, then at the toaster, which had been pulled to the edge of the counter, and again at the injured cat. What had she done?

"Sienna, did you burn this cat?"

"Yes," she said defiantly. "Bad cat."

"No, it isn't bad. It's just a baby."

"It hurts me."

Tom stood in his wet boxers in the middle of his kitchen facing his daughter, holding a dying cat and wondering what to do. He could take it to Lauren. But he couldn't afford to lose guests by not being here. Still, he couldn't quite bring himself to kill the tiny thing and end its suffering, either. "Get in the truck," he told his daughter.

Sienna ignored him.

"Damn it, Sienna. Get in the damn truck!"

☼

Tom paced back and forth in the pet clinic lobby. The receptionist sat grim-faced at her computer, glaring at Sienna, who was pulling cans of expensive pet food from the shelf and stacking them into pyramids by the color of their labels.

The woman eyed Sienna, then turned her rancorous glare on Tom. "Where did she get a kitten?"

Tom turned away, unable to escape the caustic shame he felt, knowing what the woman was thinking. "I don't know."

"Is she left unsupervised during the day?"

"No. I'm there. I mean...I can't watch her twenty-four hours a day. I have work to do." He stuttered out the words before he realized how defensive he sounded, and it made him angry that this woman had the nerve to ask these questions. And why was he answering them?

Lauren stepped out of the brightly lit exam room and pulled her glasses off. She looked over at the receptionist. "Belinda, you can go on home. I'll finish up here."

"Are you sure, Dr. Kent? I don't mind staying."

Lauren nodded and Belinda picked up her purse and trundled out. Lauren waited for the door to close before speaking. "It has internal bleeding, Tom. It's not going to make it. I think the best thing to do is put it down."

Tom winced. Then he nodded.

"Tell me again what happened."

"I don't know. I...She got angry with it and hurt it." He slumped down in a vinyl chair and rested his elbows on his knees, letting his head droop. "I don't know where she got it. You know I would never let her have a kitten."

"I know," Lauren said. "But this is pretty serious. You know that, don't you?"

"Of course I do." Tom pulled out his wallet. "What do I owe you?"

"I don't want any money."

"No, I'll pay for it."

She hesitated, searching Tom's face, then said, "Really, Tom. I don't want any money."

"How *much*?" he shouted.

"Forty-five dollars."

Tom laid the exact amount on the counter, stooped beside Sienna, and began putting the cans back on the shelf. Sienna kicked at him, enraged. The receptionist's question about Sienna's supervision still stung him as he worked blindly to right everything. What did she think? What did everyone think?

"Get in the truck," he said without looking at his daughter.

LAUREN DROPPED HER KEYS on the counter, set down the bag of groceries, and picked up the ringing phone. She'd had to drive into Hood River because the produce at the IGA in Rocket was ragged and brown. Half the shelves were empty. It had taken three hours to get groceries and return to Rocket. She flipped on the kitchen light and an amber glow warmed her bungalow. The kitchen remodel was still fresh and she swelled with delight every time she walked into the room. Her hands yet bore the calluses from cutting tile, but the manual labor had been a therapeutic endeavor.

"Hello?" she said, tucking the phone under her ear and twisting to look at the clock over the sink. It was almost nine, but she could still make it out to Tom's tonight. She set a bottle of Pinot Noir on the tiled countertop beneath a 1920s art poster of a jolly chef.

"Lauren, it's Ellie."

"Thanks for calling me back." Lauren began emptying the grocery bag, sliding a jug of milk into the refrigerator, then rolling a sack of oranges out into a purple ceramic bowl.

"What's up? Your message sounded urgent, then I couldn't get ahold of you."

Lauren stopped arranging the fruit. "It's Sienna. She killed a kitten today, or at least injured it so badly that I had to put it down." She leaned against the sink, crossing her arms over her chest and pinching the phone to her ear with her shoulder.

"Where did she get a kitten?"

"I asked that, too. Tom didn't know."

"I knew something like this was going to happen," Ellie said. "I just knew it."

"I reported it as an animal abuse case. Sheriff Turnbull is probably out there now."

"You what? Why?" Ellie's incredulity seared through the phone, startling Lauren.

"Look, I know Tom is a good father and he's doing everything he can, but...I can't let something like this go. That child needs help. This is the wake-up call Tom needs."

"Oh, Lauren..."

"I thought you'd be supportive. I called you because it was a hard thing to do and I needed a friendly voice."

"But to report it? You know what a terrible position that will put Tom in."

"Ellie, we've been through this. You know he needs to see that he can't care for Sienna by himself. I didn't do it to be malicious. You know that."

"I can't believe you reported it, though."

Lauren felt the unspoken disapproval in Ellie's voice wrap around her like cold fingers. "I thought you'd back me up on this," she said.

Ellie sighed. "How are you going to explain to Tom why you did that?"

"I wasn't the only one at the clinic. It could've been anyone who saw the kitten and put two and two together."

"You're going to let someone else take the blame?"

Lauren scowled down at her hand, realizing that she

was clenching her fingers into a tight fist. She flexed them hard. She'd expected Ellie to understand. She was a doctor, after all. "Look, I don't need your approval on this. I did what I thought was best. I did it for Sienna's sake. He doesn't see what trouble they're in. He doesn't understand how serious her behavior is. I did it for her, and you make it sound like I'm a monster. I'd hoped for a little more understanding."

"Lauren."

"I have to go. I'll talk to you later." Lauren hung up the phone and turned to stare at her reflection in the kitchen window. Had she done the wrong thing? She wasn't trying to hurt Tom. She'd done it only to help him. To help Sienna. Why couldn't Ellie see that?

When Lauren finished putting away anything that might rot in the heat, she paused in the kitchen and stared at the bottle of wine. The raspberry-colored label looked beguiling against the Mexican tile backsplash, promising better times. She hadn't planned to take it with her to Tom's, but it still seemed like a ridiculous purchase under the circumstances. It sank in then, what she'd done to Tom, and she instantly wished she could undo it. A knot had formed beneath her breastbone, a knot of dread or sorrow or anger, she couldn't discern.

☀

Sheriff Turnbull entered the motel lobby, but he didn't need to ring the bell because Tom was sitting behind the counter half expecting him. That receptionist must have called the police the moment she left the clinic, Tom thought. He'd sensed something about her, perhaps the way she eyed the scratches on his forearms, maybe something deeper. He knew the minute she looked at that kitten she'd report it as animal abuse, but by then there was nothing he could do but regret his decision and hope that Lauren would intervene on his behalf. What could that woman possibly know about raising a child with special needs? He had suffered many sharp glares and hissed comments through the years from people just like her. Once he'd even found himself wishing the worst sort of misfortune on people like that, to have a child like Sienna. A child she could not explain, control, or protect. When he'd confided this to Maria, she'd cried. He hadn't meant to hurt his wife, but thought she might share his feelings.

He and Sienna hadn't been home more than thirty minutes before the county patrol car pulled up. He had managed to wipe the grimy burger off the table and into the trash, and stack dirty dishes in the sink, a hasty attempt to make the place look less neglected.

"Sheriff," Tom said, standing off his stool. "I've been expecting you."

"I'm sorry, Tom. I wish I was here under different circumstances." Turnbull pulled at his mustache.

Tom looked at the man's perfectly pressed brown uniform, its collage of embroidered and metal badges, the radio microphone clipped to his breast pocket, and the coil of wire beneath it that ran to his earpiece. They knew each other quite well. In more prosperous summers Turnbull came often to the Jemmett Motel to break up surfer parties. The sheriff had escorted plenty of vagrants off the premises, people who thought they could just park in the lot and sleep in their vans because they knew paying guests.

"Do you want to show me where you found the cat? Tell me everything that happened and all?" Turnbull's voice failed to carry the full authority Tom knew it capable of.

"She was in the kitchen with it when I came in from cleaning rooms," Tom answered, motioning for Turnbull to follow. He led the older man into the apartment and stood in the cramped kitchen where the toaster was still perched at the very edge of the counter. The garbage had gone rancid in the heat. Tom wished he'd taken it out, even if that were all he'd done.

Turnbull eyed the appliance, then the table and the counter. He turned a full circle conducting some sort of silent inventory before looking at Tom. "Where's Sienna?"

"Sienna," Tom called over his shoulder, knowing she would ignore him. "Please come in here."

The two men looked awkwardly around at anything but each other as they waited, but she didn't appear. Finally Tom walked into the living room, the sheriff on his heels.

"Sienna," he said to her. "Sienna, I called you." He picked up the remote control and switched off the TV, silencing Homer Simpson's angry rant at Bart. When he turned back to Turnbull, the sheriff's eyes were roaming every inch of the place. Tom wished the man would leave. This was their private living space. The motel belonged to everyone, but this, their home, belonged only to Sienna and him.

"What are all the buttons for?" Turnbull touched a stack of medium-sized green ones, scattering several of them across the bookcase.

"No!" Sienna screeched. She sprang from the sofa and restacked the button tower, her face puckered into an angry wad. "Don't touch."

"I'm sorry," Turnbull said. "I won't touch them, honey, if you'll answer some questions for me."

She glared in his general direction, her dark eyes aflame.

"Where did you get the kitten you had today?" Turnbull sat on the arm of the sofa to bring himself eye-level with Sienna. "Can you tell where the kitten came from, honey?"

She glanced at Tom, who nodded for her to answer

the question, but she didn't. Instead, she glared at the buttons, her lips pursed.

"I don't know how much good it'll do to ask her questions," Tom told Turnbull. "She barely answers me. Strangers are..." He shrugged. The only words that ever came to mind to describe Sienna's behavior were insufficient catchall ones. *Weird, odd, abnormal.* The counselor called her *antisocial, obsessive-compulsive.*

"Why don't *you* tell me, then?" the sheriff said to Tom.

He agreed, but only if they could discuss it in the lobby, away from Sienna. There, Tom recounted what he'd found in the kitchen, and the reason Sienna had injured the cat.

Sheriff Turnbull made notes in his little booklet, then asked, "Does anyone supervise her while you're busy with work?"

"I do."

"So you don't have a sitter or anyone?"

Tom bit down on his lip, wishing with every ounce of himself that he didn't have to say his next words. "I can't afford it this year. I could lose everything if the wind doesn't come back. I'm behind on my mortgage."

Turnbull scowled at his pad. "I've heard that from too many business owners recently."

Tom knew that Turnbull wasn't judging him, but he couldn't escape the burn of shame.

"I know you're a good father, Tom. Everyone does."

What does that mean? Tom wondered. That this was my fault? Of course it was. He swallowed the knowledge like a stone.

"This is a sign of more serious problems, you know." Turnbull jotted another note, and Tom wished he could see what the man was writing. "She's a minor, and there are unusual circumstances here. It wouldn't serve any purpose to file charges."

The back of Tom's throat went dry. He realized his heart was hammering.

"It can't be ignored, though. You know that, Tom."

Tom nodded.

"Child welfare will be out, probably in the morning." Sheriff Turnbull inched closer to the door.

Tom walked past Turnbull and opened it wide to help move the man along. He felt like he'd swallowed rat poison, and nothing the sheriff could say to him about how they all understood Sienna's situation soothed his churning gut.

As he watched the sheriff pull away, the phone rang. It was Hap Mitsui.

"I heard the sheriff was called out to your motel," Hap said. The connection was poor and the line crackled. "Should I bother coming out? Anything interesting enough for a story going on out there?"

Tom should have expected this. Hap reported everything that happened in Rocket. *The Rocket* was less a newspaper than a community-newsletter–gossip-rag combination. Nothing escaped Hap's pen, no matter how obscure. Tom stood behind the lobby counter and gazed out at the little dots of light illuminating the doors of his empty motel rooms. If anyone had come by to check in, he hadn't been here to greet them. "I need to ask you a favor, Hap. Friend to friend. If ever I needed anything from you, it's now."

"Sure, name it."

"You can't run *this* story."

"Why not?"

"It's about Sienna. She . . ." But Tom couldn't get the words out. They choked off in his throat and tears burned his eyes. He eased himself down on the stool and tried to catch his breath, tried not to let Hap know he was crying.

"Tom?" The line buzzed. "Tom? You okay?"

"Yeah," he managed. "Come by tomorrow, Hap. I'll tell you then." He dropped the phone back on its cradle and wiped his eyes. He hadn't seen Lauren's Jeep pull up, and she startled him when she burst through the door, a sense of urgency billowing around her. Tom wondered who in Rocket *didn't* know what was going on by now with that horrible woman calling the police and probably half the town. Was there anyone? Anyone in this whole damn town who wouldn't know everything by morning?

"Tom, I'm sorry," Lauren said, rounding the counter and putting her hands on his shoulders. She kneaded the muscles at the back of his neck, but he refused to look up, embarrassed by his tears.

"That bitch receptionist of yours. What's she doing? Calling everyone in town?"

"I'll let her go." Lauren worked his muscles harder. "How are you doing?"

"Under the circumstances..."

"How's Sienna?"

Tom turned then to look at Lauren. He couldn't recall the last time she'd asked that question. "She doesn't know what she's done."

"Did...Sheriff Turnbull come out?" Lauren's voice sounded as soft and tentative as the sheriff's had, as if this new tenor were contagious.

"I should've put the kitten down myself. I shouldn't have involved you." He couldn't stop fresh tears, and knowing that made his chest tight. "Turnbull called child welfare. They could be here by morning."

Lauren winced and gave Tom a long pained stare. "I'm so sorry," she whispered.

※

Tom hadn't slept, but by morning he was grateful that
his motel was empty. He and Lauren sat in the clean-but-
scruffy kitchen, drinking coffee from mismatched mugs.
He watched her sturdy fingers as she rubbed the letters
on her cup, *UNIVERSITY OF MONTANA* printed in
large block letters. She'd come through for him in a way
he couldn't have imagined, wouldn't have predicted, and
it filled him with gratitude toward her. Overnight, Lauren
had transformed his apartment from a rat-hole to something near homey. She'd gotten on her knees and
scrubbed his grimy bathtub, mopped the floors, and
taken everything off the bookshelves to wipe away six
years of dust. She had scoured the inside of his refrigerator and arranged it so the food looked more plentiful.
She'd chipped hard-water deposits off the kitchen faucet
and swept dead flies out of the sills. He'd kept pace with
her, doing whatever she directed him to do, taking out the
trash, vacuuming the carpets, organizing the closets. The
buttons had been collected in a big glass jar and set on the
television. Tom knew Sienna would throw a tantrum
when she saw the jar, but returning them to their patterns
and color arrangements would also keep her busy.

Sienna was now asleep in the single bedroom, where
Tom had carried his sleeping daughter after he and
Lauren arranged her things in his old closet and dresser.
It would be her room from now on; he would take the
sofa.

"They can't come in here and find a twelve-year-old
sleeping on the couch every night," Lauren had told him.
"She's getting too old for that; she needs privacy."

Tom nodded. He'd thought of that before, but Sienna
was still so little-girlish to him. Until she was five, she'd
slept on the floor in his bedroom. He and Maria had
imagined they'd have a house of their own before Sienna
was old enough to need her own room.

"Does she bathe herself?" Lauren looked Tom square in the eye when she asked it, sometime around dawn.

"You know she doesn't." He was irritated by her question.

"That's not the right answer, Tom."

"But it's the truth."

Lauren bit her lip as she looked over her shoulder at Sienna asleep in her father's bed. The activity in the apartment had agitated Sienna at first, and she'd retreated to a corner of the sofa, where she pulled her legs up under her and rocked. When Tom ran the vacuum, she covered her ears and whined. The next time he checked on her, she'd fallen asleep.

"What happened yesterday was horrible. It was a tragedy that you can't ignore, Tom," Lauren urged.

"I know," he snapped.

"Look, they're going to take your daughter away from you if you don't answer the questions right."

Tom stared at her, bewildered. It hadn't occurred to him that they might actually take Sienna. He was a good father. He was doing the best he could.

"She needs help," Lauren pressed. "Help that you can't give her. Things have to change, but I don't want to see it happen this way."

The early morning conversation bounced in his head now as he sat dazed and empty across from Lauren. The feeling reminded him of being hungover, griminess coupled with a lack of sleep and suffocating stress. He reached across the table and rubbed Lauren's hand.

"I don't know what I would have done without you."

She looked up from her coffee. "Promise me something, Tom."

"What?"

"When this is over, when they've come and seen that you're a good dad, and things are back to normal again, promise me you'll look into other living options for Sienna."

He frowned. "She's my daughter. What are you asking me to do?"

"It's for her own good."

"What, you want me to stick her in a home? Like some kind of pet I don't want anymore? Is that what you're asking?"

"Tom," Lauren said with a pleading glance. "You're tired. Just . . . just think about it. Think about what's best for Sienna. How long can you go on like this?"

"Like what?" Tom shoved back his chair and dumped his coffee into the sink. "I agree that what happened was terrible. It won't happen again; I'll make sure of that. She isn't an animal. She's my daughter."

Lauren closed her eyes. She took a slow breath. Then she stood, too, and put her mug in the sink. "I'm exhausted, and I don't need to be here when they show up. I'm going home. Please call me later."

He didn't agree immediately, but stared at her, still burning over her suggestion. At last he nodded and only then did she leave. He'd pushed her away and he knew it. He always pushed people away. Why should Lauren be different? That was his prerogative, he believed, for having a daughter like Sienna.

☼

Lauren was bone tired when she got home. She showered and went into the clinic because she had appointments that she couldn't afford to reschedule. At the rate things were going, she'd never see those clients again if she wasn't available when they wanted to see her.

The clinic was dark, though Belinda should've been there by now. Lauren had given her a key so she could get the files pulled and the rooms prepped first thing.

"Where is that woman?" Lauren said under her

breath. She was simultaneously annoyed with her for her perpetual tardiness and sorry for letting Tom think the worst of Belinda in order to save her own relationship with him. Oh well, she thought, at least now I can let her go and Tom will think I did it for him. She couldn't shake the image of Tom crying from her mind. By helping him clean and coaching him on how to answer the questions that the state would ask, hadn't she somehow defeated the purpose of calling the authorities in the first place? She could have done less and Tom wouldn't have known the difference. The man was certainly in no condition to defend himself when she found him last night.

Lauren pressed the blinking light on the answering machine and listened to Belinda's gravelly voice.

*"Dr. Kent, I don't think I can work for you. I'm really sorry not to give you more notice, but after last night with that poor kitten, I just don't think I have what it takes. I hope that man gets some help for his daughter. That child is a threat to society."*

Lauren stared out into the empty parking lot as she listened, then she pulled the files for her appointments and slipped them into the slot in the wall at the back of the reception area where she could easily retrieve them. As she donned her lab coat, the phone rang.

"Dr. Kent, this is Shari O'Connor. I need to cancel the appointment for my cat today."

Here it starts, Lauren thought. "Okay, when would you like to reschedule it for?"

"I can't reschedule. My husband got transferred. They're closing the cable office."

Lauren paused over her appointment calendar. "What does that mean? No more television?"

"The Hood River office is going to service this end of the gorge from now on."

Lauren nodded. "I'm sorry to hear you're leaving Rocket."

The woman laughed, a little sarcastically. "We're just the next in a long string of people, I bet. This town is dying."

"Don't say that."

"It is, Dr. Kent. Maybe you don't feel it, but it is."

"Oh, I feel it. Believe me."

The woman laughed again. "Yeah, I guess I just canceled my appointment, didn't I?"

The woman's laughter made Lauren angry. Why did everyone assume that because she was a veterinarian she was rich and that her business was immune to a downturn in the economy? If people continued to leave Rocket at the rate they were fleeing now, she'd be out of business in six months.

"Good luck to you, Shari," Lauren said and hung up the phone without waiting for the woman to respond.

Maybe it's time to consider moving my practice, she thought. But to where? She loved Rocket for its charm, its transient ebb and swell. She loved being the big fish in this small pond. Her only competition was Ellie, and Ellie lived in Hood River and only worked in Rocket two days a week. Lauren was *the* resident doctor, a status she relished. That she dated the owner of the highway motel made her seem accessible to her clientele, something else she relished.

She didn't want to see this town die. She didn't want to start over somewhere else. Lauren was confident in her skills as a doctor, but competition made her uncomfortable. No one second-guessed her here. No one had the training to review her work, make judgments about its quality.

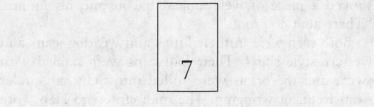

7

HAP SAT AT THE COUNTER in the Windy Point Diner and waited for his eggs Benedict. He wasn't a breakfast-eating man, but he'd resolved to patronize the businesses in town when he could in an attempt to keep them afloat. He knew that having breakfast twice a week at the diner wouldn't make that much difference toward Linda's bottom line, but it couldn't hurt, either. And maybe it would inspire others. He'd written a lengthy column for the front page of the most recent edition of *The Rocket* encouraging his fellow townsfolk to do the same, listing the casualties of this windless summer: the Rocket Kite Shop, Susan Bradford's Tiny Tots day care, the Rocky Mountain Chocolate Shop, a loss he took particularly hard, and the most recent, Yolanda's Used Books. The last one seemed too rapid to be the fault of the wind, but it all added up to bad things for Rocket.

"It's global warming," the man sitting to Hap's right commented to his companion.

Hap had thought the two men were truckers on their way through town, but now he tuned in to their conversation.

"I don't believe in that crap," the other said as he

shoved a piece of well-cooked bacon into his mouth. "There ain't no proof."

Both men were in their fifties and wearing jeans and western-style shirts. Their ball caps were stained with sweat and the brims were rolled into tight half-circles from frequent wringing. The man closest to Hap wore filthy tennis shoes.

"How can you not believe it? Just look around you. Read the papers. Watch the news. They're having hurricanes of biblical proportions in the gulf, Florida is getting their nuts frosted regularly, and we don't have any goddamn wind."

"Wind'll come back."

"When? When we're out of business?"

Hap tilted his head forward and looked down the counter. It was a small gesture that usually got him invited into the conversation. "What do you men do?"

The man next to him practically barked with credulity. "Wind turbines."

"That's a tough business in a summer like this." Hap sat back and sipped his coffee. He hadn't given much thought to the wind turbines that lined miles and miles of open prairie to the north, like an orchard of enormous tri-blade fans, or tombstones now. They were everywhere in eastern Washington, not far from Rocket. Harnessing wind to generate clean electricity was an idea he'd supported wholeheartedly. He'd even written an article a few years earlier about the first turbines to go in. The locals scoffed. They thought it was a fanciful dream and that it could never replace hydropower. Perhaps they were wiser than they had seemed at the time.

"We just finished installing the last fifty turbines last fall. Cost us a fucking fortune. And they're standing out there like great big white goddamn daisies."

Linda brushed by with the coffeepot and refilled the

line of mugs down the counter. "Nice column, Hap. I appreciate your perspective."

"Don't mention it," he said.

"It helped. I've had more people today than I think I got all last week combined."

The two men studied Hap anew.

"I edit *The Rocket Rocket*. Our local newspaper. I encouraged folks to come out and support the local businesses. We've lost more than a few lately."

"That's a neighborly thing to do. Good man."

☼

The child welfare case manager, Alexandra Metzger, arrived seconds after nine o'clock. She stood politely in the lobby, her pale eyes darting from surface to surface so that Tom wished he'd taken the same care cleaning this public entrance as he and Lauren had his apartment. But it was too late to scrub the day-old coffee stains off the table, or sweep the doughnut crumbs into the wastebasket. It was too late to vacuum up the pea gravel that made its way in from the parking lot wedged into the grids of sneaker soles.

"Good morning," she said. "Mr. Jemmett?"

"Yes," he replied and instantly heard the stiffness in his tone. "Please call me Tom."

The temperature was already in the high seventies, and the fan blew warm air around the room. He motioned toward the apartment.

"We can talk in the kitchen."

Sienna sat on the sofa, her hair in wild disarray, and stared at the *Good Morning America* reporter interviewing someone in front of a crowd of screaming people with signs. Tom poured a cup of coffee for the social worker without asking if she wanted any and set it next to her. She ignored it.

"That must be Sienna," Ms. Metzger said, gesturing through the entryway at the back of the child's head.

"Yes." Tom stood rigidly near the sink, waiting for the woman to do whatever it was she was going to do. She was younger than he'd expected, thirty-five perhaps. A boxy woman, square face, square shoulders, square hands, which were softened only by the color of her pale orange pantsuit. She pulled a notebook and pen from her briefcase, and dropped her business card on the table. "Do you mind if I take a look around?"

"Not at all," he lied.

He followed her to the bedroom. "Sienna sleeps here. We only have one bedroom. I...sleep on the sofa." He turned to find his daughter staring at him, undoubtedly wondering why he was telling this lie. He flushed with shame.

The woman nodded and opened the closet.

"She's getting older now. She needs her privacy," he said, more for Sienna's benefit than the social worker's, but then wished he hadn't.

Ms. Metzger pulled back the ripped shower curtain and stared down into the rust-stained porcelain. She made notes, then opened the medicine cabinet and examined bottles. She turned to him abruptly, holding a bottle of painkillers so long out-of-date he couldn't remember why he had them.

"You need to throw away all old prescription drugs."

"Sure," he said, suddenly annoyed with Lauren for missing that detail; she would have known to throw those out. "I forgot it was there. That must be two years old. At least."

"Everything else needs to be locked up. It can't be where Sienna can reach it."

"Okay," he said. Sienna had never gotten into the medicine cabinet, but now, as he saw the pills in the case worker's hand, he realized how lucky he'd been.

Tom followed the woman through the cramped apartment until she'd opened every cabinet, closet, and drawer. She inspected the contents of his refrigerator, its bologna, mayonnaise, and cheddar cheese. She warned him about the cleaning supplies under the sink, within Sienna's reach. He nodded, anxious to obey. Then she asked him to recount the incident with the cat. He pressed his fingers to the side of his head to ease the pounding in his temple as he spoke. Lauren had made him rehearse it word for word six or seven times during the night. He told the truth about what had happened, the damning words marching out devoid of emotion as Ms. Metzger took notes.

"I'm going to speak with Sienna now," she said.

*Good luck,* Tom thought. He stayed in the kitchen, where he could hear the social worker trying to get Sienna to talk. The woman's voice was at first sweet, then firm. Not once did he hear a response from his daughter. At last Ms. Metzger returned to the kitchen.

"Severe autism?" she asked.

Tom hated that label. Maria had hated it, too. "I've been told multiplex developmental disorder."

"Autism," she said too severely, making the short hairs on Tom's neck prickle. "Who are you working with?"

"Dr. Taglione at the Hood River Mental Health Clinic."

"Medications?"

Tom shook his head. "We've chosen not to."

Ms. Metzger jotted down the doctor's name. Her eyes studied him, chill and remote. "I don't see anything here to cause concern for the child's safety."

For the first time in hours, Tom breathed normally. But then he remembered that he hadn't told her about Sienna's accident with his truck. Should he? Would she take his daughter away if she knew? Or did she already know? Would she take her away if she found out from someone other than him?

"She needs better supervision, though. And you'll lock up all toxic substances?"

He agreed. He could always claim he'd forgotten about the truck incident—it was so minor. He'd let it go for now.

"I'll talk to Dr. Taglione this afternoon. I will be making regular visits over the next few months. Not all will be scheduled. If I find things in the same order as today, you don't have anything to worry about."

Tom felt his temper rise. This woman would be dropping by without notice to assess his parenting?

The social worker made her way out to the motel lobby, followed closely by Tom, who couldn't wait to see her off. She stopped short at the front door. "Have you figured out where she got that kitten?"

"No."

"Be sure she can't do this again." Ms. Metzger's gray eyes seemed to bore holes into Tom's forehead.

He bit the inside of his cheek as he nodded meekly. Of course he would see to it she couldn't do it again. What kind of idiot did this woman think he was?

*

Tom collapsed onto the sofa next to Sienna. She glanced at him, then back at the television screen. He studied her, the way her wavy dark hair cascaded in tangles over her olive skin. She looked so much like her mother. She seemed older now, as if she'd matured overnight. Her thin cotton nightgown clung to her body, revealing small breasts. He turned away at the sight of them.

"Daddy's beat, sweetie," he said.

She ignored him.

This never would have happened if Maria were still alive. None of this would've happened. He thought of the kitten, how its limp body curled in the palm of his hand, the tiny spot of blood in its nostril. And he thought again of his wife. He pushed the memory away, but the thin arc of blood that had soaked into his shirt all those years ago stubbornly remained. Like a bright light burnt onto his retina, holding its shape long after he'd closed his eyes.

☀

Tom was wrenched back to the present by Sienna shrieking.

"Buttons!"

She loomed over him now, holding the jar of buttons, shaking it loudly at him.

He rubbed a hand across his eyes and sighed. "We had to clean the house, Sienna. You can put them back now. Put them how you like them."

She rattled the jar furiously, then dumped the buttons out on the floor. Buttons scattered everywhere, rolling under the television and bouncing off the baseboard. The sight of her treasures, once so carefully sorted, now in a chaotic mess panicked her. She flung herself down on the floor, screeching, "My buttons, my buttons."

Tom pressed his hands over his eyes, still stung by the memory of his wife, limp and still as the kitten. He tried to tune out the tantrum, wishing he could close his ears as well against her shrill screaming. But she wailed and thrashed until he was forced to look, to be sure she was okay.

Sienna frantically scooped the buttons up again, piling them in her lap, tears and snot wetting her face. "My buttons," she wept, and bent over them tearfully, sifting them into piles by size.

☀

Tom jerked awake, sweaty and panicked. *The medicine cabinet. The cleaners.* He lurched up and staggered into the bathroom, where he stared at his unshaven face in the mirror. What was the point of this—any of this?

After urinating, he looked for Sienna. She had fallen asleep on her new bed, curled up wearing her thin cotton nightgown, which rode up her tan legs. Tom made a mental note to buy her some more shorts in that super-soft, thin material that she liked. Why did this come so hard—silly things like remembering to buy her clothes? He was a hopeless parent. Maria would have known how to manage these things. Wearily, he climbed into the shower.

※

Hap nodded at Stan Morgan, the owner of the Red Tail Tavern, and lumbered up to the bar. Barely eleven in the morning, but a few regulars sipped beer and shot pool. He slid onto a stool as the smell of grease and spilled beer slowly surfaced, but then wouldn't go away.

"Philly steak sandwich on special today," Stan said as he placed a napkin on the counter in front of Hap.

"I'll start with a dry martini."

Stan's eyebrows went up, but he remained silent as he poured the drink, carefully dropping in the olive and set-ting the glass down. "Rough day?"

Hap frowned. "What's the news in town?"

"Newspaperman is asking me?" Stan scratched his heavy mustache. "Jemmett girl and that cat is all I heard about last night. I was ready to cut the whole damn place off unless they changed the fucking subject."

"That's what I figured."

"What? You were hoping to get the jump on news like that? Better go to work in Portland, then. This is a small town. Everybody knows everything the minute it hap-pens." Stan wiped the bar as he spoke, his gray braid sweeping over his shoulder and grazing the wet surface. He wore the same black leather vest he always did over a tee shirt, his well-defined, tattooed arms bulging out at the sleeves.

"I wasn't looking to get the jump on *that* story," Hap said and sipped his martini.

Stan nodded somberly. "Yeah, that's a sad one. You talk to Tom?"

"Just came from the motel. He took it hard. Child services paid him a visit bright and early this morning."

"It ain't the end of the world. Stuff like this happens." Stan opened a can of Coke and took a deep drink. "Shit, normal kids mess up, too. Everybody's acting like she's a freak or something."

"I promised Tom I wouldn't run the story about the cat."

Stan's pale eyes came up to meet Hap's. "Best not. The wolves have had their meat. Let it lie."

※

Lauren stood in the sweltering afternoon sun, holding a cardboard box with two tiny gray kittens in the bottom. Tom's boots were all she could see of him, wedged under the shed behind the motel. She thought of the certainty of spiders in that cramped, dark place. Those creatures fascinated her with their gruesome ways, until she imagined them crawling across her skin or tangled in her hair. She shivered.

"Are there any more?" she called to him.

"One that I can see." His voice was muffled, and she wasn't sure she heard him right. Out along the back fence where Tom's property ended and the basalt bluffs jutted skyward, a calico cat lurked, watching them take her babies. Lauren crouched down and put a hand out, though the cat was several hundred feet away.

"Here, kitty kitty. Here, kitty kitty kitty," she called.

The cat slunk into the prairie grass and out of sight as

Tom inched out, ankles first, then legs, butt, back, and head. His forehead was caked with sweat and dirt, and cobwebs clung to his hair. In his outstretched hand he gripped two kittens, one orange and the other gray.

"Don't squeeze so hard," Lauren warned. "You'll hurt them."

He glared up at her as he handed them over. "You crawl under there and get them yourself if you don't want me to squeeze too hard."

Lauren scooped them up and put them in the box with their littermates.

"You see the mother?"

"She's out there in the grass. I can't get her to come anywhere near us."

He sat in the dust, gazing off toward the fence line. "Well, it's not likely Sienna will get ahold of her."

"No, but she'll have more kittens if *we* don't."

He stood up and dusted himself off, then opened the shed door. "I've got a live trap in here somewhere."

"You do?" Lauren peered into the darkness behind him. "What for?"

"Raccoons. When Maria and I first bought the place, there was a whole family of them living under the motel."

That name stung. *Maria.* Lauren hated it when Tom mentioned his dead wife, though why, she wasn't exactly sure. Maria posed no threat to their relationship, and he rarely brought her up, but it never ceased to catch Lauren by surprise when he spoke that name. It rolled off his tongue so lovingly. Maria. *Mah-ree-ah.* And it sounded so much like Sienna. *See-enn-ah.*

He emerged with the wire contraption and dropped it on the step. "You have any of that fancy cat food?"

"Milk will work."

He peered into the box at the kittens. "Cute, aren't they?"

"I'll drop them off at the shelter in Hood River to-morrow. In the meantime, I'll take them down to the clinic and give them some food." Lauren started for her Jeep.

"Thanks for helping me catch them."

She looked over her shoulder at Tom. She wanted to ask him what he was going to do about Sienna now. Just because the social worker didn't do anything didn't mean everything was fine. Did he see that his daughter needed help? Did it register that she was taking tiny kittens away in a box, not because they were feral, but to protect them from Sienna?

"I'm glad things went well this morning." Lauren hesitated, then said, "It doesn't mean you're out of woods, though."

"I know," he said, but he wouldn't look at her.

"Sienna needs help, Tom."

He said nothing, but started toward the back porch.

☼

In the house Tom found Sienna still arranging the buttons. Just when he thought she was done, she'd go back and mess with them again. She huffed with fierce concentration as she worked, clearly still angry that he'd touched them. This time, she laid out a continuous row across the windowsill from deep cobalt to sky blue to white to pale green to forest and so on. Then she ran her finger along it, naming the colors, softly. "Dark blue, light blue, white, light green, dark green, yellow, orange, light red, dark red, purple." She paused, as if expecting her chain of colors to continue, though she was at the end of the line. Her eyes skimmed backward through the buttons to the beginning, and she nodded in satisfaction. "Dark blue..." she began again.

After his second shower that day, Tom sat in the lobby exhausted, not from his usual work and lack of sleep, but the more difficult task of navigating his emotions. What Sienna had done to that kitten dredged up memories that he had worked continuously to keep at bay. They'd fought, he and Maria, the day she died. The last words spoken between them had been harsh, hateful, and accusatory. He could never right it, never take them back. Maria died angry with him. Worse, she died believing he hated her.

He pushed it away again, looking for the small things that had made them happy. Those fragments of which the sum totaled a happy marriage, not that horrible angry moment that now branded his memory. An occasional car whizzed past on the highway, but no one slowed. As the sun sank into the western sky, the river sparkled topaz and the cliffs on the Oregon side of the gorge purpled. He peered in on Sienna, who was still working her color chain, then walked out into the parking lot to escape his thoughts. It was the view that they had fallen in love with, not the motel. The motel was simply the vehicle by which he and Maria might live out their dream on the starkly beautiful plateau overlooking that generous river. She had been the one who had instantly seen its potential. Maria had talked him into reviving the place. In the beginning—years ago, they could hardly stay focused on the work at hand, constantly pausing to take in the soft scent of grass and the sight of shale, or look out at the broad Columbia and its shifting palette of green, blue, and purple. The wind had swept the dry air off the high plains and down the gorge, carrying with it the scent of hay and wheat in summers past.

She would sneak up on him as he repaired an air conditioner, or shampooed a carpet, and slide her hands along his ribs. It always gave him a start. He'd turn and she'd meet him with a smile and a kiss.

"I love this place," she loved to say. "I love this

place." She didn't mean the motel—or at least he didn't think so.

She died before the vineyard went in on the other side of the river. She would have loved that, too, with its precision rows and carefully groomed vines. They might have waited for the wine to age, then spent a Sunday afternoon in the tasting room, gazing back at their own little motel atop its bluff. They would have talked about the future. About their dreams for Sienna. When she was born, they had imagined her growing up to be a scientist or a doctor. Sienna would go to college, they agreed. She would be the first in their families to do so. They were prepared to scrub as many toilets as it would take to make sure she got that opportunity.

Tom shook the fantasy off and walked back inside. Maria had once told him if anything ever happened to her that he should remarry. He'd laughed at her when she'd said it. How could he do that when there was no woman on earth who could compare to her? Without Maria, he didn't think he could do this alone. A stepmother was not in Sienna's future, so perhaps it was time for him to look at other alternatives for her. Perhaps a group home, or assisted-living facility. He thought of the busload of retarded people. There had to be someplace that understood kids like her.

He drew up the stool and turned on the radio, hoping to catch the last few minutes of the Portland news. But the first thing he heard made his head jerk up. A perky reporter was talking about Art, his Art, the bus driver who had come through with the group of retarded people.

"... *beaten to death in a bedroom of the assisted-living facility where he worked. Several residents of Independent Living allege that Art Schlegel sodomized them repeatedly over the past several months. One of the residents, a man whose identity is being withheld, is in custody for the fatal beating.*" The reporter delivered the news neutrally, smoothly switching to the price of gasoline.

Tom suddenly felt woozy, as if he might pass out. The heat was stifling. He couldn't breathe. He clicked off the radio and staggered back out to the parking lot. Sweat dripped from his forehead and nose. And he had *just that moment* entertained the idea of putting his little girl in a place like that.

He doubled over and vomited on the sidewalk.

# 8

TOM SHOT UPRIGHT on the sofa, gasping for air. The heat felt more oppressive in the darkness. He missed his bed, and the apartment smelled like hot dust and Cheetos. He lay back on the couch again, his undershirt sticking to his body. The bell chimed in the lobby, startling him. He wondered if it was the night bell that had awakened him and not his relentless parsing of the bus driver who raped his charges. Or how the man had been so outwardly caring toward those people that Tom actually considered a facility like that for his own daughter. How could he have been so far off in his judgment of the man? He pulled his jeans on and stumbled out into the dim light.

An urchinlike man stood in the lobby, looking starved out and sleep deprived. His thin beard only partially covered the snake tattooed along his jawline, and his greasy hair hung to his shoulders, limp and stringy. "You have any rooms?"

Tom nodded and looked at the clock. It was just after two in the morning. He glanced past the man at the battered Torino, vintage 1970 and oxidized to silver-blue, idling in the turnaround. A woman sat in the passenger's seat. She'd been staring at Tom, but when their eyes met, she flinched and looked away, slumping down in the seat. But not before Tom saw her two blackened eyes and smashed nose. He turned back to the man and spoke slowly. "One bed or two?"

The man hesitated, as if he might change his mind about the room. "One."

Tom slid the registration card onto the counter. "Fill this out." He looked back at the woman, but she was turned away from him now. Tom studied the man's knuckles for evidence to the woman's condition, but his entire body was scratched and scabbed the way junkies often look. Tom thought about sending the couple away as he usually did with people like this who stopped, but the woman's condition bothered him. "Where're you from?"

The man glanced up. "Minnesota."

"Been on the road long?"

"Few days." He slid the card back, but Tom couldn't make out the writing.

"What's the name on this?"

"Bill."

"Bill . . . ?"

The man eyed Tom carefully. "Johnson."

Bill Johnson my ass, Tom thought. He took the cash Bill laid on the counter and made change, then turned to the rack of keys. He took down room ten, looked at it, then back at the car. The woman was peering at him again. She looked terrified. He put the key back and picked up room six. Its luck was running four-to-one in the negative, and he thought this man deserved a shot at either winning the lottery or being crushed by a semi. "Here you go. Six is in the corner there." He pointed out the window at the darkened unit.

Bill scooped the key up and was out the door without another word.

Tom considered calling Sheriff Turnbull, but their last meeting was still too fresh in his mind. He didn't want to remind Turnbull that his daughter had killed a kitten, or that social services had paid him a visit. Suddenly he wondered if he and Sienna were all that different from the couple in room six. He examined the scratches and bite wounds on his own arms and recalled the clean-cut man who'd sodomized the people in his care. Looks could be deceiving. Perhaps there was another reason for the made-up name. Who was he to judge?

※

At dawn Tom filled an air pot with coffee and placed it on the table in the lobby. He'd canceled the doughnut order, despite Hap's article about supporting the local businesses. No point in paying for doughnuts to go stale in the heat, and his fellow Rocketeers weren't exactly rushing out and renting rooms to keep him in business, either. He missed Lauren, or the company of an adult. Lauren was smart and funny. He enjoyed their conversations, usually. They talked politics often, though they were on opposite ends, she more conservative, he more liberal. Lauren had managed to convince him to see things her way about a few issues like the inherent rights of property owners and the responsibility of individuals to make their own way in life. But only after she'd given handicapped people like Sienna a pass, agreeing that in some circumstances society had an obligation to provide for the less capable.

Tom and Sienna had eaten bacon and eggs for breakfast, and she'd actually smiled at him in exchange for six bright blue buttons in various sizes that he'd collected for her. He'd been trying to be more attentive, guilty for entertaining the idea of putting her in an assisted-living facility.

"Blue," she'd said, leaping up from the table to work them into her elaborate array. Now, two hours later, she was still working on it, chanting, "Blue, blue, blue."

Tom poured himself a cup of strong coffee and flicked on the television, waiting for his guests to check out. Maybe he'd call Lauren later. At last the woman appeared at the door. She looked as frightened as ever, yanking the handle and rushing the desk. She reminded him a little of Sienna, her wild mannerisms, and her matted hair. And those purple-black bruises under her eyes, they made him cringe.

Tom stood. "Checking out?"

"He won't move," she said. "He just lays there like he's dead or something."

"Who?"

"Martin," she snapped, as if Tom were slow.

"You mean the man you checked in with?"

She was headed back to the room now, looking over her shoulder to see if Tom followed.

"Did you call an ambulance?" Tom asked as he caught up to her.

She shot him a look of terror. "He'd kill me if I did that."

Tom followed her to room six.

The woman refused to go inside, instead looking cautiously in from the sidewalk, keeping her distance. "He pushed the dresser up like that so I couldn't get out," she said. "He always does that."

He had to squeeze through the narrow opening where the bureau had once been shoved against the door, then pried away again. He went to the bed where Bill or Martin or whoever he was lay motionless, the orange polyester spread covering him completely. Tom approached cautiously, a part of him dreading what he might find, another part worried that this man might come up shooting.

He turned back to the woman. "I don't have any money. The register in the office is empty."

She scowled, confused, and Tom realized how ridiculous that sounded.

"Bill!" he shouted at the bed.

"His name is Martin," the woman hissed from the door.

"Martin! Are you okay? Martin?"

The man lay still as a petrified log. Tom pulled the bedspread down and choked off a gasp. Martin's eyes were open wide; his mouth, too. His thin lips were blue. Spit had trickled from the corner of his mouth and crusted into white flakes in his beard. Tom reached down to feel for a pulse, but yanked his hand back again at the thought of touching the man. He tried once more, looking at the ceiling as he ran his index finger along Martin's throat, feeling the cool, clammy skin. He found no pulse.

"Is he dead?" The woman pressed herself forward without coming inside the room.

"I think so," Tom replied. He turned, ready to console her, but she let out an enormous sigh, her shoulders loosened, and her face went slack.

"Thank God!" She squeezed past the dresser and into the room now. "He was a lunatic. Picked me up in Vegas and wouldn't let me go. I told him he got only thirty minutes." She squinted at Tom as if she could hardly believe Martin's idiocy for not understanding the time limit. She seemed old beyond her years, with puffy bags and broken teeth. Beyond the temporary bruises inflicted by Martin, a hard life had etched itself deeply.

"Excuse me?"

She huffed. "He's a john. I thought he was gonna kill me. He busted me up pretty good."

"I noticed that." Tom looked around, wondering what he should do. A half-empty bottle of Southern Comfort stood on the end table next to a homemade crack pipe, a book of matches, and a Brillo pad. He needed to call Sheriff Turnbull. Instead, he turned back to the woman. "What's your name?"

She studied him as if suddenly realizing she'd said too much. "Why? It don't matter. I didn't kill him or nothing. I told him he got thirty minutes."

Tom opened his mouth, but closed it again, not knowing what to say. She wasn't quite all there, mildly retarded maybe, or severely damaged by drugs?

"I mean I wanted to, believe me. Kill him, that is. I thought of lots of ways to do it, but this is what I got for looking at him wrong." She pulled her shirt up and turned her back to Tom, revealing the sort of angry, oozing welts he'd only seen on the backs of slaves in made-for-TV movies. "I put cocaine in his whiskey, but it just made him twice as mean. He was a *lunatic*."

"Holy mother of God." Tom whistled. "Come on. Let's get some help." He took the woman by the arm, and she came with him back to the lobby, though her feet dragged reluctantly along the sidewalk and she glanced back at the room repeatedly.

※

Hap stood with Tom and Sheriff Turnbull in the motel parking lot. They watched as the ambulance driver slammed the doors shut and pulled away. A gust of wind descended from the bluff, raising a dust devil along the highway. All three men paused to look at it, then at the sky. There was an expectant silence as they waited, holding their breath for another one. But the air went still. Their shoulders drooped in disappointment.

"How's Sienna?" Hap asked, before realizing that it was likely not a topic Tom wanted to discuss in front of the sheriff.

"Working on her buttons," Tom said. He sounded distant, as if mulling a puzzle.

"Sure been out here a lot for so little wind this summer," Turnbull remarked absently, then flushed pink. "It's busy all over," he added. "Environmentalists tried to break in to the hatchery last night. Didn't succeed. But I'm still wondering what they were planning to do. Free all the baby fish?"

Hap watched Tom, but the reference to Turnbull's visits, and the reminder that his most recent was painfully associated with Sienna, seemed to slide right by him. Tom seemed distracted to the point of not even being there. "Fish kissers at the hatch and a dead man in room six," Hap said to ensure that Tom didn't pick up on Turnbull's blunder.

"That was the second," Tom said, looking off toward room six. "No, wait—third. He was the third person to come up dead after staying in that room." He laughed.

"Three?" Turnbull asked.

"That assisted-living guy in Portland who was beat to death by the retarded people he was supposed to take care of. He stayed in there. Right after Helen Simpson."

Hap perked up. "Are you serious?"

Tom nodded at the lobby where the woman, Freda Schaffer, sat as if waiting for her fate to be dictated. "What are you going to do about her?" he asked Turnbull.

"Nothing. I got her statement. She isn't under arrest." Turnbull tucked his small notebook into his breast pocket and started for his cruiser. "Three, you say?"

Tom was looking at Freda again. Hap really noticed her for the first time then. He'd dismissed her as a prostitute caught up in a bad situation, but now, looking at her tiny frame, he wondered how she came to be a hooker in the first place. Drugs, he guessed. Wasn't it always drugs?

Tom ignored his question. "What about the car?"

"Belongs to the dead man," the sheriff answered. "I'll get it towed to impound until we figure out who to contact."

"Can't you give it to her?" Tom's eyes remained on the woman.

"By the book, Tom." Turnbull slid into the front seat of the cruiser and pulled the door shut. He sat in the air-conditioned vehicle for a few minutes, talking on the radio.

Tom shook his head. "Coldhearted bastard. If she wasn't a prostitute, he'd have made sure she got back home."

"I can give her a lift into town," Hap said. "She can catch the bus from there."

"Thanks." Tom started back to the lobby, so Hap followed. He wanted more information about these three deaths. It seemed an amazing coincidence that all had stayed in room six. Inside, Tom rounded the counter and opened his cash drawer. He counted out a hundred dollars in twenties, then slid them across the counter. Freda sat staring out the front window, her arms crossed tightly over her chest, one foot tucked up underneath her skinny frame. She hadn't even acknowledged their presence.

"Ms. Schaffer?" Tom said.

She turned to him, but didn't get up.

"Are you sure you don't want to go down to the clinic? I think someone should look at your injuries."

She shook her head.

"You can still file a report with the sheriff. It's not too late."

"What for? The asshole is dead. What are they gonna do to him now? He got what was coming to him."

"It was wrong, what happened to you," Tom told her softly.

She grunted as if everything in the world that happened to her was wrong.

"Well, at least take some money . . . to get back to Nevada. Hap here can give you a lift into Rocket. The Greyhound comes through twice a day."

She stood and picked up the cash that Tom had laid on the counter, fanning it out in front of her to see how much was there. After a moment, she put it in her jeans pocket and said, "I can repay you for it before I go, if you want me to. I do oral or—"

Tom shook his head to halt her before she could go on. "You don't have to do that."

She shrugged. "Thanks." Then she turned to Hap expectantly.

Hap wasn't ready to go, but realized it wouldn't be appropriate to grill Tom about the deaths in front of this woman. He smiled at her, wishing he'd thought to give her the money himself. Tom couldn't afford it, Hap knew. Somehow Tom always managed to teach him how to be a proper man—something he didn't know he lacked until the two of them became friends.

"Right this way," Hap said, sweeping his arm out toward his waiting van.

※

A bottle of Pinot Noir sat uncorked in the middle of Tom's kitchen table. Two stemmed glasses stood next to it, along with bread sticks in a basket from the Rocket Bakery. Lauren had heeded Hap's column, making a list of the places she should patronize until the wind came back. Each of the business owners she'd identified were also pet owners, and she made a point of asking about their dog or cat by name. Lauren had to look up the name of Petra Osterlundt's shepherd-collie mix before she bought the bread. Kaiser. Why hadn't she remembered that the only German woman in town had named her dog Kaiser?

Lauren recalled the odd conversation they'd had. Petra, who was always in the mood to talk about her dog, had brushed right past that topic to ask if Lauren had seen Hap Mitsui lately. Petra seemed overly interested in how old Lauren thought Hap was, and if she thought he'd had his teeth veneered, or if they were natural.

Lauren opened the compact oven and checked the T-bones she was broiling. They were almost done. She pulled down the only two matching plates Tom owned, and placed them neatly across from each other on the mostly white tablecloth she'd found in the pantry. Then she peeked into Sienna's room. The child sat on the floor, sifting through a giant compartmentalized tray of beads. She seemed entranced by them. Lauren could see that Sienna had already begun to sort them out by color. The kit had come sorted, but Lauren dumped them out on her own dining room table and mixed them up before bringing them over with a cheeseburger and fries from the Dairy Queen. She'd hit a home run with the kid today. There were aspects of Sienna's autism that fascinated Lauren—her amazing patience to sit for hours, even days, and work out intricate patterns. Lauren had wondered if there was some savant tendency in the girl that was yet to be discovered. Maybe some rare talent for music or numbers or dates? Hard to know and less likely to find out while Sienna was cooped up in this depressing motel apartment day and night. It was as much for Sienna's future as it was for Tom's that he needed to get the girl some help.

When Tom emerged from the shower he was cleanly shaven and his blond hair still wet and combed straight back in a way that she'd never seen it before.

"You need a haircut," Lauren said.

Tom touched his hair, but said nothing.

"You're not going to grow it out and put it in a pony-tail, are you?" She laughed. "If you start looking like a hippy, I'll have to find a new boyfriend."

He shrugged, still preoccupied with his thoughts. "No, I just haven't had time to visit the barber. Dinner smells good." He wandered out into the hallway and stood for a long moment in Sienna's doorway, watching her.

"Will you pour the wine? The steaks are almost ready."

Tom obeyed, sitting down and tipping back on the hind legs of his chair. The back rested against the wall behind him, his feet dangling bare. "Thanks for bringing Sienna those beads. You made her day. Maybe her entire year."

"I thought she'd like them." Lauren carried the food to the table in three trips, then sat across from Tom. "She has an amazing eye for colors."

"That sofa is killing my spine," Tom said as he rubbed furiously at the back of his neck.

Lauren sat perfectly still and gazed at Tom. It was now or never. The subject would be difficult regardless of when she broached it, but she was a doctor. He had to listen to reason.

"Tom." She blinked and put her napkin in her lap. "We need to talk, about Sienna."

He blew his breath out and brought the front legs of his chair down hard on the linoleum. He stabbed his fork into one of the steaks and plopped it on his plate, withering the ambiance she'd worked so hard to cultivate in his ugly little kitchen.

She forged ahead anyway. "There are places where she can have full-time attention by trained, caring people. People who know how to work with her, to bring out all her talents. She's capable of much more."

"Places like where?"

"You know, assisted-living arrangements, group homes."

Tom snorted. "Do you have any idea what goes on in places like that?"

"Yes, Tom, I think I do." She sighed. "Listen, they're

regulated. It's not like the old days when they locked people up for being mentally deficient and threw away the key."

"Mentally deficient?"

She looked away. "You know what I mean."

"You're a vet, a medical professional. Shouldn't you know the difference between a mentally retarded person and an autistic one? Sienna isn't retarded."

Lauren bristled, but tried to keep her mind focused on the bigger issue. The scraping of their knives filled the silence between them as they cut their steaks.

Finally she said, "What I meant was that there are qualified people who take care of kids like Sienna for a living. It's their calling. They're kind, patient professionals."

"Really?" He threw his napkin down on his uneaten meal. "Have you read the papers lately?"

She stared at him blankly. She rarely picked up a newspaper or turned on the television. All the talk of terrorism and global warming only depressed her.

"Remember that busload of retarded people who stayed here last week?"

"Yeah."

"Well, that driver, the one in charge of the whole damn group, was . . . was . . . raping the people in his care."

Lauren cringed and set her fork down.

"He seemed like a pretty damn nice guy to me. I would never have guessed it." The veins at Tom's temples flared, and she could see his pulse hammering away at the side of his head. "And you want me to dump my little girl off at a place like that? You must be out of your fucking mind!"

Lauren leaned back in her chair, seared by his words. She could feel the heat rising in her cheeks. "I'm out of my fucking mind? Well, excuse me. I was trying to offer some solutions here."

"You're trying to get rid of her. You've been working up to this moment for as long as we've been dating." He stood and went to the sink, where he dumped his glass of wine down the drain.

"I don't need this shit," Lauren said, getting to her feet. "If you can't see my intentions for what they are, we don't have anything more to talk about."

"You're damn right we don't have anything more to talk about." Tom refused to look at her.

Lauren scooped up her purse and stormed through the lobby. In her Jeep, hot tears splashed down her cheeks, making it impossible to see the ignition. She waited, certain that Tom would come after her once he realized that she was only trying to help. But he didn't, and after a few minutes, as her fury dried her tears and she began to think of hurtful comebacks to his reaction, she started the engine and peeled out of the gravel lot, intending never to come back.

"I'm out of my fucking mind, am I?" she seethed. "I'm not the one sleeping on the sofa! I'm not the one pretending there's nothing wrong with that girl! I'm not the one covered in bite wounds! I'm not the one trapping kittens to protect them from my killer daughter! Out of *my* fucking mind?"

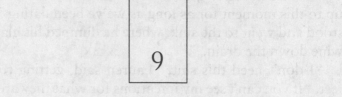

9

THE AROMA OF FRESH BREAD wafted out the storefront and over Hap as he stood on the sidewalk in front of the Rocket Bakery. He'd paused there as a breeze swirled down Main Street lifting the wind sock that had been left behind by the owner of the kite shop as a memorial to his once-thriving business. The yellow tail, sunbleached almost to white, rippled and danced, polarizing the few residents in its vicinity. Everyone halted. A man on the other side of the street pointed at it. And they waited. Another slow gust tipped the wind sock up almost parallel to the street, then eased it gently down again. No one moved. All eyes were riveted on the sock, then above to the wash of clear sky.

Hap stood motionless, as if any sudden movement might scare away this shy and tentative breeze, but after a moment he realized it was already gone. The others recognized its absence as well and went on with their business, their heads bent a little lower, their voices a lot quieter.

"Ve have pumpernickel today," Petra called from inside the bakery. "And ole veat."

Hap looked a last time at the wind sock. "Pumpernickel sounds good, Petra. I'll take a loaf of that."

✺

In the days after he and Lauren had fought over Sienna, Tom suffered a roller coaster of guilt and satisfaction. He missed Lauren, especially the sex, despite the perpetual rocky nature of their relationship. She was the only woman he'd ever dated who had a college degree, let alone a license to practice medicine on living creatures, and there was something about that fact that made her more alluring than he would have otherwise found her. She could buffalo him with her sharp wit and vast education, and he'd never know it. That excited him, the idea that he didn't have all the control in this relationship. But despite that, she needed to understand the order of things. Sienna first, girlfriend second. That's how it was, and that's how it was always going to be.

He let out a mirthless laugh. Who was he kidding? It was Maria he missed. The admission of it made him feel desperate to have her back again. He could almost feel her lay her head against the center of his back the way she always did after a fight. It was her way of letting him know that she still loved him. He'd caress her forearms and pull her more snugly around him, and the two of them would stand in a wordless embrace. They'd been through so much together between running a business and raising an autistic child; they'd fought over things big and small. But they had a ritual makeup dance. A silent communion. He would eventually turn and pull her against him, encircling her with his arms. Then she'd cry softly into his chest while he held her. They didn't need to say sorry.

✺

Tom had pulled the mattress out of room six and propped it against the wall behind the motel. He would haul it to the dump next chance he got. Even if he wanted to rent the room, which he didn't, he couldn't stomach the thought of some unsuspecting guest dozing off in that same spot where Martin's heart had seized and his bladder had failed. Tom convinced himself that the cause of the trouble with room six—the coincidence of three people dying—was somehow attached to the mattress, and one morning he loaded Sienna into his pickup and hauled the smelly thing away, stopping at the Bed Mart in Hood River on the way back to purchase a replacement. An expense he could scarcely afford.

It was Tom's custom to rent the rooms with the newest mattresses first, but even after he'd sanitized room six and made up the new bed with crisp white sheets smelling of bleach, his fingers paused only momentarily over that familiar key before he went on to grasp another. Eight people had checked in and out since Martin and his kidnapped hooker, some pleasant, some unreadable. No one who compelled Tom to try out the new bed, though.

In the dull, hot afternoons, after the chores were done and Sienna fed, he sat at the front desk and combed back through registration cards, making a list of names in chronological order on a yellow legal pad. All the people who'd stayed in room six since the day he and Maria had bought the motel. The boredom of running a motel with no guests had put him on a mission to know the score. When he was done, perhaps he'd do the same on another room just to see how they compared.

Sienna sat on the rug in the lobby, her tray of beads laid out in front of her. She picked through the colorful selection and constructed patterns, building on them, rearranging them. There were moments when just the right light hit her face, or a particular angle, that she looked exactly like Maria. She had her mother's rosebud lips and long black eyelashes. Tom cherished those glimpses. It was as if Maria lived on through their daughter.

"I love you, Sienna," he said. *"Do you love me?"* Maria sang it to Sienna every morning and every night.

Sienna didn't respond to his sentiment, but she never did.

"Do you love me? Do you love Daddy?"

Tom waited, then returned to scribbling down names, addresses, dates, on his legal pad. A woman pulled up in a nearly new Jaguar and strolled in, her stiletto heels clicking on the sidewalk, her gold bracelets clanking. Tom stared at her. He never got rich people here. Even Sienna looked up as the woman stepped around her in a waft of sweet perfume. The child's eyes followed the woman to the desk and remained on her for a long unreadable moment.

"Can I help you?" Tom asked.

"I need a room," the woman replied cheerfully.

He hesitated, as if maybe she misspoke. Then nodded and pulled out a registration card. "There's a nicer place up in Hood River," he finally said.

She flashed him a gleaming white smile. "This is fine."

He took her credit card and ran the number for confirmation, then handed her the receipt. Her manicured nails clicked lightly on the counter as she waited. He scanned the rack of keys, his fingers pausing over room six. It had a brand-new mattress. It was as clean as a hospital operating room after he'd finished with it. He pulled the key down, looked at it, turned it over in his hand. Maria's face flashed in his mind so suddenly that it startled him. He put the key back. He took down room five instead.

"Nice view of the pool from this room. Plus it has a kitchenette."

"Thanks," she said, taking the key. She turned to leave, but stopped to examine Sienna's masterpiece. "That's beautiful. I love it."

Sienna looked up again and stared at the woman's lips

with her dark eyes. Then she looked back at her creation as if seeing it for the first time. She pulled at her shirt absently, the neckline irritating against her skin, and silently mouthing the word *love*.

Tom watched, willing the child to say the word aloud.

"What is it?" the woman asked her.

Sienna pointed at the elaborate mosaic of pink, green, and red. "Watermelons. Smashed on the road."

The woman's eyebrows went up and she nodded, clearly at a loss. "Oh, how nice," she finally managed.

A shiver ripped up Tom's spine. When the woman had gone, he came out into the lobby and looked down at the design. "Sienna, what's that?" He pointed at the red and purple beads clumped together.

"Six."

※

Ellie was already seated at a table along the window when Lauren got to the Windy Point Diner. She waved, and as Lauren neared the table Ellie stood and gave her a brief, apologetic hug. They hadn't spoken since the night Sienna hurt the kitten, but their relationship had weathered many of Lauren's storms without any lasting damage. They just picked up and moved on. Let the past remain in the past.

Lauren bit her lip, tears springing to her eyes before she even sat down.

"What's wrong?" Ellie asked as she arranged her napkin on her ample lap.

Lauren shook her head, waiting for it to pass. She'd been uncharacteristically emotional since her fight with Tom. A trait she found annoying and demeaning in other women. "Nothing."

"Is business that bad?" Ellie looked out the window at the fence separating the nearly empty parking lot from the wrecking yard, with its razor wire snaking along the top.

Lauren took a breath and found her center. The momentary onslaught of emotion dissipated and she smiled again. "No. Well, yes."

Ellie nodded adamantly. "I'm pulling out of Rocket."

"What?"

"I can't keep both offices open and there are no patients here anymore. People are evacuating this town faster than they would if Mount Hood were about to blow. I receive two cancellations for every new appointment someone makes. Did you hear that the Verizon office is closing? That's eighteen people without jobs unless they opt to move into Portland."

"Yeah, I heard that."

"I don't have any choice but to move my practice to Hood River permanently."

Lauren felt the sting of returning tears. "Isn't Hood River affected by the lack of wind? It's a tourist town, too."

"Yeah, but it's got other things going on. There's the brewery, skiing, you don't need wind for that." Ellie sipped her coffee. "We've got agriculture. This is a good season for pears and you know Hood Bartletts are the best. Besides, people just like the place, wind or no wind. It's cute. It has historic buildings and quiet, tree-lined streets. Rocket is . . ." She gestured at the window. ". . . is so . . . God, look at that wrecking yard. How ugly is that to look at while you dine?"

Lauren agreed. Why the diner faced that monstrosity instead of the river on the other side was a mystery whose answer lay somewhere in the aesthetically barren eyes of its builder.

"Maybe you should consider moving your practice, too."

Lauren brushed away tears. "I have a lot invested in Rocket."

"Is this about Tom?"

"We fought the other day."

"About Sienna?"

Lauren nodded. The tears came faster.

"He'll come around."

"No he won't. He's blind to the problem." She picked up the menu and pretended to read the lunch specials as Linda came by with coffee.

"Do you need a minute to decide?"

"Just bring me a bowl of soup and a Caesar salad," Lauren said without looking at her. She thought about asking the waitress how her cat Monteaux was doing, but let it go. Lauren didn't want to advertise her emotional state to a woman with so much opportunity to spread gossip.

When Linda had gathered the menus and left the two women alone, Ellie leaned forward. "There are other fish in the sea."

"I know." Lauren bit her lip. "But I like that fish."

"Lauren, he's good-looking, but you can do a lot better. You're educated, he's not. You have ambition, he has none that I can see. What do you two have to talk about?"

Lauren nodded and fiddled with the saltshaker. Everyone believed she dated Tom because of his looks. It wasn't that. The deeper attraction was his capacity for devotion, the way he insisted on protecting his daughter. The way he guarded the memory of his dead wife. She'd only seen such devotion in dogs, never people. She was scared, scared she'd never see it again. And though she knew she was not the target of his fierce devotion, she dreamed she might be someday.

"You said yourself that you didn't want to run a motel with him."

"He could run a pet hospital with me." Lauren's voice harbored a fragile hope that she instantly regretted revealing to Ellie.

"Well, I suppose that is the practical approach. Have you asked him to?"

"Once."

"What did he say?"

"Said he liked his motel."

"See. He's a guy. His pride is at stake. You'll never convince that man to come be your assistant."

☀

Hap pulled off the road at the overlook on Highway 14 outside of Rocket to see down into the gorge. He looked at Charlene sitting in the passenger seat of his van. She was feminine beyond reason in her orange halter top and ragged cutoff shorts. Her feet were up on the dash, painted toes touching the mangle of papers he'd shoved there and never retrieved. Her tan legs were smooth as polished jasper.

"Sucks not to see any surfers," she said, her eyes riveted on the gorge below.

He nodded. He might have said *unfortunate, disappointing, economically disastrous,* but he was getting used to Charlene's unrefined vernacular. And it did pretty much sum up the way everyone was feeling.

After a moment he pulled back onto the highway. "You're a real gem for agreeing to this," he said.

"It's nothing."

"Well, it's something to Tom, I can promise you." Hap had seen the soft spot Charlene carried for Sienna and knew it sprang from a deeper, more personal place than her attraction to Tom. She never talked about her past, but he'd lived in Rocket long enough to know what had happened to her when she was a kid.

At the motel, Charlene charged right in, striding

around behind the counter and plopping down her purse. She leaned her elbows on the Formica and smiled down at Sienna. "Hey, kiddo. Want to spend the evening with me?"

Sienna held a pink bead up and examined it, then put it against her shirt, which was also pink. She dropped it and pawed through the tray for another shade and matched that to her shirt.

"Sieeeenah," Charlene sang out. "Earth to Sieeeenah."

Sienna looked up, bewildered.

Tom was staring at Charlene, surprised.

"We're here to rescue you," Hap told Tom.

"From what?"

"Boredom." Hap smiled, then gestured at Charlene. "Show her what to do because she's your desk-clerk-slash-babysitter for the evening."

Tom was already shaking his head. "I can't do that."

"The hell you can't," Charlene said. "I'm already here and I ain't going back to town."

"But, I . . . I already told you that I can't afford to hire someone this year."

"Nobody's asking for money," Hap said.

"But I can't just leave all this with her and not pay her."

"Stop talking about me like I'm not in the room," Charlene said. "And get your ass out of here, tightwad."

Tom scowled. "I don't think this is a good idea. I appreciate it, I do, but . . ."

"C'mon, Tom," Hap said. "What's the worst thing that can happen?"

"You have no idea."

"I can do this," Charlene said, her eyes fixed on Tom. "Trust me."

Tom hesitated. He looked from Charlene to Hap and back to Charlene. "Okay. But you've got to promise you'll call if anything happens."

Hap held up his cell phone. "She's already got the number."

"And it's really important that you don't cuss in front of Sienna. She'll pick those words up and never understand why she's not allowed to use them."

Charlene clamped a hand over her mouth and held two fingers to her forehead. "Scout's honor."

❋

At the Red Tail, Hap racked up a game of eight ball as Tom got a pitcher of beer. The place was dead; it was Tuesday. Stan set a bowl of tortilla chips on the table near the two men, then sat down to watch them play.

"Charlene's probably taught Sienna every cussword in the book by now," Tom muttered as he picked out a cue stick.

"There's a price to pay for everything," Hap said.

Tom nodded. "God, it feels good to get away." He broke with a loud crack, banking the twelve into the corner pocket. "I'm high, you're low."

Hap watched Tom clear the table of stripes, then call the eight and win the game before he'd even had a chance to shoot. "I wouldn't have kidnapped you if I'd known you were going to humiliate me."

Tom grinned. "Should've known better than to ask me to shoot pool."

A handful of windsurfers came in, grumbling about the lousy weather, and Stan got to his feet. Hap and Tom shot another round of pool, Hap breaking this time and pocketing three balls before Tom cleaned up. They sat down at a table and refilled their beer glasses.

"So, tell me about room six," Hap said.

"Ah, so you did have a motive for dragging me out tonight."

"Not really, but as long as we're here."

"It's just a freak thing. I mean, there can't be anything

to it." Tom sat back and took a long gulp of beer. "Spooky as hell, though."

He recounted the three deaths, as well as the woman who'd been mugged in Portland. But then he turned the conversation to Carl Warren of McCall, Idaho. "He stayed in room six and won the lottery. So it's not just *bad* luck.

"He was a nice guy. Gave Sienna a book. He could see she didn't know how to read, but he gave it to her anyway." Tom put his feet up on the chair next to him, and Hap noticed that his boot soles had worn almost completely through. "I'm making a list of all the people who ever stayed in that room. If I can get some time, I'm gonna go down to the library and use their Internet and see if I can find out anything about them. It's got me curious now."

"Give it to me. I have a computer. I can check on them."

Tom tilted his head and studied Hap. "It's confidential information. I'm just caught up in this quest to see what's up." He bugged his eyes at Hap. "Geez, do I sound like a lunatic or what?"

Hap laughed, but now he was curious, too. "It's not like I'm going to run a story on it. Nobody would believe it if I did. But it would be interesting to find out."

Tom laughed. "This is absurd."

Hap shrugged.

"All right. But you gotta promise you won't tell anyone what we're doing. I've got enough trouble with people talking about me as it is."

"Only the women; they're hot to have you."

"I wish that was true, but we both know what they're really talking about."

"Heard you and Lauren called it quits." Hap was desperate to change the subject away from Sienna. He didn't know if Tom was aware that his daughter and the kitten were the topic of nearly every conversation in town, but he guessed so.

"See what I mean?"

"Charlene was chomping at the bit to come out and help you this evening. I bet you'll find your house scrubbed from top to bottom in her quest to prove to you that she's marriage material."

"She's too young for me. God, she's just a kid."

"She's too young for me, too. But if she wanted in my drawers I'd be stripping naked in the street," Hap vowed, and they both laughed.

☼

When Hap and Tom returned to the motel, the apartment was as messy as he'd left it, maybe worse. But Sienna and Charlene were curled together on the sofa with the book Carl Warren had given Sienna, Sienna pointing at pictures. She rubbed her finger across a brightly colored rooster, and Charlene read the accompanying paragraph, then looked at the child.

"Auracana," Sienna said.

"Yup, it's an auracana. I love those kind of chickens, they lay green eggs."

Sienna's eyes studied Charlene intently. "Love green chickens," she said, but not as a statement about her own feelings. Rather, it was a way of understanding and making sense of Charlene, Tom thought.

Charlene looked at the men. "She's smart. Sienna, what animals did we read about tonight?"

"Black, yellow, green, blue, brown, spotted," Sienna counted off stiffly with her fingers.

Charlene blinked at her. "Actually, I thought it was something like newts, lynxes, poison dart frogs, blue jays, fruit bats, and leopards." She got up and picked up her purse. "Oh, and I didn't use a single cussword. But I better get out of here, because they're all knotted up and they're gonna come shooting out like bottle rockets any minute."

"Thank you," Tom said. It sounded so inadequate.

"Anytime." Charlene shook her hair out. "I mean it. It was fun."

Tom opened his mouth to protest that he couldn't prevail upon her like that, but he stayed quiet. Why not, if she wanted to?

"You sober enough to drive me home?" Charlene asked Hap. She turned back. "Hey, kiddo, I'll see you soon. Okay?"

Sienna looked suddenly dismayed as Charlene disappeared with Hap. She immediately began to rock. "She comes back. She comes back."

"Not tonight, sweetie."

"She comes back!"

"Okay, I'll see if she can come back, but not tonight. It's late; you go on to bed now."

"*No!* She comes back!"

The night surged on, sleepless, as Tom tried to calm his daughter. She screamed and cried and threw tantrums, demanding that Charlene return. Getting her into her nightgown was like wrestling a wild animal, making him wonder why he bothered. She refused to be distracted by her buttons. She went quiet only shortly after one o'clock in the morning. Tom watched her sleeping for a time, wrestling with his thoughts, then dozed on the sofa. But Sienna clocked him on the head with her book, bringing him onto his feet in a searing rage.

"Damn it, Sienna! You don't hit me!" He grabbed her arm and gave her a hard swat on the backside. She wrenched away from him, and he realized something: she was too big to spank now. "You don't hit Daddy. You don't hit *anyone*. Do you understand me?"

"She comes back," Sienna bawled, tears dripping onto her nightgown. "She comes back."

Tom sank down on the sofa and rubbed his face. His head pounded where the book had struck him. He inhaled and exhaled shakily. Sienna had never shown emotion toward another human being, not since she was a toddler. Her mother was the only one who could invoke that kind of response from her, though it had still been rare. And, in the end, fatal. How could he spank his daughter for showing an attachment to someone now? The one thing he'd most longed to see and he had punished her. He felt heartsick. He held his hand out to her.

"I will ask Charlene to come see you again."

She looked at him, her face wet with tears and snot, her hair tangled. There was a food stain on her nightgown. She refused to take his hand.

"I promise I will ask. But, Sienna, honey, Charlene is sleeping now. We should all be sleeping now. She isn't coming tonight."

Sienna crumpled to the floor, sobbing. He sat motionless until she'd cried herself to sleep. Then he carried her to bed. He pulled the sheet over her, something to cover her even in the heat. Then he lay down on the sofa again, but he could no longer find rest. Sienna and Maria had always had a tumultuous, emotional connection. Their daughter loved and hated her mother with equal intensity. Crying for Maria one moment, as if the world were collapsing around her, then slapping her viciously the next. Maria stumbled through the days haggard. Tom's stomach lurched.

# 10

LATE MORNING, after a fitful two hours of dozing, Tom wandered outside to check on the live trap he'd set up near the shed. The milk had curdled in the heat every day before it could entice the cat, and today he carried chunks of cheddar cheese to lure her. He thought about his night away from the motel and the brief but welcome release it had provided. Maybe he could splurge and hire Charlene to come out once in a while to give him a break. He immediately dismissed the idea. He was now three months behind in his mortgage payments, the bank was sending threatening letters, and he had no idea how he would catch up again. After baiting the still-empty trap, he headed for the front of the motel. Along the west wall he discovered a rusty Volkswagen van parked off the road and tucked back where it was difficult to see.

"Damn surfers," he said and pounded on the van's window.

A baby shrieked and a woman with disheveled blonde hair popped up from under a blanket, followed by a man. The side door creaked open and the nearly nude man slid out. The woman rummaged around inside the van for something to calm the baby, herself barely covered. They were older than Tom had expected—not the twenty-something surfers he usually found camped out in his lot. The vagrant before him looked to be in his forties, his face spackled with gray and black stubble. He caught a whiff of the man's unwashed body and suppressed a grimace.

"This is private property. You can't sleep here," Tom said.

"We're sorry." The man leaned in and grabbed a shirt, which he pulled over his head and covered his ribby, birdlike chest. "We didn't want to wake you up when we came in last night."

"This is a motel; we're open twenty-four hours."

"Oh, we can't afford a room." The man thrust a chapped hand forward as if to shake Tom's. "I'm Gill." He gestured at the woman inside, now breast-feeding the squirming infant. "That's Sandy and Little Gill."

After an awkward moment, Tom shook Gill's hand, embarrassed that the man was wearing no pants. "I can't help you if you're not looking for a room," he said.

"I'm looking for work, actually. I'm a good carpenter, but I can do anything—plumbing, sheetrock, laying carpet. Anything you need."

"Business has dried up this year. No wind."

Gill looked dejected.

"No wind, no surfers. No surfers, no work." Tom looked off toward the placid river, then back. "I wish I could pay for help, believe me."

Gill nodded.

"What are we going to do now?" the woman whispered to her husband.

Tom tried to not look at her, though she didn't seem concerned about baring her meager breast in front of him. He could feel her fear. A little part of him shared her fear.

Gill shifted from one bare foot to the other. "We don't have anyplace to go."

Tom didn't know what to say. The idea of giving them room six struck him. He'd put a new mattress in it. Whatever weird luck the room possessed had to have run its course. In lieu of payment, they could test his new theory about room six somehow enforcing the laws of nature. Good people hit it rich; bad people croaked. This business with room six was simply a freak coincidence.

"We used the last of our money to buy some bread and peanut butter last night. We're done. We got nothing," Gill said.

Tom stared down at the gravel, wondering how tough a man's feet had to be to stand unflinching in those sharp rocks, and what he was supposed to say to this family. It was good they had bought peanut butter with their last dollar, though—surfers would've bought beer.

After a silence, Gill said, "We'll get off your lot. We've probably got enough gas in the tank to get back to that little town we came through last night." He climbed back into the van and rummaged under the blanket, coming up with a wilted pair of jeans.

Tom looked at the cyan sky, which seemed vast and forgiving, though it brought no wind. A crop of cirrus clouds stretched leanly across the southern end. He sighed. "I can put you up for a night or two. You can do a little work for me in exchange. But I can't pay you. I'm barely treading water and I can't spare it."

Sandy let out a relieved cry.

"The Dodge Center up in Hood River has food . . . if you're desperate." Tom looked away as he directed them to the food bank.

Gill pulled his pants on, smiling. "You won't regret it. We're good people. We just hit a rough patch is all."

☀

The office chair squeaked sharply as Hap leaned back and tried to make out Tom's handwriting on the three pages that represented the history of room six. He was not a superstitious man, and the idea seemed ridiculous after a good night's rest. But Tom was a thinking man, too, and the fact that he'd created this list at all made it worth checking into. Hap laid it on his desk and took a sip of his coffee as he fired up the computer.

Charlene wandered in, looking spent, and dropped her handbag on the mail-sorting table. She turned to Hap. "Next time *you're* staying with the motel and *I'm* going out drinking with Tom."

"I thought you had a good time with Sienna."

"I did. But not the kind of *good time* I'm looking for." She made little quote marks in the air with her fingers.

"You know, Tom can look after his own damn motel and you and I could go out drinking."

She snorted with laughter.

Hap focused on his computer, trying not to let her reaction sting him so deeply. He typed in the first name on the list and clicked *Search*. A page of random links appeared.

"Did you hear that both the people who died out there this summer slept in room six?" Charlene said. "And another man died in Portland after staying in that room."

Hap looked up. "Sheriff Turnbull tell you that?" he asked. Even the sheriff was not above spreading gossip in a town like Rocket.

"Stan told me, last night." She opened a large canvas bag and emptied its contents of envelopes into a bin.

"Stan?" Hap thought of the tattooed barman. When had she seen Stan? He'd taken her straight home and it was past midnight when he dropped her off.

"Yeah, I walked over to the Red Tail and had a nightcap."

Hap leaned into his computer screen and began scanning the links. This was the place in conversations with

Charlene that he was tempted to lecture her about the wisdom of a young woman wandering the streets late at night, slipping into bars. It was just such past lectures that earned him geezer status in her eyes.

"Pretty damn freaky, if you ask me," she went on. "You should run a story on that. *That* would be news."

"That would ruin what's left of Tom's business, if you ask me."

Charlene appeared to think about his comment as she sorted mail. The front door rattled unsteadily on its frame, and Lauren Kent's face appeared in the service window. She slid a small pink paper across the counter.

"Need to pick up a parcel," she said.

"Just a sec," Charlene replied without looking up. She continued sorting. Hap had seen this little game before that Charlene sometimes played with people she didn't like, especially Lauren Kent. Charlene always made her wait, even if she wasn't doing anything important.

"Hi, Hap," Lauren said.

"How are you these days, Lauren?" he asked and sipped his coffee.

Charlene's ear bent toward the window as she continued her sorting.

"Great," Lauren said as if she wanted the people across the street to know it, too. "Really good."

Charlene smirked.

"Did you hear about that freaky stuff at the Jemmett Motel?" she asked, approaching the window at last.

Hap couldn't help listening to Charlene bait Lauren in her less-than-subtle way. Lauren scowled—a clear indication that she hadn't heard anything about it.

"Oh, I'm sorry. I thought Tom would've told you." Charlene took the slip from the counter. She made a prolonged show of reading the printing on it that had come from her own hand.

Lauren smiled brightly. "Of course he did."

"What do you make of it?" Charlene hoisted a medium-sized box onto the counter and hammered the pink slip with a rubber stamp before dropping it into a slot near the window.

"What's to make of it?" Lauren said with a shrug and picked up her box. "See you later, Hap," she called over her shoulder. Her hasty departure left Charlene in unusually high spirits for so early in the morning.

"She's lying. She doesn't know a damn thing about it," Charlene said, still watching Lauren from the window.

"That stuff with room six is just a fluke," Hap said. But even as he said it, he focused on the screen full of information about Sam Cantwell, a recent room six resident who had been bequeathed a fishing guide business on the Olympic Peninsula by an old family friend. "A surprise dream come true," Sam was quoted as saying in the Bremerton paper. "I could never have imagined that I would be fishing for a living. I love it."

Charlene turned to Hap, grinning like a mischievous child. "There're enough friggin weirdos in the world that if you ran a story about Tom's motel, people would be crawling all over this town. Who needs wind? We've got the *Jemmett Motel*!" She put her hands up as if reading a giant marquee.

Hap jotted a note about the unusual inheritance next to Sam's name, deliberately masking his reaction to Charlene's idea. He'd had the same idea himself. It woke him from a dream about a lizard with a handgun sometime after three o'clock in the morning. He had lain awake considering the scenarios that might play out in Rocket. Hearing Charlene say aloud the thought that had plagued him all morning tuned him to the tremor that was building beneath their little hamlet like a low humming from the earth itself. By the history of small towns everywhere, Hap knew the story would be told regardless of what he or Tom intended to happen. Word was out. It was *his* story, and it could be the only thing left to keep this place alive.

☀

Hot air blasted from the air conditioner in room eighteen. Gill cranked up the fan and Tom held his hand in front of the inferno.

"Give it a sec," Gill said.

Sure enough, the air cooled and was soon so frigid, Tom pulled his hand away. He nodded approvingly. "I've been fighting with that damn thing all summer."

"These older models are finicky. But they're good workhorses. Think about it. It's probably twenty-five or thirty years old."

"Older than that, I'd guess." Tom adjusted the temperature to an even seventy-two degrees and pulled the drapes shut while Gill collected his tools from the floor. He had noticed that the first thing both Gill and Sandy had done in room six was shower. He'd expected them to rest awhile, but within a half an hour, Gill was standing wet-headed in the lobby, leaning to one side under the weight of his toolbox and asking where to start. Sandy came in behind him with her baby balanced on one hip, wanting to know if Tom needed any rooms cleaned. He thought for a moment that he'd died and gone to heaven.

They returned to the motel lobby, where they gulped down paper cups of cold water, chased by coffee that had thickened in the still air. Sandy had finished the two rooms from the previous night and was sitting on the lobby sofa, her sleeping baby sprawled out in the heat, and watching Sienna make patterns with her beads.

"Look at that," Sandy said, pointing down at the elaborate design in yellow and green. It was perfectly symmetrical and scrolled lavishly outward with curling limbs like an octopus.

Sienna continued working as if she were the only person in the world.

"What did you make?" Sandy asked.

Sienna didn't respond.

"Sienna?" Sandy called.

Tom watched, wondering what Sandy thought of his daughter. Neither she nor Gill had so much as mentioned the child, though Sandy continued to behave as warmly toward Sienna as when she'd first laid on eyes on her.

"Sienna?" she said again, but didn't raise her voice.

Sienna turned, blinking as if she'd only just noticed her there. Then she turned back to admire her design.

"Did you count out how many beads so they would match?"

"One hundred." Sienna pointed at the first swirl, then at the next. "One hundred." She pointed at each one. "One hundred, one hundred, one hundred." Until she'd named them all.

"Make one with one hundred and fifty beads," Sandy said.

Sienna scowled at the design. She began flapping her hands, gently at first, then more rapidly.

"It's just a suggestion, Sienna," Tom said. "You don't have to do it."

Sienna calmed.

He shrugged at Sandy. "She's got a thing for numbers you can divide by one hundred."

Sandy seemed pleased with that and pulled a magazine from the diaper bag. Sienna glanced up at the woman twice, as if waiting for her to say something more, then bent over her beadwork, her hair over her eyes. Tom suffered a wrenching ache for the child who had no mother. Somehow, in her small way, she seemed to be reaching out. Trying at least.

"What else you got for me?" Gill asked as he dropped

his paper cup in the garbage and wiped the sheen of sweat from his forehead.

"Well, let's see." Tom looked over his maintenance log. "Faucet in room twelve is dripping and the toilet runs."

"I'm on it," Gill said, waiting for Tom to hand him the key. "God, it feels good to do an honest day's work."

Tom watched the man as he left. He felt a little pang of guilt for having put them in room six. Maybe he should make some excuse to move them.

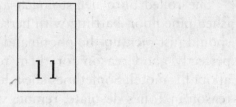

11

TWO DAYS HAD PASSED since she'd first heard the rumors about Tom's motel, and Lauren still hadn't gotten a believable explanation. She'd been told by several people, mostly pet owners visiting the clinic, about the deaths associated with room six, but Lauren could scarcely imagine Tom believed this ridiculous idea that the room was cursed. She knew him better than most, and he would never make the claims that were attributed to him.

She sprawled on her leather sofa, staring at the muted television in her starkly clean, air-conditioned home above the city park. A motorcycle roared past, and she realized how quiet this summer was without the surfers. She had hated those beach bums when they were here, always looking forward to the fall when the air turned crisp and the water icy. The sun shone nearly year-round out there on the high desert plateau, and Lauren preferred the frigid windy winters to the sweltering, congested summers. This particular summer couldn't end soon enough for her. Next year would be better. The wind would return and new life would be breathed into this town, despite the annoyance of the seasonal residents it brought with it.

She rolled onto her stomach and stared at the polished pine floor, battling with herself about whether she should just pick up the phone and call Tom. This was a perfectly good reason for them to talk, this nonsense about his motel. Sometimes she felt like the lone voice of reason in Tom's desolate, remote world—he needed her more than he realized. A good laugh might be just the icebreaker she needed. Instinctively, she glanced at the clock, though she knew he would be up. It was only eight-fifteen, early enough to drive out and see him. But still, she wanted him to be the one to call. He owed her an apology.

She picked up the phone, but dialed her sister Kelly in Pullman instead. "Hey, Sis. What's up?"

There was a silence on the other end. They hadn't actually spoken in three months. Not since Lauren spanked Kelly's four-year-old son in the grocery store for throwing a tantrum over Hershey's Kisses.

"Let me guess," Kelly said. "You split up with Tom."

Lauren cringed. "How about 'It's nice to hear from you, Lauren. What have you been up to? Seen any good movies lately? How about those Mariners?' "

Kelly laughed, and even though she didn't want to give in so quickly now that she was mad again, so did Lauren.

"How about those Mariners?" Kelly said.

"Yes, I did split up with Tom."

"Bummer. He was good-looking. I liked him. He lacked a sense of humor, though."

"We came to blows over Sienna."

"When are you going to learn that you can't tell other people how to raise their kids?"

"Who said I was telling him how to raise his daughter?"

"C'mon, Lauren, I know you." Kelly sighed into the phone. "Look, I'm sure the kid's a challenge. God, I wouldn't want to have to deal with a situation like that every day."

"She killed a kitten."

"Ugh, that's horrible."

"I just wish..." Lauren rolled onto her back again. "It just feels like that day Aunt Kathy blurted out the details of my adoption at the family dinner table like she was talking about the weather or something."

"Lauren," Kelly said with a hint of exasperation. "It's nothing like that. You always do this. Whatever bad thing happens you somehow tie it back to that."

"You don't understand," Lauren said, holding back tears.

"The hell I don't."

They'd both found out about their lack of genetic connection to the rest of the family that day over pork ribs and corn on the cob. But somehow Kelly seemed to just skim right by it, as if it had amounted to nothing more than finding a weird-shaped birthmark on her leg. Lauren, on the other hand, couldn't get over it. The ground beneath her had turned to liquid on that muggy afternoon, and she'd never found solid footing since. Why couldn't Kelly understand that?

"This breakup just makes me feel tricked. A fool. You know?"

"You're overreacting. People break up all the time. He didn't trick you."

"What if it was just physical for him? You know he's never gotten over his wife. He called me Maria once when we were having sex." Tears now streaked Lauren's face, but she worked at not sniffing into the phone so Kelly wouldn't know she was crying.

"Well, I don't know what to say about that. But what do you expect? He loved her."

"I know. But at some point you have to move on,

right?" She waited for Kelly to concur, but she wouldn't.
"I want to go out there and tell him to go to hell."

"No you don't."

Lauren sniffed hard, her nose running so badly she
could no longer hide her state, nor caring to. "You're
right. I want him to beg me to come back."

☼

"You don't know what you've done for us," Gill said
as he arranged the contents of his toolbox on the floor of
the motel lobby.

"You more than paid your way with the work you've
done. I kinda wish you weren't leaving." Tom sat down
on the stool behind the counter and leafed through a
stack of mail that had been piling up, unopened, for most
of the week.

"I'll get that bathtub in twenty-three caulked before
we leave in the morning."

Tom studied the emaciated, grease-stained man.
Looking at him, Tom would never have guessed the
breadth of knowledge Gill carried in his head for the me-
chanics of almost anything. Problems Tom had puzzled
over, Gill could fix in minutes. Together, they had tackled
three-quarters of the maintenance backlog, while Gill's
wife kept an eye on Sienna along with her own child.

"Guthry said we could have the apartment over the
shop until we find a permanent place," Gill said.

Tom pictured Guthry's auto body. All he could remember, even though he drove past it every time he went
to town, was its yellow brick facade with the Art Deco
design. He hadn't known there was an apartment on the
second floor.

"That'll be convenient for Sandy, won't it?"

Gill smiled. He adored his wife the way Tom had
adored Maria. Living in such close proximity to their
quietly intimate way with each other had proven difficult

for Tom at times. They would reach out and touch each other in passing, the way he and Maria had done. A squeeze on the shoulder, or finger hooked around finger. A brief, silent connection to let the other know they were loved. And Sandy's vast hope for Little Gill twisted some unseen knife in his heart, as if she might wake up one day and discover that her child, too, wasn't quite right. When had that moment happened to Tom and Maria? How old was Sienna when the hints became too loud to ignore? Would it be the end of Gill and Sandy's relationship, too, if they found out their son was broken? They would say no, but Tom knew otherwise.

Gill slammed his toolbox shut. "Thank you, Tom. Thank you for everything."

Tom shook the hand he thrust at him. "Don't mention it." He watched Gill sway out of the lobby with his over-sized toolbox and head to room six for one last night. Had it been room six luck that landed Gill a job as the newest mechanic in Rocket? Or had it been coincidence?

He turned to the mail and slid out an envelope from the bottom of the stack. It had sent icy spasms darting through his blood when he first laid eyes on it at the post office, and he'd buried it at the bottom of the pile so no one else would see it. He steeled himself, slipped his pocketknife blade along the seam, then extracted the crisp letter. Thirty days. That was how long he had to bring his mortgage current before the bank foreclosed.

He set the letter aside and called to his daughter, who was watching TV in the apartment. "Want to go get a hamburger?"

As usual, she didn't acknowledge him. It was as if the child were deaf. As if nothing that happened in the world around her could penetrate the silence in which she lived.

He called again, loudly.

Her head turned and she trundled up off the sagging sofa and out into the lobby, ready.

Tom picked up the phone and dialed room six. "Sandy? This is Tom. Do you think I could trouble you with one last favor before you leave?"

Sandy gladly agreed to act as stand-in desk clerk for a few hours while Tom and Sienna escaped from the motel. He pulled a pair of twenties from the cash register, suddenly not caring if it was the last forty bucks he had in the world. Soon the bank would take his motel, and he'd be starting over—just like Gill and Sandy. He pushed the thought from his head and coaxed Sienna into the truck.

※

The smoldering heat enveloped Hap the moment he stepped out the back door of the post office. He jiggled the door handle out of habit to make sure it was locked and started across the burnt asphalt toward his small house on the edge of town. On days like today he was tempted to drive home, but it was only a half mile and the bulk of age was beginning to wear on his nerves as much as his knees.

Passing the Dairy Queen, Hap did a double take, then glanced at his watch. It was too late in the evening for Tom to be in town. He cut across the parking lot and intercepted the truck before Tom could pull away from the take-out window.

"Late for you to be roaming town?" he called when Tom saw him.

"Sandy McKaherty is running the show for a couple hours."

"Who?"

"A guest. I prevailed upon her. Sienna and I are headed down to the boat launch to enjoy these burgers in peace. Wanna come?"

Hap rounded the truck and opened the passenger door. Sienna stared at him as if she'd never laid eyes on him in her life. "Hey, kiddo. Mind scooting over so I can join you?"

Sienna looked at her father. He nodded and she scooted over to make room for Hap, but kept an apprehensive eye on him. On her lap she balanced an enormous tray of beads, organized by color and size. When Hap leaned over to look at them more closely, the girl whined like an agitated dog. He straightened up hastily and pressed himself against the door and she calmed down.

At the river, Sienna sat on the picnic table with her feet up on the bench, her head bent over her beads as her milk shake went runny.

"She can't stand the feel of grass," Tom said as the two men sat down in the shade of an old poplar tree. "Or water or mud or any of the things the river has to offer."

Hap didn't know what to say, so he didn't say anything. He wanted to be supportive—one of the few who didn't judge Tom or Sienna. He wanted Tom to understand that whatever he did as a father, Hap would never question. But he couldn't comprehend Sienna as a child or as a person. He had no advice, no words of wisdom. His praise of her extraordinary memory always sounded tinny and hollow and forced when he heard the words— words that he believed—come from his own mouth.

"How'd you manage to corral a guest into working the front desk for you?" he said, finally settling on a subject that didn't involve room six, Sienna, death, or wind. He had news for Tom on that list of names, but he didn't quite know how to deliver it without sounding like a flaming psychopath.

"This couple is doing some work for me in trade for a room. They were on their last gallon of gasoline and past their last dollar."

Hap thought of the prostitute Tom had given cash to

get back to Las Vegas and the countless surfers in years past that Tom had seen home to their parents. If it were any other summer, Hap might not notice, but Tom was struggling financially. He couldn't afford to give handouts.

"I put them in room six." Tom looked guiltily at Hap, then away. "It has a new mattress. And besides, they aren't paying."

Hap forced a laugh. "Did anything happen to them?"

Tom scowled out at the water. "He got a job working for Guthry. A decent-paying job." He snapped his fingers. "Just like that, he drove into town and came back with a job. Never heard of that happening in Rocket. Ever."

"Well, if my research tells us anything, the number of good things is running about one to four on that room." Hap pulled the much-folded pages from his breast pocket and flattened them out on his thigh. "So far, I've found seventeen people on this list and every single one of them has had something significant happen to them."

"What do you mean by *significant*?"

"This one," he pointed, "received six million dollars in capital funding from an anonymous source. He went on to start the restaurant chain Nacho Papa."

"I've heard of that."

"Yup. It's doing extremely well." Hap ran his finger down the list. "This guy went to prison after his dog dug up a body part buried in his yard. It turned out to be the foot of his missing wife."

Tom grimaced. "These things could happen to anybody alive in the world and doing things they shouldn't be."

Hap shook his head. "How about this one who visited room six from Alabama? One of his tenants put a fully grown alligator in his pool knowing that the man liked to swim at night."

Tom stared at Hap. "And?"

"And he's alligator grub." Hap squinted at the list, trying to make out his own handwriting. "Oh, and this one, Cynthia Deschamps. The very day she left your motel she fell down a mine shaft in John Day. She's paralyzed from the neck down."

A visible shiver ran through Tom, which reacquainted Hap with his own physical response to this information he was sharing—an incessant ringing in his left ear.

Just then a seagull landed on the table where Sienna worked on her beads and tried to steal one. She shrieked and thrashed her arms over her head, gaining the attention of everyone at the river, no matter how far up- or downstream they sat. Tom leapt to his feet and chased the bird off. It circled and screeched as loudly as Sienna, but would not leave. Finally, Tom flung Sienna's uneaten burger into the water, sending the bird flapping away like a fiend.

When Tom returned to the tree, Hap turned his attention back to the names. He ran through the list of bizarre happenings, from one very wealthy man's loss of everything to the woman who died after a tree crushed her on a calm, blue-sky day. He realized that some of the events sounded too comical to be true. He wondered if Tom thought so, too.

"Is there anyone on that list who didn't have something happen to them?"

"There are quite a few people I haven't turned anything up on." He handed the list to Tom, who scoured it again.

"Maybe I should tell the bank my motel is haunted."

Hap looked quizzically at Tom.

Tom leaned back against the tree, defeated. "They're foreclosing. I've got thirty days to come current."

"How much do you need?"

"More than I have. More than you have."

"You don't know that."

"Yes I do." Tom sighed heavily. "It's just as well. The place is killing me. I can't keep up with the work, and poor Sienna is all but ignored. It's probably for the best."

Hap could tell Tom didn't believe those words. He'd witnessed Tom's enthusiasm for the place before. When the wind was strong and the motel was full, Tom thrived on the bustle of work. He loved the people, even though he swore he didn't. And in summers past, he could afford help.

"If you can just get through this one summer, the wind will come back. It has to."

Tom looked out at the wide, sapphire river, as placid as a bathtub. A ski boat roared up the middle, sending a slow wake toward them. "I don't know, a lot of people think it's global warming. Besides, even if the wind returns next year, that's too far off. The summer business is what carries me through the winter. It takes only one bad summer. It's over. I just need to figure out what I'm going to do, that's all."

Hap shook his head, refusing to join Tom in defeat. He wouldn't let this happen. He wouldn't see Rocket lose a man of Tom's stature. The copy was already written and sitting on his desk in a neat stack, just waiting for his editing pen and maybe some guts. Maybe he'd end up the laughingstock of journalism, but short of giving Tom the money, it was the only thing he could do. And there was something bigger at stake here, anyway.

The seagull returned to Sienna's bead collection, cawing rudely and making her shriek and cover her head. Tom got up again, more slowly this time, and dusted himself off.

"Well, I've probably taken enough advantage of my guest. We'd better get back."

☼

At six-fifteen the next morning Hap sat in the dim light of his office and e-mailed his story about the Jemmett Motel to *The Oregonian, The Seattle Times, The San Francisco Chronicle,* and *The Los Angeles Times.* In that split second after he'd launched it into cyberspace he felt dizzy, a rush of blood pounding in his ears. Despite his high standing in the community as the editor in chief of *The Rocket Rocket,* Hap was not immune to the pull of ambition. He had occasionally wondered if he could make it in a place where the news mattered. He believed he could, and now that belief would be put to the test with the most ludicrous story he'd ever reported.

It wasn't just Tom's motel, though Tom was the man Hap most cared to keep in business. It was Petra Osterlundt's bakery and Bill Guthry's auto shop, the Windy Point Diner and the pet clinic. Stan's Red Tail Tavern, the Dairy Queen, the Laundromat, the feed and seed, and the overpriced grocery on the corner with its patiently waiting mutts, and a handful of others still holding on. It was even Dillard and his annoying way of being the town know-it-all. Who would humor the unfortunate man if he had to move to the big city? It was all of them Hap hoped to save now.

# 12

TOM SAT IN THE QUIET, early-morning lobby, watching a near-full moon hang over the broad, still Columbia. It cast a luminous silver beam that stretched from Oregon to Washington like the aura of a waning dream. In front of him on the counter lay a worn photo of Maria basking in the glow of a Pacific sunset. Tom had taken it on their honeymoon in Cannon Beach. She wore an orange bikini that she had insisted, laughing, was "tangerine." He'd told her he didn't care if she thought it was an entire fruit basket, as long as she wore it. The dark glow of her skin was youthful and beckoning.

Tom rarely looked at the pictures he had of her, few as they were. They only dredged up emotions he could not control and didn't care to relive. He could no longer remember her with the warmth and affection that had been their marriage. Those early mornings they awoke with their limbs entwined, snuggled tightly against each other, reluctant to get out of bed, had all but vanished from his memory. After all these years, he felt only loss and emptiness when he thought of her. Would it ever go away? Would he ever be able to think back and laugh about some small moment without the biting sting of her absence?

"I'm sorry, Maria. I tried to keep the place," he said aloud, then felt a spark of anger and put the photo back in the little envelope where he kept it. He slipped it into the drawer under the counter. "I tried my best, darling."

He stood and made coffee, thinking he could use some. He'd suffered from insomnia nearly every night these past few days. Last night he hadn't even attempted to sleep. How could he? Between the ever-present pain in his lower back from that terrible sofa and the revelation that his work here was futile—the motel was slipping irrevocably away from him—why bother with sleep? It was Maria's presence in this place that would make losing his motel the hardest. The motel was all that kept him going. It was her dream, her vision for their future. And every day there was work to be done here. He'd never succumb to a pause long enough that he might not get moving again, which is what he had always feared he would do without her.

As the coffee splattered into the pot he began to assess his options. He could put the place up for sale. No, he really couldn't, he decided, even if he had enough time. Who would buy a motel that had no guests? The place had been sitting empty for six years when he and Maria found it. No one had wanted it but them. And that was when there was wind. He walked back to the counter and pulled out his ledgers. He had $2,614.13 in his bank account. That wouldn't even get him an apartment with first and last months' rent, deposits and all. He suddenly felt panicky. What would he do? Where would he and Sienna go?

"Morning," Gill said, startling him. "I just wanted to say again how much Sandy and I appreciate what you've done for us." He set the key to room six on the counter.

Tom shook his head. "It was nothing."

"Wasn't nothing to us. Well . . . gotta be to work this

morning. Can't be late on my first day. We'll see you around town, I guess."

"Sure."

He watched Gill climb into the van and waved at Sandy as they drove out of his lot, leaving his motel in finer condition than they'd found it, but still utterly deserted. Then Tom sat down with his coffee and speculated about these two. They were like Carl Warren: good. And something good happened to them. It probably wasn't room six but life itself, setting things right. Giving people exactly what they deserved, just as he could be certain that his misdeeds had sentenced him to life with a broken child who could never be fixed, stumbling toward an elusive sort of redemption that could not be honestly fathomed. But in the absence of grievous sins, what exactly defines a good person? he wondered. Someone who helps others? What if they do good out of selfishness?

"Motive," he said aloud to his empty lobby. "Motive and outcome. The combination of pure motives and positive outcome." But then he thought of his own daughter and the kitten she'd injured so badly they had to end its suffering, and he had a sickening ache in his belly. Outcome could not be factored in. He swirled his coffee and stared into the cup. Motive. What was Sienna's motive in anything she did? Selfish—he knew. She was not capable of selflessness. His theory collapsed like a house of cards. He decided to check the live trap and see if he'd had any luck catching the mother cat.

☼

Hap drummed his fingers on his desk as he waited for his e-mail to load. Suddenly his in-box had three new messages: *Cheap prescription-free Viagra, Investor alert, Enlarge your peni$...* No word about his article. He waited ten minutes and clicked the Refresh button. Nothing.

"You're awfully quiet over there," Charlene said.

He pushed back in his chair and looked at her. "Just tired, I guess."

"You've been staring at that computer all morning. Haven't said two words to me."

"Sorry." He got up and filled the plastic cup he kept on his desk with water from the cooler. "Didn't get much sleep last night."

"I heard the older you get, the less sleep you need," Charlene said as she dumped a mailbag on the counter.

"What's that supposed to mean?"

She looked up. "I'm teasing you. Don't be so sensitive, asshole."

He grimaced. "I'm just not in the mood today, okay?"

"Today? You're never in the mood. You haven't got a humorous bone in your entire body."

Hap dropped into his chair and sipped his water as he waited for his e-mail to refresh. Still nothing. He gathered his notepad and a pen. "I'm leaving for a while. See if anything is going on in town."

Charlene glowered at him. "We live in Rocket. What are you expecting to find?"

Hap didn't answer or say good-bye but left through the back door, where he stood on the sweltering pavement, the heat seeping through the soles of his shoes, and stared out at the Dairy Queen and the windless gorge beyond. His muscles felt hot and achy. His neck was sore from stooping over his computer screen, waiting for an e-mail that might never come. What editor would run his unbelievable story? If someone had submitted it to him, he'd have laughed and tossed it in the garbage. The glaring sun was giving him a headache. He wandered past his Econoline van, down Chemeketa, an empty back street that ran parallel to Main, toward his home. He didn't know what else to do. Charlene was right—they lived in Rocket and nothing was going on in Rocket.

☼

Lauren pulled up in front of the Jemmett Motel, but she didn't get out of her Jeep. She stared into the bleak little lobby with its outdated colors and ancient sofa. She could smell the carpet just glancing at it. *What am I doing here?* she wondered.

Tom rounded the exterior wall just as she finally climbed out of her Jeep, raking a hand through her wind-whipped hair. He carried the live trap with a calico cat in it. "Thanks for coming."

"No problem," she said. Seeing Tom, his broad shoulders and tan arms, made her stomach do a little flip-flop. She'd missed him almost constantly. *That's* what I'm doing here, she thought.

He placed the cage on her passenger seat, then turned to her. "How are you doing?"

She shrugged. "Things have been better."

They waited awkwardly, each for the other to speak, then Tom put his hand on the cage again. "She was a bugger to catch. Cheese was the thing that finally got her. I doubt the shelter will be able to find a home for a cat this wild."

Lauren peeked in at the creature, which hunched in a frightened ball at the corner of the small enclosure. When Tom called asking for directions to the animal shelter, she couldn't help herself, she had to see him. She'd been looking for any stupid excuse to come out and talk to him. She had expected him to apologize. Now, when he didn't, she didn't know what to say.

"Probably not," she answered. "They'll have to put her down."

Tom's forehead creased and he studied the cat. "I don't want that."

"I don't think it's your call."

He lifted the cage out again and stood on the walkway with it dangling at his side.

"It's humane. She won't suffer."

"I don't want to kill her."

Lauren felt instantly furious. He was so difficult. "What are you going to do with it, then? You can't keep it. And you can't allow it to have more kittens for..." Her words fell away as she groped for the right way to say it.

"For what? For Sienna to hurt?"

"That's not what I was going to say, Tom."

They stared at each other a moment longer, and finally Lauren said, "Just let me take the cat."

Tom shook his head and tears streaked his face. Lauren was stunned. She'd never seen the man cry before. She stepped forward, but he turned away.

"What is it?" she asked.

"Nothing. I...just haven't had any sleep." He composed himself. "It's been a rougher than normal week."

"Sienna?"

He shook his head, but she thought he was lying to her.

"Tom," Lauren said. But she didn't know where to go from there. "Tom, let me help you."

"How?" He set the cat down on the sidewalk and took a soft breath. "How can you help me?"

The question hung there, its sarcastic edge cutting into her. She climbed back into her Jeep, frustrated. She had imagined that he called her this morning because he wanted to see her, too. She wasn't the only person in Rocket with directions to the animal shelter. He could've called the damn place and just asked how to get there, if he hadn't wanted to see her.

"I don't know," she said. "But maybe if you told me what you need or want, I could."

He said nothing as she fastened her seat belt. He just stood there next to the caged cat, its huge terror-filled eyes watching them. She considered spaying the cat and turning it loose again, but she could not afford to do any more free work.

"At least let me take the cat," she said.

Tom stepped forward and leaned into the Jeep from the passenger side. "Tell me something."

"Anything."

"What do you think makes a person good?"

Lauren shook her head. "You're losing it, Tom."

"It's a simple question."

Lauren sighed and sat back to think. "Someone who pulls their own weight in the world—doesn't freeload off the rest of us. Someone who doesn't commit crimes or waste their talents. That's what makes a person good."

"Thank you," he said quietly.

Lauren couldn't believe that was the end of the conversation. She rolled her eyes and then it dawned on her. "Does this have something to do with all that bullshit about your motel and room six? Is that what that question was about?"

Tom shook his head, but she didn't believe him.

"Tell me you don't buy that crap. I can't believe the stuff people in town are saying."

"What kind of moron do you think I am?"

Lauren smiled weakly. "You had me worried."

Tom didn't smile but stared down at the cat.

She waited, but the conversation seemed to be over. "Let me have the cat, Tom."

"No. I'll take it up to the fish hatchery and let it go. Won't do any worse than here."

"Tom! No! It's a feral cat. It'll breed and have feral

kittens. The world does not need more unwanted cats. *Please*. Let me have it."

Tom picked up the cage and looked once more at the animal, then deposited it on Lauren's seat. "Fine. But tell them to at least *try* to find it a home."

"I'll tell them." Lauren started the Jeep, but didn't put it in gear. "Are you okay? I've been worried."

"I'm fine."

"I hear ridiculous stories about this place, you practically break down for no reason, and you don't want to part with a feral cat. Tom...are you sure I can't help somehow?"

"You *have* helped. By taking this cat, you've helped a lot. Thank you."

She nodded and pulled out, knowing that things were more complicated than they seemed. Something was wrong with him. The heaviness of frustration and longing sat on her now. She wanted to go back and hug him, make him see that she was there for him. But to what end?

## 13

IN THREE DAYS not a single guest had checked in to the motel. A few semis blew past on their way to Golden or Hood River, but Tom hadn't seen a single car in the past hour. He thought of Lauren and regretted having called her for help with the wild cat. It hadn't been his intent to lead her on, but she interpreted his request as something more than it was. He liked Lauren, but it was clear to him that they would never make it as a couple.

He watched his daughter sort her beads into the baby food jars that he'd found in the shed, leftovers from a previous owner and bygone era. With each jar she chanted softly the name of the color as if it were a mantra: *blue blue blue blue blue, purple purple purple purple*. When she was finished, she lined them up along the lobby windowsill from red to green in graduating hues. The setting sun backlit the jars in a blaze of color, forcing her to further refine the assortment by separating the green-blue beads from the green-yellow beads and inserting the jars in the correct order. At last she sat back on her heels and stared at them, her eyes shifting from one to the next and down the line again and again.

Then she turned abruptly to her father and said, "Done."

"Done?"

She nodded and looked back at the beads.

"That's it? You're not going to play with them anymore?"

"They're put away." She got to her feet and looked out the window, then back at Tom.

His hope flared. He seized this unusual moment with Sienna when she was actively engaging him. "I love you," he said, then waited, heart quickening, for a response.

She searched the highway with her eyes.

"Do you love me?"

"Where's that girl?"

"What girl, sweetie?"

"That *girrrrl*," she whined, twisting her torso and stretching her arms out like a baby bird preparing for flight. "That girl that reads to me."

"You mean Charlene?"

"Where is she?"

Tom sighed. "She's in town."

"She comes back." Sienna's voice pitched higher and louder. "She comes back. She comes back."

He glanced at the phone and wondered if he could call Charlene. What would he say? *Come out and babysit my daughter, please? Oh, but I can't pay you. Do you mind?* Then he remembered Lauren's assertion that Charlene just wanted to sleep with him. He could ask her on a date—a date with the two of them. They could have both their needs met. Tom realized he was being a pig, yet the idea lingered. He liked Charlene for reasons he couldn't explain. She had a way of occupying his thoughts and giving him a nice escape from the drudgery of his daily work, even though it was pure fantasy. He imagined that he would enjoy spending time with her, if he wasn't aware of the sheer numbers of men who had already explored that territory.

"Let's go to town," he said to Sienna, surprising

himself when he said it. "Nothing going on here." He walked out into the lobby and looked down at his daughter. "Listen, sweetie." He pulled her chin up, but she wrenched away. "We probably won't see Charlene. I don't know where she is. But we may as well get out of here and do something. Okay?"

☼

Hap sat at the bar in the dimly lit Red Tail Tavern, listening to Stan and Jorge Fernandez speculate about the goings-on at the Jemmett Motel.

"Coincidence. That's all," Stan said, pouring a gin and tonic for the sun-blackened, wrinkled man.

"Karma," Jorge said with a heavy Mexican accent. "All the karma in the world is concentrated in that one spot. It's the place where you get what's coming to ya."

Stan scoffed, but Hap pondered the idea. Could there be such a place where karma could be cashed?

"Check in to room six, then," Stan said, handing over the drink.

"You, if you don't believe it."

Stan gave the matter some thought, then turned to Hap. "What about you? What do you think of all this?"

Hap swallowed the last of his porter and shoved the glass away. Should he tell his fellow Rocketeers that he tried to run a story on it, but no paper would pick such nonsense up? "I think it's bizarre. But it's nothing more than that."

"See," Stan told Jorge. "Hap here is the expert. He writes all the news. If he don't think something freaky is going on out there, it ain't."

Jorge shook his head stubbornly. "Sleep in room six and I'll believe you. If there wasn't some little voice working at you, you'd do it. You can feel it, can't you?" He sipped his gin. "Tom tells it that woman who got hit by the truck was a royal pain in the ass. And then that other dude—he was a kidnapper."

"When did you talk to Tom?" Hap asked.

"I heard that's what he said."

Stan filled a new glass of beer and slid it over the counter to Hap. "Tell Jorge that it's nothing. There ain't nothing going on out there."

"You're the one scared to stay out there," Hap challenged. "What's stopping you?"

"Shit." Stan spat and shook his head. "I ain't staying out there. Even if it is just a weird coincidence, I'm not taking any chances. If karma has anything to do with it, I'd be fucked."

"See," Jorge said. "Told you."

"Why not you, Hap?" Stan said. "You'd stand about the best chance of any of us. You'd finally get laid. Maybe Charlene would give you head. Why don't you give it a shot?"

It wasn't the first time Hap had thought about what might happen to him if he stayed in room six. The possibilities could go either way. He did his best to improve the world around him, live lightly, and take little. But he wasn't always that way. He'd wronged a few in his lifetime—most notably his ex-wife. He had a fleeting memory of Joanne, the twenty-one-year-old neighbor who'd infiltrated his marriage bed, and he realized that she had looked a little like Charlene.

"I'll do it," Jorge said.

Both men turned to him.

"I will." His black eyes shone with the prospect of adventure. "I came through 115 degrees, rattlesnakes, and scorpions so I could work my ass off at the winery out there from sunup to sundown, six days a week, cutting vines and picking grapes for shit pay. I left my family and everything so I can send all my money back to Mexico while I sleep in a shack with five other smelly, ugly men and no running water. Hell, yeah, I'll do it. My grandmother used to say 'Live with a good spirit and die rich.' If there's something good coming to me, I want it now."

Hap and Stan were silent. Finally Stan said, "I'll pay for the room."

The post office was closed when Tom drove by. He looked over at Sienna, who was biting her fingernail. A trickle of blood ran down her lip, but she didn't seem to notice.

"Stop biting," he said.

She pulled her finger from her mouth and examined the tip. She'd torn the ragged nail back, creating a crimson pool. She flicked it, splattering tiny drops of blood across the windshield, laughed, and flicked it again. "Red."

"Stop it!"

She ignored him, sucking her finger back in her mouth and gnawing at it.

He pulled in to the parking lot alongside the Red Tail Tavern and said, "Proper young ladies don't bite their nails." But he wondered why he bothered with this level of instruction—any level of instruction. It was a miracle that Sienna was even toilet trained. If she didn't hate the feel of shitty, wet pants, she wouldn't be, and he knew it. Convincing her to stop biting her nails was like asking a dog to wipe its feet.

Lauren was right about one thing: Sienna was more than he could handle. What if he was doing his daughter a disservice, trying to raise her himself? He felt desperate to protect her, but what if he was smothering her? He'd read countless articles about autistic people living productive lives, some even becoming professionals. It wasn't beyond comprehension—or at least it hadn't been in the beginning. But the school counselors and teachers had never offered much hope. They merely accommodated Sienna as the law required, putting her in with the mentally retarded boy and the deaf girl in the portable classroom behind the building. A speech therapist visited her once a week, a counselor once a month. The last, a matronly and tired woman who often called Tom to suggest potential medications. They had tried the medications, despite his early convictions against them. But by the second grade Sienna had taken fourteen different prescription drugs. None helped, at least not consistently. He concluded for the second time that she was better off without them. She was better off as nature had intended her to be. Tom pitched the drugs into the garbage and never regretted it. But now he wondered if it might be a good idea to explore those options once again. Maybe there were new discoveries that could make her closer to normal. He knew he was holding her back by cooping her up in that mind-numbing motel day and night, but he guessed it didn't matter just now, as that mind-numbing motel was slipping away from him. Perhaps it was divine providence—something Maria had believed in fervently.

"Listen, Sienna," he said, taking her chin in hand. "You have to be on your best behavior. Daddy will buy you a hamburger and a pop. But you have to sit still and be quiet."

Surprisingly, she didn't twist away but listened to him.

"What do I want you to do?"

She watched his mouth as he spoke.

"Sit quietly," he said.

Her eyes followed his lips.

"Can you say that for me?"

She said nothing.

"Sit quietly," he repeated and turned off the engine.

Inside, Stan waved at Tom, then shook his head when he saw Sienna trailing him. "Tom, she's a minor; she can't come in here."

Hap slid off his stool and carried his beer over to greet Tom. "C'mon, Stan, it's not going to hurt anything," he said over his shoulder.

Stan looked uncertain, but didn't protest.

"I promise she'll be quiet and well behaved," Tom said, following Hap to a booth on the other side of the pool table.

"Quiet isn't what I'm worried about," Stan said. "Shit, my customers aren't quiet. It's the cussing."

"Well, cut it out, then," Tom said, taking in the handful of people eating and minding their own business.

"That and Turnbull."

"Turnbull is up in Wishram. Heard him called out to a domestic dispute just before I came in," Hap said, waving the bartender off. He turned back to Tom and said, "Jorge over here—" He gestured, but there was no one at the bar. He twisted in his seat and looked around the room. "Hey, Stan, where's Jorge?"

Stan pointed at the door. "Just bugged out."

Hap turned back, shaking his head. He fiddled with the saltshaker. "That liar."

"Wanna fill me in?" Tom said, giving Sienna a packet of sugar.

"Jorge took a dare to stay in room six. Stan volunteered to pay for it."

"Well, that would've made one guest tonight."

"Guess he got scared." Hap smiled at Sienna, but she wouldn't look at him. She licked the tip of her finger, dipped it in the pile of sugar she'd poured out on the stained table, and sucked it off.

"Hey," Hap called to Stan, "get this kid some French fries and a Coke."

"You seen Charlene around?" Tom asked.

Sienna turned and stared at her father, waiting for his next words.

"Saw her a couple hours ago, at the post office," Hap said. "Why?"

"Sienna is driving me crazy begging for Charlene to come visit her."

Stan sloshed a pitcher of beer down hard on the table and gave Sienna a glass of Coke with a big red straw. He grunted as he turned away, mumbling something about burgers on the grill.

"Thought I might run into her here," Tom said, pouring himself a glass.

"She's probably down at the river doing a wind dance—or a man dance. She's hard up." Hap wished he hadn't said that last part. Charlene wasn't hard up enough to take him up on his repeated offers of dinner, drinks, dancing, anything he could think of.

Tom sipped the foam off his beer, then took a long drink. "That tastes good; I love beer."

Sienna looked again at her father and mouthed the word *love* without sound. Then she slid off the seat and under the table. Tom hauled her back up and gave her a sharp glare. She twisted out of his grip and sipped her Coke, making a low growling sound like a cornered animal ready to lunge.

"How are things with the motel?" Hap asked, knowing the answer. Why else would Tom be here instead of checking in guests?

"Lost cause. Guess I better start looking for a job," Tom sighed. "Need a place to stay, too. Know of any place with cheap rent?"

"Alan Camper has that little house on Fifth up for rent."

Tom scratched his chin. "Which one?"

"You know, it's bright yellow. Shingle siding. One-bedroom."

"I'm done sleeping on the sofa. Gotta have two bedrooms. Besides, isn't that place right next to the wrecking yard?"

Hap shrugged. "You said cheap."

"Guess it doesn't make sense anyway to rent a place in Rocket. I'll probably have to move to Portland to find work."

Sienna slid off her seat again, like a melting cartoon character.

"Get out of there," Tom said.

Hap could feel her crawling across his feet and imagined the filth down there. Stan did a decent job with his bar and kitchen, but he wholly neglected the cement floor, which was sticky with spilled beer and ground-in fries.

"Sienna," Tom boomed, drawing the attention of a couple sitting in a booth across the room. "Get out of there—now." He stood and dragged her out by her arm and plopped her down next to him. "Stay put!"

She sat for a second, looking stunned, then let out a slicing screech. She flopped off the bench and under the table again, this time flailing and screaming as if she were being beaten. She knocked the table and her Coke tipped over, spilling into Tom's lap and onto the seat.

The other customers stared and shook their heads.

Hap sat helpless, watching the color drain from Tom's face as he resolved the problem by pulling out his wallet and laying a ten-dollar bill on the table next to his own spilled beer, then extracting his now sopping, clawing daughter from under the table, hoisting her onto his shoulder like a bagged animal and lumbering out of the tavern. As the door closed behind him, Hap got up to follow, wishing he'd said something. Paid the damn tab. Done anything but sit there. When he reached the parking lot, Tom's truck was already headed east up Highway 14, black exhaust boiling from its tailpipe. Hap stood beneath the purple sky, the dry air hot and dusty in his nostrils. He felt burdened and heavy with the understanding that Tom had given up on his motel and Rocket. And sickened, too, that he was embarrassed and ashamed of his daughter.

He wandered across the street to the post office, where he went around the back and unlocked the door. Inside he flipped on his computer, opened his notebook, and reviewed the list of less reputable tabloids he'd collected in the consuming silence that his article had garnered from the big papers.

## 14

CHARLENE STARTLED TOM when he responded to the lobby bell and found her standing there. She paced along the counter, running her hand over the smooth surface, her eyebrows pressed tightly together as if she had grave concerns on her mind. Her hair was loose and tangled from driving with the windows down. Tom instinctively looked past her at the empty turnaround, half expecting to find a strapping young windsurfer waiting for her in a van.

"Charlene," he said. "What brings you out?"

"Hap said you were looking for me." She glanced around the motel lobby as if there must be some other message, but she couldn't remember it. "Nice doorbell," she said and pressed the chime again for effect.

"We were hoping to run into you in town. Sienna," he said, gesturing at his apartment. "She's been begging me to invite you back ever since that night." He looked down at the stained carpet, trying to formulate his thoughts better. He was barefoot, and his white skin looked pale and unhealthy against the green pile.

"Well, here I am. It's not too late to stop by, is it?"

"No, of course not. Come in." He glanced at his

watch—it was only eight-thirty—and stepped aside to allow Charlene into the apartment. "It's . . . it's kind of a mess."

Charlene brushed against Tom's arm as she passed, and he caught a whiff of her perfume, soft and floral. She wore a miniskirt with pumps and a tight tee shirt. Tom's eyes slipped down the backs of her bronze legs before he caught himself.

"Can I get you something to drink?"

"Beer if you have it," she said, flinging her purse down on the table and continuing into the living room. "Hey there, Sienna. You okay, kiddo? Heard you had a rough day."

Sienna leapt up, her dark eyes shining, a grin so big Tom stared into it with awe. "My book," she said, and ran to her room for it. "My book."

Charlene followed her, but stopped at the door and turned to Tom. "Hap said it was a bad scene at the tavern."

"No worse than other scenes. He's just not used to it, I guess." He was aware of the edge in his tone, but didn't care. It was time people realized that things were not perfect with him. Things were far from perfect.

"You shouldn't have taken her to a bar." Charlene disappeared into Sienna's bedroom, and Tom felt his face flush hot. He'd been reprimanded by a surfer girl with the morals of an alley cat and the mouth of a trucker. That she was right made it all the more maddening.

When Charlene didn't reappear, Tom took the beer he'd opened for her into Sienna's room. The two were sitting on the bed, Sienna pointing at pictures, Charlene reading the captions.

"Here," he said, handing her a cold Henry's.

"Thanks." Charlene took a long drink, then set the beer on the nightstand and continued reading.

Tom listened, but now as he stood there, Charlene's words grew suddenly stiff and she stumbled over phrases.

"I'll just be out in the living room," he said, but didn't go. It struck him how desperately his daughter had craved this attention, and shamed him that he hadn't read for her himself. A simple enough task that he'd put behind a million other things that at the time seemed more important. But now, in the face of losing his motel, those tasks were so amazingly trivial.

Thirty minutes later, Charlene appeared in the living room alone. Tom was watching a mindless sitcom, listening hard for the lobby bell, hoping for at least one guest. He muted the television.

"Um," Charlene started. She hesitated, looking back at the bedroom. "You know, she's really . . . dirty. Sticky, you know."

Tom fiddled with the buttons on the remote control. He'd never known Charlene to be hesitant or lacking for words. In fact, her entire demeanor this evening was different—barely recognizable.

"I mean . . . what I'm saying is that, she well, she could use a bath."

"I imagine she could," Tom said, anger rising, but for what reason he didn't know. He looked at Charlene, tried to stare her right in the face, but her gaze was too earnest for him to be truly angry. "But bathing Sienna is like bathing a ninety-pound house cat. Maybe worse. You tend to let it go awhile, if you know what I mean."

Charlene stared down at the floor as she tried again. "Maybe she'd let me. If you don't mind."

Tom thought about it. Would Sienna be any better behaved for Charlene than she was for him? And this, this horrible aspect of their lives, this terrible intimate ritual—

could he trust Charlene with the rawness of it? What if she shared some detail about it in town? Especially knowing that he was the one fighting Sienna every week, not a licensed caregiver as Lauren suggested, or . . . a mother. It was a thought he hoped no one in Rocket paused to ponder.

"She smells, Tom," Charlene said.

"I know." They stared at each other for a second, then Tom said, "If you're up for it."

Charlene disappeared, a moment later leading Sienna into the bathroom with clean clothes draped over her arm, leaving Tom to wonder why she was volunteering for this.

☼

Tom sat tensely on the sofa, listening to his daughter's whine turn to a hard, urgent scream. He stood up and paced the living room, then walked down the hall and stood outside the bathroom door. He could hear the tub filling with water, and Charlene speaking in a soft, soothing voice. Sienna went silent a moment, then started the long, anxious whine again. As it came to a nerve-ripping crescendo, Tom knocked.

"Need some help?" he called.

"No. We're fine. Girls only—ow, ow, no, *ow!* Sienna, let go of my hair. Let go."

Tom winced, thinking of Charlene with Sienna's fingers tangled around her long hair, dragging her head forward. "I can help," he said again.

"We're *fine.*"

"Sure," he muttered and went to the kitchen for a beer. He sat at the table, but he didn't drink from the bottle he'd opened. He stared at the bathroom door, rolling the beer cap between his fingers, pressing the sharp ridges into his palm with the intensity to match his daughter's squeals, until his hand was a collage of circular red impressions. He was inspecting the deeper ruts when he realized that the bathroom had fallen silent. He leaned forward, trying to listen, then got up and walked to the door. He pressed his ear against it.

"Isn't it better to be clean?" Charlene said.

If Sienna responded, Tom could not hear her through the door.

"Look, we'll braid your hair. It'll stay cleaner that way and it won't bug you. Can I do that?" Charlene's voice was sweet and melodic. "I'll bring you some conditioner next time so it won't be hard to comb."

Conditioner, Tom thought. That would make her hair easier to comb?

"Okay, sit down here and watch me in the mirror. I'll try to be gentle."

As Tom returned to the table he heard Sienna's whine start up again. He dreaded combing her hair. He had taken to whacking it off as she slept, using his utility scissors. He'd waited too long this time and it was horribly knotted when Charlene took Sienna into the bathroom. He sat down and sipped his beer, feeling impossibly tired. When the door opened, Sienna emerged first, pink and shiny. Her hair was wet, but parted in the middle and braided in two plaits that ended abruptly below her ears with one noticeably longer than the other. She was wearing a clean tee shirt and shorts, and she looked at her father with large sad eyes, then whirled and glanced back at Charlene, as if for assurance. Something about the look hurt him—a stab in his chest.

"Go get in bed and I'll come say good night," Charlene promised as she flipped off the bathroom light. She paused in the hallway, then held up her severely scratched arms for Tom to see. There was evidence of tooth marks, though not as deep as he had suffered on occasion.

"I see how you might let it go awhile," she said and smiled sympathetically. Then she went to Sienna's room and talked to her for several minutes before coming out and closing the door behind her.

"She won't stay in there," he said.

"She's asleep."

Tom couldn't believe that and let his mouth gape before he recovered his wits. "She never falls asleep like that. She's usually up until midnight, one ... later."

"A warm bath will do that to you. Even on a hot night like this."

Charlene's neck glistened beneath a sweaty sheen, her hair sticking to her forehead and her tee shirt ringed at the armpits.

"Beer?"

Charlene looked at her watch, then out at the black night. She seemed unsure of herself now, without Sienna there to draw her attention away. Tom thought it was oddly out of character for her—or at least how he thought she'd be. She'd always come across as brash and outspoken, but here she stood in his kitchen looking shy and even a little innocent.

"I better go home. It's late."

"Okay," he said, but wished he could think of one single reason that she should stay. "You're amazing with Sienna. Thank you for coming out to see her. For doing this."

"She's just lonely." Charlene gathered her purse. "We all get lonely."

Tom followed her out of the apartment and into the lobby.

"I told her I'd come see her again next week. I hope that's okay."

"Of course it is. I just wish I could pay you."

Charlene turned on her heel, her face suddenly hard. "Pay me? I'm not a babysitter."

"I didn't mean that. Not like that," he stammered.

"I like Sienna. She reminds me of someone I used to know. I could never take money for visiting her."

☼

Hap wandered back across Main Street to the Red Tail after double-checking that the back door of his office was locked. Charlene had surprised him when she popped in to retrieve her forgotten purse. He hadn't noticed it sitting on the counter or he would have delivered it to her. And he suffered another jealous pang as she rushed out to see Sienna. Tom, more likely. He wished now that he'd gone with Charlene to Tom's place instead of sending off all those pointless e-mail queries to editors who would scoff at his article, no matter how questionable the integrity of their own tabloids.

As he crossed the hot, deserted street, Hap paused and looked up at the apartment over Guthry's auto body. He'd never seen the light on up there before—hadn't even realized there was an apartment on the second floor. He studied the other buildings along that stretch of old Rocket. Dignified brick storefronts from a bygone era with their boxy, Art Deco details and big picture windows. Half were empty now, some with broken glass, taped over or boarded up. A few with their *Going out of Business* signs still pasted in the windows, fading and curling up at the corners. On one end was the original Rocket Hotel with its ornate Victorian turret on the upper corner. It now housed a dingy, overpriced convenience store that no one seemed to go in or out of, though it always seemed that some dog or other waited on the sidewalk. Gaudy hand-painted signs advertised cigarettes and beer. If the wind comes back, Hap thought, Tom could convert that back to a hotel and we could open a tasting room and wine bar like the ones springing up in towns all along the Columbia—a real upscale place here in Rocket.

He pushed into the Red Tail and took a seat at the bar.

"Thought I got rid of you for tonight," Stan said. "What're you drinking?"

"Better stick with beer or I'll have a headache tomorrow," Hap said. He looked over at the woman next to him and realized it was Lauren Kent. He nodded to her. "Lauren, how are you?"

She rolled her eyes. Hap could see she'd had a couple drinks already—something mixed, tall with orange juice.

"How's the pet clinic?" he asked, wondering if it was too late for a beer, after all. It would take more than beer to make a conversation with Lauren interesting, he thought.

"Just hopping. How about the paper?"

"Slow. No wind and all."

"I've heard that before."

They sat in awkward silence for a moment, then Lauren asked, "Did you grow up here?"

He shook his head, wondering where that question came from. "Hood River."

She studied him. "Were you always a reporter?"

"No. I was city planner in Marysville, California, for twenty years."

Lauren's eyes widened. "Why'd you move to Rocket?"

Stan set a pint of beer on the bar in front of Hap.

He took his time sipping the foam off before answering. "It's pretty close to home without really being home. It's small and dry. I always liked the river."

She nodded as if she understood completely. "No family in California?"

"No, just a couple of rental houses and an ex-wife. What about you?"

"I'm from Pullman. I thought this would be a nice place to live and there was no vet here."

"It is a nice place to live."

She shrugged. "It was when there were people with pets."

"Wind'll come back. Has to."

She looked at Hap again with interest. She suddenly appeared stone sober. "What do you make of these rumors about Tom's motel?"

"In the absence of wind, people need something to keep them busy."

"Is that all it is?" She stared intently with her green eyes.

Hap imagined she could intimidate almost anyone she set her mind to. "It does seem weird. I'll give you that."

"So you do believe it!" she snapped, as if she'd caught him in a trap.

"Doesn't matter what I think. I'm no authority."

Stan appeared again at the bar. "Another gin?" he asked Lauren. She nodded and he poured a straight shot for her, then disappeared into the kitchen.

Lauren raised the glass and examined it a moment, then threw it back and swallowed.

Hap waited for a tremor to run through her, a shiver, anything to prove that she was human, but she set the glass on the counter and leaned back smoothly. She picked up the tall glass and sucked the last of it up through her straw, making a childlike racket with her ice cubes, then dug in her purse for a few bills. She laid them on the counter, and looked again at Hap.

"I'm worried about him," she said.

"Tom?"

"He's acting crazy."

Hap said nothing.

"Well, if that room six produces the miracles everybody claims it does, maybe Tom should put his daughter up for the night in there." She started for the door, but tipped slightly sideways as she pulled it open and waved good night to Hap.

# 15

"CHECKOUT IS NOON, but since the sun is already up, I'll let you stay until three." Tom handed a room key to a gray-haired man with dark bags under his eyes and a bristle of black stubble on his chin.

The man glanced at the number and scanned the motel through the lobby window.

"Room ten is on the second floor along this wing," Tom said, pointing.

The man dumped the key on the counter. "Gimme something on the ground floor."

"All right." Tom turned to his key rack.

"Make it a quiet one, too. I need some sleep," the man ordered.

Tom scowled and took down the key to room six. He tossed it on the counter without a word, and his guest picked it up. Tom pointed to the corner room and the man disappeared without thanking him for the extra three hours.

Tom shook his head as he watched the man unlock the door and disappear into room six. Maybe he'll get a new job just like Gill had. He thought about the past events with room six with the same skeptical slant he always did during the day. It was only when he awoke in the middle of the night, short of breath, having suffered a nightmare about being held personally responsible for the things that had happened, did he wonder if something was really going on in there. Now, wide-awake, the list of unfortunates and fishing guide beneficiaries aside, the idea seemed horribly misguided—insane.

"When . . . when . . . wh . . ."

Tom turned to find Sienna behind him, gazing out at the parking lot, her new braids fuzzy and her face cherubic in its scrubbed sleepiness.

"When is she coming back?" Sienna finally managed.

"Charlene. Can you say her name for me?"

"When is Charlene coming back?"

Tom nodded approvingly and smiled. "Next week, she said."

"She comes back now."

"Next week, Sienna."

"Who's that?" She pointed out the window.

A battered Toyota Celica that looked about thirty years old rattled into the grassy field next to the motel. The parched ground boiled with dust that drifted against the lobby windows. A man climbed out wearing a decaying black suit. He was tall and thin with a dark mustache, his hair parted down the middle. He put his hands on his lower back and stretched hard as he looked around.

"No idea. You stay here." But when Tom turned to Sienna she was already gone, back into the apartment. He heard the TV come on. Tom waited for the man to do something. There was no law against stretching, and he wasn't technically parked on Tom's property, but the way this stranger sized up his building bothered him.

"Can I help you?" Tom said, approaching the car.

"The end is nigh, my brother," the man said. "The end is nigh."

Tom thought of the bank drafting foreclosure papers. "You could be right on that one."

"I am indeed. We must repent and beg for mercy or God's vengeance will rain down on us."

"I don't think it's *that* bad." Tom eyed the man warily. He'd had his share of Holy Rollers and doomsayers come through, especially in more prosperous years when his rooms were filled with single young fornicators. The first summer he and Maria ran the motel it was as if they'd stepped back forty years. Tom was too young to have fully enjoyed the sixties, and already settled into marriage with a baby on the way when he encountered this carefree counterculture on the steppes above the Columbia. These people were simply a new generation of hippies with their patchouli and clove cigarettes, except that they had a singular purpose: windsurfing. And because of that purpose, they had abandoned him for windier climes.

The preacher leaned into his car and pulled out a stack of small green booklets rubber-banded together. He snapped one free and thrust it into Tom's hand. "Your soul is all you have, my man."

"You can't park here," Tom said, trying to hand back the booklet.

"I've been sent by God to pray for those who come to this crossroads of evil."

"Evil?"

"I know about your motel, my brother."

"I'm not your brother. And this—"

"We are all brothers in the Lord." The preacher bowed his head slightly as if to ask God for patience with Tom.

"Look, I don't know who you are—"

"Reverend Shelly. You may call me Reverend."

"Well, Reverend, like I said, you can't park here."

The reverend smiled, but not in a friendly manner. He gestured at the open lot. "This, my brother, is not your property."

Tom imagined this man had been kicked off enough properties to do his homework up front. The reverend was right, it was not his property. "Have you received permission from the landowner to be here?"

The reverend didn't answer, and Tom didn't know what else to say because he didn't know the man who owned that property, either. All he had was a name on his escrow papers listed under "adjacent property owner."

"Your motel, my friend, is a mecca of evil."

"In case you hadn't noticed, *my friend,* my motel is empty. There's no one here for you to pray for. They've gone with the wind. If you want to pray, pray for wind."

Reverend Shelly leaned into his car once again and pulled out a single page of a newspaper. He pointed at the headline "Spooky Doin's in Rocket, Washington." "Says here that people who stay in your motel die, Brother Jemmett." The reverend stared him in the face with a defiance that gave Tom a shiver.

"Let me see that." Tom took the paper and scanned the article. It summed up the deaths of Helen Simpson, Art Schlegel, and the kidnapping john from Las Vegas. It went on to talk about the others—the people Hap had researched and scribbled out on their shared pages of yellow legal paper listing the guest history of room six. Tom's blood was rising. He could hear his pulse pounding in his ears, and he didn't have to look at the byline to know that Hap Mitsui had used him. He'd blatantly lied about not running a story, and here was the evidence. Tom stalked back to his motel, gripping the tract in one hand and the paper in his other.

"You can keep that, my friend," Reverend Shelly called after him.

☼

Hap opened his e-mail messages and cheered at the response he'd received from *The Sasquatch,* a regional

paper in Northern California known mainly for reporting conspiracy theories and UFO sightings. He didn't
care. It was a victory, albeit small. The note said simply:

> Dear Mr. Mitsui,
>     Thanks for the informative article. We've
> run it in this week's edition on page eight
> with a byline. A check for $50 is on its way
> along with tear sheets.

"This week? Thanks for the advance notice," he said
to his monitor.

"Who are you talking to?" Charlene asked from her
honeycomb of mailboxes.

Hap hesitated. "No one."

She snorted. "You're so friggin weird."

"How was your visit with Tom last night?" He sat
back, feeling satisfied with himself and more than a little
curious about Charlene and Tom.

"I didn't visit Tom. I visited Sienna." She dumped a
sack of mail out on her sorting table and tossed the canvas bag in the corner. The sound of peeping birds, which
had serenaded them since they'd arrived, became loud
and urgent. "Oops," she said. "Forgot about those
chicks. I wish Patrick would get down here and pick those
poor things up. I will never understand how people can
ship day-old baby chicks through the mail. Did you know
that if you order twenty-five they actually ship thirty-five
because they figure ten will die? That's just sick."

Hap was not aware of that, and got up to inspect the
box with holes in its lid and *LIVE CHICKS* stamped on
its side in big red letters along with arrows to ensure the
carriers didn't flip them over. A pungent odor of chicken
shit seeped from the box. "Think you should put them
under a light for warmth or something?"

Charlene looked uncertain. "You think?"

He shrugged. "Couldn't hurt." He took the box back to his desk and set it under his library lamp. He could see the yellow down through the holes as the tiny birds crowded to the end where the bulb shone brightest. After a moment they settled down to a rhythmic peeping once again.

"Old Patrick doesn't need any more chickens. Have you seen his place lately?" Charlene said.

"Can't miss it, right there on the road."

"I bet he's got a hundred birds in his yard already. What's he want with these poor things?"

"He sells eggs."

"To who?"

To *whom,* Hap thought, but remained quiet. "How was Sienna? She get over her ordeal at the Red Tail?"

"Tom should never have taken that little girl to a bar. What the hell was he thinking? *Idiot.*"

"Come on, Charlene, he was just trying to relax."

"Well, relax at the Dairy Queen or the diner. You don't take your twelve-year-old to the tavern."

Hap had never heard Charlene espouse parenting advice before, and he thought it was touching, if not a little out of place coming from her. "You're pretty opinionated about this. Does this mean you're ready to settle down and have a family of your own?"

She stopped what she was doing to give Hap a hard stare. "You jackass."

"What? What'd I say?" Hap retreated to his computer, embarrassed. He knew instinctively that what he'd said to her had been callous and insensitive. But he hadn't meant it that way. Charlene seemed so well adjusted, considering what she'd been through with her family, that he often forgot about it completely. He wished he could take back his question.

Lauren's head ached as she drove through Rocket to the pet clinic on the west end of town. What on earth was she thinking, going to the tavern and doing shots on a Thursday evening? She sped down Main Street hoping that her newest assistant, Anna, a single mom with three kids under ten, was already there. Patrick Wilson had called her emergency number and told her that his dog had been hit by a car. He was meeting her at the clinic.

Inside, Lauren found Anna pulling files and setting up the exam rooms.

"I need the O.R. prepped for surgery right away. Patrick Wilson's dog got hit by a car this morning. He thinks its front left leg is broken. We'll need X-rays," Lauren said. "You up for assisting on a long surgery if that's what's needed?"

Anna shrugged, which annoyed Lauren. *Yes or no,* Lauren wanted to implore, *not a shrug.* But so far Anna had proven to be reliable, if silent.

Anna turned her crimson face toward Lauren, her acne as angry as Lauren had ever seen on anyone. "Patrick Wilson's dog? That little border collie of his?"

"Yeah, his name is Crispy."

Anna scrunched up her face. "Patrick can't pay for this. You know that, don't you?" Patrick was seventy-seven years old, living on an income that wasn't enough to cover his expenses twenty years ago.

"I know." Lauren sighed, walking down the hall toward the operating room. "No one in this damn town can afford to pay me for my services. But what would you have me do? Turn them away?"

"I would," Anna said unapologetically.

Lauren turned to face the girl with new interest. "Oh?"

"Well, why do you think all these businesses are going under?"

"Because there are no tourists this year?" Lauren said.

"Because everyone's giving free stuff away," Anna declared.

Lauren watched as Anna moved efficiently through the O.R., inventorying the instruments that Lauren had detailed for her only a few days earlier. Anna had an amazing memory. She hadn't asked any questions, just listened quietly and nodded as Lauren described the purpose of each one and when she would need to use it. Lauren had imagined she'd be repeating herself later, training Anna again and again and again, as she usually did with the staff she could find in Rocket. But Anna laid out the instruments she'd need without a single question, and when she was finished she stood back looking at Lauren for confirmation.

"Perfect," Lauren said as she heard the bell chime on the front door. "That's Patrick."

## 16

MID-MORNING Reverend Shelly set up a portable canvas gazebo to shield himself from the scorching sun. On it he hung a large hand-painted sign that read *Repent now! The end is near.* What business Tom might have seen would surely be driven away by this spectacle. An occasional semi blew its horn at the reverend as it thundered past. Tom watched from his lobby, where he pored over Hap's story in *The Sasquatch* three more times. He didn't know whether to call the son of a bitch up or drive into town and face Hap in person. Or maybe he'd just turn his back on the friendship—a friendship that he had obviously valued much more highly than Hap had. He was reeling so thoroughly from the betrayal that he didn't immediately register the sound of breaking glass in the apartment. Then he wondered if he'd imagined it. But there it was again, a combination of popping and smashing.

In the kitchen Sienna stood with a jar of relish over her head. At her feet were smashed jars of mayonnaise and pickles. She looked up at her father, startled by his sudden appearance, screwed up her face angrily, and pelted the jar down with as much power as she could put into it. Flecks of green relish exploded at her feet, splattering the cabinets, the inside of the open refrigerator, and both of their legs.

"What are you doing?" he demanded.

Sienna's face went hard and she turned toward the refrigerator, but Tom slammed the door shut before she could reach for a half-full jar of cherry peppers.

"Answer me. Why have you done this?" He grabbed his daughter by the arm and dragged her toward him, her feet slipping in the gooey mess.

"She comes back!" Sienna shrieked. "She comes *back!*"

"This is not how you ask someone to come back." Dots of spit landed on the girl's face, making her pull away. "This is not how you get someone to come see you."

Sienna twisted and screeched, trying to wrench out of Tom's grasp. She lost her footing in the slime on the floor and slid, but Tom hauled her off her feet with brute force because broken glass lay everywhere. He slung her over his shoulder and felt the mayonnaise and relish squish against him, soaking into his shirt. Sienna thrashed, kicking her feet and bruising his ribs with her knees. When did she get so heavy? he wondered as new pain shot through his lower back.

He carried her to the bathroom, where he intended to strip her down and force her into the shower, but he found the floor smeared with toothpaste and shampoo. The mirror was covered in shaving cream and his heart thudded to a momentary halt when he recognized his safety razor in the bottom of the sink. He scanned the room for blood, but there was none.

"She comes back!" Sienna screamed, pounding Tom on the shoulders and head. Her fist came down hard on his ear, sending hot sparks deep into his brain.

Tom skidded on the sticky floor, but found purchase on the matted hall carpet. He carried Sienna to the bedroom where he threw her down onto the bed. She bounced and fell on the floor, and he picked her up and tossed her on the bed again. She was crying hysterically. He felt as if he could beat the child. He wanted to spank her, to slap her, to make her stop. He wanted to hit her and hit her and hit her. He imagined wrapping his fingers around her throat and choking her.

Tom's breath came up short and the room swirled around him. He yanked the door shut, holding the knob as Sienna flailed against it, bawling. He couldn't believe he'd just entertained those thoughts. How could he have imagined such a thing? How could he?

The lobby bell rang, jolting Tom back to the moment. It rang again.

"Just a minute," he yelled. He couldn't let go of the door. She'd be out and into the broken glass in seconds. He looked around. The bell rang again. "I said just a goddamn minute!"

At last he shoved the hall bookcase in front of the door, cursing the fact that bedroom doors didn't lock from the outside. Didn't anyone ever need to lock someone *in*?

In the lobby, Tom found a middle-aged couple waiting for him. The woman, a bleached blonde in a tight-fitting blouse, looked him up and down suspiciously.

"Whacha got back there, a wildcat?" the man asked. "That's a serious ruckus you got going on."

"What do you want?"

"A room," the woman said coolly.

Tom opened the drawer where he kept the registration cards, but paused.

"What's up with the preacher out there?" the man said, pointing out the window at Reverend Shelly. "Tried to tell us we'd come to the crossroads of evil." He laughed. "Crossroads of evil ..." The man marveled at the words as he stared out at the reverend.

Tom looked down at the contents of the drawer as the

woman tapped her fingernails on the counter, waiting. He shoved the drawer closed. "Sorry. The motel is closed."

"Closed?" the woman said. "But the—"

"It's closed," he said. "Forever."

The couple stared at him a moment, then looked at each other.

"You'll have to find some other place. I'm done." Tom turned and walked back into his apartment, past the broken jars and smeared condiments, past the sticky bathroom and Sienna's room, where she continued to sob and kick the back of the bookcase, knocking the books onto the hall floor a few at a time. He sank down on the sofa.

The lobby bell chimed again. "Go away," he shouted. "Don't you get it? I'm closed. I'm done."

Tom stared at the floor, and realized that there were beads and buttons everywhere. She'd emptied the baby food jars onto the carpet and scattered them across the furniture.

"She comes back," Sienna gurgled through snot and tears. "She comes *back*."

"Damn you, Maria," Tom whispered. "*Damn you!*"

The room was now still and quiet, but his wish to hurt his daughter had placed a heavy pall in the air that he couldn't put out of his mind. For all the frustration and anger Sienna could conjure in him, he had never wanted to kill her before. Thinking about it now gave him a dull, nauseous feeling. The sharp, tangy smell of relish and vinegar permeated the apartment. He stood, feeling stiff. He wanted a drink, but that was the last thing he needed. It would be too difficult to stop if he went down that path tonight. Instead, he shoved the bookcase away from Sienna's door. She was lying on the floor staring up at him, her face swollen and red, her tears spent. She'd wet her pants and taken them off and thrown them in the corner in a ball. The bedroom reeked of urine. She lay with her legs spread, uncaring or unaware of her exposed genitals. Tom pulled her up to a standing position. Her hair was slimy with mayonnaise.

"You're too old to behave this way. You're twelve, not two." As he said it, he choked back the urge to cry. She was an animal. An infant. A permanently damaged child who would never amount to anything, and he needed to face that. She'd burden him for the remainder of his days—and then he'd die. And then who would protect her?

"C'mon. We're moving in to room five. You need a bath."

She whined.

"Not today." He pulled her bathrobe from the closet and draped it around her shoulders.

Room five was the only ground-floor unit with two queen beds and a kitchenette. Tom brought a handful of things to the room: clean clothes, Sienna's pillow, her book. It would have to do until he made a plan. The motel would be foreclosed on in three quick weeks; he needed to figure out where they were going. He couldn't sit here any longer, stupidly waiting for a miracle that would never come.

On the way through the lobby, Tom found the key to room six on the counter. He glanced out to see if Reverend Shelly was still picketing and found his last guest standing with him, talking. When Tom came back for some coffee grounds, the two men were down on their knees praying. Tom shook his head at the idea anyone would give this bogus preacher the time of day, let alone pray with him on the side of a sweltering highway in the middle of nowhere. He took out the registration card and read the name of the guest: Mike Naylor. Then he turned the *Closed* sign to face the driveway and switched off the neon on his highway sign—an act that sent a stabbing pain through his chest. That sign had never been turned off since the day it was redone with Tom Jemmett's name on it, and he felt as though he were betraying Maria by closing the door on their shared dream. The motel was the last good memory he had of her, and with the flip of a switch he'd condemned her to death all over again.

Tom took the cash from the drawer, put it in his wallet, and locked the lobby. The preacher and Mike Naylor looked on as Tom wandered down the sidewalk to room five, where Sienna sat in front of the TV, stinking. He groaned at the chore that lay ahead of him.

Lauren opened her post office box and removed a single envelope—a telephone bill. She peered down the long shaft of polished metal, hoping she'd missed something, but it was empty. Hap Mitsui's voice echoed back at her, as if he held a can on the other end of a string. She couldn't quite make out his words, but before she closed the small door, she heard Charlene's response.

"I'll go out and check on Sienna tomorrow. That child is desperately lonely."

Lauren paused, her heart suddenly pounding madly in her throat. She tipped her head forward and pretended to concentrate on the envelope as Patrick Wilson lumbered arthritically into the lobby. His hat was missing and his bald head was sunburned.

"See if you can get Tom to come in for a beer," Hap said.

"Hello there," Patrick said to Lauren. He was a cheerful old man who could be difficult to escape once he started talking. "How's my Crispy-dog doin'?"

Lauren resented the interruption, but smiled at

Patrick anyway. "His leg is going to heal, but it'll take some time. He'll limp, maybe for the rest of his life. Have you been over to see him yet?"

"No, but I'm gonna go over in a little bit. I kept tellin' that damn dog he was gonna git run over."

"Well, you know how dogs are," Lauren said and turned back to her mailbox, straining to hear the conversation in the back and hoping Patrick would see that she was busy.

"Thinks he's gonna catch a semi."

"He's lucky to be alive. You better keep him in the yard or he won't be for long."

Patrick nodded, and went to the window where he slowly pressed the service button.

Realizing she'd heard all she was going to, Lauren slammed her mailbox shut and struggled with the key. It always stuck in the lock as if the mailbox didn't want to let go of it. She'd complained, but Charlene shrugged it off with some lame excuse that they were all that way.

The service window opened and Charlene popped into view. "Damn it, Patrick, where the hell have you been? These baby chicks are dying in here. I called you five hours ago."

"I'm sorry," the old man said. "Crispy got run over this morning."

Charlene gasped. "I'm sorry, Patrick." Her voice had gone quiet and serious. "I didn't know. Is he...did he...?"

"He's gonna make it," Patrick said. "Thanks to Dr. Kent here." He gestured at Lauren.

Lauren passed behind the old man on her way to the door and she and Charlene glimpsed each other. Lauren felt suddenly self-conscious with her hair pulled sharply back in a ponytail, no makeup, her surgical scrubs work-worn and too long. A little tight in the thighs. What did

Charlene know about Sienna? How could *she* say whether the girl was lonely?

☼

Hap listened to Patrick tell Charlene about his dog as Lauren Kent slipped out the front door. Ever since he'd run into her at the Red Tail, she'd been on his mind. She seemed to have lost some of her hard edge since splitting up with Tom, and Hap wondered if the woman really was the she-devil he'd always believed her to be. There was something sad about her now, but he couldn't quite put his finger on it. Maybe it was just seeing her drunk on gin on a Thursday night.

Tom's recent display of generosity with Gill and Sandy, the vagrants he found on his lot, and the prostitute from Nevada had caused Hap to think more carefully about the way he judged people. Not just Lauren Kent but Dillard, too. Hap wondered what sort of childhood had produced that insecure man and his desperate search for acceptance. Neglect? Perhaps a sharply disapproving parent? We all have our skeletons, Hap decided, looking at Charlene. No one ever talked about Charlene's past. She had the most sensational and tragic story—not just in Rocket, but perhaps the entire state of Washington. He'd often wondered why she chose to stay here. Had it been him, he'd have long left for places he could be anonymous. Somewhere that people didn't know enough to speculate or pity.

He turned his attention back to Lauren as she retreated across the parking lot toward the clinic. Her hair was pulled back today and her faded medical scrubs made her backside look rounder and softer. She wasn't really as unattractive as he'd always thought.

☼

Tom waited until Sienna had fallen soundly asleep, then went back to the apartment for a few more things. When he reached the lobby door, key in hand, there was a note taped to it. It simply said, *I'm going to sue you, you son of a bitch!* Tom took the note down and looked around at the empty parking lot. No one was there but the preacher in the adjacent field, leaning against his car with his arms crossed, staring at Tom.

Tom went inside, but the note bothered him. Who had left it there? Instead of looking for Hap's number straight off, he walked out to where the reverend lounged. The setting sun put a golden hue over the landscape, making it appear as though the preacher stood in a field of fire.

"You see who put this note on my door?" Tom asked, holding it up, but not handing it to the preacher.

"I believe that would be our brother in God, Mr. Naylor."

Tom looked again at the note. "Oh, so you've convinced him he's damned because he stayed here and now he's making to sue me?"

"I didn't have to convince him, my friend. He experienced firsthand the evil that lurks here."

"What are you talking about? I saw him out here with you earlier. He was fine."

The preacher smiled his unfriendly smile at Tom.

"Why am I even bothering to talk to you?" Tom said and turned back. The preacher said nothing, and Tom found his passkey in the lobby, then wandered down to room six. The door stuck and he had to put some shoulder into it to get it open. He hadn't actually been inside the room for several days—maybe a week. At first the place seemed nearly untouched. The bedspread had a small crinkle in it and the pillow was flattened, but the bed was still made. Dust motes floated in the air. The buzzing of an insect or two against the window. Or maybe three. Tom flipped the light switch that lit the bed-side lamp and noticed a yellow jacket crawling across the shade. He stepped forward to get a cup from the bath-room and put the creature outside when he saw another on the wall above the lamp. He paused and listened. The room hummed unnaturally. Tom went to the window and pulled back the drapes, but found himself suddenly standing in a swarm of yellow jackets. He batted them and turned in circles trying to get away. Dozens of them came at him, diving for Tom's head. One landed on the back of his hand and as he brushed it away he trapped another between his fingers, causing it to sting. The pain burned across his skin as he felt another crawling up the back of his sweaty neck, and he ducked out the door, only to be stung on the forearm as he tried rid himself of another.

*"Goddammit!"* he shouted through deep searing pain. But the yellow jackets kept coming, chasing him out into the parking lot. One had gotten down his shirt and commenced to sting him again and again on the torso. Tom yanked his shirt over his head as another stung him on the temple, and he sprinted desperately for the pool. He plunged in feetfirst and let the cool water envelop him. As he drifted toward the bottom, his denim jeans pulling him down, he imagined hot coals pressed against his skin in ten or twelve places, unquenchable hot spots that scorched into his flesh. A black and yellow body floated past his face on its way back to the surface, and his hand grew thick and tight with swelling before he resurfaced for air.

# 17

AS SHE SAT at her desk finishing her paperwork Lauren stewed about Charlene's assertion that Sienna was lonely. What did Charlene know? Was she a trained professional? Of course not, she was a postal clerk, and barely qualified to do that.

"The O.R. is clean and prepped for tomorrow," Anna said from the doorway, her purse slung over her bony shoulder. "So are the exam rooms. I've pulled the files for your morning appointments, but I'll be here at eight."

Lauren looked up and smiled. "You're the best assistant I've had in a long time," she said.

Anna stared morosely at Lauren. "I looked in on Patrick's dog. He's still groggy from the surgery. Do you want me to come back later?"

"Do you mind?" Lauren had planned to do that herself, but if Anna was willing, she could go out to Tom's instead. She'd come to the devastating conclusion that morning as she pieced Crispy's leg back together that Tom was not going to call her or come after her. He was willing to let her go. She wished she could accept that, but she simply couldn't. She hadn't realized how much Tom needed her until her trip to the post office. Charlene didn't care about Sienna, she was after Tom, but he wouldn't see it.

"It's on the clock, right?" Anna asked.

"Yes."

"Then I'll come back. I need the money."

Lauren nodded. Anna didn't have much personality, but Lauren didn't care as long as she was reliable.

☼

The welts Tom had suffered from the yellow jackets swelled and smoldered, leaving him stiff and achy. His temple had a knot the size of a tangerine and his throat had gone dry and scratchy. He had waited for the cloud of yellow jackets to clear before leaving the pool, then quietly closed the door to room six. He didn't care where the insects had come from, and he wasn't going to deal with them now, or ever. From outside, the window was a blur, teeming with black and yellow—a frenetic throng of hundreds, maybe thousands. Back in room five he stripped down and inspected himself, counting fourteen volcano-like wounds, a mashed yellow jacket still clinging to his wet belly. Sienna slept on for another hour, and when she finally awoke he forced a Benadryl tablet down her, then took one himself so he could rest. He fed her a cup of instant noodles and the antihistamine quickly put her back to sleep. But rest eluded him. He watched Sienna doze fitfully on the bed next to his, and wished he hadn't resorted to drugging her. He knew in his heart that it was time to seek better help—perhaps even the medications he'd refused all these years. The names floated back to him now: Tenex, clonidine, Ritalin. And so did their side effects: weight loss, agitation, drowsiness, liver damage. But Sienna needed help. *He* needed help if he was going to manage her spiraling behavior. Today had been a wake-up call. He no longer trusted himself with the task of caring for this child—a failure too great to contemplate.

He squeezed his eyes shut, but his mind wound through the loss of his motel, the escalating demands of his daughter, Hap's betrayal. He'd never, felt so profoundly alone, so without direction. He looked again at his daughter. Charlene had commented that Sienna was lonely. Indeed. They were both lonely. He could scarcely fathom the future—a future devoid of hope or happiness.

Lauren pulled up in front of the Jemmett Motel about half past nine at night. She slid out of her Jeep and stood in the eerily dark parking lot. A half moon hanging in the deep-cobalt sky illuminated the white trim of the building, making it look like the cover of some cheap horror novel. It took a moment before she realized that the neon sign was black. She turned a full circle and looked out over the vacant lot next door, where a strange man sat next to his car in a lawn chair. She couldn't make out the signs he displayed, but the way he stared at her with his arms folded across his chest made her feel naked and exposed. There was something curious about him. Something not unfriendly.

She tugged the door to the darkened lobby, but it was locked, so she pulled the keys from the Jeep's ignition and walked around to the back door of Tom's apartment. His pickup was there where he always parked it, but no light came from inside. She fumbled with the key he'd given her months ago, but never used, as she tried to insert it into the lock, finally managing to unlock the door. It creaked on its hinges as she pushed it open and peered into the dark room. She was immediately struck by the vinegar smell of pickles and relish, followed rapidly by the stench of rotting food.

"Tom?" she called, but the place was still and obviously abandoned.

Lauren turned on a lamp in the living room and looked around in the dim glow at the buttons and beads flung everywhere. The sofa cushions were in disarray and a bookcase had been shoved into the hallway. Books lay scattered, some open, their pages creased and torn. She found her way into the kitchen and halted at the crunch of glass beneath her feet, feeling along the wall for the light. When she finally found the switch, she gasped at the mess. She peeked into the bathroom.

"*My God,*" she said. "That child is an animal."

Lauren wandered out into the lobby and scanned the motel from the window. Was Tom even here? Where would he go without his truck? Short of knocking on every door, she didn't know how she'd find him. She'd never convinced him to get a cell phone—he claimed he rarely went anywhere so there was no need. Perhaps he'd left with someone tonight. Perhaps he was with Charlene.

The odd man sat in his chair, staring at the building. Lauren went back into the apartment, pulling the door closed behind her. She looked into the bedroom, which smelled of urine. She noticed the photograph of Maria that Tom kept displayed for Sienna still sat on the dresser. He wouldn't have left it behind if he were gone for good, that she was sure of.

"Tom, what are you going to do with this child?" she said quietly, still stunned by the magnitude of the mess. "Why won't you listen to me?"

Then it came to her—a way to prove how much he needed her. He would at last see. She would show him. Lauren walked through the apartment, turning on every light. She found an old work shirt of Tom's and changed into it, rolling the sleeves up, then pulled on the rubber dish gloves he kept under the sink in the kitchen. She started with the glass, picking up the large pieces, then wiping up the goo with paper towels. Next she found the mop and a bucket. After an hour or so, she turned on the television to keep her company as she worked, her resolve deepening as she cleaned. She finished the kitchen, then the bathroom, then she shoved the bookcase back to its place in the hallway, stacking its books neatly onto their shelves. As she worked, she imagined Tom's face when he came home. He'd be expecting to have to tackle this mess himself and would find it done for him. If he couldn't see that she was there for him—truly cared about him . . .

The last thing Lauren did before leaving was collect the beads and buttons into a plastic bag. After straightening the bedroom and throwing the soiled laundry into the washer, she set the bag in the middle of Sienna's bed.

It was nearly midnight by the time the apartment was finally restored to its dingy but clean self. Lauren looked at her watch and wondered if it would be best to call now, or wait until morning. She knew there would be a night answering service taking calls, and decided that was better because they wouldn't recognize her voice from the last time she'd called. Lauren picked up the phone and dialed the number of Child Protective Services.

"Is this an emergency?" the night clerk asked.

"No. But I think someone should check on the little girl who lives out at the Jemmett Motel."

"What is your name, please?"

"I don't want to give my name."

"Is the child in immediate danger?"

Lauren hesitated. "No," she said. "I just think they need some help. I think her dad is trying to take care of her, but I think he's in over his head."

"Can you give me more information?" the clerk asked.

Lauren's fingers were shaking. She struggled for something to say. When she'd called before, they had treated her differently because she was the veterinarian reporting an animal abuse case. Now she was just an anonymous caller. She didn't want to ruin Tom, only scare him into seeing that he needed help.

"Ma'am?" the clerk said. "What's happening with the girl? What are you concerned about?"

Lauren banged down the phone. She sat in the quiet apartment, trembling but feeling oddly satisfied. Finally, she got up, gathered her keys, and went out the back door, locking it behind her. She looked for the strange man. His car was still there, but the lawn chair was empty now as she pulled away from the motel.

☀

Around dawn Tom was awakened from a fitful slumber by a loud racket in the parking lot. He peered out between the drapes to see a cluster of people standing on the sidewalk. A battered van with clumsily painted slogans and graffiti on it sat in the turnaround, and someone was rapping on the locked door to the lobby. He reached for his clothes.

Outside, he got a better look at the group. They appeared to be a band of some sort, all dressed in black with army boots and brightly colored hair. One had a Mohawk. They reminded him of the punk bands that had been popular during the eighties. Several had safety pins in their lips and ears and eyebrows. Tom cringed at the idea of sticking something sharp through flesh so near the eye. Their shirts were torn, and the lone woman in the group wore a miniskirt with fishnet stockings that had seen better days.

"The motel is closed," Tom said as he approached them, buttoning his shirt.

"It's full up?" a tall boy asked. He looked about

twenty and was so thin he might've been able to tread water in a garden hose.

"No, it's shut down. Closed."

"No way, dude. We've come all the way from Grants Pass to stay in room six."

Tom blinked at the group. They must've read Hap's little article in *The Sasquatch*. "It's closed," he repeated.

"Aw, come on. Just let us stay in room six. We'll pay for it." The woman puffed up her lips in a mock pout and made eyes at him in a way that put Tom off. She looked half his age, but twice as used.

"Even if it was open, you can't stay in there, it's full of bees."

"Bees!" the tall boy shouted, throwing his head back as if he'd been granted an amazing gift. "Awesome."

Tom shook his head. "You'll have to find another place to stay."

"We'll pay double," another man said. He was leaning against their van with one foot crossed over the other. His demeanor and graying temples indicated that he called the shots.

"It's full of bees," Tom said again.

"So?"

Tom stared at the group a moment, then pulled his shirt off to show them his welts. "See. Bees." He thought maybe they didn't get it.

The tall boy erupted in laughter. "See bees. Get it? Seabees."

The others laughed.

"C'mon, dude. We left a gig and drove all night to get here. Don't turn us away."

Tom put his shirt back on, then shrugged. "If you sign a statement that you won't sue me, fine, you can stay in room six."

The group cheered.

"Seriously, the room is full of bees and I'm not doing anything about it."

☼

Hap walked up Chemeketa toward the post office on his way in to work, eyeing the cars parked along the curb. It was early yet, barely past dawn, but there were six or seven vehicles in that empty stretch, which only two days ago had none. He paused at the overlook and peered down at the glassy river. The beach was empty, the wind nowhere to be witnessed. He crossed the street and took a back alley past the Dairy Queen and came out on Main a few blocks west of the post office. Traffic was thicker, there was no question. A couple emerged from the little all-night grocery on the corner as another group went in, forcing a bottleneck on the sidewalk. The small crowd exchanged words, one person pointing up the highway, another flinging his hands out as if frustrated.

As Hap neared the group of people, a woman turned to him. She was wearing a large purple crystal around her neck and a cotton dress with a blazing yellow print. The hem dragged along the ground, gray and ragged.

"Excuse me," she said. "Can you tell us where the Jemmett Motel is?"

They all turned to Hap, expectantly.

"It's a few miles east of town," he said, pointing up Highway 14. He noticed the rolled-up newspaper in her hand then, and guessed it was *The Sasquatch*. So it had worked, after all. He'd brought tourists back to Rocket.

At the post office, Charlene was busy parsing out the mail. "I hate this job," she said by way of greeting. "It sucks."

"Notice anything different about town today?"

She looked up, then out at the street. "No."

"Busier."

She leaned over to get a better look outside. "You're delusional."

Maybe she was right, he thought as he sat down at his desk. So what if seven people showed up as a result of his article? It wouldn't save Tom's motel. And it sure wouldn't bring life back to Rocket.

※

Lauren rushed out the door. She'd overslept after returning from Tom's. She needed to get down to the clinic to check on Patrick's dog and meet Mrs. Cohen and her obese cat, Winsor. But as she unlocked her Jeep she noticed it had a flat tire.

"Damn it," she snarled, and opened the back, where she rummaged for her rusty jack. She took it in hand and studied it, trying to remember how it worked. It had been a long time since she'd changed a tire. She glanced up the street, then down, looking for a man who might help her, but the place was empty. For the first time, she realized how many *For Sale* signs dotted the front yards: six on her side of the street alone, four more on the opposite side. She turned to look at her own house, wondering how she'd sell it with so much competition. It was the nicest house on the block with its new siding and pale yellow paint, its upgraded plumbing, fresh wiring, and two-year-old roof. She'd put everything into refurbishing it, making it her own. And although she hadn't thought seriously of selling, it struck her now that she'd never get her money out of it if she were forced to let it go. She turned her attention back to the tire. The jack was rusted into a frozen hunk of metal. She should've replaced it.

After thirty minutes of fighting with the stupid thing, she lifted it over her head and slammed it down on a rock near the end of the driveway. The jack rolled into the flower bed and hit a ceramic rabbit, splitting it in two.

"*Fuck!*" she shouted as Mrs. Horn, the next-door

neighbor and chairwoman of the Rocket Methodist Women's Club, who came out onto her porch to see what was going on. The old woman pursed her lips and went back inside. They'd never been particularly friendly.

Lauren peered down at the decapitated rabbit, its nose pointing at the cloudless, sun-bleached sky, and kicked the jack. She would regret this outburst when Mrs. Horn's elderly poodle was in need of dentistry.

Lauren gave up and started walking the half mile to the clinic.

☼

Between the music thudding through the wall from room six and the yellow jackets next door, which had begun working their way through a tiny hole in the corner, by ten o'clock room five seemed a lot less appealing to Tom. Sienna had awakened like a badger. Tom didn't know if it was the effects of too much sleep or the throbbing bass, but she whined constantly and finally lodged herself between the toilet and tub so tightly that he could not extract her without the risk of breaking bones. He finally lured her out with the promise of a doughnut, which he knew he'd have to drive into Rocket to get. As he got her ready, he wondered about the band next door and what kind of drugs one had to take in order to withstand angry yellow jackets. He'd heard them shouting and the woman shrieked every once in a while, but for what reason he couldn't discern. He just shook his head, and reminded himself that he'd done well to have them sign a liability waiver. But a small part of him admired the group for their carefree, risk-seeking attitude. It must be a luxury, he thought, to be able to pick up and go looking for adventure in a haunted motel in eastern Washington.

On the sidewalk between his door and the door to room six, he found several spray cans of Bee Gone, which he collected with the intent to take around back and throw away in the Dumpster. The band was on his mind constantly now, making him reconsider throwing in the towel. Maria would never forgive him if he walked away from their dream. Better to have it wrenched from his grip by the bank than to leave of his own accord. Besides, what did he have left? Where would they go?

"Excuse me," a man called from behind him.

Tom turned, and that's when he noticed that there were four cars in the lot.

"Do you know who runs this place?" A middle-aged man with thinning hair strode across the parking lot toward him. He seemed urgent, as did the others who followed.

"I do."

"I was here first," an old man said, pushing his way in front.

Tom turned to Sienna, who was retreating back to room five. "Come on, sweetie, let's go to the lobby."

She followed reluctantly, dogging close on Tom's heels with her face pressed into a hard, tight frown. He unlocked the lobby door and took his place on that familiar stool behind the desk. Sienna started for the apartment, but Tom called her back, thinking of the mess and broken glass inside.

"Sit right here a sec. We'll get you a doughnut in a few minutes." He stood and patted the stool, but she'd already found her familiar place between the file cabinet and the wall. A good, safe spot, Tom thought, and turned to his guests.

Six people poured into the room, cramping the tiny space. Tom listened as the group, clearly not traveling together, clamored and squabbled about who had gotten there first. A fight broke out between the elderly man and a woman standing near the coffeemaker. She wore a yellow tie-dyed skirt and a crystal around her neck, making

Tom think she'd never found her way out of the sixties. She called the old man a geezer and he called her a cow in return. A bidding war ensued, and the offer for room six reached a hundred and fifty dollars.

What kind of lunatics had descended on his motel? "Thank you, Hap Mitsui," he said under his breath, punctuating each syllable. "Wait 'til I get my hands on you." Tom waited for the crowd to calm down. Finally, he held up a hand. "Listen," he called. Then he raised his voice. "Listen to me."

The crowd quieted. All eyes turned to Tom.

"It's not room six like the paper said. It's the entire motel . . . All the rooms produce amazing things."

The crowd was silent, and Tom thought they didn't believe him.

"It's true."

"I still want room six!" the old man shouted, and the group went wild again. The bid shot up to two hundred dollars.

"Two-fifty," snarled a tanned young man in the front wearing a finely pressed business suit.

"That's not fair. Some of us don't have that kind of money," the woman with the yellow skirt screeched over the hum.

Damn, Tom thought. *Two hundred and fifty dollars!* For a fifty-nine-dollar room? How many nights would it take to bring him current with the bank?

"Okay," he said to the tan man. "It's yours."

The crowd erupted in anger, protesting the decision as the man stepped up to the counter and opened his wallet.

"You'll have to wait for the folks who have it now to check out. Then I'll need to clean it," Tom said, pushing a registration card forward. "Fill that out."

The well-groomed man took a flashy silver pen from his inner suit pocket and started listing his information. Tom noticed his sleek, manicured hands. "What do you do?"

The man paused from his task and said, "I own a casino down on the south coast."

"A gambling man," Tom said. "I'll need to have you sign a waiver."

"What for?"

"So you don't sue me. Anything could happen, you know. You might walk away dripping in diamonds, but then again..." Tom gave the man a grave look. "You might not walk away at all."

The casino man grinned as if he and Tom shared a secret. "Okay."

Tom turned to the others in the lobby. "Anyone else want to get in line for room six for two hundred and fifty dollars a night?"

Two people took the offer and put their names down.

"I still have twenty-five other rooms. And I'm serious, they're all the same. Room six isn't any more haunted or charmed or whatever you want to call it than the others." The group mulled the idea while Tom rented two more rooms at the regular price. The lobby emptied, leaving him with the sudden awareness of sobbing behind him. Sienna was crouched down in the corner, her head tucked under and her arms wrapped tightly around her legs as she rocked and cried.

"Sweetie, I'm sorry," he said, touching her hair, but she pushed his hand away.

"Hey," someone called from the open door. "You got a fight goin' on out here."

Tom stood up to see what was happening. Two men who'd been standing in the lobby, but declined to rent a room, were now shoving Reverend Shelly around in the field next door, puffing out their chests and shouting in the preacher's face.

"That's not my property," Tom said. But he could see that the preacher needed help, so he called the sheriff's office and the dispatcher agreed to send Turnbull out.

Tom turned back to Sienna, but before he could do anything, another guest came in imploring Tom to help the preacher.

"You better go help that guy," the guest said, pointing. The reverend had been shoved to the ground and was trying to get to his feet.

Tom clenched his teeth. The last thing he wanted to do was protect that freak. He would sooner join in the fun and beat the arrogant attitude right out of the man. But instead, he collected the baseball bat he kept behind the counter for just such situations and hoisted it over his shoulder. He strode outside with confidence, which he'd learned to do the first season he ran the motel. The bigger and more menacing he looked, the better his odds of a peaceful end.

"Live by the sword, die by the sword," Reverend Shelly said as Tom approached.

"Shut up," Tom told him. "Can't you see I'm here to help you?"

The two men sized Tom up.

"This asshole is telling everybody that they're sinners," one said. They were young—late teens, early twenties maybe. The smaller of the two was well built, but the other was thin and oily.

"He's a pain in the ass, I agree, but you don't have to listen to him," Tom said.

"How come you let him stand here shouting at people? He doesn't know anything about us."

"I don't *let* him do anything. He's not my pet and he's not on my property. He can do what he wants. So can you, but the sheriff is gonna be here any minute. So whatever you're gonna do, you better hurry up."

The two boys looked at each other, perplexed, then at Tom.

"Well, what're you gonna do?" Tom said, nodding at the reverend.

"We weren't gonna do anything," the smaller one said and sneered at Reverend Shelly. The other shrugged and they began to walk away.

Tom called after them, "If you don't have a room, you need to clear out of here." He turned back to Reverend Shelly. "I should've let those two beat the shit out of you, you self-righteous son of a bitch."

The reverend brushed the dust from his clothes, but didn't thank Tom.

"Just because I stepped in once doesn't mean I'll do it again. If you don't leave my guests alone, I'll beat you within an inch of your life myself. You got that, Preacher?"

As Tom turned back to his motel, he found himself staring at Ms. Metzger, the woman from social services. She was standing behind him, listening, her square frame accentuated by the way she folded her arms tightly across her chest. Her eyes were hard and narrow as she scrutinized Tom.

"Busy morning, Mr. Jemmett?" she asked.

18

TOM'S PULSE SKIDDED to a halt, then, as quickly, raced forward. He looked at the hard-faced social worker standing before him, her hair aflame in orange beneath the searing sun. But instead what he saw was the broken glass littering his kitchen floor, the smeared condiments, the razor in the bathroom sink, and the books strewn through the hallway. He recalled Sienna's sobbing and turned toward the lobby, glimpsing through the large window his apartment door standing, not closed as he'd left it, but slightly ajar. His stomach turned to gelatin.

Without waiting for the social worker, he sprinted toward the motel.

"Sienna," he called as he burst through the lobby door. "Sienna!"

"Mr. Jemmett," Ms. Metzger called from behind him. *"Mr. Jemmett!"* Her tone was sharp, the unmistakable air of authority issuing from her squat frame.

He ignored her, imagining his daughter sliced and bleeding. "Sienna?"

Inside, he found his daughter watching *General Hospital,* sitting on the sofa as if nothing had ever been wrong. Only the faint tang of vinegar remained as testament to her emotional meltdown. He glanced into the kitchen, then crossed the hall to the bathroom, finally poking his head inside Sienna's neat and tidy bedroom. Had he dreamed it?

"Mr. Jemmett," Ms. Metzger said, gaining the entry-way to the apartment, her breath coming up short from trying to catch up with him. "Is something wrong?"

"I . . . I . . ." Tom looked around in disbelief.

The social worker walked past him and into the living room, where Sienna stared at the television as if in some sort of trance. Ms. Metzger turned in a circle, her eyes assessing the room, then resting on the girl. Sienna didn't look up or acknowledge the woman's presence.

"I just . . . had promised her a doughnut and I . . ." But even as he said it, he realized how ridiculous he sounded. "I don't like to leave her alone. Not even for a moment. But with that fight going on, I didn't have a choice." He shrugged, miming helplessness. His thoughts churned.

Ms. Metzger's expression softened and she nodded. "I understand, Mr. Jemmett. We don't expect that she'll never be out of your sight. That wouldn't be practical."

Tom flushed, embarrassed, and vaguely angry. Too stunned to make sense of things. Who had cleaned his apartment?

The social worker had moved into the kitchen and was looking inside the refrigerator. "You need to buy some groceries," she called.

"Yes, I know. We're headed to town this morning."

The woman peered into Sienna's room and nodded approvingly. "Did you lock up the cleaners and medicines?"

"Yes," he said and walked to the tall, narrow pantry at the back of the kitchen, which was snugly padlocked. He rattled the lock for effect.

"Excellent," she said. "I'm just going to talk to Sienna,

then I'll be finished. You're doing a good job, Mr. Jemmett."

Gratitude coursed through Tom, although he knew her approval was nothing he should have to earn. He was a good father. He'd always been a good father.

After an unsuccessful ten minutes with Sienna, which sparked in the child an animal-like whine that only became shriller for the woman's efforts to get Sienna to answer questions, Ms. Metzger closed her notebook and walked out of the apartment. Tom followed her. She paused in the lobby and pointed at Reverend Shelly, who had resumed his place under the handmade sign.

"No one needs that kind of persecution when they're trying to run a business," she said.

Tom looked out at the smug preacher and felt his jaw clench.

"Nonetheless, I hope that was an empty threat I overheard you make. I have made a note of it."

"I've never hit anyone in my life," Tom lied. "I just met the end of my patience is all."

"A man in your position requires an abundance of patience. It can't be any other way. I don't need to tell you that."

Tom watched the social worker leave as a long-suppressed memory of Maria flashed through his mind. He pushed it away. But he couldn't shake the image of her sprawled on the floor as Sienna stood over her.

☼

Hap took a deliberate step toward the door as he bit into one of Petra's hot cheese rolls.

"It is good, yes?" she asked, watching him with her watery blue eyes, a twinkle of excitement bringing them to life for the first time in months. Dark bags and deep jowls gave her the appearance of a Saint Bernard.

He nodded. "Excellent, Petra."

"You take some cookies, too." She snapped a paper bag open and reached into the glass case, pausing over snickerdoodles the size of hubcaps. "Vhat about sugar cookies. You like?"

"You don't have to do that. The bread is enough. I need to watch my diet," he said, rubbing his paunch.

She giggled, giving him a chill. Her steel-blue hair stuck to her sweaty forehead as her upper arms jiggled. "You are my best customer."

Hap imagined he was everybody's best customer these days, except for Lauren Kent's, because he was allergic to cats and dogs. He was the only regular most businesses were still seeing. When he'd started arriving every morning at the Rocket Bakery for a loaf of bread, it had never occurred to him that he might give this poor woman the wrong impression.

"You save those for paying customers. Don't give them away," he said.

She winked at him and picked up a fudge brownie with walnuts and dropped it in the sack, too. "Hov old are you?" she asked as she thrust the goodies over the counter at him.

"Now, that's a personal question, Petra."

She smiled and he could see that she had a full set of dentures—uppers and lowers. "I bet you are older zan me."

He hesitated. This was dangerous water. "I'm certain I am," he finally said. "But you don't have to make an old man feel worse by pointing it out."

She giggled again.

Hap took the sack of goodies, gathered up the loaf he'd paid for, and started for the door. A group of middle-aged hippies in their Birkenstocks and elk teeth necklaces wandered past on the street. He turned back to Petra.

"Have you seen more people the last day or two?"

She nodded resolutely. "Zay all vant to know vhere ze motel is."

"A lot?"

"No. Maybe six or seven."

He stepped out into the heat, but called back to her, "Make them buy something before you tell them where the motel is."

Back at his office, Hap picked up a message from a newspaper reporter in Portland. She left only her name and that she was a freelancer for *The Westerner.* He wrote the number down, thinking it was too bad that she wasn't with *The Oregonian* or *The Statesman Journal,* but *The Westerner* was a clear step up from *The Sasquatch.*

Charlene belted out a wordless rock-and-roll tune, bobbing her head wildly and tossing envelopes from one bin to another on her side of the room. He listened, but couldn't make out the song, then punched the numbers on the phone, waiting for Kristen Montella to answer.

"This is Hap Mitsui out in Rocket," he said when he heard the woman's crisp voice come on the line.

"Ah, the man with the haunted motel," she said.

"Not my motel. I just wrote the story on it."

She laughed as if his story were amateur scribbling. "Do you have time for an interview tomorrow morning?"

"Sure, what time?"

"It'll take a couple hours for me to drive out there from Portland, so let's say eleven."

"Okay, you'll find me at the post office."

Hap set the phone down and leaned back in his chair. It wasn't quite the flood of curiosity seekers he'd hoped to bring in, but a slow and steady trickle couldn't hurt. The good of the town was what mattered.

"Hey," Charlene hollered out the service window at a group of teens in the parking lot. "You can't park there."

The group didn't hear her, and she flew out the service

door and opened the glass door at the front of the building. "This is the post office parking lot. You can't leave your car here."

They sneered at her, then got back in, peeling out and smoking their tires on the pavement.

"Assholes," she said.

Hap had followed her out into the lobby and peered over her shoulder. "Just like old times," he said, beaming.

Charlene surveyed the street. "There's a space right there." She pointed at the curb in front of Dillard's antiques store. "And one right there," she huffed. "Idiots think they can park in the post office lot."

She returned to the back room, but Hap stayed at the door. There were available spaces, for sure, but a lot less of them.

"It's busier today," he said. "Did you notice?"

"You're going senile," she called.

"You should've seen it," Lauren said as she sat back in her desk chair and twirled the phone cord with her finger. "I've never witnessed anything like it in my life."

"What did you do?" Ellie asked. Since Ellie had closed her office in Rocket the two women hadn't spoken much. Only the occasional phone call and attempt at scheduling a lunch date that invariably ended up canceled at the last minute.

"I cleaned it." Lauren peered through the open door at Anna, who was working diligently on the computer in the reception area. Lauren stood and pushed the office door closed. She was exhausted, but needed to stay until Patrick came by to pick up his dog. She was reluctant to let the old man take the dog, but it was costing her too much money to keep Crispy at the clinic. She needed to impress upon Patrick the importance of keeping the dog confined until his leg healed. Otherwise she'd be amputating it in a month, and probably for free.

"You cleaned it?" Ellie sounded put off, and for the first time since Lauren had called, she gave the conversation her full attention.

"Well, yeah. I want Tom to know that I'm here for him."

"But you said he wasn't even home."

"He has to come home sometime. Besides, his truck was there. My guess is that he was in one of the rooms." A shiver ran across Lauren's arms as she imagined sleeping on those well-used, nasty beds in one of Tom's motel rooms. "He probably didn't want to deal with it then. I'll go out this afternoon and see how things are going. I'm a little surprised he hasn't called me yet."

"You're amazing," Ellie said. "I wouldn't have done it. I would've left the mess and left the man, too."

There was a long silence as both women avoided the fact that Tom and Lauren had already broken up.

"I didn't want him to call Charlene. That little slut has her sights on him. I overheard her one day at the post office talking about Sienna and how lonely the child is."

Ellie was silent.

"How could Charlene Anderson possibly know anything about Sienna?"

"Lauren..." Ellie said tentatively. "I keep forgetting that you're not from Rocket."

"So?" Lauren pulled an emery board from her pencil drawer and began whittling down the rough edge of her thumbnail where it'd torn during a struggle with an angry Chihuahua. Last summer she'd considered turning Mrs. Vernon away because her dog was so awful. Thank God she hadn't.

"No one's ever told you about Charlene's brother?"

Lauren put the emery board down and sat up, pressing

her elbows against the polished cherrywood desk. "What brother?"

Ellie sighed. "It's a long story. We should probably save it for lunch or something."

"Tell me now."

"I don't know. It's ..."

"It's what, Ellie?"

"Charlene had a younger brother named Stephen who was diagnosed with schizophrenia when he was about thirteen. He did some crazy stuff like climb to the top of the radio tower up on the hill and try to swim across the Columbia. The coast guard had to rescue him both times. He thought the government was tapping their phone and that everybody in Rocket was a government spy, even though he knew us all. It was ... really sad."

"How come I've never heard this before?" Lauren looked out at Highway 14 and the heat squirming off the pavement under the midday sun. She thought she knew everything about Rocket. What other secrets lurked in its past? "People love this kind of stuff. Everyone should be talking about it, even if it happened a hundred years ago."

"People don't talk about *this*," Ellie said quietly.

"Why not?" Lauren's hard edge came back.

"Charlene's mom was single. She was actually a lot like Charlene, now that I think about it—loose. No one knew who the kids' dad was, but everyone still liked her. She grew up here and she was fun to be around. Her name was Karla; she was a big partyer. Anyway, she worked as the receptionist at the trucking company that used to be here. It's been out of business for a long time."

Lauren tried to place Karla Anderson's name, but no face came to mind. Lauren had always imagined that

Charlene moved here to be where the windsurfers were. She didn't realize the girl had grown up in Rocket.

"Stephen was messed up from the start, from way before the actual diagnosis. Everybody knew there was something wrong, but it took a long time before anyone knew what. He had trouble in school, he was hyper—he was the kid who pulls the produce down at the grocery store, then has a screaming, thrashing tantrum in the aisle. You know the kind."

Lauren remembered her nephew's meltdown over the Hershey's Kisses and how she'd swatted him on the butt because her sister, Kelly, wouldn't.

"So where is he now?" Lauren asked.

"Dead."

"What happened?"

"Charlene's mom shot him one night. Then shot herself."

Lauren gasped.

"No one talks about it."

"God, that's horrible. Why did she do that?"

"He did something, but no one knows what. The only one who was there was Charlene, and she refuses to talk about it."

"Wasn't there a police report?"

"Yeah, but Charlene wouldn't tell anyone what happened, not even Turnbull. He tried to get the story out of her for years, but I don't think she ever talked."

"How old was she?"

"Sixteen." Ellie was quiet awhile as the story took hold in Lauren's mind. "She still lives in the house where it happened. She's been supporting herself on that postal job and behaving like any normal citizen. We've all worried about her, but she seems fine."

"I guess that's all the more reason Charlene shouldn't be anywhere near Sienna," Lauren said.

Tom didn't have time to call Charlene and thank her
for cleaning his apartment, or to invite her out, as he'd
planned. He felt bad that they had missed her the night
before while holed up in room five, injured and raw. He
was also embarrassed that she'd found the apartment
that way, especially without benefit of some explanation.
Of course, there was no explanation Tom could give that
would help anyone understand his daughter's behavior.
For that, he'd first have to understand it himself.

Nor did Tom have time to drive into Rocket for groceries or Sienna's promised doughnut. He poured his
daughter a bowl of Cheerios and gave it to her dry,
knowing he'd be vacuuming most of it out of the carpet
later. A steady stream of people inquiring about room six
had pressed him into service all morning long. Most were
hippies long past their prime, searching for some universal karma depot, for which they believed room six was
the answer.

Tom was coming to see the humor in what Hap had
done, though not ready to forgive the man for his betrayal. He had even turned his neon sign back on, de-
lighting in the sound it made as it popped and buzzed,
finally burning an electric pink *Jemmett Motel* into the
dry, hot sky.

Room six had a waiting list a week long now, and the
rest of the rooms were renting at a hundred dollars
apiece. For the first time since he'd received the notice
from the bank, he imagined he might just have a chance
of turning things around. He'd even called the bakery to
renew his daily doughnut delivery.

The band strolled up the sidewalk and into the lobby,
looking for coffee. They were cheerful and talkative,
flashing him youthful smiles.

"How was it?" he asked.

"Dude, that was awesome," the tall boy with the Mohawk said.

"Bees didn't bother you?"

The bandleader leaned forward and said in a confiding tone, "Those are yellow jackets."

Tom nodded, amused by the simplicity of what concerned some people. Obviously, this man didn't have the sort of problems Tom did, to be concerned with this.

"There's a difference between bees and yellow jackets, you know. They aren't all the same. People tend to lump them together because they have stingers, you know. Yellow jackets, hornets, wasps, bees. But they're different species altogether."

"Leave him alone, Pete," the woman shouted from near the coffeepot. She turned to Tom. "Pete feels the need to educate everyone he meets on stupid shit like the difference between bees and yellow jackets. It's all we heard last night. We're all fucking experts on insects now." She pivoted on her feet and came face-to-face with Pete. "Or are those even insects? Maybe they belong in the ornithology group."

Pete winked at Tom and smiled.

"I guess the yellow jackets didn't bother you, then?" Tom tried again.

The band didn't answer but sugared their coffees and joked about feeling like a million bucks as they made their way back outside to their waiting van.

Tom watched them go, dying to ask if anyone had been stung. His own wounds were still painfully tender and swollen, but he saw no evidence of the same on any of these people. He shook his head, mystified, then collected his passkey and cleaning supplies so he could make the room ready for the casino man who was in his Speedo, reddening by the minute next to the pool.

Tom waved at him on the way back and pointed at room six, holding up a bottle of cleanser and pushing a vacuum cleaner full with dead yellow jackets. He had made a mental note that the Bee Gone had been a pretty effective poison and wondered what toxic chemicals it might have left behind in the room. Marie had always worried about poisons, especially with Sienna a toddler. He'd scrubbed everything extra well, including the walls, just to make sure.

The casino man paid him no attention, railing to someone on his cell phone about the cost of good labor. "How can you deal blackjack if you can't even speak English?" he asked. "Christ, get me some red-blooded Americans, would you?" He hung up without saying good-bye and tossed the cell phone onto the small glass table next to his lawn chair.

"Room is ready," Tom called, but he had trouble masking the disdain in his tone. He recognized this man as the same sort who had always assumed Maria was Tom's servant because she was Mexican. They'd run into people like that often during their marriage, especially after purchasing the motel. But Maria always shrugged it off.

"They're ignorant," she'd say. "You don't have to educate them, Tom. Divine providence will do that."

*Divine providence,* he thought and glanced back at room six. "Maybe."

# 19

"WHAT DO YOU KNOW about Charlene Anderson?" Lauren asked Anna as she filled prescription bottles for Patrick's dog.

Anna crooned to the dog as she lifted him out of the kennel and set him on the linoleum floor. The dog sported a bright purple cast from his shoulder to his paw on which Anna had applied a clover leaf cut out of green vet wrap. "For luck," she had told the dog. After situating Crispy so he could manage a three-legged hop down the corridor to his waiting master, Anna looked up at Lauren.

"We went to school together," she said, but her tone showed no emotion. She slipped a noose-style leash over the dog's head and called Crispy to follow her.

"Did you know her brother?" Lauren asked without looking at Anna. But when Anna didn't respond she glanced over.

Anna was paused in the corridor, her deep-set eyes staring back warily. "I don't really remember him much. He was younger than me."

Lauren scooped pills into a container and pasted a label on the outside, trying not to show too much interest. "Quite a tragedy, I hear. I mean, what happened to him."

Anna looked down at the dog for an extended period, then back at Lauren. "I don't like to talk about folks, Dr. Kent. Especially after they die." She then led the dog out to the waiting room.

Lauren heard Patrick's excited voice as he greeted his dog. She scooped up the bottles of pills and followed Anna out to meet Patrick and explain how much of each medication and how often to give the dog. But Lauren couldn't help feeling reprimanded by her assistant. She was finding Anna's lack of personality grating, but the holier-than-thou attitude was simply more than Lauren could swallow.

Patrick was down on his knees snuggling his dog when Lauren walked out into the lobby. Crispy's entire back end wagged wildly as he licked the old man's face. Patrick let him, closing his eyes and rubbing the dog's ears. It was small consolation to see this happy man, considering he would never be able to pay her for the work she'd done on his pet.

"Patrick," she said, "I have some instructions for you."

He opened his eyes and looked up at Lauren through tears of joy, then got stiffly to his feet. He sniffed hard and gazed down at his dog awhile. Finally, he said, "Thank you for saving his leg, Dr. Kent."

"Well, we're not out of the woods yet, Patrick," Lauren said, going on to explain that he needed to keep the dog confined, that Crispy shouldn't go up and down steps, and that he had to keep the leg clean and dry. Patrick nodded, giving her his full attention. She explained the medications—painkillers and anti-inflammation pills.

"He could still end up losing the leg. It's very important that you follow these instructions to the letter," she said.

"I will. I promise."

"Okay. Now, about payment . . ."

Patrick stared quietly at the floor. "I called my son in Seattle. He said he'd send me some money, but it's not going to be enough to cover everything." He looked at Lauren, then at Anna, the papery skin of his cheeks pinkening with embarrassment. "I was wondering if maybe you'd consider a trade of some kind?"

Lauren looked at the dog, not Patrick. "How much will you be short?"

"About five hundred dollars."

She sighed. "That's a lot."

"I know. I'm really sorry. I just don't have it."

Anna stepped toward him and touched Patrick on the shoulder, but said nothing. He wiped his eyes before tears fell.

"What did you have in mind for a trade?" Lauren asked.

He glanced out the glass front door toward his dilapidated shack on the outskirts of town. Lauren couldn't imagine this old man had anything she might want. She had noticed that he'd spread a tarp over his roof to keep it from leaking this past winter. It was a tiny house; it wouldn't take much in roofing materials to fix. She had paused to consider how much worse the things that couldn't be seen from the road must be if the roof was not a priority for Patrick. And she could never eat enough eggs for him to repay his debt that way.

"I have some antiques. I can bring them in and you can look at them."

"What sort of antiques?" Lauren said, but she was suddenly aware of Anna's cold eyes on her. She looked at her assistant, who stared incredulously at Lauren. Lauren stared back as if to tell the girl to mind her own business. Wasn't Anna the one who had suggested that every business in town was going under because people were giving away free stuff?

"I have some paintings and some dishes that were my mother's. I have a few other odds and ends that I've picked up here and there."

Anna wouldn't look away, no matter how fiercely Lauren stared back at her. "Well, I don't have much need for paintings or dishes, but why don't you bring a few things in later this week and I'll take a look. We'll work something out, Patrick. In the meantime I want you to take good care of Crispy. Don't let him get loose, understand?"

He agreed, and the two women watched him lead his limping dog out into the bright day.

"I can't believe you'd take that old man's family heirlooms," Anna said as soon as the door closed.

"Excuse me, but no one asked you. This is a business. And when people owe money we sometimes look at creative ways to collect." Lauren swept up Crispy's file and took it to her office with the intent to finish her notes before handing it over to Anna to be filed. She stopped in the doorway. "You were the one who suggested I put the dog down. Remember?"

Anna's eyes followed Patrick and Crispy out to the parking lot, where the old man lifted the dog into his car. "I didn't think it would be like this. He was so happy to see that dog he cried. And he's just an old man. That dog is all he has. I never thought of it like that before."

"Welcome to veterinary medicine," Lauren said and shoved the door shut with her foot. She slumped down in her chair, exhausted. Why hadn't Tom called? She suddenly wondered if he was even still in town. Maybe he'd left for good. But where had he gone?

Lauren snapped up the phone and punched in Tom's number. It rang three times before he picked up.

"Jemmett Motel," he chirped.

Her stomach emptied, then fluttered as if it were suddenly brimming with birds.

"Hello?" he said.

"It's me, Lauren."

There was a pause. "Lauren. How are you?"

"Good—great. I was just calling to ask *you* that question."

Tom laughed jovially. "Good. Things seem to be turning finally."

"Turning?" Lauren got up and peeked through her office window up the street, expecting to see the wind sock in front of the old kite shop blowing in a stiff breeze. But it hung limply in the heat. "What do you mean?"

"Business. I've rented half the motel for double the going rate. Got a waiting list on . . ."

"On what?"

"You'll think I'm out of my mind."

"Try me," she said.

"On room six."

"Oh, brother! Don't tell me people still believe something is going on with that room? It was coincidence, Tom."

"Yeah, maybe so. But Hap, that dirty son of a bitch, wrote a story about the motel without my knowledge and now I'm overrun with freaks and weirdos."

"Are you serious?"

"Had a retro band drive all the way up from southern Oregon just to spend the night in room six with a bunch of bees. Or I guess they were yellow jackets."

"There's a difference," she said.

"Anyway, can't talk long."

Lauren scowled at the phone. He wasn't going to thank her for cleaning up that mess?

"Run into you sometime in town maybe," he said.

"Wait. Did you . . ." She wasn't sure how to ask. Or if to ask. But how could he let it go? Didn't he realize how much work it had been for her to restore his apartment?

"Did I what?"

"Do you . . . want to get together? I could maybe come out?"

Another long silence. "Lauren . . ." His voice had gone soft. "I'm not sure it's a good idea. We gave it a solid try, but we just don't seem to be a good fit. You said so yourself."

Lauren felt her cheeks flush hot and she didn't know what to say. He could so easily let her go? "I guess I didn't think we were finished trying. Or at least . . . I wasn't finished trying. I wish we'd had this conversation before I cleaned your apartment last night."

She heard him draw a deep breath. "That was you?"

She sighed heavily. "Yeah, that was me. Who the hell did you think it was, the tooth fairy?" She dropped the receiver back in its cradle and bit her lip, struggling against a scorching onslaught of tears.

☼

Tom listened to the buzz of dial tone in his ear. It was Lauren who cleaned the apartment? He closed his eyes, an instant flood of remorse. *Shit.* Lauren had saved him from terrible consequences with the social worker showing up unexpectedly that morning. And he'd assumed it was someone else who'd helped him. How could he possibly repay her? He dialed the number at the clinic and the receptionist picked up.

"Is Lauren—I mean Dr. Kent in?"

"Who's calling please?"

"This is Tom Jemmett."

"Just a sec," she said.

Tom waited on hold, listening to Mozart and feeling like the biggest jerk on the planet. He hadn't given Lauren a second thought after they split. He'd even been a little relieved that it was over. *I'm such an ass,* he thought.

"She can't come to the phone right now," the receptionist said. "Can I take a message?"

"No—well, yeah. Tell her Tom called."

The receptionist agreed, and Tom hung up, wondering if Lauren really was busy or just too pissed off to talk to him. He guessed the latter. He thought about driving into Rocket to apologize in person, perhaps with the aid of some fresh flowers, but how could he with all these guests? It was only four o'clock, and his odds of filling the place were pretty good today. He considered Lauren's selflessness as he watched the woman in the yellow skirt construct a roadside stand in the vacant lot right next to Reverend Shelly. The preacher looked on disdainfully as she laid out an assortment of stones and other mystical items, stringing crystals along the perimeter of her table so that the sun caught them and cast bright strobes of yellow and purple light toward the motel. Tom picked up the phone again and dialed Hap's number.

"Hello," Hap answered on the first ring.

"Listen to me, newspaperman."

"Who is this?"

"Tom. I'm not done being pissed off at you for writing that article after you said you wouldn't, but I need some help. And the way I see it, you owe me."

"Tom, I was planning to come out there tomorrow and talk to you. I only wrote that article to help bring some business back to Rocket. We need it. It's working, isn't it?" Hap's voice sounded tentative and vaguely apologetic, which pleased Tom.

"If you consider turning a respectable motel into a roadside circus, then I guess you could say it's working."

"Weirdos have money to spend, too, Tom." Hap laughed nervously.

"Look, I need some groceries or my daughter is going to starve. I can't get away. It's the least you can do. Then you can help me with all these freaks you've summoned from the four corners of the earth."

"No problem. I'm on it. I'll have food for Sienna out to you in two hours."

"Make it one. You can stand watch while I run an errand, and then you can tell me what other surprises I can hope to find in the coming days."

☼

Hap wandered the aisles of the Rocket IGA trying to remember what a twelve-year-old eats. He dropped some boxes of macaroni and cheese into his basket, then an assortment of breakfast cereals.

"Pay dirt," he said to himself when he found the soup aisle. He pulled in cans of tomato and chicken noodle, cream of celery and minestrone. One could not go wrong with soup, he decided. He added boxes of crackers to his basket, and as he worked his way toward the dairy case at the back of the store, the soles of his shoes stuck to the floor. The light above the milk and yogurt fluttered and threatened to go out. Hap scanned the dates on the jugs, but they had expired. He pushed them aside, reaching into the bowels of the cooler, searching for the fresher cartons they kept in the back. It was empty. He leaned down and peered through the space he'd created at the dirty glass window on the other side. Beyond it, boxes were stacked haphazardly, rotting fruit perched on top. He straightened and looked around the store. A faintly moldy smell had surfaced somewhere in that back area and he sniffed the air to find the culprit. It came from the produce section to his right, so Hap steered his cart away from it, peering down at its contents. He decided the prepackaged stuff was safest anyway and abandoned the milk and cheese altogether.

At the register Hap surveyed the unswept floor and the empty racks that had once been arranged with colorful and enticing displays of candy and magazines. Colleen, the octogenarian checkout clerk, watched unenthusiastically as he deposited his groceries on her conveyor belt. Her hair looked punkishly blue beneath the fluorescent light.

"Afternoon," he said.

She nodded and began scanning his items, shoving them onto the end of the counter where the bagger usually stood waiting.

"The milk is outdated." Hap pointed at the dairy case as if Colleen could see the dates on the cartons from where she stood.

She sighed as she punched codes into the register with her spotted and arthritically misshapen fingers. "Sorry."

Hap looked around for the owner, Jim Dublin. "Everything okay, Colleen?"

She glanced at Hap over her bifocal lenses, then back toward the office where Jim usually perched, scanning the store for shoplifters. He wasn't there today. "Does it look okay?" she asked.

Hap didn't answer. It was rhetorical, he guessed.

She took his money, then began bagging his groceries. "I'll be looking for work soon, I imagine. Keep an eye out for me, would you?"

Hap nodded, but couldn't look the woman in the eye. She'd worked at the IGA as long as he'd lived in Rocket, and probably from the beginning of time. Where would she get a job?

He hoisted the sack up and started for the door, then turned to Colleen. "Let me know if you need anything."

She smiled sadly.

☼

Lauren uncorked a bottle of Shiraz and poured herself a large glass, uncaring that the wine sloshed down the sides, staining her fingers burgundy. She kicked her shoes off and pulled the drapes closed with one hand, balancing her drink in the other. Then she slumped down on the sofa and sucked off the top inch in a single swallow. The dry, woody flavor soothed her some and she took another long sip. She let her head drop back against the soft leather of her overstuffed couch and closed her eyes. Tom's apartment the way it had been when she found it the night before was the image she couldn't eradicate from her brain. She'd been so stupid. She tipped her head up and finished the glass, quickly standing up to refill it. She'd drink the bottle in its entirety—she already knew she would. Did that make her an alcoholic? Or just a fool?

She brought the bottle into the living room with her and set it on the coffee table. It was early yet, about six-thirty, but she didn't care. She pulled out the drawer beneath the table and pawed through its contents, eventually coming up with an old family photo album. She slid the wine bottle aside and spread the book out on the oak surface, opening it carefully to the first page where black-and-white faces smiled up at her. She ran her fingers over a picture of two young girls—she and Kelly when they were still in single digits. Kelly was tall and lean, Lauren short and stout. She recalled the envy she'd carried for Kelly's beauty even at that innocent age. Kelly was a dark-eyed firecracker with a sharp tongue but a beguiling smile. She still was, even as she approached middle age. Kelly had always made Lauren feel clumsy and white and flabby and outdated in her presence. A thing that only seemed to become more pronounced as the years behind them amassed and Kelly raised her family with her devoted husband, while Lauren grasped at impossible men like Tom.

She turned the page and lingered over her parents' wedding photo from 1958. Her mother wore black cat's-eye glasses. Her father had a flattop crew cut. The two smiled lovingly at each other as if they could scarcely fathom their luck. Lauren had to give them that—they'd had a solid marriage filled with laughter. So why did she feel so empty whenever she looked at this picture? Had they hoped for children of their own? Of course they had, or they would never have kept Kelly's and her adoption a secret from them. She moved on to photos of cousins, aunts, uncles—people she could hardly remember and had no desire to reconnect with, especially now that her parents were gone. As she turned the pages, Lauren felt a burning sense of loss. Not simply because her parents were dead—each of cancer two years apart. But as if Tom's rejection were preordained, a statement about her life, an indicator of her worth. Had he seen in her the very thing she was trying to hide? Had he recognized her as the damaged goods she was—an unwanted child, the second choice for a barren couple?

Lauren reached for her wine with a shaky hand, spilling it across a picture of her childhood horse, Ranger. She mopped it up with her cast-off sock, but the photo warped and buckled. Ranger's dark eyes blurred and his pale coat turned crimson. She suddenly found herself sobbing as she tried to restore his image.

She was startled by a knock at the door. She set the picture aside and wiped her face, then scrambled up and looked around at the maniacally clean room. The visitor knocked again, louder. She ducked into the kitchen, hiding. She didn't need to answer the door. But what if it's an emergency? she thought. No, they would have called. The knock came louder, followed by her name, shouted.

"Lauren? It's Tom. Please open the door. I know you're in there."

Her limbs went weak and quivered. Should she answer the door? She was a mess. But she had to.

"Lauren, please. I'm sorry."

She straightened and took a breath, then wiped her

face again. She walked to the door, trying to compose herself, but her fingers shook as she reached for the handle. The lock clicked and she pulled the door open a crack. Through the slim gap she saw his face, which made her insides tumble. He gripped a bouquet of lilies in that awkward manner of men.

"I'm sorry," he said again. "I didn't know. I...I should've known."

She opened the door a little farther and witnessed the horror on his face when he saw her tears. She left it open and stalked back into the living room where she sat down on the sofa and took up her wineglass. He followed her inside and stood nervously in the entry.

"Who's watching your motel?" she asked.

"Hap." Tom looked down at the flowers, then thrust them at her. "These are for you."

She took them and held them to her nose. Their sweet fragrance was almost too much, and she felt a sneeze coming.

"Got a glass of wine for me?" he asked tentatively. A look of hope glazed his eyes.

She stood and took the flowers to the kitchen, putting them into a vase and getting a wineglass for Tom. She brought it out and handed it to him, then handed him the bottle. It was nearly empty. Its contents only filled half his glass.

"You're here only because I did you a favor, Tom. Not because you care about me."

"That isn't true. I just didn't know it was you. I mean, that kind of work is not for you. You're the vet, the town doctor. Not a maid." He tilted his head to one side, looking pained as he said it. "I never expected you to do that, and it never occurred to me that you would."

"I can contribute just like anyone when there's a need. Having a medical degree doesn't make me some kind of princess."

"I know. I'm sorry."

Lauren smiled weakly. He was trying so hard, how could she not feel a little sympathy toward him? "It looked like you needed some help. So I just did it. I wasn't expecting you to thank me for it, but I also didn't think we'd called it quits forever."

Tom approached her carefully, as if she might lash out when he came within reach. He touched her hair, and tears spilled again. He pulled her against him and kissed her head. She sobbed drunkenly. Sad, happy, and terrified all at once.

# 20

HAP SAT ON THE STOOL behind the reception desk in Tom's motel. Sienna sat on the floor next to him, eating a bowl of dry cereal and behaving as if he weren't there. The child made him nervous; he'd seen the tantrum in the tavern. He wished Tom had taken the girl along with him, but Hap was in no position to request it.

It was the first lull he'd had since reluctantly taking over for Tom an hour ago, but so far he hadn't succeeded in selling a single room. He'd fielded questions about the pool, the ice machine, the makeshift camp next door, and room six. Most of his answers were pure fabrications. Through the front window Hap watched the preacher converse stiffly with the woman who'd set up a roadside table selling brightly colored stones. She was the same woman he'd seen in town, and he marveled at how well read *The Sasquatch* had turned out to be. Tom was right, these were mostly freaks that he had summoned with his article, but *The Westerner* might draw a slightly more centered crowd—though barely so. At the pool a sunburned man talked on his cell phone and watched a woman in her midfifties strip off her top as she dangled her legs in the water. Her small breasts sagged over her belly, but the man on the cell phone didn't seem to mind.

He flashed her a grin and gave her the thumbs-up sign. Hap wondered if Tom wanted him to referee these people. He couldn't imagine how to do that, so instead he turned his stool to face the highway, pretending not to see it at all. Cars had filled the empty lot next door— battered relics from prior decades all. A handful of pup tents had gone up, dotting the parched ground with an array of muted colors.

The air inside the lobby was thick and the place felt like an inferno. Hap reached up and turned on the little oscillating fan, trying for any small relief.

"Air-conditioning, Tom," he muttered. "Air-conditioning."

Sienna glanced up at him, staring intently at his mouth as though she'd only just realized he was there. But the moment the fan blew air across her, she shrieked and leapt to her feet, leaving an upturned bowl of Froot Loops behind.

"Shit!" Hap quickly snapped the fan off and followed the child into the apartment. "I'm sorry," he called after. "I turned it off. It's okay. You can come back."

She gazed in his general direction from the other end of the room, but didn't make eye contact. She reminded him of a wild animal that had been coaxed into society, but still spooked at the slightest provocation.

"It's okay. The fan is off."

She peered around as if looking for her father. Her eyes were filled with uncertainty and even a little terror.

The lobby bell rang and Hap looked from Sienna to the door, then back at Sienna. "You can come back. It's okay."

She didn't move, and the bell chimed again, pulling him away.

"Okay, I'll be right back. You just stay here." He patted the air, as if to communicate through sign language.

In the lobby a man leaned on the counter, waiting. His

beard was braided into a point that jutted down his front, ending raggedly near his navel. His thinning hair was pulled back into another braid that ran the full length of his back. Hap had a random thought that two people could pull the man's head and jaw apart by grasping a braid each and yanking straight down.

When the man opened his mouth to speak his front teeth, uppers and lowers, were missing. "I'd like room six, please."

Hap shook his head. "Won't be available until the middle of next week."

The man leaned back on his heels and surveyed the motel.

"I can put you in another room. They're all the same, according to the owner."

"No they're not," the man said with clear agitation. He drew out a folded copy of *The Neskowin Register* and pressed it flat on the counter. "Says here room six is special."

Hap peered at the paper, not recognizing it. "Can I see that?"

The man shoved it across the counter at him.

Hap skimmed his article. How had they gotten it? He flushed with anger at finding his work printed without permission, payment, or byline.

The man on the other side of the counter snatched the paper back. "I need that."

Hap nodded. "Well, I can add you to the waiting list. The price for room six is two hundred and fifty."

"What kind of bullshit is this?" The man moved menacingly toward the counter. "You trying to scam people?"

Hap swallowed and stepped back. "Look, this isn't even my motel. I'm just filling in. Two-fifty is what people are willing to pay for room six. We had a bidding war here earlier. It was the guests who set that price, not the owner."

The man scratched his belly, then rested his hand on the sheath of a large hunting knife dangling from his belt. Hap eyed it, then the man. Was he strong enough to take this guy? Hap was bigger, but it was these scrawny guys who always surprised people. He took another step back and scanned his side of the counter. Tom's baseball bat rested upright in the corner. For the first time, Hap fully appreciated the daily challenges of running a motel. It was clearly not as easy as he'd imagined. He stepped casually toward the bat, pulling out a registration card with one hand and resting his other hand on the smooth wooden handle.

"Can I put you up in room sixteen, maybe?" he asked, sliding the card over the counter.

The man fingered his knife and glared at Hap. "This is fucking bullshit."

"I can put you on the waiting list. What will it hurt? You can take your time deciding if you want to pay two-fifty before it's your turn." Hap felt a bead of sweat sprout on his forehead.

The man fiddled with the knife and looked out at the pool, pausing for a long moment to assess the topless woman now smoking a cigarette. He turned and looked then at the preacher and the woman with the crystals. He lingered on them a longer while. Finally, he turned back to Hap. "You think those two are together?" he asked, gesturing at the preacher and his companion.

"No idea. But somehow I don't get the feeling they are."

The man nodded. "She's something. Ain't she?"

Hap studied the woman. She was rotund, with silver-blonde hair and large breasts. Her shirt gaped low, showing off a liberal swath of deeply tanned skin and cleavage. "Maybe you should go check out her merchandise," Hap suggested.

The man grinned widely, showing off his pink gums, and gave Hap a knowing look. "Yeah, maybe I should." He started for the door.

"You want me to put your name down for room six?" Hap called after him.

"Not for that price. Besides, I just might've found what I was looking for." He sauntered out of the lobby and straight across the open field with purpose.

The woman greeted him with her eyes long before he reached her on foot. The reverend stood to speak to him, but the man brushed past without a glance, leaving the preacher talking to himself. The woman smiled and got to her feet, laughing at something the toothless man said. She tossed her hair over her shoulder and lifted a stone to his waiting palm.

Hap jotted a note to himself for his next column. "Love blossoms in unlikely places," he said aloud. Then he picked up the phone and called Charlene's house.

"Hello?"

"Charlene, it's Hap. What are you doing?"

There was a long pause. "Why?"

"I'm out at Tom's motel. He asked me to watch the place while he runs some errands."

"Oh, are you watching over his one guest?" She snorted at her own joke. "Or does he even have that many?"

Hap rolled his eyes. She could be so mean sometimes. "I think I've scared Sienna. She won't come near me."

"Hap." She sounded exasperated. "What did you do?"

"Nothing. I just turned on the fan and she ran out of the room screaming."

"Is she okay?"

"Yeah, she's in the apartment. But I think she's too scared to come back out." Hap peeked through the door and saw the top of Sienna's head over the couch. She rocked forward and back rhythmically. The television was off.

"You want me to come out there?"

"Would you?"

She sighed. "Yeah, I can do that."

"You're a gem."

"Tell that to Tom, would you?"

Hap suffered a pang of jealousy, but nodded. "Sure. I'll tell him."

☼

Tom looked at his watch; he'd been at Lauren's for an hour and a half. He worried about Hap alone with his motel, alone with a bunch of freaks, alone with unpredictable, hard-to-please Sienna. He trusted Hap, but doubted the man would know what to do if Sienna became anxious. Then he worried about Sienna alone with a man she wouldn't recognize no matter how many times she'd seen him. If she paused to pay attention to Hap's presence, she might get scared.

Lauren had opened a second bottle of wine. She swallowed the last of what was in her glass, then swooped at the bottle and sloshed in more. They'd discussed Tom's insensitivity and her desire to help. He'd apologized more times than he could count, but somehow he didn't really get the feeling that she'd forgiven him. So far they hadn't talked about Sienna. He wondered if Lauren would triumph in knowing that the social worker had paid him a surprise visit, and if it hadn't been for her, things would have turned out much differently this morning. He owed her that acknowledgement, but something held him back. He knew it was just a matter of time before Lauren started in on him about Sienna, and honestly, he thought he might be ready to hear her out. She did have medical training, after all. And God knew he wasn't handling the situation any better by pretending

Sienna's problems weren't real—or rather, by imagining that she was as nature had intended her to be. He couldn't quite buy in to that idea anymore. Certainly there was more for Sienna than this. Lauren could be right; maybe there were options he hadn't considered.

"Sweetheart," Tom said, "I'd love to stay, but Hap has probably ruined my motel by now."

Lauren paused mid-sentence from her diatribe about how Rocket was going under and the proof was that Ellie Mercer had closed her medical office. "Doesn't it matter to you?"

"It matters," he said. "It matters to everyone. We're all disappointed to lose our only physician."

Lauren bristled. "I'm a physician, too, you know."

He closed his eyes. Even when she was drunk he managed to stick his foot in his mouth. "I meant *people* doctor. It must be hard for you to lose the only person even close to being your equal in this town."

She nodded. "You know what that means, don't you? People are going to start coming to me when they have emergencies. I'll be setting bones and delivering babies before long."

Tom thought that was far-fetched, since Dr. Mercer's office was only open two days a week as it was. People in Rocket were used to driving up to Hood River, or just calling an ambulance. Besides, there were still a handful of volunteer EMTs in town, although they were a dwindling lot.

"What are we going to do?" she asked, thrusting her hand toward the front window and ignoring Tom's attempt to leave. "My neighbors all have their houses up for sale. But I'll never be able to sell mine."

"Of course you will," he said, looking around at the surgically clean bungalow. It was the sort of place that Maria would've loved to have had, but she never asked for pretty houses or nice cars. She'd always been willing to cast her desires aside for their shared dream—whatever it was at the time. "It's a beautiful house."

"I know it is. That's the point. It's the best place in Rocket. I'll never get out of it what I've put into it."

Tom sighed and stood to go. "Do you want to come out to my place tonight? I can't stay here."

She swayed to her feet and nodded. "I'll get my keys."

"I'll drive," he said, knowing she was in no condition.

"But I have to be into the clinic early tomorrow."

"Lauren, I don't think you should drive." He smiled at her, trying to make his tone light. "You've had a few glasses of wine."

She scowled at the two bottles on the coffee table. "So have you."

"Uh, not that much." He took her by the arm before she could protest. "C'mon. I'll drive and I'll arrange for you to get back to town in the morning."

She wrenched away from his grip.

"Or, I guess you can stay here," he said, shrugging. "But really, you shouldn't drive."

His forceful words seemed to bring her to her senses. "Okay, if you promise to get me back to town by eight."

"No problem," he said, wondering how he was going to pull that off. "Do you mind if I use your phone? I want to call and see how things are going with Hap."

She shrugged and disappeared into the bedroom.

"Hap?" Tom said, when he heard the voice on the other end speaking the name of his motel.

"Where the hell are you? This place is a zoo," Hap said.

"No one to blame but yourself for that. How many rooms you rent?"

"None. Not one! These people are crazy. They don't want rooms; they want to camp out in your field."

Tom shook his head. "You're supposed to tell them no. *Make* them rent rooms."

"Yeah, like that nutball with the hunting knife?"

"I'm on my way there now. I was just calling to see how Sienna is doing." Tom smiled at Lauren as she emerged with a small bag. She leaned against the door jamb and waited for him to finish.

"She's scared of me, so I called Charlene. She's coming out to help."

"Charlene's coming?" Tom said it before he thought. He glanced at Lauren as she straightened up, her hackles rising with her. "Sienna will like that." Tom said goodbye and hung up, but didn't look at Lauren.

"Tom," she said as grimly as he'd ever heard her. "You don't want Charlene Anderson around Sienna."

He laughed uncomfortably. "Why not?"

"Haven't you heard about her brother?"

"What brother?" Tom started for the door, certain that he didn't want to hear whatever gossip Lauren was about to share.

"I just found out myself," Lauren said, a hint of a smile on her face. "He was schizophrenic."

Tom paused with a hand on the knob. The information surprised him, but also shed some light on why Charlene was so patient with Sienna. "So?" he said. "A lot of people have problems like that."

"So he did something horrendous and Charlene's mother shot him. Then shot herself. It was a murder-suicide. And the only one who witnessed it was Charlene."

Could this be true? Tom felt himself struggling for breath. It had to be a lie. "I've never heard this," he said in a soft voice, still breathless.

"You can't trust her with your daughter."

"What the hell are you talking about?" He still didn't fully grasp what Lauren had told him. "She's great with Sienna."

"Are you out of your mind?" Lauren was facing him now, only a few inches away, with a beseeching, urgent look on her face. "Who knows what really happened in that family? Who knows what Charlene might do?"

"This sounds like the worst kind of small-town gossip I've ever heard," he muttered, turning the knob and letting the infernal evening air wash over his skin. "I don't believe this."

Lauren sighed. "I heard it from Ellie."

Tom looked back at Lauren from the open door. He didn't know what to think, but there was something terribly wrong with the way she was sharing this information. Something perverse.

"Tom," Lauren said with renewed urgency. "Her mother *killed* her brother. What kind of family does that?"

"I don't think you should come with me after all," he heard himself say. "I'm sorry, Lauren. I need to think things over and you're drunk."

She stared dumbly, her mouth slightly agape. "But—"

"I don't want to hear any more of this. I have to go." He took the front steps two at a time on his way back to his pickup.

※

As he drove the seven miles from Rocket to his motel, Tom went over the information again and again. It couldn't be true, could it? He hadn't lived in Rocket long enough to know the history of its residents, but people talk. And no one had mentioned this. Then again, he was sequestered out there on Highway 14—apart from the others. It was conceivable that no one would tell *him*. Especially him, with his handicapped daughter. People had a way of censoring information like that because they somehow believed that talking about it called attention to Sienna. He felt sick to his stomach. The idea that Charlene could have survived something so horrific didn't make him wary of her—on the contrary. Instead it made him ache for her loss. He'd lost someone he loved, too.

Somewhere along the high bluffs overlooking the Columbia, with the setting sun blazing in his rearview mirror, he realized that he was following Charlene. A lump rose in his throat and he tried to imagine what he would say to her. Would she know he knew by looking at his face? He tried to dismiss the story. There was no proof that it was true, though Ellie would know because she was from Rocket—the reason she'd kept her practice open so long after business dried up. He wondered briefly if Lauren had lied, but he'd never known her to be dishonest. Lauren was a lot of things, but even she valued the truth.

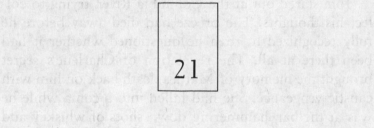

## 21

TOM PULLED TO THE SIDE of the road at the overlook and sat in his pickup. He wanted to give Charlene a head start so they wouldn't be walking in together. The more Tom thought about what Lauren had told him, the more he wondered why Charlene had never said anything—especially to him, knowing what he was going through every single day with Sienna. She'd had the opportunity that night in his apartment when she volunteered for the unpleasant task of bathing his daughter. He slid out and stood on the edge of the precipice, where the guardrail had crumbled down the steep slope and come to rest a few feet from the water. A breeze whipped up from the river, bringing with it the scent of baked basalt, dead grass, and fish. It lifted his hair up on end as it hit him in the face and he closed his eyes, swimming between two emotions, neither of which he believed he had any right to feel: protective of Charlene for her broken life and some odd kinship with her. Tom possessed a wholly new perspective of her that explained the dozens of men she'd accompanied to his motel. Thinking about it now made him despise himself. Why hadn't he understood her behavior for what it was—emptiness and desperation? Instead, he had only judged.

Tom stared out at the Columbia River, trying to collect his thoughts. The breeze had died away before he fully recognized it, then he questioned whether it had been there at all. The revelation of Charlene's secret brought the memory of Maria's death back on him with caustic vengeance. She had fallen into a coma while he was at the bar, hammering down shots of whiskey and cursing her name. He stared into that memory, his stomach knotting and tears coming to his eyes, when a car whizzed past him on the highway, kicking up a rogue stone and sending it into the gravel at his feet. It pulled him back to the moment, and he took a raspy breath, shaking off the specter. He turned his thoughts again to Charlene. What images did she carry in the deep recesses of her brain? Did she push them away with the same reflexive force that he did? Did those memories prey on her in the darkest hours of the night when her guard was down and she lay in her bed? He didn't want to think about it anymore.

He climbed back into his truck and pulled onto the highway. When he reached his motel, he parked in the back, barely glancing at the campground that had sprung up in the field next door. Inside the apartment Charlene was on the floor with Sienna, a huge sketchpad laid out between them. Sienna was pressing a red crayon back and forth in rhythmic motion, forcing the hue to a deeper crimson with each stroke.

Charlene glanced up at Tom and smiled. "Hap called me. Hope you don't mind."

Tom smiled, too, but it faltered and he wondered if she could read his thoughts. "Not at all. Thanks for coming out."

"He doesn't know what to do with kids. It's a serious character flaw, but I didn't think Sienna should have to suffer because of it."

Tom forced a laugh and stepped past them, then turned back. "She'll eat those crayons if she gets a chance."

Charlene looked long at Sienna, then back at Tom. "How long has it been since she's had crayons?"

It was an odd question, Tom thought. He shrugged, trying to remember. "A while."

"She's older now. I doubt she'll eat them." She handed Sienna a purple crayon and the girl took it without looking up. She began to work it back and forth along the lower edge of the red stripe she'd made. "She was so excited to have them I kind of felt sorry for her," Charlene added.

Tom watched his daughter, another wave of shame coursing through him as he faced his latest shortcoming as a father. Why hadn't he bought her crayons? Why had he imagined that she would simply remain the same all these years?

"Why do you do this?" he asked Charlene.

She glanced up. "Do what?"

"Spend time with her?"

Charlene stared at Tom, unwilling to answer. When he didn't leave or change the subject she looked away. "I want to."

"Why?"

"Why not?" She sounded vaguely angry. "Don't you want me to?"

"Of course I do," he whispered. "But you're the only one who ever *wanted* to."

She scrambled to her feet then, and Tom immediately regretted pushing her. Was she leaving? She walked into the kitchen, away from Sienna.

He followed her.

"I guess you don't know about my brother," she said as she took a Henry's from his refrigerator.

He stood mutely behind her.

"He wasn't autistic." Charlene twisted the cap off with her bare hands and flicked it into the trash at the end of the counter. "That would have been a blessing."

*A blessing?*

"He was schizophrenic." She looked at Tom for his reaction.

Tom took a breath, trying to act as though he were hearing it for the first time. "I'm sorry."

"Yeah, well . . ." Charlene leaned against the counter. "He's passed away now. I miss him, though. And there's something about Sienna that reminds me of him. I don't know what. Just that . . . that vulnerability."

"Why didn't you say something before?"

She turned her gaze on him and held it a long time, making him flinch. "Do you ever get those people here who see that something is wrong with Sienna and then tell you all about the problem their kid has?"

"All the time," he said, thinking of the innumerable motel guests who had instantly drawn a connection to Tom because their child had ADD or was mentally retarded. They always began by asking about Sienna, but it was nothing more than a way of launching a sorrowful tale about their own troubles. They expected Tom to listen and understand by default.

"Those people would corner my mother at school or in the grocery store to commiserate about their kids' problems with her as if what they were going through was anything like our situation. I hated their arrogant presumptions. I hated *them,* and I hated my brother for attracting them." Charlene drank several swallows of her beer. "Call it penance or guilt or whatever you want, but when I see Sienna I wish I hadn't had those thoughts about Stephen. And that makes me want to help her."

"You *have* helped her," Tom said. "You've helped her a lot."

"Not really. It's mostly selfish."

Just then Hap poked his head into the apartment. "I thought I saw you come in. You gonna leave me out here to manage this place by myself?"

Tom didn't look at Hap but kept his eyes fixed on Charlene. Tonight he didn't pay attention to her beauty, although he wasn't blind to it, either. Tonight he saw only her soul. "Sienna's not the only one happy to see you, you know?"

Hap's face went pink and he disappeared.

Charlene smiled softly at her beer.

Tom didn't know what else to say. "I guess I better go relieve Hap."

☀

Hap's stomach churned so violently it felt like he'd swallowed a sturgeon. Leaving Charlene and Tom smiling shyly at each other gave him hope for the two people he cared most about in Rocket, but also left him a little angry. How could she see in Tom what she couldn't in him? Hap understood that Tom was almost two decades younger than himself, and certainly better looking, but Hap's intent was the same—perhaps even purer.

Tom was so taken with Charlene that he didn't seem to care when Hap told him that he was bringing a reporter from *The Westerner* out the next day. He even laughed about the business Hap had brought him—a one-eighty from when he'd called earlier demanding help.

Hap had warned Tom about that preacher, though. "He's rallying the tent city next door to unify them against the motel. He's claiming that something evil is lurking over here."

Tom only laughed.

Hap changed the subject because the reverend gave him the creeps. "Weren't you going to Lauren's house? How come she didn't come back with you?"

Tom had shrugged and said simply, "Lost cause."

"Who's the lost cause here?" Hap asked himself, thumping his finger on the steering wheel. But even as he wrestled with his jealousy, he believed Charlene was in good hands. If he couldn't be the one who offered her the comfort she sought, at least it was Tom. And Tom deserved her, too, after losing Maria.

Running Tom's motel had worn him out, and he was hungry. He sighed as he pulled off the road at the Windy Point Diner. Hap didn't know how Tom could stand dealing with those throngs of people coming and going at all hours of the day and night like that. It was like being a damned referee with all those idiots arguing and taking off their clothes, leaving their children in the pool unattended. One woman asked him if he'd please run off the preacher because the man made her nervous, a thought that had crossed Hap's mind repeatedly all evening. He prized his solitude, just like he'd told Dillard Meek. And that creepy preacher, he was too much, Hap thought. He'd be inclined to chase the man away with the .38 Special he kept in the glove compartment of his van.

Linda greeted Hap as he took his familiar stool at the counter. "Coffee?" she asked.

"Too late for that. I'll never sleep. Just water."

She placed a menu in front of him and disappeared.

Hap glanced down the counter. The place was quiet but for the usual handful of truckers eating alone at the counter as they made their way across the vast stretch of eastern Washington farm country on their way to Portland or Pendleton, Spokane or Kennewick. Dillard raised his coffee cup and stood off his stool, walking over to join Hap at the other end.

Hap groaned inwardly, but smiled at the man anyway. "Evening, Dillard."

"Hey, Hap." Dillard slapped a hand down on Hap's shoulder as if they were old buddies.

"What's the word, Dillard?"

Dillard cut his eyes down the row of truckers, who were quietly eating and minding their own business. Then he lowered his voice as if speaking confidentially. "That Jemmett girl . . . what's her name?"

"Sienna?"

"Yeah, Sienna. Isn't that a color?" Dillard sipped his coffee and fiddled with the menu.

"Yes. It's a burnt orange-brown. A very rich color." Hap tried to recall if he'd ever really seen the color sienna in its full glory anywhere but in an oil painting. It was a tough color to live up to.

Dillard nodded thoughtfully. "This business with that fleabag motel and room six. You've heard about it, haven't you?"

"It's just talk. Talk in a windless summer, that's all." Hap brushed a hand in the air to wave it off.

Dillard shook his head, giving Hap a grave look. "It's a poltergeist."

"A what?"

"Girl's what? Fourteen?"

"No, she's twelve."

Dillard nodded as if that proved everything. "She's going through puberty. That's when it happens."

Hap ignored the man. Dillard was the freak, not Sienna.

"She's summoned some sort of supernatural force and it's wreaking havoc on the people who check in to that motel."

Linda set a glass down in front of Hap and drew out her order pad. Hap's appetite had evaporated.

"What can I get you?"

"I haven't decided yet. Another minute?" He picked up the menu and flipped it open.

"Sure. I'll come back."

As Linda moved down the counter, Dillard leaned in. "She's a strange kid. She's not right." He twirled his index finger around his ear.

"She's a kid with special needs, Dillard. That's all."

"I'm not the only one that thinks something is wrong with her. It's all over town that she's what's causing all this—this, you know . . ." He raised an eyebrow.

Hap didn't think he could loathe Dillard any more than he already did, but he was finding new depths of hatred for the man.

"Look, I know something about poltergeists. I've researched them."

"Have you, now?" What a surprise, Hap thought.

Dillard nodded confidently. "She's channeling her dead mother. How old was she when Tom's wife died?"

Hap pulled the menu close to his face. "I don't know. I don't remember."

"You know a poltergeist needs an agent, and that kid is the agent. They're always female and they're always under the age of twenty. *Pubescent girls.* Oftentimes poltergeists happen in places where there's been a violent death."

Hap waited for Dillard to make his point, but the man went silent and stared earnestly at the side of Hap's face.

"Maria Jemmett suffered a brain hemorrhage after she fell cleaning the pool. A violent death usually implies ill intent. Hers was a tragic accident," he clarified, hoping Dillard might see how absurd his theory was.

"She fell?"

"Yes, she fell. Are you suggesting something else happened?" Hap dropped the menu on the counter and turned to face Dillard. *Enough,* he thought. He raised his voice to draw attention. "What exactly are you saying, Dillard?"

Dillard's gaze faltered and he glanced around nervously. Hap knew the man didn't have the guts or the confidence to hold his ground when confronted, and he relished forcing this man to retreat.

Dillard got up and dropped some bills on the counter. "I'm not the only one who thinks that girl is bad news," he said under his breath before he walked out.

Hap watched him go. When he turned back, Linda was standing in front of him. He couldn't tell if she'd overheard the conversation.

"You decide what you want?"

"What's the special?"

"Cedar plank salmon with apricot sauce."

"I'll have that." Hap kept his eyes on Linda. She was somber tonight. "People been talking about the Jemmett girl a lot?"

She nodded. "It's all I hear about. The girl and the motel and the girl and room six and the girl."

"What do you think?"

She scooped up the menu and tucked it under her arm. "Seems a bit odd—all this stuff. I'm of the opinion that something sparks these things. There has to be some nugget of truth in it. Stories like this don't just spring to life one day without provocation."

"Maybe, but you don't think Sienna has anything to do with it, do you?"

"I don't know what to think. I know she's the same age as my son Taylor and none of the kids at school like her."

"She's autistic, and kids are mean at that age. They don't like anyone who's different."

Linda shook her head, looking uncertain. "No, it's different than that. They're afraid of her."

☼

Tom tossed around on the sofa, wishing he had followed his instincts and romanced Charlene into spending the night. Just thinking about her now with her supple skin and sweet perfume gave him a hard-on. It wouldn't have been difficult to initiate that first kiss, which he imagined they would both have called a *good-night kiss,* despite its depth and duration. He could have drawn her back into the apartment and onto the sofa. She'd been flirtatious with him, following him out into the lobby and asking probing questions about his childhood in Wyoming and his family. He enjoyed the interrogation, though he found her questions difficult to answer now that he understood something about her own past. And he'd been afraid to ask her those same questions out of fear that he'd break the spell between them and send her away in pain. As it was, explaining that he'd never been close to his family, that his parents were both dead more than fifteen years, and that he'd lost touch with his only brother over a decade ago was tough enough. It made him feel as though he'd been hard and uncaring, that he'd thrown away important people in his life. Had he simply not taken the time for them? He understood how selfish he'd been, focused only on what was right in front of him, and he also realized that Charlene had a way of illuminating that ugly flaw. He hoped that she wasn't home lying in her own bed right now thinking he was a jerk.

Tom tried to imagine how he'd ever come to know Charlene without asking prying questions about her family, as those are the things two people want to know when they are trying to understand each other. She intrigued him now and he wondered if it was real or just

morbid curiosity. One thing was certain: he didn't want
to rush this—whatever it was. Not only was she a lot
younger than he, but she had a connection with Sienna
that was bigger and more important than his sex life. If
things didn't work out, it would be his daughter who suffered the most. Where Sienna hadn't even noticed
Lauren's presence, let alone her absence, Charlene was
everything to her.

And Tom couldn't stop thinking about Charlene's
mother—this woman who had killed her son, then
turned the gun on herself. Why hadn't anyone told him
about that? A part of him admired her for her courage.
He knew that was an abnormal response to such a trau-
matic event. If he stated that idea aloud to anyone they
wouldn't understand, but it was precisely what he felt.
Admiration.

The lobby bell chimed, rousing Tom from a deep
slumber. He panicked when he saw the time. Eight
o'clock. How had he overslept? No one had started the
coffee, or put the doughnuts out. He pulled on his jeans
and a tee shirt and scrambled out into a scalding light,
far brighter than the day. He shrank back, his eyes sting-
ing. A woman wearing a crisp red suit and an unearthly
amount of makeup greeted him by thrusting something
into his face. She was accompanied by a man packing a
huge camera on one shoulder. When Tom got his bearings he realized it was a microphone that she was waving
about. It was adorned with a giant stylized logo that he
recognized from the cable station known for their off-
beat shows, such as *Raw Nerve,* in which people attempted dangerous stunts in the nude.

"Mr. Jemmett?" the woman said crisply. "We'd like
to ask you a few questions about your motel. Is it true
that strange things have been happening out here?"

As Tom opened his mouth to speak the cameraman adjusted the light, blinding Tom. He instinctively covered his face, shielding his eyes. "Geez! Turn that thing off."

"You'll get used to it in a second," the woman said. "We need the light for the camera."

"Who are you?" Tom demanded.

"Washington's channel eleven—Vancouver. We've heard bizarre things are going on in room six of your motel. Can you comment? Tell us, what do you think it is?"

Tom put his hand down, squinting at the pair. "There's nothing going on in my motel."

"Really?" the woman said in a tone of obvious disbelief. "Why are all those people camped in the lot next door? Why aren't they sleeping in the motel?"

"They can't afford to stay in the rooms."

"What about Robert Hemphill?"

"Who?"

"He was mauled by two bullmastiffs yesterday. In his interview, he claimed he stayed in room six right here." She pulled out a crinkled copy of *The Sasquatch*. "He gave us this."

The cameraman shuffled forward, bringing his lens within inches of Tom's face.

"According to locals three people have died after staying in that room," the woman pressed on. "And now a mauling? Don't you think that's odd?"

"It's coincidence," Tom said, turning back to his apartment to escape the pair. They seemed to consume every square inch of the tiny lobby.

"That's not what people in town are saying," the reporter persisted.

"That's enough," Tom said. "I'm not answering these questions. You need to leave."

"Mr. Jemmett, how many people have been injured or died after staying in room six?"

Her question stunned him. He had sudden visions of being sued by everyone who'd ever set foot on the premises. "No one has been injured."

"Martin Orr wasn't injured in your motel? I guess dying isn't the same as being injured, is it, Mr. Jemmett?"

"He died of a heart attack. It would have happened if he'd been here or somewhere else. He was snorting enough coke to kill a rhino."

"So you're not denying that a man died in your motel?"

Tom stared at the camera.

"And Helen Simpson?"

Tom shook his head, flustered. "She pulled out onto the highway in front of a semi. That had nothing to do with this motel."

"But it happened right out front. And after she'd stayed in room six, do you deny that?"

Tom struggled to collect his thoughts. The woman was twisting things, making them sound sensational. She wasn't listening to him.

"Helen Simpson died the morning after she slept in your room six? Isn't that right, Mr. Jemmett?"

He wished she would stop repeating his name like that. "Look," he said. "It was just a coincidence."

"Coincidence? Was it coincidence that Art Schlegel was beaten to death a few days after he stayed in room six?"

"Get out!" Tom shouted. He stepped forward, crowding them.

The cameraman didn't move.

Tom shoved him. "I said get out. This is private property."

"Are you denying that these things happened in your motel, Mr. Jemmett?" the reporter went on. "Can we see room six?"

"*Out!*" Tom roared. He turned and retreated into his

apartment, slamming the door behind him. In the dark hallway he tripped over Sienna, who was standing motionless. She concentrated on Tom's face, her brows knitted and her lips pursed in concentration.

"Six," she said.

## 22

CHARLENE WHISTLED A SWEET, soft tune as she sorted the mail, distracting Hap from his task of editing the final copy for the next edition of *The Rocket*. He'd included a shorter version of the story about Tom's motel that he'd sent off to *The Sasquatch*, seeing no point in pretending nothing was going on now that people were showing up to gawk at the place. And he'd followed up with a humorous paragraph about how coincidence had allowed them all a good laugh and some hard-won tourists, but of course no one actually believed any of this nonsense was true.

"I saw that article you wrote about Tom's motel," Charlene said as she filled out the morning batch of parcel notices. "Someone left a copy at the Red Tail and Stan pinned it up outside the bathroom. What was that you were telling me about ruining Tom's business?"

Hap sat back and shrugged.

"Just admit that it was my idea."

"It certainly was not. I had that idea long before you caught on. In fact I'd already written the copy by the time you suggested it." He tossed his editing pencil down and drank the last of his water before standing to refill the cup. "I didn't tell you because you'd have spread it from here to Hood River by noon and it takes time to get an article—an honest accounting of the facts—in print."

"I was right all the same. There are enough friggin weirdos in this world that we don't need wind to keep this place alive."

"Sad but true, my dear." Hap sat down, his chair squeaking beneath him. "You enjoy your evening with Mr. Jemmett?"

"Mister?"

"You know who I mean."

Charlene smiled and it warmed Hap's heart, even as he wished she would smile like that for him.

"Just be careful you don't hurt Sienna if you get involved with him. I don't think the child gave a rat's patootie about Lauren, but you're different."

Charlene gazed past Hap at some indistinct point behind him. She seemed to be at a historic loss for words. Her smile faded and she started writing out notices again, silently this time.

"You okay?" Hap asked.

She nodded, but he didn't believe her. Why hadn't he kept his mouth shut and refrained from offering advice? No wonder she didn't want to date him: he behaved like her father.

Hap glimpsed a white van passing by on Main Street with a satellite dish mounted on its roof. He stood to get a better look, but it was gone. He wandered out into the lobby and looked through the large plate-glass windows up the street. A blue number eleven was painted on the back of the van.

"Isn't channel eleven a cable station?" he called to Charlene.

"How should I know?"

Hap watched the van on its way out of Rocket toward Hood River and the cities beyond. "It is. They have that show *Pacific Northweird* where they track down bizarre things going on around the region."

"Never seen it."

"You know the show. They did a big special on the Shanghai tunnels in Portland last Halloween and how they're haunted by the ghosts of prostitutes and murdered sailors."

"Is this what you watch on TV?" Charlene whistled. "No wonder you're so friggin weird."

The van disappeared and he thought about calling Tom to find out if reporters had been out to his motel. Why else would they be in town? He glanced at his watch. He still had a couple of hours before the reporter from *The Westerner* was due, so he walked up the street to the bakery.

Petra immediately got to her feet when she saw him, beaming. "Morning, Hap. Hov are you today?"

The enticing aroma of fresh bread was the true reason he came back day after day, despite the mixed message his presence was sending this woman. He glanced around at the empty tables. "I'm good. What's the special?"

"Ve have Jemmett bread on special today."

"What?"

She grinned, her big dentures slipping so that she had to suck them back into her mouth with an unpleasant pop. "I bake it in ze shape of a zeex."

Hap didn't know what to say. He stared through the glass top at the shelves of bread loaves, each carefully bent into the number six.

"It is vhat people vant. I sold eight loaves yesterday. And ze television crew from Vancouver bought five zis morning." She smiled down at her work as if eminently pleased with herself.

"That TV crew came in here?"

She nodded again, still smiling.

"They ask questions?"

"Yes, lots of questions. Zey vant to know if ze motel is haunted."

"What did you tell them?"

She shrugged. "I told zem ve had a haunted motel in Germany ver I come from. No one stays zere but people vanting to be frightened." She twisted her finger around her ear to indicate that these people of whom she spoke were crazy. "Ze man zat owns it makes a lot of money on zese ding-dongs."

Hap drew the connection to Tom and hoped he was just dishonest enough to do the same, but he didn't think Tom would completely abandon his morals for money. "Well, I'm glad to see you found a profitable angle for business."

"Ah, yes," she said enthusiastically. "It is ze best money I have made all summer."

"I'll take one of those Jemmett loaves," Hap said.

Petra examined each loaf before selecting the right one for him. "Zis one has nice crust. Just right." She slid it inside a bag, eyeing Hap solicitously as she moved. "You zink zat girl has somezing to do viz zis stuff?"

"What girl?"

"Ze little one—at ze motel."

"Why would she have anything to do with this?" Was this an original thought of Petra's? Or had Dillard planted the idea? There were only a handful of businesses left in Rocket, and Petra's and Dillard's were only a couple of doors apart. Though they professed to hate each other, certainly the man wandered down for a hot ham and cheese once in a while.

"I know about ze kitten she killed. Belinda Melton tells me about it a couple of days ago. I zink ze girl is . . . how do you say it?" Petra trawled for the right English word, her eyes roaming the ceiling as if she might find it there. "Possessed!"

"*Possessed?*" Hap stepped back, instinctively distancing himself from that word. "Petra, don't say things like that. Especially about a child."

"I zink it is true. Ze devil's vork is going on out zere."

"And what do you call this?" Hap picked up the loaf of Jemmett bread and thrust it at her.

"Just a little fun. No harm in zat. No one dies vhen ze eat my bread."

Hap stared at the woman, a mixture of amazement and disgust at her convoluted logic. "Did you tell the news crew anything about Sienna Jemmett?"

"Don't be silly. I am not a gossip."

Hap turned to leave, rendered speechless by the conversation.

"You forgot your bread," she hollered after him.

"You keep it. I don't want it." He strode outside and stood on the walk.

"You are not so good-looking of a man, anyvay," she called after him.

☀

Sheriff Turnbull pulled in to the motel turnaround at half past eleven as Tom was finishing up cleaning room three. Tom shoved the vacuum out onto the cracked sidewalk and went back for the dirty sheets and towels, which he dropped into a large canvas laundry basket on wheels.

"Morning, Tom," Turnbull said in his most authoritative voice. Clearly he wasn't just out patrolling but had in mind to put an end to something.

"Sheriff," Tom said. His pulse quickened as he thought of the possibilities. Was he here about Sienna?

"This little tent city . . ." Turnbull brushed a hand out

toward the lot next door, which was packed with tran-
sients. There were about twenty tents of various shapes
and sizes; a half-dozen other people slept on the open
ground, and a few in their cars and trucks. An aging
school bus, painted white, sat along the far side. Its windows were draped with tie-dyed scarves and blankets to
protect the privacy of its occupants. "Yours?"

Tom shook his head. "Are you kidding me? They'd be
paying for rooms if I had my way. They aren't doing me
any good sleeping out there."

The sheriff assessed Tom impassively. "Been hearing
some weird stuff about this place in recent days."

"Yeah, I imagine you have."

"Like to hear your explanation."

Tom glanced at his watch. "Coffee?"

"Sure. You have any doughnuts?"

"Yep." Tom led the sheriff back to the lobby and
poured them each a cup of coffee while Turnbull swallowed a maple bar in three enormous bites.

"So? What's all this nonsense?" Turnbull brushed
crumbs from his neatly pressed uniform, then blew the
steam off his coffee.

"Just that. Nonsense." Tom sat on the stool and pulled
out his ledger, marking down which rooms he'd cleaned.
"Remember those two people who died out here?"

"Most excitement we've had all summer."

"Well, Hap Mitsui decided he'd save my motel from
foreclosure and wrote some ridiculous story for some little paper out of northern California. I think it was *The
Bigfoot* or something like that. Apparently it's well sub-
scribed to by all these"—he gestured at the tent city—
"these drugged out goofballs. So here they are. Come to
cash in at the universal karma depot."

Turnbull laughed. "So he made it all up?"

Tom paused. "No, I don't think he did, actually. It's
pretty much the truth."

Turnbull seemed to mull that a moment. "That your property next door?"

"Hell no. If it was I'd have run them all off by now."

"Well, they need to move, that's for certain. It's a hazard. Fire danger is extreme right now. I can name off at least twenty laws they're breaking."

"Run that preacher off first, would you?"

Turnbull squinted out at Reverend Shelly's canvas gazebo with its handmade signs and a slow smile dawned over his face—a private smile. Tom suddenly understood a little about the man behind the uniform. The sheriff drew a keen pleasure from what he was about to do. The idea bothered Tom a little, despite the fact that it was directed at Reverend Shelly.

☼

As Turnbull strode out of the lobby on his way to disperse the tent city, Tom slipped into the apartment to check on Sienna. She'd been sleeping when he started his cleaning routine that morning and time had gotten away from him. She was down on the floor, hunched over her new sketchpad, grinding an orange crayon down to a nub. Little flecks of wax adorned the page where she'd pressed so hard the crayon had disintegrated.

He looked long at the picture, then at her. What would he do with her? What would he do with this child he was bound by fate to protect?

"I love you," Tom said. When she didn't respond he abandoned the useless question of whether she loved him, too. Emotions, it seemed, were too complex for her to articulate. He wondered if she understood them at all. "You eat something. Sienna?"

She turned her eyes on him then, hot and angry. She'd been crying. "She comes back!"

Tom took a hard breath. Not another day of this. Was it worth it to have Charlene spend time with his daughter if it only meant that he suffered severe backlash when the woman was gone? "She will. She will, sweetie."

Sienna flung the crayon down onto the paper and he recognized the raw, red-orange fury she'd illustrated. It was like looking into the crater of an angry volcano. "She comes back!"

"Sienna," he warned. "Don't you do this now. Daddy is very busy today. I won't tolerate bad behavior."

Sienna grasped the drawing and ripped it from the sketchpad, tearing it in half and shoving it at him. "She comes back! She comes back!"

"No." He took her by the wrist and pulled her into the bedroom. "No. Now sit down." He shoved her down on the bed.

She thrashed and kicked, catching him hard in the crotch with the top of her foot, then pulling back and nailing him again with the ball of her heel. Tom's world fluttered black and he found himself lying on his side, the smell of old urine seeping up out of the green carpet. She was on top of him, biting and scratching, digging her fingernails into his flesh. He gasped for breath, holding himself between the legs. Blinding pain seared through him. He couldn't get his words out as she bit into his ear, bringing up hot blood.

☼

Hap paced the post office lobby waiting for the reporter from *The Westerner*. She was late by nearly an hour. Had she gotten lost? A napkin blew down the street, rousing his interest, but it got hung up on a dead shrub in front of the empty storefront across the way. He scanned the sky, then the hills, for any sign of wind. It was probably a passing car that had dislodged it from its prior resting place. He'd been unable to concentrate on anything that morning, thinking of Petra and the gossip she was spreading about Sienna Jemmett. He wondered, not for the first time, if he'd made a huge mistake by running that story. The very advice he'd given Charlene about not hurting the girl was what he himself seemed to need more than anyone. How had he overlooked this probability? Of course people would draw conclusions.

"You should see the pictures Sienna makes," Charlene said. "The colors are so rich. I've never seen anyone get that kind of depth from a crayon. I think she has real talent."

"She's a genius, I think," Hap said on his way back to his desk. He felt sick, thinking about that little girl. Only Charlene would see talents in the child's messy habits. He leaned into his computer, but his eyes drifted to Charlene and back again.

"Why do you keep looking at me?" she demanded.

"I'm not."

"Yes you are. You've been staring at me all morning."

"I just had a really disturbing conversation with Petra."

Charlene rolled her eyes. "What's so surprising about that?"

"She's a crazy old bitch."

Charlene paused from her work to look at Hap. He could guess what she was thinking. He made a point of saying only positive things about people behind their backs, and he'd just broken that rule with highly uncharacteristic profanity.

"What did she say?" Charlene asked, her eyes narrowing.

"She thinks this stuff about Tom's motel is because..." He didn't know how to finish now that he'd started. He wished he'd kept his mouth shut. Charlene didn't need to hear Petra's stupid suspicions.

Charlene waited for him to continue.

"Never mind."

"No, tell me."

"It's stupid. The woman is insane."

"It's about Sienna, isn't it? She thinks this stuff is happening because of her."

Hap nodded.

"That fucking bitch!"

"I shouldn't have said anything. Everyone knows that's not true. No one would believe that."

"The hell they won't!" Charlene moved swiftly to the service window and looked up the street toward the bakery. "I'm gonna go over there and set that stupid Nazi cunt straight."

"Whoa, Charlene. Hold up a minute."

"She has no right talking about people like that. What the hell does she know about Sienna? And since when does being autistic give a person special powers that... that... kill people?"

"It doesn't. Everyone knows that."

Charlene spun on her heels to face Hap, who had joined her at the window. Her cheeks were flaming red. "What exactly did that bitch say?"

He hesitated. "It's not important."

"Tell me."

"That Sienna is possessed."

"Oh, that... that..." She picked up her purse and started for the door.

Hap grabbed her arm and pulled her back. "You're too angry to go talk to her now."

"Talk? I'm gonna beat the shit out of her."

"Charlene, sit down," he snapped, with an authority that surprised them both. He guided her to a plastic chair along the wall. "Think about what you're doing. Beating up an old woman will not change anything for Sienna."

Charlene sat rigidly in the chair, glaring at Hap's feet. Then, to his astonishment, she hunched over into a tight ball and began to sob.

Hap watched as her body shuddered quietly, not

knowing what to do. It was the last thing he expected to happen. He'd never known how to behave when a woman started crying. His ex-wife had accused him of not caring. He hadn't seen this coming, but he rarely did. He reached out and touched Charlene's hair, then pulled away, then reached a tentative hand to touch her again. She didn't recoil so he patted her back. "What's all this about?"

She pushed his hand away, but couldn't catch her breath.

"It'll be okay. She's just a stupid, crazy woman. People know Sienna is not responsible for this." Hap stood next to her, his hands at his sides, wondering what he was supposed to do. Wondering why he never quite knew what to do.

Charlene struggled to get her breath. "I hate that woman. She used to say the same thing about my brother. She'd stand in her little bakery all high and mighty and tell everyone who would listen what a threat he was to society."

Hap shifted from one foot to the other, feeling awkward and useless. This was more information than she'd ever shared with him about her brother.

Charlene wiped her eyes and drew a deep breath. She looked up at Hap, her face contorting, even as she struggled to compose herself. "Petra Osterlundt is the person I blame most for what happened."

"What do you mean?"

She shook her head and gathered her purse, getting to her feet. "You know what I mean." Charlene strode out the back door.

Hap listened to the seconds tick by on the large clock in the lobby, echoing in the emptiness. That night when Charlene lost everyone, he'd heard the police dispatcher call Turnbull out to the Anderson home. He'd written a brief story about the tragedy, covering the scarce facts he could glean. It had barely been a two-inch piece of copy, and it left more questions than answers. Stephen Anderson was dead, shot by his mother, who had then turned the gun on herself. He'd also written the obituaries for Charlene's mother and brother—another brief accounting of the facts. And when Charlene came to work at the post office, moved into the shared space, he'd feared what she thought of him for his part in that public accounting.

Hap slumped down in the chair where Charlene had been, smearing her tears across the cement floor with the sole of his shoe. When he'd first moved to Rocket, Petra had warned him, too, about Stephen Anderson; she'd called him a monster. But Hap didn't walk out and refuse to buy bread from her. He didn't even express disapproval of her spiteful gossip. He'd simply listened, and nodded, and watched the boy meander past the window with his hands in his pockets and his head hung low.

※

Lauren stood next to Anna in the pet clinic lobby. There wasn't a single appointment scheduled that day, and Anna had already filed, scrubbed, disinfected, and restocked everything in the building.

"Well, I guess you can go home," Lauren said.

Anna frowned. "I thought this was going to be a full-time job."

"I can't pay you to do nothing, can I?"

"What if I went outside with a sign, like those people who stand on the corner and advertise sales?"

Lauren stared at the scrawny woman. She had such bizarre logic. "That might work for selling sofas, but people usually need a reason to bring their dogs and cats to see the vet."

"Well, you could run a special on vaccinations. Or maybe spaying and neutering."

"Wouldn't a newspaper ad be more effective for that?" It wasn't a bad idea, though. Lauren filed it away for later use.

As Anna procrastinated punching out for the afternoon, Patrick pulled in to the parking lot.

"Look, a client," Anna said, hopeful.

"That's Patrick. Oh God, he's probably bringing in those things he wants to trade."

"You're going to take his family heirlooms?"

Lauren shook her head, exasperated. "You don't need to stick around to see what he brought."

Anna's deep-set eyes were rimmed in purple, making her look perpetually sleep deprived. "I really need the hours, Dr. Kent. I've got kids to feed."

"All right, but we don't need your opinions on this transaction. Is that clear?" She'd regret letting Anna stay, Lauren knew that already.

Anna nodded.

The lobby bell chimed as Patrick shuffled in with a battered cardboard box in his arms.

"Hello, Patrick," Lauren said. "How's Crispy doing?"

"Good, good," the old man said. "I'm taking good care of him. He has his own little space in the kitchen where he can't get too rambunctious. And I take him out twice a day so he can do his business, but I don't take my eyes off him."

"That's great, Patrick. Are you keeping up on the pills?"

"Oh, yeah. He likes 'em with cheese."

Anna giggled and Lauren gave her a sharp glare. Anna shrunk away, and Lauren realized that the reprimand hadn't been necessary.

"Brought you some stuff to look at, Dr. Kent. In trade for what I owe you." He lifted the box onto the counter and small clouds of dust boiled out of its rickety corners.

"Let's see what you've got," Lauren said, stepping tentatively toward the relics.

Patrick pulled out an old book that was missing its cover. The pages were yellowed and flaking. "This here is an eighteenth-century Bible," he said, plopping it down.

Anna stepped forward, too, and peered at it.

"It's in German," Patrick said.

"I can't read German. Sorry." Lauren hoped the man had something better than this, but it looked doubtful.

"I wondered about that," he said. "I have this other thing; it's a part of Rocket history. Dillard once offered me seventy-five dollars for the thing it's in." He rummaged in the box.

Lauren stepped closer, wondering what Patrick had that the antiques dealer was willing to pay seventy-five dollars for. She knew Dillard would offer half the value or less if he intended to make a profit on it.

Patrick looked up and grinned, enjoying the moment of anticipation as the two women waited.

"What is it?" Anna said, then immediately gave Lauren an apologetic glance.

His smile widened and he pulled out an old brown canning jar and rattled its contents.

"That's just an old fruit jar, Patrick," Lauren said. "And not a very pretty one."

"What's in it?" Anna asked.

He didn't seem deterred, despite Lauren's waning interest in his treasure. "It was the jar Dillard wanted. It's rare. He has a big red book in his shop that has all the manufacturers and colors of all the fruit jars ever made and how much they're worth. It's not supposed to be brown. That's the result of a screwup at the factory."

Lauren sighed. What would she do with a brown jar that had come into being as a screwup, and how on earth could he imagine it was a piece of Rocket history? "Why don't you sell it to Dillard and then you can use the money to pay on what you owe me?"

Anna shook her head and eyed Patrick as if sending him a private message, but she stayed quiet.

"Oh no, the jar belonged to my grandmother on my mother's side. It's all I have of hers. I'd rather not sell it. It's what's in it that I thought you might be interested in." He pried at the zinc screw top, but it wouldn't budge. He placed the jar between his thin, bowlegged thighs and tried harder to twist it off with his misshapen fingers. Finally it creaked, loosing sand and grit onto the polished linoleum floor. Patrick straightened up and poured the contents onto the counter.

Lauren frowned at the mess; Anna would get more time now just cleaning up after this old man. She assessed the lump on the counter, and it took a moment for her to understand what she was looking at. It first appeared to be an ancient dirt clod, but then she made out the slim lines and arcs of corroding metal. It was a unified hunk of ancient coins that had nearly fused together over the years in that ugly brown jar.

Patrick pulled his pocketknife out and began separating the wad into individual coins, some gold, some copper, some silver.

Anna gasped. "It's money."

"Money in very poor condition," Lauren reminded her. "Patrick, these coins haven't been well preserved. You can hardly make them out. I doubt they're still worth anything."

"Sure they are," he said, undaunted. "They're part of our history. I bet you didn't know that a steamboat sank in the Columbia out here, did you? Right off the end of the Rocket jetty."

"When?" Lauren asked.

"Eighteen ninety-three. These coins came from the wreck. My great-uncle Nelson salvaged them when they were cleaning up the wreckage."

"I heard about that wreck." Anna's eyes twinkled over the mess on the counter, then at Patrick. "I had to write a report about it when I was in the fifth grade."

Lauren looked at the coins with mildly renewed interest. "That's fascinating, but I still don't think they're worth anything. It's just interesting history."

"I think they're cool, Patrick," Anna said, leaning in so close that her nose was only inches from the blade of Patrick's knife as he wrenched them apart.

He looked at Anna as if seeing her for the very first time. His eyes lingered over her face and she gave him a shy smile. He picked up a five-cent piece and wiped it on his jeans, then held it out to her. Just the outline of a woman's profile was visible, and the faint numbers of a date.

Anna took it in her fingers and examined it. "Eighteen eighty-seven." She looked up at Patrick, radiant with curiosity and wonder. "Wow, that's so cool."

"I'm sorry, Patrick, but I don't think I can use any of this stuff. I'll just hold your account open and you can make payments on it until we're good."

Patrick's face fell and he began scooping the coins back into the fruit jar.

"I'll pay his balance," Anna told Lauren. "You can take it out of my paychecks."

Lauren was stunned, and realized that she was gawking with her mouth open. What happened to the hungry kids?

"No, I can't let you do that," Patrick said. "It's nice of you to offer, though."

"But I want to—really. I've been thinking about it since you were here last time."

Patrick was quiet a moment. He looked at the coins, then at Anna. Finally, he said, "You want these coins, hon?"

Anna blushed, and Lauren was repulsed by what she

read in her face. Anna was attracted to the man, Lauren was certain of it. There had to be forty years between the two of them, if not more. It was obscene.

"Why don't you come over and we can clean them and catalog them together? You can tell me all about them. If you're hungry I can make you supper."

Patrick looked at Lauren, embarrassed and flustered, confirming Lauren's suspicion. He looked back at Anna, but couldn't quite bring himself to look her in the eye. "No, I can't do that."

Anna nodded urgently at him. "You'll need to tell me what each one is. I've never seen anything like them before. Please?" Anna waited expectantly for an answer. Her skin glowed in a way Lauren had not seen before.

He laughed. "Well, I can come by for a little while, I guess."

Anna scrambled to get her purse and scooped up the box containing Patrick's treasures. She paused to look at Lauren. "You said I could I go home, remember?"

Lauren shrugged, still not comprehending what had just happened between these two.

"Thanks, Dr. Kent. I'll see you in the morning," Anna said, leading Patrick out the door. Lauren found herself standing in the empty lobby, looking at the pile of grit on the floor in amazed and lonely silence. How was it that these two could find some remote spark of romance when she, a woman with so much to offer, found only rejection and heartache?

# 23

TOM DABBED RUBBING ALCOHOL on his ear and paused to let the burn sink in, closing his eyes against the pain. When it let up a little he examined the bite wound. There would be no hiding this one; anyone within a twenty-foot radius would recognize the ring of deep punctures for what they were. Tom pressed his hands against the cool porcelain sink and let his upper body slump forward. The sound of Sienna kicking the wall reverberated through the apartment. He'd hastily removed everything in the room except the bed and her clothes, then shoved it all into a heap in the hallway. The dresser had blocked her exit until he'd hammered up a slide lock. The child screamed for over an hour without reprieve, only just now falling into a steady pounding with her foot against the secured door. Tom felt drained, empty of all energy or emotion. He would call Dr. Taglione and ask for help—ask for drugs.

He blew out his breath, his eyes fixed on the rust stain at the base of the drain, afraid to look at himself in the mirror. Though he had not done so, he'd imagined hurting his daughter with graphic clarity. Not simply hitting her, but killing her. He had gone through the motions in his mind of bringing her into the bathroom, drawing a bath, and drowning her like an unwanted kitten. *Kitten.* He recalled the tiny orange creature that she had burned and mauled. No—like a rat. A nuisance, an inconvenience, a . . . a burden to be cast off.

He drew his face up and peered into the mirror. He was a monster. A dark, dark creature lurked inside him and Tom could barely stand to live with it another moment. He would cut it out with a butcher knife, or burn it out with fire. He studied his blue irises and tiny pupils in the mirror. His eyes were bloodshot and his face shadowed in stubble. He ran a finger over the scarlet wound again, thinking of how he might asphyxiate them both with exhaust fumes from his pickup.

The lobby bell chimed, startling him. He looked again at the man in the mirror, but he seemed suddenly normal again. Weary and tired and beaten, but normal. The bell chimed again.

"Just a sec," he hollered, then took up his comb and did the best he could to hide the bite under his hair.

☼

Hap handed Lauren a parcel for the pet clinic through the service window. He stamped the little pink slip and dropped it into the box where it belonged. He'd seen Charlene go through the motions so many times that he had no trouble falling into the clerk's routine as postal patrons arrived with their packages and questions, their orders for stamps and requests for governmental forms. He'd thought of closing up for the day, but didn't want to put Charlene at risk of losing her job, and the reporter from *The Westerner* had never showed up, anyway. It was almost three o'clock; he doubted she was coming at all.

"Where's Charlene?" Lauren asked as she took the package.

Hap shrugged. "She wasn't feeling well."

Lauren looked suspiciously around the corner of the

service window, as if Charlene might be hiding in the back somewhere. "Doesn't she have someone she can call to fill in for her?"

"Yeah, but it was sudden. She got . . . food poisoning . . . or something. Had to leave on short notice. You know how that belly waug can be." He made a face and touched his stomach tentatively.

"Belly waug?"

Hap realized that he'd used a long-lost family term for stomachache, a term his mother had been fond of. "Nausea."

Lauren snorted. "I like the other phrase better." She took her package and started for the door. "I'll remember that one. Belly waug." She repeated the term on her way out the door, but she turned around again and walked back to the window.

"You've lived in Rocket awhile," she said.

" 'Bout twenty years."

"So you know about Charlene's brother and mother."

Hap wanted to slam the window closed and go sit down. He wasn't going to have this conversation with Lauren Kent or anyone else. "I don't know anything more than anyone else."

She studied him. "There are things this town doesn't talk about. Have you noticed that?"

"For good reason. It's a painful memory and there's no point in picking at an old scab."

"I guess." Lauren ran her hand over the label on her package thoughtfully, taking her time. "Do you know what happened to Maria Jemmett?"

Hap blinked at her. "What do you mean?"

"I mean, how did she die?"

"Didn't Tom tell you?"

Lauren shook her head, her eyes focused on Hap. "He doesn't talk about it."

Hap shrugged. "Well, she fell while cleaning the pool."

Lauren remained there in the doorway, waiting for Hap to elaborate.

He shifted his weight, hoping she'd leave, but she stubbornly stayed. "She had a . . ." He searched for the words he'd once put down in newsprint. ". . . a brain hemorrhage."

"They couldn't save her?"

"She didn't make it to the hospital in time. She lay down to rest and just slipped into a coma."

Lauren lingered at the counter as she digested the information, her eyes resting on the small space between them, making Hap more uncomfortable with each passing second. He didn't like telling Tom's past, especially given that this woman had recently been the man's main squeeze and he hadn't told her himself. Somehow it felt as though Hap were betraying Tom—again.

Lauren homed in on Hap. Those green eyes seemed to probe his insides like lasers, they were so intense. "He's never gotten over her, you know."

"I guess you don't get over things like that."

She nodded, but only as an acknowledgement of his point, not as though she agreed with it. "Gonna be a long, lonely life if he doesn't."

Hap scowled at the little pink parcel slips near his hand. When he looked up, Lauren was gone, crossing the parking lot toward her clinic at a stiff and rapid clip.

☼

Tom checked in three guests, wondering what the point of it all was. The waiting list for room six was fifteen days. He'd been pressed into service twice to plug a hole between the bedroom and the bathroom where the yellow jackets had started working their way back into that room. If he saved his motel, he'd need an exterminator.

The lot next door was empty now, the dead grass

flattened with patches of bare, powdery dirt showing through. Litter was strewn everywhere—paper cups and scraps of canvas, the bent aluminum poles of an old army tent. A mud hole had formed on the far end where the campers had relieved themselves, and without the barrier of the blankets they had used for privacy or the tents between it and the motel, its smell burned hot and pungent in the afternoon sun. Turnbull had succeeded in clearing the area out, leaving behind an incessant loneliness about the place that Tom had never noticed before. Where had those crazy people gone? he wondered.

He opened a small address book, picked up the phone, and dialed the number of the Hood River Mental Health Clinic. When the receptionist picked up, he asked for Dr. Taglione, and was promptly forwarded to her voice mail. He turned and looked into the apartment and down the hallway as the recording advised him to hang up and dial 9-1-1 if this was an emergency. Was it? The apartment was quiet, and Tom decided that Sienna had cried herself to sleep. She usually did after an emotional storm of this proportion. When he heard the beep signaling him to leave his message, he put the phone down. What would he say? Was it Sienna who needed a psychiatrist or himself? He ran his fingers over the back of the phone, leaving a sweaty streak and regretting that he hadn't left his number. But for some reason he was unwilling to call back.

As he thought about the logical next steps—steps he and Sienna had already been through too many times and with too little success in the years since Maria died— he could hear his dead wife's voice. It always came to him in these moments when he decided to try again, this time as clearly as the day they had fought about the decision he wrestled with now.

"It's the only answer, Tom." Maria had stood by the

lobby door, blocking his exit and forcing him to listen to her.

He hadn't listened but picked up his toolbox and started for room six. *Room six,* he thought now. It had had a broken air conditioner on that day, and he'd been fighting with it all morning, but to no avail. He'd only come back for his socket wrenches and a glass of water; the day had been so hot—just like today.

Maria had followed him out of the lobby and down the sidewalk, talking to his back. Imploring him to see reason. It wasn't the first conversation they'd had about this. "Sienna is not getting better. She's getting worse!"

"Worse than what?" he had snapped over his shoulder as he entered the room.

"She bit me this morning."

"She's a child. Children bite."

"Tom, listen to me!" Maria insisted, grabbing him by the arm and pulling him around to face her. She was silhouetted in the doorframe, the blinding sun lighting the sidewalk behind her in hot white. Maria had bared her shoulder and was leaning in to show him a deep purple wound along the soft curve below her neck. It had bled. "I can't deal with this kind of behavior. What will she do next?"

"What are you suggesting, then?" He knew exactly what she was suggesting. They'd been fighting about it for weeks by now. She wanted to try the prescriptions that neither of them could pronounce. Their agreement to let their daughter be who she was—not pollute her system with chemicals that did God knew what—was now lost to Maria. She was going back on her word. Changing her mind, her resolve weakening under the pressure.

"It's time we tried the medication. We were wrong. We were . . . we were idealistic, Tom. It just isn't the way we imagined it would be."

"I'm not putting our little girl on drugs," he had said, turning toward the dismantled air conditioner. His anger was near the breaking point, his head aching and his stomach in a knot. Maria could never stick to a plan; she always gave up too soon. But he wasn't backing down this time. It was too important. "We agreed. *You* agreed."

She didn't speak for a moment, her face stiff. When she did, the words flew from her lips in a poisonous rush. "You're not the one stuck dealing with her every minute of every hour of every day. Damn you, Tom! *You* can go find something to do. *You* can ignore the situation—pretend it's not so bad. Easy for *you!*"

Tom had rounded on her. "Listen to yourself."

"She frightens me sometimes, Tom. She has violent moments when I can't control her. I'm afraid for myself. I...sometimes I hate her."

The lobby door opened and in stepped Charlene. Startled by her arrival, Tom was jolted out of the past. Yet the memory clung to him—a pall he could not shake.

Charlene stood by the door, not smiling, not speaking. "Hi," she said at last.

"Hi." His head swam as he tried to return to the present.

"I...was in the area." She turned and looked out at the highway. It was late summer and farmers were harvesting their wheat fields to the north, sending the chaff and dust drifting down into the gorge like smoke from a forest fire. The air was brown and thick.

Tom thought of the mess in the apartment, his daughter locked in her room like a caged beast. "Charlene..." he started, but he didn't want to send her away. As much as he also didn't want her to see the state of things, he couldn't bear the idea of her leaving again now that she was standing in front of him. Her company seemed a sudden necessity, a precious gift that he was compelled to accept.

"What?" Oddly, she didn't approach the desk or start toward the apartment. She simply stood there, as if frightened or injured.

"Are you okay?"

She tensed and shook her head. "I don't think so."

He slid off the stool and came around the end of the counter and she rushed into him. He embraced her, and she pressed herself so tightly against him it was as though she had never felt the touch of another human being before.

After a moment, she pulled away and gave him an apologetic look. He pulled her back. He wasn't sorry.

"I didn't know where to go," she said. "I've just been wandering around all afternoon wanting to murder someone." Charlene's eyes went straight to Tom's ear. She walked into the apartment, leaving him in the hot, rank odor of the campsite toilet.

"I'm sorry," he called after her, but it was Maria he watched walk away. "I'm sorry," he whispered again, this time to Charlene. Would she hate him when she saw how he had locked his daughter up? He followed her, wanting to offer some explanation, but there was nothing he could say.

"Tom," she said, stepping over the mess in the hallway. "What happened?"

"She had a tantrum because she wanted you to come back. Every time you leave, she puts me through hell demanding that you return. I've wondered if you should visit her at all."

He bent and began picking up the things that had been on Sienna's dresser: the picture of Maria, a hairbrush, the sketchbook Charlene had brought her. "I took everything out of the room so she wouldn't hurt herself."

Charlene knelt down and began gathering up the crayons. She examined them, the way they had been chewed and broken.

"I know what you must think," Tom said.

Her head snapped up. "No. You don't."

"Then tell me."

She sat back on her heels and looked again at the mess. "You're in over your head."

He gazed down at the things in his hands and nodded.

"If you don't get help, this situation will ruin you. I know how this goes."

"What help is there?" Tom said, mostly to himself as he stacked the items against the wall. "We've tried the medications, the therapy. She only gets worse."

"What are you looking for? A miracle?"

Tom didn't know what to say. Yes? That sounded asinine from a grown man. No? That was a lie. Of course he was looking for a miracle. He'd always been looking for a miracle.

"There is no magic bullet. She's never going to be normal."

Such harsh words. Tom stared at Charlene. No one ever said these things, even if they thought them.

"All you can do is start where you are and make steps toward good. Every step is progress. Then, over time, you look back and see how far you've come. But there's no express train to where she's going."

"I don't know how much strength I have left."

Charlene touched his hand. "What other choice do you have?"

☀

Lauren slipped onto the bar stool at the Red Tail. "Evening, Stan."

"Dr. Kent," he said, placing a napkin on the bar in front of her. The jukebox played a Mark Knopfler tune, the whine of an electric guitar making Lauren feel lonelier than she already was.

"Call me Lauren. Please."

"What'll it be, Lauren?"

"Whiskey and ginger ale."

Stan went to work on her drink, and Lauren surveyed the smattering of patrons. A few stools down Dillard Meek watched muted NASCAR racing over a half-drunk pint of dark beer. She thought of the ugly brown fruit jar that Patrick had brought in, a sting of annoyance that the old man might be having sex with her assistant right now. The idea disgusted her, just like those pictures of Anna Nicole Smith and her oil tycoon husband. It was like a scene out of *Tales from the Crypt,* a decaying, wrinkled corpse and a young vibrant girl coupling like freaks.

Stan set the drink down and gave Lauren his best customer-service smile. He was a good bartender, she thought. He knew how to make people feel like the Red Tail was their own living room. She wondered how he was faring in this windless summer. Did he have his finances in order? Could he coast through a bad year? Or did he wake up at night with sharp anxiety over losing everything the way she did?

"Get you something to eat?"

She shook her head, but kept his attention with her gaze. "Tell me something."

"Name it."

"What's the scoop on Charlene Anderson's family?" Lauren picked up her drink and sipped it through the tiny straw designed for stirring.

Stan glanced down the bar. He seemed reluctant, which irritated Lauren. Why did everyone clam up about this? "I don't know much. What you've heard is what I've heard."

She cocked her head. "What have I heard?"

He studied her a moment, and she found herself drawn to his well-defined biceps and broad chest. He was a good-looking man, and would be better without the tattoos. "Let's not play games," he said.

"Let's not."

He stayed quiet, still contemplating her with his pale eyes, then said, "Charlene's a good kid. I don't want to disrespect her by dredging up the past. It was a terrible thing and talking about it won't change anything."

"That seems to be the party line." Lauren set her drink down, but noticed out of the corner of her eye that Dillard was leaning a little in her direction. He watched the television above the bar, but looked over just often enough for her to recognize that he was listening. "Same true of Maria Jemmett?" Lauren asked Stan a little louder.

"That was a sad accident, that's what that was."

"Brain hemorrhage, wasn't it?"

Stan nodded, then picked up his bar rag and swept it over the counter, making his way down the line and away from Lauren. She imagined he'd learned early how to gracefully extract himself from conversations he didn't want to have in order to be successful in this business. She watched the television awhile, then turned sideways on her stool and stared directly at the side of Dillard's head.

He glanced over once, then again. Each time quickly looking away, back to the television. Finally, when Lauren refused to leave him alone, he turned to her and nodded. "Evening, Dr. Kent."

"Hi, Dillard," she said and continued to stare.

He sipped his beer and tried to focus on the race, even cheering for one of the drivers, but he couldn't concentrate, and Lauren knew it.

She picked up her drink and moved down two stools to sit next to him. "How's business?"

He turned to her, but wouldn't make eye contact.

He'd always stammered and quaked in her presence. It had once annoyed her, but she'd come to find some perverse enjoyment in intimidating the man, though Lauren didn't believe she alone possessed any special power over him. He was just the insecure sort.

"Slow," he said. "But it doesn't matter. I'm not really in it for the money."

Lauren raised her eyebrows. "You're not?"

Dillard glanced at her quickly, then away. "No. I got that business from my father. It was paid for—even the building."

"Patrick came by today to show me an old canning jar he had."

Dillard perked up. "Was it amber colored?"

"Yeah, I guess you can call it that. Looked brown to me."

"I've been trying to get him to sell that to me for three years. It's rare." Dillard cut his eyes down the empty bar in each direction. "Don't tell Pat, but that jar is worth four hundred bucks."

"Really?"

"I've got a guy out in Connecticut who buys 'em. He's looking for one just like that."

"Patrick told me he wouldn't sell it."

Dillard slumped forward. "I know." Then he turned to Lauren with new interest. "How come Pat was showing you his fruit jar?"

"He owes me money for fixing up his dog."

Dillard nodded thoughtfully.

"If I can get that jar from him, how much will you give me for it?"

Dillard thought on it, scrutinizing Lauren. "I gotta make a profit."

"Thought you weren't in it for the money."

"Well, what's the point if I don't make anything?" He scratched his chin. "Two hundred."

"Three."

"That only leaves me a hundred bucks."

"More than you'll get if it stays with Patrick." Lauren didn't know why she was making this deal; three hundred dollars wasn't going to make much difference in her business finances. But there was something fun about the challenge. And she believed that Dillard would be more forthcoming with information if he viewed her as an ally. "How badly does this guy want it? Would he pay four-fifty? Five hundred? Not everyone is suffering like the folks around here, you know?"

Dillard smiled quietly to himself. "Get the jar and I'll find out."

She nodded and ordered another whiskey and ginger ale. "What do you make of this crazy business with the Jemmett Motel?"

Dillard's eyes lit up, but he quickly reined in his enthusiasm. "Aren't you going out with Tom?"

The question cut through her like a hot blade, but she didn't let on. "We're taking a little time off to reevaluate things."

"So you broke up?"

She winced inwardly. "I guess you could say that."

He leaned in and took on a confidential tone. "It's the little girl." He nodded and straightened up.

"How so?"

"She's the agent for a poltergeist."

Lauren couldn't stop herself from smiling.

"She is. I think it's her dead mother." Dillard's voice dropped to a whisper. "That question you just asked Stan—about Maria Jemmett." He gulped down the last of his beer and shoved the glass toward the other side of the bar. "Nobody knows what really happened. Tom says he left her alone with the girl. He came in here—this very tavern—to shoot pool. When he got home she was unconscious."

"You don't believe that?"

"Well, I think there's more to it than that. Poltergeists happen in places where there's been a violent death. It all adds up, if you think about it. Maria's death, the little girl now going into puberty, the strange things happening out there, people dying. Dying!" He went quiet as Stan set Lauren's drink on the counter.

"Another one?" Stan asked, collecting Dillard's glass. Dillard nodded and waited for Stan to fill a new pint and set it down. After the bartender had moved on, Dillard looked Lauren in the eye. "Her death had to have been violent, or this wouldn't be happening now. I think the little girl somehow killed her. She killed a kitten a couple weeks ago; she's got a violent streak."

As Lauren was trying to come up with a response to this odd information, a young couple she'd met once at the clinic burst through the front door. The man had a cell phone pressed to his ear.

"Turn on channel eleven," he shouted. The two stood expectantly as Stan fumbled for the remote control.

"The motel is on *Pacific Northweird*," the woman said, pointing when Stan had found the right channel.

A reporter in a bright red suit was shoving her microphone into Tom's face. His hair was mussed and he looked as if he'd just awakened from hibernation. He stammered out some words that Lauren couldn't make out, and scowled irritably at the camera. He looked as insane as any person she'd ever seen on this show. But that didn't stop her heart from fluttering and her hands tingling at the sight of him. The footage abruptly cut to the reporter on Main Street in Rocket, the bakery and the antiques shop behind her.

"Turn it up," Dillard said. "That's my store."

"There's no question, but *something* weird is going on at the Jemmett Motel. Some have gone so far as to suggest there's a child involved," the reporter said. "This is

Wendy Castle for *Pacific Northweird,* back to you, Charles."

Lauren turned to Dillard, suddenly suspicious. "Were you the one who suggested a child was involved?"

He shook his head, and kept shaking it with absolute resolve. "It was Petra. They interviewed her. Even bought some of her Jemmett bread."

" 'Jemmett bread'?" Lauren slumped back on her stool. What the hell was going on with this town?

"She bakes it in the shape of a six," Dillard said.

Stan shook his head with vehement disapproval. "And people eat that shit up. Morons!" He picked up the bar rag and started sweeping it across the already-clean counter. "They better leave that girl alone."

24

TOM STOOD IN THE HALL as Charlene coaxed Sienna into bed. It was late; past eleven. He'd had to give his daughter an antihistamine tablet to make her drowsy, not only because she'd slept for several hours after her tantrum and showed no signs of being ready for bed, but because he wanted a little time alone with Charlene. Since she'd arrived, he could hardly keep from touching her—a hand on her shoulder, a finger stroke along her hair. She didn't seem to mind, in fact paused several times to press against his skin as if to savor a fleeting moment. He felt flooded with happiness.

She'd spent the evening talking to Sienna and asking her funny questions. They were sprawled on the floor in the living room, the crayons and paper between them— Charlene always got down on Sienna's level, he noticed.

"Do you think the color yellow likes the others?" Charlene asked.

Sienna at first just scowled at the ideas Charlene was tossing around, fingering the yellow crayon, which was now only an inch long, then pawing through the pile of crayons for others that were close to it in hue.

"Do you think blue is a boy or a girl?" Charlene asked.

"Girl," Sienna said without hesitation.

Charlene found a dark blue crayon in the pile, then looked for another that was sky blue. She held the two up. "Are they both girls?"

Sienna grunted an affirmative.

Tom wondered how Charlene had thought of these questions and why. It was interesting; he'd certainly never considered colors to be gender specific before.

"What about numbers?" Charlene said. "Do you think the number eight is a boy or a girl?"

"Boy," Sienna said and began coloring. "A brown boy."

Charlene looked for the brown crayon and began to draw a circle on the corner of Sienna's paper, but the child swatted at her hand, pushing her away and whining.

"No," Sienna said in an angry, high-pitched tone. "It's not for him."

Charlene merely nodded and dropped the crayon on the pile. After watching Sienna for a few minutes, she said, "You can just say no. You don't have to hit me. I don't like to be hit."

Sienna glanced at Charlene, then turned back to her drawing.

"Do *you* like to be hit?"

"No."

"I won't hit you if you won't hit me, okay?"

Sienna look up and nodded, agreeing to the terms. Tom smiled. He'd had moments like this with Sienna, too, though they were rare. She would occasionally grasp, with intense clarity, a concept that had previously been too difficult or elusive. He had come to understand that it was just these kinds of instances that seemed to stick the best. It was a moment like this when he finally potty trained her. She was five, almost six, and he was getting nasty notes from the school along with plastic bags filled with wet and soiled clothes. He hadn't actually been trying at the time—he'd already tried every-thing he could think of by then. He was simply so ex-hausted and frustrated that he said matter-of-factly that he didn't like to smell bad and wear wet pants, so he used the toilet. She had looked at him a long time, then agreed, and mostly did, too, after that.

"Daddy hits me," Sienna said, still hunched over the drawing.

Tom's cheeks burned hot as Charlene glanced up at him. "Only an occasional, well-deserved spanking."

Charlene looked back at Sienna. "I don't think spank-ing translates to well deserved in her mind. But I can un-derstand your frustration."

"Can you? Can anyone?" he asked.

"Yes, I can." Her response resonated with surety.

He was satisfied with that. Charlene wasn't judging him but teaching him. And that was perhaps a more dif-ficult thing to accept. Shouldn't he know how to deal with Sienna by now? Shouldn't he be the one teaching others? He left the two of them in the living room and made spaghetti and meatballs.

The phone had rung and rung throughout the evening, but Tom refused to answer it. Room six was booked for twenty days, and he figured if he didn't an-swer the phone anyone serious about staying in room six would simply show up in person. Then he could con-vince them to rent another room instead. His mind occa-sionally floated over the reporter's claim that a man had been mauled by bullmastiffs after staying in that room, but he hadn't gone back to verify the name. He would do it later. A part of him didn't really want to know if it was true. It was easier to imagine it was all simply coinci-dence if he didn't know the names of room six's past guests or the fates that had befallen them. He had never been a superstitious man.

Now, as he watched Sienna's eyes close while Charlene

read from the ragged encyclopedia that was missing its cover, he decided he should buy her more books. Maybe things weren't as bad as they had seemed. Charlene's presence had a soothing effect on everything, and Tom began wondering what it would be like to have a wife again. He'd never given it any serious consideration since Maria died, for reasons too numerous to ponder. But he didn't want to go back to the way it had been as recently as this morning; he needed someone—especially someone who was good with Sienna. And yet, he didn't want to mistake his gratitude for more significant feelings.

When Sienna fell asleep, Charlene closed the book and turned off the light. After she'd pulled the door shut and joined Tom in the hall, she tipped her chin up and gazed at him. Her cheeks were red and her forehead shiny in the late-summer heat. He felt like Goliath next to this small, fierce woman, and he placed his broad hands on both sides of her face, drawing her closer. She didn't protest, and he bent to gently kiss her.

"You're an angel from heaven. I swear you are," he whispered.

She giggled. He kissed her again, deeply, and they moved into the living room and onto the sofa, where they made love quietly and slowly. Each move came deliberately, every touch savored and reciprocated. And for a brief time all his troubles vanished and he was safe in the arms of someone who understood.

Hap climbed into his van early the next morning, bored and seeking some small news item to keep him busy. It was Saturday, and he was glad. He needed a break from the post office, and a break, too, from Charlene. He'd really screwed up yesterday by sharing Petra's absurd and hurtful comments, and he had suffered mightily for his insensitivity. He'd tossed all night, unable to sleep, thinking about the boy, Stephen Anderson, and how he himself had so easily fallen into step with the town's way of thinking. Stephen had never been real to Hap. He was just the town freak—every town has one. Even after Charlene took the job as Rocket's postal clerk, Hap hadn't given the boy much thought. Oh, he'd recalled the incident—the murder-suicide. How could he not? But so much time had passed by then that he simply didn't consider Stephen a real person anymore, just a victim of a tragic event he could turn into a headline.

Hap hated himself this morning. Not only had he ruined Charlene's day, but when he turned on one of his favorite television shows, Tom was there stammering like a madman while the reporter accused him of running a dangerous motel. And with Petra and Dillard pumping stories into everyone's heads about Sienna...Hap wanted to take back the article. He imagined it would've been better if Rocket had simply dried up and died in this blazing summer bereft of tourists.

As he pulled onto Main, fiddling with the air conditioner, trying to get some cool air flowing, Hap noticed a handwritten sign leaning against the wall in front of the bakery. He drove slowly past in order to read it. He'd made out *The End* and *Repent* by the time Hap recognized that weird preacher sitting at one of Petra's sidewalk tables, a cup of coffee and a cinnamon roll in front of him. His long legs were folded up under him like a cricket and his greasy hair was carefully parted in the center of his head and combed straight down over his ears. The preacher glowered at Hap as he passed.

Hap drove on, wondering if there was more to this connection between Petra and the itinerant preacher than baker and patron. She'd go in for his brand of logic, Hap imagined. It was bad for Rocket to have this man standing on Main Street, though. Certainly Petra would recognize that. As he passed the Windy Point Diner, the lot was crammed with buses and cars that looked strangely familiar. He was several miles up Highway 14, gazing out at a fishing boat bobbing in the sapphire river, when he realized those were the same vehicles that'd been parked in the lot next to Tom's motel. Someone—or something—had driven them off. He circled back into town, deciding to get breakfast at the diner to hear Linda's perspective of this group, then stop at the motel.

☼

Tom hummed a tune to himself as he set out the morning doughnuts. The thought of Charlene, still sleeping tangled in a sheet on his living room floor, made his palms tingle. He imagined that last night was the best night he'd had in ten years. He felt somehow younger today, more energetic and ready to take on the day—whatever it brought.

The latest room-six guest appeared in the lobby, a middle-aged man with thinning hair and skinny arms.

"Morning," Tom said. "Coffee's hot and doughnuts are fresh."

The man rubbed his hand over his head and nodded. He looked as though he hadn't gotten much sleep.

"How was the room?"

The man glanced up, then poured some coffee for himself. "Had weird dreams all night. First I was being chased by a snake, then it was a spider, then it was a man with a yellow raincoat." He methodically emptied five packets of sugar, pouring each one into the cup and throwing away the paper before tearing open the next. "I got up and watched TV for a while, but I kept hearing this screaming. I even walked out into the parking lot, but I could only hear it in the room."

"What kind of screaming? I didn't hear anything."

"I don't know, like a woman or something. Not like a terrified scream...more like a mad scream."

"You get back to sleep?" Tom thought of Sienna, but dismissed the idea, then considered the seven or so other guests that had checked in the night before. There had been a family next door in room five, but they'd left before the sun was up, dropping their key on the counter and not bothering to wait for coffee or doughnuts.

The man nodded. "Yeah, but then I dreamed I was on a barge going down the Columbia and it wouldn't dock. I was stuck on it. The only way to get to shore was to jump in and swim."

Tom didn't know what to say, so he just listened.

"I can't swim. And that water is treacherous. Have you seen those currents?" The man shivered at the thought, then stirred his coffee and took a sip.

"So what do you think it all means?" Tom asked. After all, this man had forked out two hundred and fifty dollars to stay in that room.

"It's an omen. I always have bad dreams before I win something."

Tom nodded, and looked his guest over more carefully. The man didn't immediately present himself as crazy, but with some people he had to let them talk awhile before it became clear.

The man opened his wallet and pulled out a Powerball ticket. "This is it. Tonight's the night." He held it up for Tom to see. "Two hundred and eighty million bucks." He returned the ticket to his billfold and fished in his front pocket, coming up with the key to room six. He tossed it on the counter with a clatter and nodded to Tom, then disappeared out the front door.

"Good luck," Tom said as the man pulled onto the highway. He mulled what the man had said about the screaming. No one had complained. Someone always complained about things like that. It left him with an un-settled feeling.

"Do you need some help cleaning rooms today?" Charlene was standing in the doorway, wearing his shirt. Her tan legs were bare and her hair was messy.

Tom's crotch swelled at the sight of her. "Hello there."

She smiled and waited for an answer to her question.

"It's Saturday. That's your day off. I can handle this stuff in my sleep."

"I don't mind." She joined him behind the desk where he sat on the stool.

He pulled her close, straddling her, and they ex-changed a passionate morning kiss. "Wanna move in together?"

She smiled. "We only started seeing each other."

"I know, but you know when things are right. And this is right."

"Will we always have to sleep on the floor?"

He thought about this. "Just until the bank takes my motel, then we can look for a house."

She pulled back and looked at him. "What do you mean? Are you that close to losing this place?"

He nodded.

"But I thought you were doing better since Hap wrote that article."

"Too little, too late, I think. I can't make up three months of missed payments, even renting that one room for four times the price."

"What are you going to do?"

"Hmm..." Tom ran his fingers up and down Charlene's spine, feeling each vertebra through the cot-ton of his smelly shirt. "I don't exactly know. I was thinking I'd have to move to Portland and get a job."

"Portland?" She looked horrified.

"It's not such a bad place."

"It's huge. It's a big city. And there's no surfing. It's so . . ."

The phone rang and Tom looked at it, but didn't pick it up.

"Aren't you going to answer that?"

"Why? They want to know if they can stay in room six, but it's booked up until the bank comes. What's the point?"

Charlene picked it up. "Jemmett Motel."

Tom enjoyed the sound of his name coming from Charlene's lips.

"He's . . . not here. Can I take a message?" She listened. "Benjamin Leesburg? Never heard of him." She paused to listen as someone went on at length. "Yeah, well, a lot of people have stayed out here. This motel was built in the sixties, you know."

Tom remembered the reporter and the bullmastiffs, but that wasn't the name she'd given. He opened the drawer where he kept his ledger and pulled out the scrap of paper with the name Hemphill on it.

"I see," Charlene said. "I'll tell him." She hung up and turned to Tom. "That TV show *Pacific Northweird* did a story on your motel last night."

"She didn't tell me she was with *Pacific Northweird*. She just said channel eleven. I thought it was the news. I would've been a lot nicer if I'd known it was that show."

"Well, they've had a bunch of people calling their studio claiming they stayed in room six and they want to be compensated for damages. This Benjamin Leesburg has hired an attorney. He says he came down with a rare form of cancer after checking out of room six. They want you to verify that he stayed here for their story."

Tom laughed.

"This isn't funny, Tom."

"Sure it is. How's he gonna prove that?"

"It's going to cost you a fortune to defend yourself."

"Baby, I'm broke. It doesn't matter what they do. Those people are after money, and I don't have any. Come the end of the month, I won't have property, either. Unless I can convince the bank to give me more time. I'm sorry the guy has cancer, but it's not my fault, and he's not going to cash in on me."

☼

Lauren lounged in bed, thinking about Tom and his motel. He looked like a complete lunatic on television, and that put her off. It's what he deserved for getting on his high horse about Charlene while he was tricking people into paying two hundred dollars for a supposedly haunted room in his motel. And though she didn't believe that Sienna had anything to do with the incidents in room six—those were purely coincidental—Lauren thought the fact that everyone else in Rocket believed it should be one more clue for Tom that he needed to get some help for that girl.

She looked at the clock; it was past nine. Anna would be at the clinic, doing nothing right now and getting paid for it, too. Sitting in front of the computer, not answering the phone, not making appointments, not cleaning the exam rooms, all because no one was calling, no one was asking to see the vet, and no one was bringing in their pets. Lauren doubted that Anna would even spend the time surfing the Internet. She was too uptight and rigid to break a rule, even when no one was there to see her do it.

Lauren rolled to a sitting position and put her feet on the cool wood floor. Her head spun from the four whiskies and ginger ales she'd had the night before. The Red Tail had enjoyed a brief but lively crowd after *Pacific Northweird* aired the segment on the Jemmett Motel. Locals excited to see their tiny hamlet on television and anxious to tell everyone about their connection to the motel, however questionable or tentative, turned out in surprising numbers. They mingled casually with an odd crowd of disgruntled, smelly hippies who had been chased out of their campsite by the sheriff. After wandering around Rocket for several hours, the transient group had gotten permission to camp in the parking lot of the Windy Point Diner for twenty-four hours so long as they agreed to use the indoor facilities and promised to buy at least one meal each. Lauren had marveled at how low Rocket's business sector was willing to stoop in order to hold on.

Dillard had been in fine form, espousing his theories about poltergeists. The crowd listened intently, nodding and adding their assent. He'd finally found the perfect format and the willing audience he'd been craving. He didn't drink; he was too busy enjoying himself. Only one person disagreed with Dillard about the poltergeist, suggesting that it was global warming that had caused these unusual things to happen. Lauren's memory was fuzzy after that because the drinks had kicked in and she was more interested in flirting with Stan, who was too busy to give her his full attention. She guessed he was also a little intimidated by her. Blue-collar men usually were.

She stared down at her feet, which were swollen, her toes little round sausages with pink nails. She held up her hand and examined her fingers and wrist. She needed to lay off the alcohol; it always made her puffy. She rubbed her other hand over her lower abdomen, assessing the damage. She'd gained six pounds since she and Tom first argued about Sienna. If she didn't get things on track soon, she'd need a shopping day in Portland for larger clothes, a thought that irritated her and made her want to drink. Her pants were already too tight, and those were her fat pants. Facing her closet in the morning was rapidly becoming the most unpleasant task of the day. She was disgusted with herself.

At the clinic, Lauren found Anna sitting quietly behind the reception desk, watching traffic go by on Main Street.

"Morning, Dr. Kent," she said cheerfully. "How are you today?"

Lauren frowned. "Anyone call?"

"No."

"What have you been doing all morning?"

Anna looked dismayed. "The exam rooms are clean and all the filing is done. I've been waiting for appointments to come in."

"Is there anything on the schedule?" Lauren looked over Anna's shoulder at the computer monitor. She'd spent an ungodly amount of money on this state-of-the-art practice-management system, but she hated it because it was too complicated to use. She didn't know how to get a report out of the damn thing, and it never seemed to support the features that she wanted, like sorting her client list by the breed of pet they owned. It offered only cat, dog, bird, rabbit, and so on, as if there was no difference between a person who owned a Chihuahua, someone with a golden retriever, and someone with a pit bull.

"Patrick is bringing Crispy in for his one-week check this afternoon." Anna's face flushed pink at the mention of Patrick's name.

Lauren paused and watched her. "So...how was your evening with Patrick? Did you get those coins cleaned and cataloged?"

"Oh, yes. We had a lot of fun. Patrick brought his dog over and my kids took turns pretending to be nurses taking care of him."

Oh, barf, Lauren thought. "That must have been fun. Did Patrick stay late?"

Anna blushed a deeper purple, and Lauren knew the answer. After an awkwardly silent moment, Anna said, "Don't forget to take Patrick's balance out of my check."

"How are you going to feed your kids if you pay his bill for him?"

"I called my ex this morning and told him he better pony up some money for his kids or I'm gonna take him back to court. He's so far behind in his payments that they'll garnish his wages if I make a big deal about it, and he knows it. He's bringing some money over tonight."

Lauren picked up Crispy's file to review and took it to her office. She paused in the doorway. "Did you see the motel on *Pacific Northweird* last night?"

Anna stared at her blankly.

"I guess you don't watch that show, huh?"

"I don't have a television."

Lauren scowled. No wonder the girl was so strange.

"I've heard the rumors about that place, though," Anna said. "I think it's God's punishment for all the sins that have been committed in those rooms."

"You do?"

Anna nodded vigorously. "You know what those people do who stay out there in that motel?"

"What?" Lauren struggled with the urge to point out that Anna had just slept with a man three times her age, and on the first date, if she would even call it a date.

"Those surfers are all drug addicts."

Lauren decided to let it go. "I'll be in my office if anyone needs me. And if you get a call, try and convince them to bring their pet in. I don't care if it's a broken toenail; tell them they need to see me right away."

"But, Dr. Kent, that's not honest."

Lauren closed her eyes, willing herself to have patience. "Anna? Do you want to have a job tomorrow?"

"Of course, I do. I need this job."

"Well then, do what it takes to bring in business. Without it, I won't need an assistant anymore." Lauren closed the door and blew out her breath. *Stupid girl.* She sat down at her desk, opened the drawer, and pulled out a bottle of aspirin. What she really wanted was a glass of wine. It was going to be a long day. After swallowing two pills dry, she started to put the bottle back in her drawer, but something occurred to her. Aspirin. Blood thinner. Commonly involved in deaths from brain hemorrhage. She thought of Maria Jemmett and booted up her computer. She opened an Internet reference site for physicians and typed in *coup–contrecoup injuries*. A page came up describing the usual scenario: a blow to the head with very little outward injury, the inertia of the brain causing it to slap the opposite side of the skull hard enough to lead to a subdural hematoma. The patient suffers a gradual decline to confusion, loss of consciousness, then death.

Lauren made notes on a piece of paper, recalling Dillard's claim that Maria must have died a violent death. There would have been an autopsy in a death like Maria's. Perhaps she could get the records—Ellie certainly could.

## 25

TOM SNAPPED A CLEAN SHEET over the bed in room six and tucked the corners tightly under. He'd always loved the smell of freshly bleached sheets—one reason he didn't really mind the housekeeping chores. But as he made up the bed he felt guilty about owing Hood River Laundry for two months of service that he'd never be able to pay. He'd once considered installing an industrial washer and drier and doing the laundry himself, but he'd never get the sheets and pillowcases pressed so crisply, and he prided himself on that aspect of his motel. Besides, the soiled sheets and towels could be pretty rank after some of his guests, and it made him nervous to handle them. He'd just as soon let the laundry service take the risk of infectious diseases.

As he wiped down the surfaces of the room, not allowing any dust to collect anywhere, he thought of Charlene, still in his apartment, spending more time with Sienna. What could he do to convince her to stay forever?

The bright day outside hurt his eyes to look through the open door and he turned away from it, but not before he glimpsed some small movement there along the sidewalk. He paused, expecting someone to come in, but no one was there. Then he remembered the way Maria had been in this precise space, the way her form was silhouetted against the hot day, her hips round and her waist tight. Had he forgotten that she had hit him at that moment? Maybe. And where had Sienna come from? She hadn't been there with them, not at first. The sequence of events tangled in his memory when he allowed himself to think about it. He couldn't sort out what exactly happened. Sometimes he couldn't even remember how Maria got hurt. He hoped that Sienna couldn't, either.

"Hello?" he called, but no one answered. He waited. He'd seen something, he was certain of it. An odd sensation pulled at his insides, some strain of fear, or dread. "Hello?" he called again.

But no one answered.

Tom walked into the bathroom to make a final check of his work. He'd once forgotten to look behind the door and the next guest to check in was greeted by a dirty pair of panties. It was clean this time, so he returned to the main room, still plagued by an uneasiness he'd never experienced here before. It occurred to him how odd it was that he could come and go in this room day after day after day without feeling something. But it hadn't been here that he'd found Maria. He'd found her on their bed. Maybe *found* was not the right word. He'd stumbled in around two in the morning, drunk, thrown up in the bathroom, then flopped onto their bed and passed out sprawled next to her. He never knew that she was unconscious—perhaps already too deeply injured to save. It wasn't until morning when he'd been up for nearly an hour, fed their daughter, and checked out two guests, but she was still sleeping, that he came in to yell at her to get up and help him with the chores if she was going to stay, after all.

His own cruelty is what haunted him most about that

day. The fury he still felt for her a day after they had fought, his anger burning hot and long. That was his downfall—Maria had always said so—his inability to let things go. He wasn't about to forgive Maria or make peace that day, either. He had intended to make her life as miserable as possible while she remained there. So when he realized that something was wrong, he just stood there, staring at his wife's motionless body. He had no idea how long it was before he picked up the phone and dialed 9-1-1. He couldn't find a pulse and neither could the paramedics.

"What happened to her?" one of the responders had asked. "Did she hit her head or something? How did she lose consciousness?"

*Yes*, he thought. *She hit her head, but that was yesterday. She was fine. She hit her head, but she got up and walked away.*

"Do you know if she hit her head?" the man repeated.

Tom had nodded, not thinking things all the way through.

"How did she hit her head?" The paramedic was about Tom's age at the time, early thirties. He was looking intently at Tom, speaking to him like he was a frightened child. "Try and remember."

Tom remembered, but fear was suddenly gripping him, causing his blood to pulse through his ears at the same volume as the questions that were coming at him.

"Mr. Jemmett? Did you see your wife hit her head?"

He'd nodded, his mind racing. The pool. The pool was empty. They'd just drained it with the intent to clean it. It was cement and deep. "She . . . she was cleaning the pool and slipped."

"Did she fall?"

"Yes," Tom said, looking the paramedic in the eye. Tom still remembered the yellow-brown color of those eyes—kind eyes. "Yes, she fell in at the deep end."

"Did she hit her head when she fell?"

"I—I don't know. Maybe. Yes, I think she said her head hurt."

"But she was conscious?"

"Yes, yes. She got up and..." Tom paused and watched the others wheel Maria out on a stretcher. They were hurrying, snapping orders to each other. "She walked back to our apartment."

Tom had packed up his three-year-old daughter and followed them to the hospital, where he answered the same question so many times that he could tell the lie forward and backward by then without thinking. Only one person, the nurse who tended Maria in the emergency room, cocked her head to one side, eyed Sienna through the open door, and asked the question in a way that made Tom know that she didn't believe his story. She didn't believe it was an innocent fall. It frightened Tom so badly that he found himself relieved when the doctor laid his hand on Tom's shoulder and broke the news that Maria was gone. She would never be able tell them what had really happened.

The uneasiness in Tom's stomach was growing like an air bubble as he recalled those moments. His obscene first response to his beloved wife's passing. He looked out the window again, but no one was there. He picked up his cleaning supplies, and wheeled the vacuum out onto the sidewalk where he left it. His next room-six guest awaited.

☀

"Ellie? It's Lauren." Lauren got up to check that her office door was latched, stretching the phone cord across the room like a tether. "How's business in Hood River?"

"You really need to consider moving up here," Ellie said. "There's plenty of room for one more vet. People are moving here in droves. You'll be a rich woman."

"Maybe," Lauren said, no longer averse to the idea of leaving Rocket. What was here for her now?

"Did you hear about that game farm in central Idaho?"

"No," Lauren said, trying to think of the best way to ask Ellie the question she'd intended.

"This guy has a whole herd of elk down there that just got loose. Now he fesses up that he hadn't been keeping records. Fish and Game think the elk might be carrying red deer."

Lauren recalled the virus from vet school. "That'll spread to the wild population."

"Yeah, no shit," Ellie said. "The bastard ought to go to prison."

Lauren was surprised by Ellie's passionate response on the issue, but Ellie was an animal lover at heart. She probably should have been a vet. That didn't matter, though, Lauren hadn't called to talk about diseases in big-game herds. "Hey, do you still have that friend at the coroner's office in Portland?"

"Yeah, why?"

"Think she can get ahold of Maria Jemmett's autopsy report?"

*"Lauren!"*

"Look, I got some information the other day that sounded suspicious. I just want to follow up on it, that's all."

"I don't know. You can't just go pulling records like that, you know. We have laws. I'm sure you've heard of HIPAA."

Lauren rolled her eyes. "Of course I have."

"Well, this isn't like veterinary medicine. These aren't beagles, they're real people. With privacy rights."

Lauren was quiet, her chest tight with anger. How stupid did Ellie think she was? And what kind of friend questioned motives like this? She was tiring of Ellie's holier-than-thou attitude.

"Lauren, it's time you let this whole thing with Tom go. Move up here, leave it behind."

Lauren slammed down the receiver and flipped her middle finger at the phone. "Fuck you!"

☀

Hap swung into the motel parking lot behind Charlene's dented Ford Focus with the faded windsurfing decals in the back window. He stared at it a moment, nodding his head. "Spent the night, did we?" He slid out and started for the lobby, where he found his blonde officemate perched on the stool behind the desk.

"Hap," she said and smiled. "What are you doing here?"

"I should be asking you that question."

Charlene shrugged and smiled again, a little more shyly this time.

"What happened to the transient camp next door?" He swept his hand out at the empty lot. A dust devil danced along the roadway, but he figured it was kicked up by a passing car. He knew better than to get his hopes up about the wind anymore.

"Sheriff Turnbull cleared them out."

"Cleared them all into town is what he did. Now they're camped outside the Windy Point Diner."

"That place is a dive, anyway."

Hap scratched his chin. He'd never paid much attention to Charlene's preferences on eating establishments, but he was coming to see that it was the all-night grocery with the variety of waiting mutts or the Red Tail for her. The bakery was out, and he didn't think Charlene spent enough time at home to buy groceries. "It's not that bad."

She grimaced. "Yeah, if you don't mind cardboard and glue for lunch."

"Linda makes a mean cherry pie." When Charlene didn't comment, Hap looked around for Tom and Sienna. "You holding down the fort?"

"Sienna's watching TV, and Tom is cleaning rooms. I was gonna go home for a shower and a change of clothes, but I thought I'd wait until he was done in case Sienna needs anything. I think I'm going to bring her some paint, but don't tell Tom. He'll be all worried about her eating it or something."

Hap peered down the row of rooms to see where Tom was. He knew Tom always started at the far end and worked his way back toward the lobby. The laundry cart, which was heaping with knotted yellow sheets, was sitting outside room two.

"Can I ask you something?" Charlene said.

"Sure."

"That stuff you wrote about room six—you and Tom just made that up, right?"

Hap shifted his weight from one foot to the other. "What makes you think we made it up?"

"I know there were a couple of accidents—the woman who was run over and then that guy who died of a heart attack. But those were isolated events, right?"

"Don't forget about the guy who won the lottery."

She ran her fingers through her hair and examined the ragged ends. "What I'm asking is, do *you* believe something supernatural is happening here?" Her eyes came up to meet his and he believed there was a little fear in them.

"Supernatural?" He shrugged. "I don't think so. Something weird, maybe. It's probably just coincidence."

"So you do think something is going on in room six?"

"Why? Are you planning to stay in there?" Hap laughed, trying to lighten the mood. "What would happen to you if you did?"

"I don't believe in karma, if that's what you're asking.

There's no way you can convince me that people get what they have coming. Some never get what's coming to them and others get way more."

Hap felt like a heel for teasing her. To suggest that karma was real to Charlene was to imply that she'd done something to deserve the pain she'd suffered in her short life. Whatever transient affinity he himself had felt for the idea of karma dissolved right then. "No, I'm sure you're right about that."

"I just want to know if you two really believe this or if Tom is hiking the price up on that room knowing that it's a joke."

Hap shook his head. "It's not a joke, and Tom isn't behind it. I wrote that article without his knowledge or his permission. I thought it would bring in some tourists is all. You thought it would, too, remember? Tom is just accepting what these people are willing to pay. He didn't set that price, they did."

"I know, but I heard him tell a man this morning that someone who stayed in room eight met the girl of his dreams at the swimming pool last week."

"Maybe it's true."

She peered doubtfully out the lobby window at the pool. "He was asking ninety-nine a night for that room. It usually goes for fifty-nine."

Hap sighed. "Cut Tom a break, will you, Charlene? He's trying to save his motel."

"That's just it; I don't think he is. He said it was too little, too late."

"Are you the moral police now?"

"Screw you," she said and got up from the stool. She left him in the lobby and went into the apartment.

"There's the Charlene I love," he called after her.

Hap wandered outside and found Tom rolling the laundry cart into the small room off the lobby where there were shelves of neatly folded white towels and sheets on one side and a rack of spray bottles with various cleaners on the other. In the back, like side-by-side sentinels, stood the vacuum and the carpet shampooer.

"Mitsui," Tom said.

"Got a beer for a thirsty friend?"

"Sure." Tom pulled the door shut and jiggled the knob to make sure it was locked.

"You got Charlene working as a desk clerk now?" Hap said to Tom's back as he followed him into the lobby.

"Are you kidding? She can lie around and do absolutely nothing as far as I'm concerned."

Hap had already figured that.

Tom disappeared into the apartment for a few minutes, and Hap could hear him talking to Charlene. "Will I see you later?" he asked. She said he would, followed by a silence during which Hap guessed that they were kissing, then she left through the back door, letting the screen slap back loudly against the jamb. Tom returned to the lobby with two beers and handed one to Hap.

Hap leaned against the counter and cracked his beer open while Tom looked up his next room-six guest and dialed the cell number he'd left.

"Your room is ready," he said and waited. "Room six. The Jemmett Motel. You reserved it earlier in the week."

Hap could hear the man make some excuse about being too far away now.

"Gonna charge your Visa. You guaranteed your reservation."

The man was outraged, and his voice carried through the line. "Give the room to someone else."

"That's why we call it a guarantee," Tom said. "You understood that when you gave me the card number."

The man called Tom an asshole and hung up.

"People still paying four times the rate?" Hap asked.

"You heard him. Guess not. I've been expecting a no-show any day."

"At least you can still charge him. Is the extra business gonna pull you through?"

"Doubt it. But it's been a fun way to go out."

"What are you going to do?"

Tom sipped his beer and shrugged. "I don't know. Guess it depends some on what Charlene wants to do."

"That sounds pretty serious. You two just started seeing each other."

"It's right, though. Don't ask me how I know. It's just right."

Hap thought on that a moment, wondering if Charlene felt the same way. She'd been on a fishing expedition to catch Tom for as long as they'd shared office space, but she didn't impress Hap as having found Mr. Right when he encountered her here behind the desk a short time ago. Maybe it was simply the conquest that excited her. Was she marriage material? Hap had never thought so before and didn't have evidence to support the idea now.

"I'm gonna call some of these people and see if anyone else wants the room tonight," Tom said, looking over his list. "Maybe I can get double the income on it tonight."

"You don't really believe something is going on in room six, do you?" Hap asked.

Tom looked up from the list. It took him a long time to answer. "I don't know. I like to think I don't."

Hap nodded. As long as Tom didn't believe it, what harm could there be in leaving the question out there for other people to ponder?

Lauren slid onto the now familiar stool at the Red Tail, and Stan greeted her by first name.

"Whiskey–ginger ale?" he asked.

"No, make it a snowshoe."

"Don't know that one."

"Brandy on the rocks with a shot of peppermint schnapps floating on top."

He nodded and went to work on the drink. After he'd delivered it, Stan pulled a small book from a drawer beneath the cash register. It was an address book, and he opened it to the letter *s*. The pages were crowded with small, tight script. He found the alphabetical location for *snowshoe,* but there was no space to make the entry. He drew a careful line to the margin and added the new drink as Lauren watched.

"Do I get a free one for teaching you a new recipe?"

He gazed at her a moment, then said, "Why not?"

She smiled, trying to think of something else to say. The more time she spent here, and it was becoming a nightly ritual, the more attractive she found this bartender. There was something about his standoffishness that piqued her interest. "How long have you lived in Rocket?"

A man had come in and taken the stool next to her. Stan didn't immediately answer Lauren but first took the customer's order for a beer. An unimaginative drink, she thought. Tom preferred beer, too. He never caught on to the fine wines she'd exposed him to while they dated, and he kept only one bottle of hard liquor in his kitchen—or had until she drank it. He never replaced it.

Stan set a pint of ale on the counter in front of the man and turned back to Lauren. "I've lived in Rocket all my life. I bought this bar from Ken Wartliner the minute it came up for sale. I had my first drink here, learned to shoot pool here, got laid the first time by a girl I found in that booth right there," he said, pointing over at a red vinyl booth along the far wall. It looked the same as all the others.

"How old were you?"

"Not a polite question," he said, but he answered it anyway. "Sixteen."

"That's young. You've been around some."

He regarded her carefully, as if he wasn't sure if she was teasing or not.

"Ever married?"

"Yeah," he said. "I gave that a try once."

Dillard came in and stood in the doorway a moment, looking around the room before he took the stool on the other side of the gentleman with the beer. Stan seemed relieved to have another customer to tend to and immediately pulled out a cold glass and poured Dillard a draft beer.

Dillard learned forward to see Lauren around the man between them. "Did you get that jar from Pat?"

She shook her head. "I haven't seen Pat." She'd forgotten about the jar. In truth never actually intended to get it. "Next time he brings his dog in for a check, I'll ask." Lauren took the opportunity to assess the man next to her. He appeared to be in his midfifties, with brilliant silver hair and tanned skin. He was thin, but well built. She figured him for a runner.

He looked at her, but didn't smile, and she felt suddenly embarrassed. He didn't look away, but stared her back to facing forward, keeping his eyes on her until his cell phone rang. He pulled it from a holster on his belt and flipped it open the way Spock would open his transceiver on *Star Trek*. He answered it with a clipped "Yes?"

Lauren could see Dillard's reflection in the mirror over the bar as he tilted his head slightly toward the man. She refrained from doing the same.

"How come they canceled?" the man asked. He listened a moment. "Well, I'm not ready. I reserved the room for tomorrow. I'll be ready tomorrow. I'm not ready today." Then he hung up without saying good-bye.

Dillard's eyes were round and Lauren wondered if he was concluding the same as she. This man was planning to stay in room six. Oh, brother! And she'd thought he might be a good catch. She glanced over at him once more, but he stared her back again. He didn't look crazy. You just can't tell by looking anymore, she decided.

"Couldn't help but overhear your conversation," Dillard said.

The man turned to him. "No, but you can help from rudely commenting on it."

Dillard was either unfazed or simply clueless. Lauren imagined he received so many insults on any given day that he didn't even feel them anymore.

"Are you gonna stay at the Jemmett Motel?" he persisted.

"What if I am?" The man looked away annoyed and reached for his beer.

"Are you gonna stay in room six?" Dillard asked, his breath coming up short in his excitement.

The man turned and glared. "Yeah, I am. What's it to you?"

Dillard shook his head as if he couldn't imagine the man's bravery or foolishness. It was difficult for Lauren to tell which. "It's a poltergeist causing the problems out there."

The man seemed amused by this. "Really?"

Dillard nodded. "A woman died out there about ten years ago." He looked at Lauren as if something had just occurred to him. "What time of year did Maria die?"

She shrugged. "I didn't live here then."

Dillard turned to Stan, who was pretending to mind his own business drying glasses and putting them away under the counter. "Stan, what month did Maria die?"

Stan didn't look up, but shook his head. "Summer-time."

Dillard's eyes went so round, Lauren was reminded of a cartoon character. "That's why it's happening now," he said ominously. "It's the ten-year anniversary of Maria's death."

Stan shook his head again and turned away.

"Maria, you say?" the man asked.

Dillard nodded.

"Maria," the man repeated. He let the name hang there between them, then said it again more slowly. "Ma-ri-a."

Lauren cringed. Enough of that name, she thought.

"I guess I'll go have a consultation with Maria, then," the man concluded. He scowled suddenly, as if coming back to the moment, and swigged down the rest of his beer before standing up. He clipped his cell phone back onto his belt and paid his tab without acknowledging Dillard's theory, then left as Dillard watched him out the door with awe.

## 26

SIENNA SCREECHED and flung her crayons at Tom's head. He threw an arm up to shield his eyes from the waxy projectiles.

"Stop. Now." He took ahold of her, pulling her face up and trying to make eye contact. "Listen to me. Charlene is coming back. You need to be patient."

"She comes back now!" Sienna spat through clenched teeth.

"She will, but you need to wait."

"Now!"

Tom let his daughter go and watched her closely. She scowled at the picture she'd made—some swirling tumultuous band of purple against a brilliant orange and red background. When Tom first saw it, he was struck by its beauty. There was something about the colors that drew his eye in again and again: He'd complimented her on it, and that was when she looked up and realized that Charlene was gone. How had Sienna missed Charlene leaving? It had been hours ago. Had she been working on this picture steadily all afternoon? Tom was ashamed when he recognized his own inattentiveness. She'd been busy, and he'd left it at that. Grateful.

"Are you hungry, Sienna?"

Her face came up to meet his, though she still did not look him in the eye. Her mouth was set, her face implacable. "She comes back!"

Tom blew out his breath. "She will!"

"Now!" Sienna stomped her foot to punctuate the demand.

Tom turned to walk away. He'd make supper. Maybe Sienna would eat something and it would calm her. As he stepped through the doorway, he heard her footsteps behind him and turned as she advanced on him. She pinched his arm, digging her nails into his skin. He worked to peel her off, and she sank her teeth into his wrist.

"Damn you!" he howled.

"Stop it. Both of you." Charlene rushed through the back door, dropping her purse on the couch and reaching for Sienna. "Sienna, don't hurt Daddy."

Sienna let go and stared at Charlene, bewildered, then smiled as if nothing had happened.

Tom shook his wrist, trying to cut the sting as blood came to the surface where Sienna's teeth had nearly broken the skin.

"What's going on here?" Charlene demanded. She was staring at Tom, as if he'd done something to provoke the child.

He gestured helplessly at his daughter. "She wanted you to come back and when I didn't produce you on demand, she attacked me."

Charlene turned to Sienna and studied her. "Sienna? Why do you want to hurt Daddy?"

Sienna looked at Tom, then back at Charlene, but only said, "My book." She started toward her room.

Charlene stepped in front of her. "No, not right now. We're talking, Sienna. You need to answer me."

Sienna screwed up her face and began to twist her torso back and forth.

Tom shook his head, thinking, *Good luck*.

"Sienna?" Charlene began again. "Tell me why you want to hurt Daddy."

Sienna only twisted faster.

"You can't hurt people. It's not nice, and it's not okay."

"I *hate* Daddy."

Tom felt a stab in his chest. Hate? Why? She'd never said that before. He'd always imagined the moment when she'd look at him and say that she loved him. All these years asking her if she loved him and never getting an answer. Until now. *She hates me*, he thought. *All this time, she's hated me*.

"No, no. Don't say that," Charlene said softly.

Tom looked at the child. She seemed so alien to him, so unknowable. "Well, maybe I hate you, too," he heard himself say.

Charlene turned sharply. "I can't believe you said that!"

Tom shook his head. "I didn't mean it. I'm sorry, Sienna. You know how much Daddy loves you."

☼

Lauren ordered a fourth snowshoe, thinking she should probably ask Stan for the tab or a burger. She needed the food; drinking on an empty stomach was a stupid thing to do. She knew it. But she was enjoying the buzz, and what else would she do with her evening?

Dillard flipped through the channels with the remote control. He stopped when he found *The Tonight Show*, and Lauren was shocked at how late it was. She looked at her watch, but the numbers wouldn't remain still long enough for her to read them, rolling upward like the vertical hold on an old television.

"What time is it?" she asked.

Stan pointed at the large clock above the bar, but that one had the same trouble as her watch.

"Eleven-fifteen," he said.

"I gotta get home." She slid off the stool and picked up her purse.

Stan stepped up to the bar and started punching numbers into his register.

Lauren waved at Dillard and started for the door.

"Hey, Dr. Kent?" Stan called. "Don't forget your tab."

Lauren flushed with embarrassment. "Sorry. Thought you were going to bill me," she said.

Stan snorted. "I'd be out of business if I billed people."

"Shhh!" Dillard shouted. "Leno is talking about Rocket."

Stan turned the volume up on the television and a handful of people crowded in to see the comedian holding up a few lines of newsprint.

"According to this, people who stay in room six of the Jemmett Motel find themselves the victims *or recipients* of strange things. You might just as easily die, inherit a fishing business on the Olympic Peninsula, fall down a mine shaft, or win the lottery."

"Where's this?" Demi Moore was sitting in the chair next to him, looking sleek and at least twenty years younger than she should have. Lauren tried to remember how old the woman was. Older than herself. It made her feel dumpy to think there were ten years between them.

"Rocket, Washington," Leno said, running the *r* upward like a sports announcer.

"Sounds made-up," Demi said dismissively in her gravelly voice.

"The story or the town?"

"Both. Where do you get this stuff?"

Leno examined the newsprint a moment. "Reported by *The Sasquatch*." He looked at the camera. "Has to be true if it's in *The Sasquatch*." He emphasized the name of the paper, as if it were *The New York Times* or *The Washington Post*. The audience roared with laughter. He then announced they'd be right back with Brad Pitt. Demi smiled and raised her eyebrows seductively.

"We're in for it now," Stan said. "We thought we were overrun by crazy people before."

"Good for business," Dillard said. "I better tell Petra. She's gonna need lots of Jemmett bread when they get here." He dropped a twenty on the counter, adjusted his baggy trousers, and left.

Lauren stared at the twenty. Dillard had remembered to pay his tab.

"Thirty bucks," Stan said to Lauren.

"Thirty bucks? For four drinks?"

Stan looked wary, biting his lip. "A few more than four, and I gave you a free one for the recipe."

☼

Tom sat on the sofa and listened to Charlene talk to Sienna in the bedroom about love and how people are here to help her. He was grateful for Charlene's soft touch with Sienna, but a little resentful that this near-stranger had the power to resonate with his daughter so easily. He'd worked himself to death trying to communicate all the same thoughts and ideas to her, but she'd remained closed to him. And now she told him why. She hated him—probably always had.

Tom fingered the tubes of paint Charlene had brought, wondering if she was prepared to clean up the mess Sienna would make with these. When Charlene finally came out of the bedroom it was past midnight. She sat tentatively on the end of the sofa, out of reach. "She's asleep now."

He nodded. "I didn't mean what I said. I was just frustrated."

Charlene said nothing, but looked at Tom in that way she had that made him believe she was reading his mind. Finally, she picked up her purse and gathered her keys.

"Are you leaving?"

She looked toward the door as if unsure, then nodded. "I need to think about this."

"About what?"

She closed her eyes a moment. "I . . . this is . . ."

Tom scowled. He was being dumped, he could see it now.

"I love Sienna," she said.

"But?"

"But this just feels a little too familiar. I've already lived this. I don't know if I can do it again."

Tom said nothing. What could he say? Would he volunteer for this?

Charlene brushed away a tear. "I'm sure you've heard what happened to my brother."

Tom nodded. What was the point in pretending he hadn't?

"I know people talk. And I know what they say. It didn't happen the way they tell it. Stephen didn't do anything horrendous or illegal that night. And my mother's decision wasn't a desperate act in the heat of the moment. It was premeditated."

Tom looked away, understanding that scenario too well.

"She didn't want Stephen to know what was coming," Charlene said softly. "She made him his favorite meal—scalloped potatoes with ham. She even bought him root beer. He never got root beer because it made him jittery and his meds didn't work as well." She drew a breath and stared out the window at the black night. "I was supposed to be spending the night with a friend, but I surprised her when I came home instead after the football game."

"You don't have to tell me this."

She looked away from the window, at Tom. "You're the only one I *can* tell."

He fidgeted awkwardly, wondering if he should comfort her. But he couldn't. He didn't want to hear this.

"I guess I kind of already knew what she was planning to do. We'd had Stephen admitted to the mental ward at the hospital three times that fall. The last time he'd spent five weeks there before they were able to get his meds right. He hallucinated that Mom and I were spies sent by the government to keep track of him. He was terrified of us both. He put razor blades in our soup." Charlene fiddled with her keys as if putting the sequence together after such a long time. "My mother was standing in the kitchen loading a pistol while Stephen was watching a movie in the living room. She'd obviously practiced. When I walked in I startled her, and she made up some dumb excuse about a prowler, but I knew. And she knew I knew. Then she begged me to leave. I . . . tried to talk her out of it. It was unreal, like a bad dream. Me begging her not to do it, her begging me to forgive her. She was standing there with a loaded pistol in her hand, pleading with her sixteen-year-old daughter to forgive her. She just kept saying that it was better this way. He would never have to be locked up again. Can you imagine?"

Tom could imagine.

"I ran to the phone, to call the police. And that's when she did it. The dispatcher picked up and I heard the shot. I couldn't say anything. Then came another one."

Without thinking, Tom reached out, and Charlene took his hand. She brushed her fingertips over his, smoothing his skin, tracing the bite marks Sienna had left on his wrist.

"It sounds unbelievable, but I didn't know she was going to kill herself, too."

"I'm sorry," he said.

Charlene looked at him. "Why? It isn't your fault."

"You know what I mean."

She nodded. "All I can really remember with any certainty is her begging me to forgive her."

"Have you?"

"I've tried to do that every day of my life. But she gave up on my brother. She stopped believing in him."

"Why are you telling me this?"

"People are saying things about Sienna. About what's going on with your motel."

Tom was instantly furious, a hot spark flaring in his chest. "She has nothing to do with that."

"I know. But people always find some way to blame the weak—the ones who can't defend themselves. I'm telling you this because my mother thought what she was doing would put an end to that." Charlene laughed bitterly. "The irony is that it only fueled the stories. Nobody remembers Stephen's laugh, or his sense of humor. No one remembers that he saved Willy Baker from drowning in the Columbia when they were eight. Or that he won the fifth-grade spelling bee." Silent tears slipped over her cheeks, but she seemed not to notice them. "He's a legend now—a legendary monster. But my brother wasn't a monster. He was just a frightened, confused little boy."

Charlene's fingertips touched the bite mark on Tom's hand, then she got to her feet. "Don't let them do that to Sienna."

Tom stood as well. "Don't leave. Please?"

She looked up at him, her eyes glistening. "I need some time to think. I don't know if I can do this. And I don't want to hurt her more by staying now and leaving later."

Tom was silent as he watched Charlene go. He stood in his quiet living room, trying to sort out all that she'd told him, bouncing between devastation and fury. Why would they blame Sienna?

Hap awoke to the sound of a car alarm outside his house. He sat up and rubbed his head. He'd slept late, but it was Sunday. The alarm turned itself off intermittently before sounding again. Finally, he pulled his clothes on and looked out the window. Both sides of the street were lined with cars. He stepped out onto the porch to get a better look. Several cars passed his house, moving slowly.

A red pickup stopped in the middle of the street. The driver rolled down his window and hollered to Hap, "Where's the Jemmett Motel? I've been all over this town and can't find it."

"It's not actually in Rocket. It's out on Highway 14 about seven miles."

"Which way?"

"East." Hap pointed toward the sunrise, and the man thanked him.

Hap went back inside, showered, and then walked up to the all-night grocery. He barely knew the man who owned it. He was Ukrainian, but Hap didn't know his name. The store had changed hands so many times over the years that Rocket residents didn't bother to get to know any specific proprietor anymore, if they ever had. The place carried packaged stuff, like little powdered doughnuts that had been made weeks ago in a factory somewhere in the Midwest and were swaddled in cellophane. Or little cans of finger sausages. Hap viewed the fare as subpar and possibly even dangerous to his health, but since he'd sworn off the bakery, had no tolerance for talking to Dillard Meek, and had no reason to visit the pet clinic, this was the last remaining business on Main Street.

"Morning," the owner said as Hap stepped inside the

cramped, dingy store. The rotting floorboards sagged and creaked beneath his feet. The owner sat behind a crowded counter with an old cash register, key rings in the shape of sailboards, tiny flashlights, and chocolate eggs left over from last Easter. Behind him were rows of cigarettes, bottles of Mad Dog 20/20 and Boone's Farm wines in berry flavors with screw tops.

The place bustled with activity, reminding Hap of summers past. "What's all the commotion?"

"You didn't see?"

"See what?" Hap asked, stepping aside so the man could ring up a package of Doritos.

"*The Tonight Show.*" The owner had a barely detectable accent. "He talked about the motel."

"On *The Tonight Show*?"

"Yes. Good news for me. I need to clear out this inventory. I was afraid I would have to dump it all."

"What do you mean?"

"I'm closing. Just a couple of days to the end."

Hap shook his head. "The IGA is about done, too."

The customer at the counter turned to Hap. "It's boarded up. I went there first."

☼

A van with a satellite dish on its roof sat in the turnaround of Tom's motel. Another one sat in the parking lot and a third in the empty lot next door. ABC, NBC, and FOX had turned out from Portland bright and early. Tom had barely slept, thinking of Charlene's confession and fighting an ever-increasing curiosity about her mother. Somehow he felt like he knew the woman, though he'd never met her. He could see her so clearly, a woman in her midthirties, petite and blonde like Charlene. Dark circles under her eyes, wrinkles two decades before their rightful time. He could hear her laugh as well as her cry. A woman alone, no one to lend a hand. But he couldn't think about those things now. Not with these reporters swarming all over his motel, accosting his guests, asking questions. He'd missed his motel's fifteen seconds of fame on *The Tonight Show,* but it had lightened his mood a little this morning when he found out.

The question had been put to him so many times this morning that it now echoed in his brain. *"Do you believe something supernatural is going on in room six?"*

*Supernatural,* he thought. *No ... well ...* Tom watched a reporter powder his face and position his earpiece in preparation for a live broadcast on the morning news, standing beneath the neon motel sign, and he contemplated room six. Since Hap's article, Tom had taken a humorous approach to it all, as if it were simply a funny story. The people who had turned out to rent the room lent themselves to that idea. The motel had enjoyed a carnival freak show atmosphere. Nothing anyone took too seriously. And Tom hadn't suffered the pang of guilt when handing over the key with the six on it since Gill and Sandy left. The humor had kept the truth of what happened in that room at bay. A part of him could no longer deny the coincidence.

☼

By midday, Tom's motel was sold out and he'd been interviewed and reinterviewed eight times by different reporters. Curiosity seekers from Portland, Vancouver, Salem, Eugene, Pendleton, Bend, Olympia, Spokane, and the Tri-Cities had converged on the steps above the Columbia. They posed beneath the neon sign, or in front of the door to room six, some next to the pool. They laughed and made jokes, and pretended to get run over. Tom didn't know what to make of it all. It gave him a gnawingly uncomfortable feeling, especially since he still harbored guilt over shuttling Helen Simpson out the door and into the path of a melon-laden semi. Sienna lay quietly on her belly on the lobby floor, crayon gripped tightly in her fingers, coloring an abstract image of hot pink and yellow, laced through with eerie bands of cobalt-blue.

One man paused to gaze down at the drawing for several long minutes. Tom watched him like a German shepherd ready to lunge, hypersensitive to the fact that people were drawing unholy connections between his daughter and his motel. He stood up from his stool when the man continued to stare, preparing to send him off with a sharp word. Tom memorized his features—a dark mustache, shiny but thinning black hair, well dressed in a linen shirt and trousers. At last the man looked up and flushed pink when he realized Tom was keeping such a fierce eye on him.

"She's a fantastic artist," the man said.

Tom nodded and sat back down.

"I know art. I own the Yamhill Gallery in Carlton, Oregon." He pulled out a business card and laid it on the counter. "Has she ever exhibited her work?"

"Exhibited?" Tom looked at his daughter, who was completely oblivious to the conversation above her. "She's just a child."

The man shook his head, impressed. "Just imagine the career she has ahead of her with that kind of talent."

Tom studied his daughter, then the man. Was he a scam artist? Was he just another freak chasing karma to a motel in eastern Washington? "You didn't come to look at art."

The man flashed Tom a wide white smile. "No. I stopped to see if you have a public bathroom." He turned and looked out the front window. "What's with all the news crews?"

Tom relaxed. "I don't know. Some people think weird things are happening in one of my rooms. It's all nonsense, but it's been a bad summer and people need something to talk about."

The man laughed. "So, do you have a public bathroom?"

Tom shook his head. "Sorry. But there's a highway rest area about three miles west."

"Thanks," he said. "Any chance I can buy that piece?" He pointed at Sienna's drawing. "Or just take it on commission?"

Tom thought about taking the drawing away from Sienna and the scene that would ensue. Like taking meat from a grizzly. "She's not done with it yet, but we have another one I can show you." He went into the apartment and returned with Sienna's latest drawing.

The man's mouth came open and his eyes sparkled at the sight of it.

Tom picked up the business card on the counter and read the name: George Frazier.

"How much?"

Tom shrugged. "Do I look like an art dealer?"

"Tell you what, I'll take it with me, have it framed, then display it in my gallery. When it sells, I'll deduct the cost of the framing and my commission. Let's just see how it's received. Maybe we'll do a show for her this fall." He looked at Sienna, who still did not notice him. "Does she have any oils or pastels? Crayon will be hard to sell. How old is she?"

"Twelve. Almost thirteen."

George Frazier gave Sienna a sideways glance, now frowning thoughtfully.

"She's autistic," Tom said, reading the man's mind.

"Ah, what a wonderful story. Listen, let me get a notepad and ask you some questions. I also have an agreement form for you to sign that allows me to exhibit the painting. It protects you."

*Protects us from what?* Tom wondered, but waited for the man as he went out to his car. When he returned, Tom showed him the bathroom in the apartment.

George Frazier asked as many questions as the news reporters, but they were a welcome change of pace. Upbeat and positive, as if Sienna's future career and success as an artist were assured. He only touched on the loss of her mother, not prying too deeply. He laughed when he asked Tom how old Sienna was when they first noticed her extraordinary talent and Tom said, "Twelve, almost thirteen."

The gallery owner suggested new materials for Sienna—canvases, real paint, solvents that Tom instantly worried she'd poison herself with. He made a list of them and left it with Tom, urging him to think about it. These things would make her work more salable.

When the man drove away with the drawing carefully laid out on the seat next to him, Tom felt abandoned to the hungry, greedy wolves in his parking lot once again, and he found himself wishing George Frazier would return.

# 27

LAUREN'S HEAD ACHED as she clipped the toenails of a dachshund named Tweeter. Anna held the dog firmly, but gently, talking softly to it. She seemed pleased with herself for bringing in business, just like Lauren had asked her to do. Though today, Lauren would just as soon have had an empty schedule so she could go home and lay down. She was ignoring the messages from Ellie, pleading with her to call back. She'd left three since this morning, and Lauren thought it was good that Ellie felt bad. She'd let her suffer a little longer.

"Are we closing early today?" Anna asked.

Lauren looked up from her task. "Why? I thought you needed the hours."

"Patrick and I are going to Portland this afternoon. We'd like to get an early start if possible."

"What's in Portland?" Lauren clipped too close to the quick and Tweeter let out a yelp.

"A rare-coin dealer."

Lauren smiled to herself. They still believed those corroded hunks of metal that had once been currency were worth something. She imagined that Anna was an eternal optimist.

"I sent him photos of one of the coins through e-mail.

My mom got a new digital camera last week. It came in handy. I thought maybe one of the coins we have is rare, and this guy in Portland got really excited about it."

"What is it?"

"It's a ten-dollar Liberty Head from 1858."

Lauren nodded, though she knew nothing about coins. "It didn't look like any of those coins were in very good shape."

"This one's not bad. I was worried that it was a fake because it doesn't have a mint mark."

"Can you hand me that towel?" Lauren asked, slightly annoyed that Anna wasn't paying attention. A good assistant should anticipate her needs before she has them.

Anna grabbed the towel and placed it under Tweeter's bleeding toenail. "But it turns out that's what makes it rare."

"So how much is it worth? Twenty, thirty bucks?"

Anna shook her head. "No. He's offering us five big ones for it."

Lauren's head snapped up, and with it an ache the size of Alaska. "Five hundred dollars?" she clarified.

"No, five thousand." Anna met Lauren's gaze with those unmistakably honest eyes. "We'll be able to pay you the balance we owe for Crispy."

Lauren took in a long, slow breath. That money could have been hers.

"Are you okay, Dr. Kent?"

"Yeah, fine." She slipped the nail clippers into the drawer and did a cursory check of Tweeter's eyes and ears. "He's done." And she left Anna to ring up the bill and collect payment for the dog's unnecessary visit.

In her office, Lauren picked up the phone and called Ellie. She needed a friend right now and guessed she couldn't afford to casually throw them away.

"Ellie, it's Lauren," she said when Ellie answered.

"Oh, Lauren. Listen, I'm sorry about yesterday."

"It's okay."

"Good news. I got the autopsy report for you. But you have to promise me you won't tell anyone where you got it, okay? I don't want to jeopardize anyone's professional standing, my own included."

"I'm just curious," Lauren said. "Someone told me that Maria died of a brain hemorrhage and it sounded odd. With modern medicine and all, I wanted to know more about why they couldn't save her."

"It's true. I read through the report. Subdural hematoma. It says she fell while cleaning the swimming pool."

"Does it say anything else? I mean anything medically significant?"

"Well, I was wondering about one thing. There was a clean break in her scalp—a straight line, as if she hit a sharp edge. It's not mentioned in the report, but there's a photo of it. It had bled, but it didn't look like much from the picture."

"A sharp edge?"

"Yeah. I'm not a pool expert, but that didn't quite make sense. Aren't the edges of pools rounded for this specific reason?"

Lauren bit her lip as she thought about it. "Yes, they are."

"Wonder what it means?"

"Well, at least one person in Rocket thinks someone was involved in Maria Jemmett's death."

"What are you suggesting?" Ellie sounded worried. "You don't think Tom had anything to do with it?"

"No. But Sienna might have. She's violent. Always has been."

Ellie was silent.

Lauren realized that she needed to keep this to herself. "It's just a story that's been floating around. Well, thanks for getting that report."

"Does it satisfy your curiosity?" Ellie's voice was heavy with apprehension.

"Yeah. Hey, what are you doing next Saturday? Maybe I'll drive up there and have a look-see at Hood River. You really think there's room for another vet?"

☀

Tom handed Cesar DeRosa the key to room six. The thin, silver-haired man took it and rolled it over in his palm as if it were some sort of talisman. He appeared somber and purposeful, on a mission of grave importance. Tom watched the man, wondering what his story was. Why did he want to stay in room six? What was he hoping to find here?

"It's down at the end, in the corner." Tom pointed.

DeRosa followed his finger and looked through the lobby window, past the full parking lot and the dozen or so people enjoying the pool, then back at Tom. DeRosa scrutinized Tom for a long, uncomfortable moment, reacquainting him with the familiar unease he'd experienced in that room as he cleaned it last.

"Look," Tom said, "I don't believe anything is going on in that room. If you want your money back, I'll give it to you. There're a bunch of people waiting to rent it. You don't have to take it tonight, and I won't hold you to the guarantee."

DeRosa seized the key hard with his fist. "It's mine for the night and I'm ready now."

Tom shrugged and watched the strange man leave. The thumping of Sienna's foot against her bedroom door matched the man's footfalls on the walkway outside. Thump, thump, thump, thump. Methodical and determined. Tom had anticipated the storm this time. Sienna hadn't managed to bite him or kick him in the nuts when he could not produce Charlene. She had cried and screamed and raged against the door for nearly two hours—an all-time record, he thought. Then she fell into a rhythm of kicking it as she neared the point of crying herself out. He wasn't sure which of them was more devastated by Charlene's absence. Though he imagined it was he. He had, for some brief time, allowed himself to believe that he'd found someone to love. It made him feel foolish now.

※

Hap stood in the crowded entryway of the Windy Point Diner as a hostess he'd never seen before took names down on a piece of paper. He'd decided to leave by the time she had reached him, but Linda spotted him standing there and ushered him to the counter, where a lone stool awaited, the previous occupant's dishes still scattered on the counter with crumbs and water rings.

"Come sit, Hap," she called. "Isn't this wonderful? I'm back in business."

Hap sat down, shoving the dishes away. Three waitresses bustled through the packed dining room. "Where did you find all these employees on such short notice?"

"They sort of volunteered on the spot when they realized I had no staff." Linda nodded at a portly woman carrying a tray stacked with entrées. "That's Rhonda. She's been working since breakfast. I hope she decides to stay in Rocket; I could use a powerhouse like her. She just came out for the day to see the motel. Poor thing hasn't gotten out there yet."

"Where are the hippies? I didn't see them in the lot outside."

"Oh God, I had to have the sheriff run them off." Linda poured Hap a cup of coffee and handed him a menu. "They were shitting in the storm drain." Her voice was hushed, but the customer next to Hap grimaced at his patty melt.

"Lovely," he said.

"They promised to buy a meal each, but what a bunch of tightwads. They'd come in here and order one meal, then ask for three extra plates and split it among them."

"They didn't look like they had a lot of money to me." Hap had wondered why she thought she could get anything but trouble in the first place out of that group.

"Doesn't matter. We've got customers now. And just in the nick of time. Another week and I would have had to close my doors."

Lauren stood in the parking lot of her clinic, trying to decide where to go. She wanted to slip into the Red Tail to take the edge off, but she hadn't yet recovered from her last hangover. Besides, she couldn't afford to drop thirty bucks every night on cocktails. She didn't want to go home, that much she was certain about. She would only sit in that lonely house, thinking about Tom, Tom's daughter, and the mysterious death of her mother. Had the man been hiding something all these years? Perhaps that explained his unwavering devotion to Maria's memory. Maybe that was why he wouldn't accept anyone's advice about his daughter. He could be protecting them, not her. It made Lauren long for him—long to know the truth.

She sighed and started up Main Street, deciding to stop at the bakery for a crescent roll with cheese and a cup of coffee. Petra was usually good for a story or two, though Lauren had always believed the woman was daft.

"Afternoon, Dr. Kent," Petra and the smell of sweet, hot pastries greeted Lauren as she walked in.

A small crowd of people turned to look at her. Jay Leno had done Rocket a service, she thought. The place was packed. Too bad these people hadn't brought any pets with them. When Lauren realized there was no place to sit, she walked up to the counter, wondering if she could turn around and leave without being rude, but Petra was already talking to her in that thick German accent.

"Ve have banana bread today. Viz valnuts."

"Thanks, but I think I'll have a crescent roll."

"Coming up," Petra said. "You go sit. I bring it to you."

Lauren turned and surveyed the small dining area again. Sit where? The place was jammed. She walked to the register on the far end of the counter and leaned against the wall, waiting for Petra.

"My child," a voice said, and Lauren jumped. A tall man with straight black hair and a dark suit stood behind her. He was gangly and odd with his mothball clothes and dusty hair, but inviting in a way she couldn't quite put her finger on. Pleasingly eccentric.

"Please join me, my child." He gestured at a table in front of the window with two chairs. A mug sat on one side.

She hesitated. He seemed familiar. "Have we met?"

He smiled. "I am your brother in God."

She shook her head. "I'm not a believer." She made little quote marks in the air when she said *believer*.

He kept his eyes on her and his smile only deepened, bringing up creases in his tanned skin. It was a sympathetic smile, and he seemed harmless. She followed him to the table and sat down.

"I've seen you before," she said at last. "You were out at the motel." She began to get up again, realizing this was the man who had picketed Tom.

He put his hand on her arm to prevent her from leaving. "My work is nearly done here. I want to talk to you."

"Me? Why me?"

"Please," he said, gesturing at the seat. "Sit."

"Have you saved the motel from the influence of evil?" she asked, sitting down. She remembered now the signs he'd hung on his canvas gazebo. And the way he'd sat in his lawn chair with his arms crossed the night she cleaned Tom's apartment.

"We never truly know the impact we make. It's not for us to know. Only He knows." He pointed at the ceiling.

"So that's it? You don't know if what you've done has made a difference, but you're okay with that?"

"Ah, zer you are." Petra set Lauren's order on the table. "I see you have met ze reverend."

Lauren looked at the preacher and smiled. What was it about him?

"You, my child, must let go," he said, still looking Lauren in the eye.

Lauren gaped. She turned, embarrassed that Petra had heard, but the woman was already busy with another customer.

"Prestige and material possessions will ruin you."

Prestige? Material possessions? She squinted at him.

"You are the doctor," he said. "Do good. Use your gift to please the Lord."

Lauren was confused. She stared down at the crescent roll. "I'm not in this for prestige or material possessions. If I were, I wouldn't be living and working in Rocket."

He sat back and studied her. She felt as though his eyes were routing lies from beneath her ribs.

She ate her roll with unease as he sipped his coffee. What did he mean?

Later, at the Red Tail, after several shots of whiskey, she scoffed at the conversation. What did that weird preacher know about her? How arrogant he was to presume so much. She stared at a cable show about house makeovers on the muted television as a man who looked quite similar to Tom carried his bride over the threshold of their newly remodeled home. Letting go was not what she needed to do. She thought about Sienna. Had the child always been violent? Leopards don't change their spots, she decided. Even a toddler was capable of doing damage, especially in a full-blown rage. Tom needed her. If he couldn't see it, she'd have to show him. Lauren looked at the clock above the bar: it was eleven-thirty. Pulling out a twenty, she got up and said good night to Stan. He looked at the bill she'd left on the counter and waved.

Though Highway 14 was dark, it stubbornly held on to the day's heat, and Lauren drove the seven miles east of Rocket with her windows down. Her hair whipped around in the breeze, slapping against her skin, and it felt good. Her senses felt alive. The taste of the dry air, the smell of basalt and parched grass, made her giddy.

She took a deep breath as she neared the motel, its pink neon sign burning a hole in the black sky. It was the first time she could recall seeing the *No* in front of *Vacancy* lit up. She hadn't spent any time here before she and Tom began dating, and the place had always seemed like an empty wayside husk to her. The parking lot was full, so she pulled in to the field next door and killed the engine, then her lights, and sat there looking at the little lobby. Tom always left a small lamp with a low-watt bulb on at night. He'd be in bed, she thought. He wasn't one to stay up late. Early to bed, early to rise. She'd never heard him say that and, as she thought about it now, realized it was likelier the interruption of the previous night's sleep that had caused him to sink into bed by ten.

At midnight Lauren slid out of her Jeep and walked to the lobby, pulling the door open quietly and slipping over the ugly green carpet. The smell of coffee grounds and bleach burned her nostrils.

The door to Tom's apartment was closed, and the night bell sat in its place on the counter. She paused to study a beautiful drawing that was lying on the sofa. She had trouble making out the colors in the dim light, but she liked the way dark threads moved through the image like currents of raw emotion. She wondered who the artist was and how it had ended up there. Someone had probably purchased it at the Maryhill Museum gift shop—an inexpensive reproduction of a famous painting—then forgotten it. Impulsively, she rolled it up and taped the edge down with a square of tape from Tom's desk, then slipped it into her oversized purse. What would he do with it? He had no appreciation for aesthetics.

She knocked lightly on the apartment door, but when Tom didn't open it, she tried again, a little louder. After a moment he appeared, his hair wild, his face unshaven. Her eyes went immediately to his ear and the beacon of red sores.

"Lauren," he said. "What are you doing here?"

"I came to talk to you."

He rubbed a hand over his face, appearing annoyed. Clearly not happy to see her. "Talk about what?"

"I need to know what happened to Maria."

His lips thinned. "How much have you had to drink tonight? I can smell it from here."

Lauren ignored the comment. "Just tell me about Maria's death."

"Why?" he asked after a long silence.

"She didn't fall cleaning the pool."

"What makes you say that?" His face went dark, igniting an ember of fear in her.

Lauren chose her words carefully. "She had a clean break in her scalp. Swimming pools don't have hard edges."

His nostrils flared as he took in what she said.

She tried a softer tone. "Just tell me what really happened. I'm here to help you."

"You're pathetic," he said. "Coming out here drunk,

tossing around accusations about the death of my wife. This is because of Charlene, isn't it?"

*Charlene.* The name zinged through her.

"Well, you can go on home and quit worrying, because she dumped me."

Dumped him? Did this mean . . . Had they slept together? Anger and humiliation surged through her, each fighting for prominence.

"You really have a problem, Lauren," he said. "You're sick. Get some help." He started for his apartment.

She followed, grabbing his arm, trying to pull him toward her. "I could take this information to the authorities. Even if it was an accident, they'll lock Sienna up when they find out she killed Maria."

He turned on her, raising a fist as if to strike. She shrank back, anticipating the blow. But he didn't strike her. He held his fist in the air over her head, his fingers white with tension, his arm wound and ready to release. His face twisted with anger, and she could see that he hated her. In a sudden rush, he shoved her to the door.

"Get out," he said. "Get out before you push me too far."

☀

Tom sat on the floor of Sienna's bedroom, his back against the bed, facing away from the blood-smeared wall. He listened to his daughter howl like a worn-out coyote. Low and guttural, just a moan really. He looked at his watch. It was nearly one in the morning. He rubbed a hand through his hair, exhausted, but afraid to leave her alone. He thought through the exchange with Lauren. She *would* go to the authorities, he could count on that. He knew about the clean slice in Maria's scalp; he'd seen it that morning when he realized something was wrong with her, but he hadn't understood its significance to the lie he stammered out only a short time later. It hadn't crossed his mind until they waited for the autopsy report. Then he was certain that they would find out, and that, once they did, Sheriff Turnbull would come.

The scenario was no different today. If they investigated what had happened, they would immediately take Sienna into state custody. If he was lucky, she'd be placed in a foster home. But more likely a hospital mental ward in some run-down urban area. She'd be shoulder-to-shoulder with truly crazy people. Dangerous people.

Sienna howled. She lay on the bloody sheets, her eyes squeezed shut, her voice raw and hoarse. How would he ever explain to his daughter what a menstrual cycle was? How would he teach her to deal with it? There was only one person who would understand enough to help him. But that person understood *too* well and, because of it, had opted out.

He thought again about the mental ward; it seemed his only option. But Art Schlegel came to mind. Sienna, his teenage daughter—his beautiful, *adult* daughter. She would never escape the certainty of being victimized. Sexually assaulted, raped, sodomized. What would they do to her? He closed his eyes and tears seeped out from under his lids. He was unable to live with her, but he could never allow those things to happen to her. He owed that to Maria. He was the only barrier standing between his daughter and the depraved men who prey on the weak and helpless. It was his duty to care for this child for the remainder of his days. It was his curse: to love a child who could only bring him heartache.

"Mommy," she called.

A chill ripped across his shoulder blades. *Mommy.* She'd never said that before. He scrambled to his knees.

"I want Mommy," she moaned.

He bit down on his lip, until it hurt. He'd never known for sure whether Sienna even remembered her mother, though he'd talked about her often, showing her the picture that he kept on the dresser. Tom lifted it from its place and stared into the woman's face. He no longer recognized her, no longer felt her. He tossed the photo in the garbage, frame and all.

His eyes took in the blood on the wall again. Deep swaths of crimson, laid out like a river canyon. Mount Hood's ominous peak towering over the landscape, as if the volcano had erupted, showering the world in blood. Soon the cough medicine would kick in and she would sleep. Then he'd try to clean her up.

☀

A loud pop jolted Tom, searing across his frayed nerves. A car backfiring? But it sounded like it had come from the other direction—the back of the motel. He listened, but all was quiet. A heavy sense of dread pressed down on him. Then came voices, people shouting in the parking lot. He went out into the lobby, forgetting that his clothes were stained with Sienna's blood.

As he pushed through the front doors a man ran up the sidewalk toward him.

"Did you hear that?" the man rasped. "It was a gunshot. It came from one of those rooms." He pointed toward the corner, toward room six.

Tom pivoted, heading back for his passkey. A handful of people had emerged from their rooms and were standing bleary-eyed in their robes and underwear, asking what was going on.

"What room did you say?" Tom asked the man, hoping it was a mistake, a different room.

A woman standing on the sidewalk in front of room five pointed at a door. "Six. It came from in there. Sounded like it blasted a hole through the wall."

Tom glared at the too-familiar door. Why room six? Why not room three, or eighteen, or twenty-two? Why six? The door was dimly lit, its paint scuffed and peeling along the bottom. The knob had tarnished, as had the brass number. The numeral seemed to sneer at him. He didn't want to go inside, didn't want to know what awaited him.

"Aren't you going to do something?" someone behind him asked.

He took a tentative step forward. He knocked, but there was no answer. "Hello?" he called. "Are you okay in there?"

Nothing.

"Better go in and see," urged a man who stood on the other side of a large pickup truck. He was peering over its hood as if something might explode out of room six at any second.

"Should I call the police?" the woman asked.

"No," Tom said. "We don't know that anything is wrong." But his gut told him otherwise. The question wasn't *whether* something was wrong but *how* wrong it was?

"That was a gunshot," called another woman from the balcony above. "I'm calling the police."

An upstairs door slammed and the woman was gone. A few people hung over the railing, trying to get a better look. Tom turned back to the door, his instincts warning him off. He pounded hard on it. "Are you okay in there?"

Still nothing.

He slipped his key into the lock and felt the latch spring. He pushed the door open, then realized people were crowding in behind him. "Step back," he said. "If this was your room, would you want a bunch of people gawking at you?"

The crowd refused to move back, but didn't come any closer.

The bathroom light cast a strip of orange across the otherwise dark floor. Tom groped along the wall to the switch that lit the bedside lamp. His eyes skimmed the room, coming to rest on the mirror above the vanity. He heard a strange animal-like groan, then realized it came from himself. Tom's knees buckled and he caught hold of the drapes to steady himself. Someone had scrawled a message on the mirror in ugly red streaks. *Take me home, MARIA!*

A high-heeled foot in black stockings protruded from the bathroom, resting almost delicately on the shabby carpet. Hadn't he checked a man in to this room? Tom's attention bounced between the foot and the message on the mirror. Was this some kind of joke? The message was rendered in scarlet lipstick, his dead wife's name in large, deliberate letters.

He shoved the bathroom door open, scraping it against the body on the floor, hearing the worried murmurs behind him. The silver-haired man lay on the linoleum. He wore a black teddy with red lace, his crotch bulging grotesquely beneath the elastic edges of the negligee. Lipstick and eye shadow marred his face in garish colors. Blood pooled on the floor beneath his head, trickling into the space between the tub and toilet. A small black hole was burned into the center of the dead man's forehead. That was when Tom saw the gun, carelessly released and lying in the mess. A limp finger with bright red painted nails still curled around the trigger.

Tom read the message on the mirror again, numb and unable to collect his thoughts. He picked up a hand towel and wiped his wife's name from the glass, smearing the lipstick into a greasy mess. He worked harder, ignoring the voices behind him, scrubbing to eradicate the jeering letters. *How did this man know about you, Maria?* The name wouldn't go away. It seemed forever etched onto the surface. He worked at it, pressing all his strength into the task, now desperate to erase Maria from this place. Was she here? Was *she* doing these things?

"Maria?" he said desperately. "Are you here?"

He balled up the greasy towel and dropped it on the floor, the mirror still marred with the outline of her name.

Tom emerged from room six and into a mob of people who were noisily waiting for an explanation.

"What did you find?" asked the man who had first summoned him.

"Call the police," Tom said softly. "A man is dead." And he walked back to the lobby.

"Was it a gunshot?" someone yelled after him. "Hey! Are you okay?"

Tom didn't answer. His vision was dark, and his ears buzzed. He staggered toward the apartment door, clumsily working the knob. He yanked the door closed behind him and sank to the floor in the dark hallway outside of Sienna's bedroom, the vision of Maria's name looping around in his head.

## 28

HAP HEARD THE CALL on the police scanner summoning the sheriff out to the Jemmett Motel and recognized the dispatch code as a shooting. He hurried into his clothes, his knees stiff and painful at that hour of the night. He reheated yesterday morning's coffee in a travel mug by the eerie green glow of the oven clock, found his keys, and was heading east up Highway 14 by 2:05. The acidic liquid brought up heartburn as he swigged it down, trying to wake himself.

The drive seemed to take forever as Hap worked through scenarios. Tom was shot. Some crazy that he himself had brought out with his stupid article had killed Tom. Hap's heart walloped in his chest and he stomped down on the accelerator until his ancient van shook and rattled, trying to meet his demand.

At the motel, he pulled in along the west wall, parking out of the way of the police cruiser. The volunteer fire department had dispatched the big truck, but there was no smoke to be seen in the moonlit sky. Before he'd gotten out of his seat, an ambulance swung silently into the turnaround, its lights splashing bright colors around in the dark.

Hap found the sheriff taping off the area and taking

statements. Every guest in the place was standing in the parking lot, trying to get a glimpse inside room six.

"What happened?" Hap asked Turnbull, his breath coming hard as if he'd run the seven miles on foot.

"Looks like a suicide."

Hap scanned the crowd. "Where's Tom?"

The sheriff shook his head. "I haven't spoken with him yet."

Hap felt suddenly drained, the anxiety that had him on the drive out seeping away. Why had he imagined that Tom was the victim? He went to the lobby and knocked on the apartment door, but there was no answer. After several tries, he walked around to Tom's back door, worry on a new and urgent rise once again.

"Tom," he called. "Are you in there?" Standing on the dark stoop, he took in the desolate bluffs behind the motel, black against the inky sky. The moon cast a ruthless beam across the landscape, outlining Tom's thirty-year-old pickup. *He has to be here,* Hap thought. He tried again. "Tom? It's Hap. You okay?"

When Tom did not come to the door, Hap tried the knob. The door was unlocked. He peered into the darkened living room. He could see down the hallway and the door to the lobby. A shadowy figure hunched on the floor there.

"Tom? Is that you?"

Hap stepped tentatively inside, leaving the door behind him standing open and wondering if he should return to the van for his gun.

"Are you okay?" He moved cautiously toward the person. "Tom? Hey, what's wrong?" Hap knelt down and scanned for wounds or other evidence that might explain his behavior. "Tom?"

Tom met Hap's eyes with a hollow, devastated gaze. Hap thought of the suicide Turnbull had told him about in room six, and wondered what the scene there must have been.

"It's Maria. She's here. She's doing this."

"Doing what?" Hap asked, bewildered.

"Room six."

"What are you talking about? Maria is dead." Hap articulated it softly, gently, as if breaking the news to Tom for the first time.

"I *know*," Tom said with sudden anger.

"No, it isn't Maria." Hap scrambled for meaning in what Tom was saying. This was crazy talk.

"It's her," Tom insisted. "And everyone thinks it's Sienna."

"Tom, nothing is happening in room six. I made that stuff up."

Tom's forehead creased and he scowled at Hap. He seemed not to understand.

Hap searched for words. This had gone on for too long. "That article was mostly fabricated. I couldn't stand by and watch Rocket dry up and die without doing something. It was just a dumb story to bring tourists in."

"Dumb story? You call what happened to Helen Simpson a dumb story?" Tom sat up now, as if finding his bearings. "What about Art Schlegel or Martin whatever-his-name-was? Did you make up those dead bodies?"

"Of course not, but that was just the seed. The rest was fiction."

"Fiction? There's a man with a bullet in his head in room six. Right now as you stand here." Tom's voice rose. "Is that *fiction*?"

"Listen to me. This, tonight, it's . . . it's nothing more than a self-fulfilling prophecy. Whoever died there tonight chose room six because of what it represented. If he hadn't killed himself here, he would have done it somewhere else. Tom, nobody fell down a mine shaft in John Day. And no one was eaten by an alligator, or had a tree fall on them. I made it up."

Tom shook his head. "It's *her*."

Hap looked down at his friend, the man who always took things in stride. The motel operator who couldn't be ruffled. The father of a severely handicapped girl who stood by her side, no matter what. Tom's skin was gray, his eyes wild.

"It isn't Maria," Hap said.

"Don't tell me about my dead wife!" Tom shouted, getting to his feet. "She's all over this place. Her name is on the mirror in room six. Her daughter is screaming for her."

"Tom, look at me. Think about what you're saying. You're tired. You've been under a lot of stress. But this isn't Maria's doing."

"That man knew her name. How did he know her name? He's never been here before."

"What man?"

"The dead man in room six!"

Hap didn't know what to say.

"He asked her to take him home." Tom paced the tiny hallway. "He called her up from the dead to take him to the other side. Or she called him to her."

Someone knocked on the apartment door. Tom paid no attention to it.

"That's Sheriff Turnbull," Hap said. "He'll have questions."

"I'm not talking to him."

Hap thought that was probably the soundest idea Tom had had this evening, but he knew it would be a hard sell with the sheriff.

"Look, I'll talk to the sheriff for you—" he offered.

"Tell him whatever the hell you want, but you'd

better not go writing another goddamn article about my motel," Tom raged. His face was white with fury.

Hap worried Tom might actually attack him. "I'm not going to write an article, Tom. I promise."

"Promise? From a man who makes up lies about my life?"

Hap drew a breath against the accusation. True though it was, the loss of Tom's respect peeled him to the core, stripping away his worth and self-respect like a dead husk. "I'll talk to Turnbull," he said quietly.

Tom turned stiffly. "Don't let him in here," he warned. "I don't want anyone near my daughter."

Hap slipped out into the lobby, where Sheriff Turnbull waited.

"Where's Tom?" the older man asked.

"He's . . . pretty shook up. I don't think this is the best time to question him."

Turnbull considered this, turning around and looking out the lobby window at the parking lot, now filling with cars and people, then at room six. "I need to know who this guy was."

Hap rummaged through the stack of cards in the drawer beneath the counter, looking for the one with a handwritten six. When he found it, he handed it to the sheriff. "His name was Cesar DeRosa."

☼

Tom watched the door close behind Hap, looked in on his sleeping daughter, then stepped out onto the back porch and into the warm night air, tipping his head back to view the sky. Stars twinkled down at him in overwhelming numbers, like a jury of ghostly spirits judging him. He thought of Sienna and her cries for a woman who would never come to her aid. A woman who could not offer her comfort. Despite everything, he couldn't fathom why God would punish the child.

And Hap's admission that he'd made up everything in that article—Tom couldn't grasp that. Hap didn't make up what he'd seen on the mirror.

He walked around the side of the motel where Gill and Sandy had parked that first morning he'd met them. What about those two? They were not fabrications, were they? He hadn't seen them since the day they moved to the apartment above the auto shop, their future suddenly bright with possibility. Had he only imagined them?

Tom spotted Hap's van where he expected to find it. He peered through the windshield, then around the corner of the building to make sure no one could see him. He didn't want to answer any more stupid questions. He was done answering questions. Cars were pulling out and onto the highway, one after another, his guests streaming away in a current of red taillights. Scared off. That suited him fine. He wanted to be left alone. He thought again of that lying son of a bitch; there was only one thing he wanted from Hap now.

Tom opened the van door with a creak and popped the glove compartment. He knew Hap kept a gun in there; the man had told him so when they were first getting to know each other on one of Hap's visits to deliver papers. Tom felt around inside until his fingers closed on a cool, smooth object. He pulled it out and stared down at the shiny metal. He slid the gun into his jeans pocket and shut the door.

Inside his apartment he placed the gun under the sofa cushion, then listened through the door as Turnbull questioned Hap and Hap made a reasonable show of answering. Others were there, too, the boldest, nosiest people who had urged him into room six.

"I need to talk to Tom," he heard Turnbull say.

"Can it wait?" Hap asked. "He's not dealing with this well."

Tom snorted. He heard the sheriff agree by way of a grunt, and a moment later Hap came through the door.

"They're taking the body away now," Hap said. "But Turnbull wants the room left as it is until the investigation is complete."

They could have the whole fucking motel; Tom didn't care.

"Just as well, I guess. Tom—you need some help. Can I call someone?"

"There's no one to call."

"What about Charlene?"

Tom laughed.

Hap watched him warily. "Can I take you somewhere?"

"You can leave—leave my motel, leave my life. Just get the hell out of here. You've done enough damage, haven't you?"

Hap lingered, as if unsure whether he should agree to these terms, but after a moment he seemed to understand that it was not his choice. "Sheriff evacuated the motel. Everyone is leaving. He was afraid someone would tamper with the room if you weren't available to watch over it until morning."

When Tom said nothing, Hap left quietly.

☼

Tom roused Sienna and handed her a doughnut before she was fully awake. The Rocket bakery had left them on the front step as if nothing had happened the previous night, as if he had a motel full of guests and room six wasn't saturated with blood and lipstick. Tom had first laughed aloud at the absurdity of finding the pastries there, but immediately recognized their value.

"I love you, sweetie," he told her.

Sienna blinked at the blood-smeared wall as she bit into the powdered doughnut. She seemed not to recall where this came from.

"Today you can have as many of those doughnuts as you want."

She reached into the box and grabbed the two nearest to her, hugging them protectively against her stomach. She's no dummy, he thought. Take 'em while they're offered and don't trust promises. He smiled at her, but she didn't look at him.

"Come on, sweetie. Get up and get dressed. We're going for a ride today, you and me."

She stuffed the rest of the powdered doughnut into her mouth, crumbs and sugar cascading down her front like a snowy landslide, then grabbed two more with her free hand.

Tom pushed the box toward her. "You carry the doughnuts."

She dropped the pastries back in with the two dozen others and got up, looking down at the bulge in her panties from the sanitary pad with a mix of confusion and worry.

"Leave the Band-Aids and let's go potty."

She did as he asked, surprising him.

Tom put the new paints that Charlene had brought for Sienna, along with her crayons and paper, on the pickup seat. He added a small sack with extra clothes, knowing they wouldn't likely need them. As Sienna dressed in the bedroom, he examined the gun. The .38 Special was old, but it was loaded. He wondered if he needed to practice with it first. He could stop and buy more ammunition, then take it out onto the open prairie and squeeze off a few rounds to make sure it worked properly. He thought only briefly of Hap and his lies. It didn't matter anymore; Tom had dismissed the friendship, refusing to feel anything for the man. The suicide and Maria's presence was still raw in his mind, though the daylight brought new perspective and he no longer imagined that Maria was responsible for what had happened here. She was simply finishing her business with him. He had always known that he'd failed her by allowing her to fall into a coma and die. His lack of attentiveness haunted him and it was because of that that he'd been so devoted to Sienna. But he'd failed Sienna, too. It had been folly to ever imagine he could protect the child. That's what his dead wife had returned to point out—as if he needed anyone to tell him so. He needed to get Sienna in the truck and out of here before Hap found his gun missing.

Tom didn't look back at his motel as he pulled onto the highway in the crisp morning sunlight. The summer haze had cleared, leaving the sky such a deep blue that it had penetrated his single-mindedness for a moment, causing him to briefly contemplate the coming fall. He didn't bother to turn off the neon sign or lock his apartment. He didn't close the pool gate or turn off the coffeepot in the lobby. The smooth pavement rolled under them as his pickup strained to accelerate, its engine knocking. Sienna destroyed the rest of the doughnuts by crushing them into piles of crumbs, unwilling to let go of her treasure even now that she was too full of sugar and grease to eat them.

Tom thought of Charlene. Did he owe her anything? He guessed he didn't. She'd chosen her path and so had he. She was the only person who had come to mind as he worked through the individual tasks of his plan. He understood that he was in love with her, the only woman who had stirred that emotion in him since his wife. But there was nothing more for them to say to each other, and no reason to consider the other's feelings. He could appreciate the brief joy she'd brought him and his daughter, but not the vacuum she'd left behind. And for that—perhaps—the reason for the pain he was about to knowingly cause her would be understood, if not forgiven.

# 29

HAP STARED AT THE CLOCK, counting every second before finally calling Charlene at six a.m. and waking her up.

"God, Hap. It's not even seven yet," she wailed, her tone heavily laden with annoyance and sleep.

"It's Tom. I'm worried about him."

Charlene made grunting noises on the other end of the line. "So you call me? Go wake *him* up."

"I . . . I can't."

"Christ. And men say they can't understand women." Her irritation seemed only to grow. "Why can't you?"

"It's a long story."

"Well, I'm up now. So you better start singing."

"Remember that article I wrote?"

"Yeah," she said, yawning.

"Well, I made most of it up."

"I *knew* it!"

Hap could hear her moving around now. "I did it because I thought it might help bring in some business and save Tom's motel—not to mention the rest of Rocket."

"Oh, nice try."

"Truly. I never—"

"Wait, wait, wait," she interrupted. "At least two

people died out there this summer. You didn't make that up."

"No, but I made up all the rest."

"I can't believe you two would try and trick people like that."

"I didn't tell Tom. He didn't know."

"You fucking idiot."

"It's worse," he said. "Last night someone committed suicide in room six."

Charlene went silent.

"Somehow the guy got Maria's name and scrawled it on the mirror before he dressed up as a female prostitute and shot himself." Hap waited for a response. He heard nothing. He wasn't sure Charlene was still there. "Tom lost it. I've never seen him like that. He kept babbling about Maria being responsible for the stuff going on in room six. He thinks it's her."

Charlene still didn't speak.

"Charlene?"

"You are so fucking stupid," she said.

Hap sighed. He reckoned he deserved this. At least she was still speaking to him.

"I'm going out there," she said quietly.

"Wait, I'll come with you."

"Fine. Pick me up in ten minutes."

Tom slowed as he came into Rocket, but kept a keen eye out for Hap Mitsui. He didn't want to run into that lying bastard today or ever. As he passed the auto body shop, Gill and Sandy were standing on the street. Little Gill was perched in Sandy's arms, wearing a white sun hat. The family smiled and waved at Tom, watching him go by with Sienna. He nodded, but didn't smile in return. They were real, though. He hadn't imagined them.

He turned off the highway at the all-night grocery and took Park Street up one short block, pulling in along the sidewalk behind the old sandstone facade of the Rocket Hotel. A place where people wouldn't see his truck and he could get what he needed before heading out of town. He glanced over at Sienna, who was sifting the doughnut crumbs into a gooey mess.

"Sweetie?"

She didn't look his way, too deeply immersed in what she was doing.

He reached over and touched her chin. "Sienna?"

She looked at him then, but pulled away from his touch.

"I need to go inside the store, but I'll be right back. I'll bring you a pop if you're a good girl and don't get out of the truck."

She followed his mouth as he spoke.

"Can you do that?"

"Yes."

"I won't be very long." He slid out of the truck, locking his door. Hers was perpetually locked. He paused to make sure she would do as he asked, but she had gone back to sifting through the remains of the doughnuts, her hands slimy with maple syrup and sugar. She occasionally lifted a finger to taste test her creation. The novelty would keep hold of her attention for hours.

The store was long and narrow with high ceilings. Tom had been inside only once before and had admired it then for what it had once been: the elegant lobby of a grand hotel. He'd imagined its parquet floor and ornate chandeliers, its carved mahogany parlor sets with marble-top tables. Gutted now, and replaced with second-rate and extremely overpriced merchandise. Today he simply stepped up to the counter and purchased a box of .38 shells for the gun, a short case of Budweiser—the only brand left—and the last can of

Mountain Dew in the refrigerated case. He regretted that
the lack of choices had left him with a highly caffeinated
beverage, but a promise was a promise. And on this day
in particular he was not going to disappoint his daughter.

The shopkeeper had glanced repeatedly at Tom as he
wended his way through the store, collecting his odd assortment.

When Tom pulled cash from his wallet, the storekeeper said, "You own the motel out on the highway."

"Did. Belongs to the bank and Satan now."

The man took Tom's money, eyeing him warily.
"Bank owns this place, too. Or will the end of the week.
Closing at noon today, and never opening the doors
again."

Tom looked around the dingy store with its empty
shelves, then up at the stamped tin ceiling, the last rem-
nant of its high-Victorian styling. "This was the first hotel in Rocket," he said, mostly to himself. It still had a
way of invoking romantic ideas.

The man couldn't take his eyes off Tom's ear. "It's a
dump now."

"Too bad. It has good bones," he said, touching the
bite wound that had scabbed into a ridge of rough knots.

The man then joined Tom in studying the ceiling,
shaking his head. "Someone should burn it down."

Tom picked up the sack with his box of shells, his
beer, and the can of soda, and started for the door. But
wishing not to be recognized on the street, he turned
back to the man. "Is there a back door?"

The store owner nodded and pointed to a gap between the coolers at the back. "It's not for public use, but
I don't care if you go out that way. Just be sure you shut
the door behind you."

"Thanks," Tom said and worked his way down the
rows. Beyond the coolers was a tiny, filthy bathroom,
then a storage area cluttered with cleaning supplies and a

huge cast-iron sink. A mousetrap sat near the splattered
baseboard, a nearly decapitated rodent with bulging eyes
in its jaws. He pushed through the last door, and came
into a small vestibule with a glass door facing the street
where his pickup was parked. The floor was decorated in
tiny octagonal tiles in muted brown and blue, giving it
the appearance of an ancient Greek mosaic. To his left
was a lathe-turned newel post at the base of an ornate
open staircase. Tom paused to peer up at the second-
floor landing, illuminated in purple and yellow by the
stained-glass window there. He looked back at his truck
and Sienna, her head bent low over her creation.

Tom thought a moment. It had been his intent to find
a quiet, remote road that led into the basalt rocks.
Someplace where Sienna could paint or color, while he
practiced with the pistol. But he hadn't any particular
place in mind. He was woefully unfamiliar with the landscape out there. He'd been chained to the motel all the
years he lived in eastern Washington. And he wondered
if practicing might somehow make the ultimate chore
more difficult. Perhaps it was best done cold.

He looked up the stairway again, wondering what
was up there. Would it suit his purpose? It was somehow
poetically appropriate, he believed, that the end would
come in a defunct hotel on the bluffs overlooking the
Columbia.

Tom crept up the stairs and onto the second-floor
landing. The boards squeaked beneath him, but the
building was sound and straight. A long hallway, stud-
ded with doors, jutted away from him, toward the front
of the hotel and Main Street. At the back was another
door to what looked like a small apartment. Probably
the proprietor's quarters, he thought. Not wanting to
alert the shopkeeper downstairs, he stepped to the door
at the back of the building and tried it. It stuck at first,
then shuddered open, kicking up a cloud of dust. The

room held a tattered sofa beneath the window and a cast-iron bed with a sagging mattress, striped and stained. An ornate woodstove sat to the left, and a refrigerator from the 1950s stood in the tiny yellow kitchenette. The sink and pine cupboards appeared to have been an afterthought. Three doors along the far wall led to two tiny bedrooms and a bath. The apartment sat above the city park and Lauren's street, but he didn't imagine he could hold that against the place. Except for decades of dust and dead flies, it was empty.

He heard someone shouting on the street below and peered through the window. Two young boys were dancing around his pickup, making faces at Sienna, taunting her. They appeared to be close to her age, perhaps a little older. One leered at her through the window, contorting his face as he stood inches from the glass.

Tom took the steps two at a time, forgetting about the noise, and leaving behind the sack. He burst through the back door, leaving it standing open, as one boy was baring his ass for Sienna, and the other was shouting "freak" at the window. When they saw Tom, they scattered, but the one with his pants down couldn't get away. Tom snagged him by the shirtsleeve. The other ran up the street with the speed of an Olympic sprinter and didn't look back.

"What the fuck do you think you're doing?" Tom snarled.

The boy stammered and coughed.

"Answer me, you little shit!"

The boy wailed, tears spilling over his freckled cheeks. Tom shoved him to the ground.

"Who's the freak here? Who's sitting in the dirt with their ass on parade?" Tom kicked gravel at the boy, his fury burning out. He looked through the windshield at his daughter, who stared out with wide eyes.

The boy got to his feet, cowering in Tom's shadow. "I—I—I didn't mean it," he stammered.

Tom looked at the child. He *was* just a child. And he saw himself in the boy. He had been that way, too. Stupid and unsympathetic. He had taunted the retarded kids and made fun of them on the school bus.

He reached down and took hold of the kid's face, bending low. "Why did you do that?" he asked.

"Miles," the boy said, pointing up the empty street where the other kid had disappeared. "Miles said she was ... she was ..."

"She was what?"

"She was the devil."

Tom pulled the boy's chin up sharply. "Why would he say that?"

"C-cuz of what's happening at the motel."

"Well, you give Miles a message for me. You tell Miles that *I'm* the devil. And that I'm gonna come after him if he keeps spreading lies. Tell him his ass is mine." Tom let the boy go and watched him struggle not to sob. "You got that?"

"Y-yes."

"Then get the fuck out of here!"

❖

Charlene climbed into Hap's van with her face set in a hard scowl, angrily silent.

"Morning," he said cautiously.

"Well, it sure as hell ain't a *good* morning."

Hap didn't respond but pulled onto the highway and drove through Rocket, barely keeping his speed down to the limit.

"Why didn't you call me last night?" she demanded.

"I almost did."

"Well, you should have."

"Tom made it sound as if you two were . . ."

Charlene sat stiffly in her seat, glaring out the window. She wouldn't look at him. "How's Sienna?"

"I don't know; she slept through all the commotion."

"Well, thank God for small miracles."

As they passed the bakery Hap and Charlene both scrutinized the place. "That preacher is always camped out there now," Hap said. Reverend Shelly's handmade signs were propped inside the window again.

"Nazi bitch," Charlene said as Petra stepped out on the sidewalk to clear the tables.

At the motel, they found several news crews in the empty field next door, undoubtedly banished from the premises by Sheriff Turnbull. Hap overheard one talking about the suicide. The sheriff and a team were going through room six with gloved hands and tweezers. A photographer was taking pictures.

Charlene brushed into the empty apartment. Hap followed on her heels. She searched from room to room, pausing in the bedroom doorway, turning visibly pale. She just stared in, drawing conclusions Hap could not read.

He stepped in to see what she saw. The place was awash in bloodstains, from the bedclothes to the walls. "What happened here?" he asked shakily.

Charlene turned back toward the lobby, but Hap lingered a moment, mesmerized by the mess.

"Coming or staying?" she called to him. It sounded like a taunt to Hap.

☀

Tom peered through the storage room and into the grocery store, watching the shopkeeper count out his till. The commotion had not roused the man from his spot, and Tom had been divided about simply going back for the sack and then heading out into the gorge in search of some private spot, or staying here. He liked this building, though. It offered some unarticulated comfort. He turned back to the tiny vestibule and the now-locked door and coaxed his daughter upstairs and into the apartment. Once inside, he gave her the can of soda pop, which she took to the dusty sofa and examined closely, fascinated by the metallic green design.

He laid out her crayons and paper. He'd need to keep her quiet until the shopkeeper was gone. He opened the paint set that Charlene had brought. It had fat plastic tubes of red, yellow, blue, black, and white. He wondered about purple and orange, green and brown, but reckoned that Sienna would be happy with any colors, she loved them so. There were two paintbrushes inside: a large one and a small one. He set them next to the tubes. She'll have fun making a mess with that, he thought.

Tom opened a beer and went to the window in the corner, from which he looked down Park Street at Lauren's bungalow. Her Jeep was missing from the driveway, and he briefly wondered what she would think when she heard the news. She would righteously conclude that Sienna had in fact killed her mother, and she would be vindicated. Would she spread the news the way she talked about Charlene's mother? Was Charlene's warning, in fact, a prediction?

He drank down half the can, leaning against the glass there, surveying the little town of Rocket. Most of the homes along this street had *For Sale* signs optimistically planted in their yards. Half again had *Price Reduced* stickers pasted over the original signs. On the eastern horizon a row of wind turbines stood stoically still. Monuments to man's foolishness. Nature always gets the last word, he thought. Sienna was all the proof needed.

He turned back to her. "I love you, Sienna," he said, but he wondered if he really did. He couldn't feel it anymore.

She ran her finger over the smooth surface of the Mountain Dew, can then licked off the condensation, oblivious to his sentiment.

"I really do," he said, trying to convince himself.

☼

Lauren found the preacher sitting at his familiar table inside the Rocket bakery. His signs were propped in the window, and he sipped a cup of coffee while staring out at the quiet street. She'd not slept the night before, thinking about Tom. He'd frightened her, and she had considered several ideas, from trying to convince the sheriff that Maria's death couldn't have been a simple fall, to calling social services again. But ultimately, it was the preacher's words that resonated. She must let go—let go of Tom. She understood that. She was ready—more so than she'd ever been. She had one last thing to do first, and she sought the preacher's advice. This odd man intrigued her and drew her in.

"Sunday morning and the reverend is having coffee," she said. She felt her face flush, and she was suddenly self-conscious. How could she speak so casually to this man? As if they were old friends.

As he turned to her and smiled, all her hesitation departed.

"I thought you might be gone already," she said.

He nodded. "My work is now done."

"It isn't, though," she said.

Reverend Shelly stood and pulled the chair out for her to sit, gazing down on her like a benevolent father. He made her feel like a little girl in his presence—innocent, small, and without knowledge. When they were seated and eye to eye, she could hardly hold his gaze.

When he didn't answer her question, she said, "Tell me what I should do. I know about the murder of Tom Jemmett's wife and I need your help."

He took her hand, sending a jolt of electricity coursing up her arm. "Your work with animals is noble in the
eyes of the Lord."

She stared into his dark eyes, confused. "But—"

"Shh," he said. "Let go of your head."

She scowled and tried to pull her hand back, but he
held it tightly. "What do you mean?"

*"Feel it,"* he said.

She stared at the strange man.

"Let go," he urged. "What do you see?"

"Someone has to do something. Sienna Jemmett is
growing up. She's violent. She'll hurt others."

The preacher sat silently waiting. He shook his head.

"Don't you understand?" she asked, frustrated. "I
need your help."

But he refused to speak. He only stared into her with
that intense gaze, as if he looked upon her soul. He caressed her hand.

"Do you see the elk?" he asked.

"Elk?"

"They are not God's pure creation."

She scowled, remembering the conversation with
Ellie. "Yes, yes, I know. They carry red deer. But . . ."

He let go, leaving her hand cold and clammy and
sipped his coffee, casually looking at her. "Those are
game-farm elk. They'll kill the wild population now that
they're loose. You have work to do."

"But—but I'm not a game vet. That's not why I came."

He got to his feet again, this time as if leaving.

"Wait," she said.

"You no longer need me."

"But I do." She followed him out into the hot morning and stood on the sidewalk, shielding her eyes against
the sun as she tried to read his face. "You picked the
Jemmett Motel because you knew terrible things were
happening there. It isn't over. She's still a threat."

"I have the Lord's work to do and so do you. You
must let go." And he lumbered down the street away
from her.

☼

Tom opened his third can of beer. It had begun to
warm, but he saw no point in checking to see if the tiny
refrigerator worked. Sienna lay on her belly in the dust
and debris, smearing paint around on her sketchpad with
her fingers. Her face was streaked in yellow and red
where she'd pushed her hair from her eyes, making her
look as though she had donned war paint. Tom had first
worried about the mouse droppings on the floor, but dismissed the threat of disease. Sienna had far more to fear
today than that. He walked to the window again and
gazed down at the street, watching the shopkeeper carry
several boxes to his car and return to the building. When
would this man finally leave? Tom wondered.

He walked out into the hallway and stared down the
long corridor. He tried the doors, peeking inside the
empty rooms, their wallpaper faded and peeling. Seeking
some unknown thing that might ground him again and
prevent him from carrying out his terrible plan. He examined the bare bulbs hanging down like suicide victims
in their stark loneliness, and envied them. He ran his fingers over the warped glass panes, and watched Lauren
Kent follow the itinerant reverend up the street. She
talked at him in her usual rapid-fire way, her hands moving around her, jerking this way and that. What was she
telling this man? It didn't matter.

At last, the storekeeper pulled away, leaving Tom and
Sienna alone in the hotel. Tom swallowed hard and
turned back down the hallway. Inside the apartment he
threw back the last of the beer in his can in one long swig
and examined the pistol. He'd had little experience with
guns, only having ever owned a .22 rifle for hunting. But

he'd been too softhearted to actually shoot an animal—a flaw that had bothered him as a young man living in Wyoming. He made sure it was loaded, then opened another beer and sat down on the sofa with the gun resting quietly against his thigh as he watched his daughter mix the colors into orange and purple and deep, deep brown. Sienna, he thought. She's found sienna.

Her cheeks were flushed in the stuffy room, and he let his eyes slip over her every curve and feature. Her nubby nose and long, black eyelashes. Her rosebud lips, pressed tight in concentration. Her hair, tangled and matted, caught a ray of sun from the window, alighting it in auburn so red he wondered if they should have named her that instead. She looked so much like her mother just then, Tom winced and looked away. When he looked back, she had paused from her work to taste the paint. It was nontoxic, of course. Charlene would not have made that mistake.

Tom set the beer can aside and scooted down onto the floor next to his daughter. She didn't acknowledge him. He touched her hair, running the back of his hand along her forehead. She tipped away from him slightly.

"You look just like her, you know?" he said softly. "She loved you, Sienna. Mommy loved you."

Sienna looked up for the briefest of moments, her brows pressed tightly together as if the statement hurt.

"You're right to hate me. I . . . I am a bad man."

"Bad." Sienna echoed without looking up.

"Yes," Tom said. "Bad." He drew a long breath. She deserved to know the truth. "I hit your mother and she fell."

Sienna looked up again. "Hitting is bad."

"Yes, it is." The memory flashed through his mind. Maria rushing at him, slapping him. Shouting that she couldn't take it anymore.

Maria had pleaded with him that day. "She's too

much for me to handle. She scares me. Tom, you have to *listen* to me. We have to do something."

Tom had turned his back on her. He wouldn't listen to this nonsense. He wouldn't drug his daughter. They had agreed. But Maria came after him and struck him hard on the shoulder with the heavy rotary-dial telephone he'd just replaced and set near the door. Pain seared through his shoulder as the phone clattered to the floor, the bell chiming out of tune.

"I hate the child!" Maria shouted. "Sometimes I want to kill her!"

He closed his eyes now in the hot upstairs apartment, but it didn't stop the image of Maria's head snapping back as he backhanded her across the cheek. He'd lashed out without thinking, just wanting to put an end to her furious words. She slammed against the door jamb and slid onto the carpet at his feet, screaming and holding the side of her head. Then she went quiet a moment, lying motionless, her arms and legs limp. Silhouetted in the doorway behind her stood Sienna. She stared down at her mother with curiosity. Before Tom reached Maria, she'd staggered to her feet and was on her way back to the apartment, crying and swearing that she hated him with all her heart.

"I didn't mean to hit her so hard," Tom told his daughter.

Sienna smeared the rich paint around on the dusty floorboards, lost again to her own world.

"Silly Daddy. I thought if I was the best father you could ever have, it would take the bad away. You know, sweetie?"

Sienna didn't respond, and Tom felt empty. He could confess his deepest sins to this child and still she did not know him. She'd never know him.

"I killed your mother," he whispered. "But they think it was you. I'm so sorry, baby. All I can do is protect you, sweetheart. And this is the only way I can see to really protect you."

He lifted the gun and put it near his daughter's temple, but his hand trembled uncontrollably and he set it down again. After a moment, he put the gun to his own temple and breathed in and out until his hand steadied. Then he turned it back on her. He set the barrel lightly against her skin.

"Forgive me," he whispered. "I love you."

She reached up to push the object away, grasping hold of the polished metal. He jerked back, but the gun was now in her line of sight and she stared at it with fascination, running her hand over it. Feeling it. Her thin fingers, spattered with paint, curled around the barrel as she looked at him, her eyes coming up to his lips, then his nose. Finally, she met his eyes, sending a shock rocketing through him.

"Let go," he said softly.

She grasped the gun tighter, pulling it toward her chest.

Tom pulled it back, suddenly afraid she would hurt herself, but she wouldn't let go. She tried to wrench it away from him, squeezing down on his fingers so tightly he thought she would cause the gun to fire.

"No! Let go!" he said.

She refused, fascinated and using both hands now to take this strange object into her possession.

"Sienna, please," he begged.

She looked up again, still gripping the barrel of the gun. She smiled, mesmerizing him. Then she said, "I... love... Daddy."

Tom's breath flew away like a rush of startled birds. He instinctively released the gun to her and reached for her, pulling her into him.

She struggled to get away, whining. "No," she said. "No touch."

He kissed her, hugging her against him.

"No, Daddy. No touch." She was flailing to get free.

The shock of the percussion took a moment to register. Tom turned, and searched madly for assurance that she was not injured. His daughter stared at him, blinking and stunned as the gun clattered to the floor. Then she screeched so loudly that Tom winced from the pain of it. She dropped backward with a thud, and Tom felt frantically along her arms and legs and over her body for wounds, but he found nothing. He kicked the gun away and it went skidding under the sofa, then he released his shrieking daughter. It had been the noise that frightened her, he thought. He closed his eyes. It was only the noise.

Tom sat on the floor, horrified that he had endangered his daughter and grateful that nothing had come of it. What kind of man was he to do such a thing? He didn't want to kill his little girl. He didn't want to kill himself. How could he have ever imagined that he did? It wasn't until he opened his eyes that he saw the blood pooling on the floor. He struggled to his feet, trying to reach Sienna, who had rolled into a ball in the corner of the room, sobbing.

"Sienna?" he called. "Sienna, are you okay?"

But it was he who was bleeding, and he realized that now as he tried to stand. His shoulder was thick and numb and his left arm dangled strangely at his side. His vision clouded, and then went dark.

## 30

WHEN TOM REGAINED consciousness he was sprawled across the floor and Sienna was standing at the wall, painting a ruby scene, some familiar place of sweeping hills beneath a sky of rose-colored clouds. He swam through a tide of emotion, tossed around between delight and despair, hope and helplessness. *Everything* had changed. This connection he'd so long sought, suddenly and fleetingly there, then gone again. But its presence had been real. The words she spoke—*I love Daddy*—had reached into him and taken hold of every trace of his soul. He finally felt her.

And now he lay bleeding at her feet, unable to help himself. He slipped in and out of wakefulness as he watched her work, stroke by stroke, building an image, creating a whole. It struck him, what Charlene had meant now: steps toward good. One foot in front of the other, until they could look back and see how far they'd come. Patience and persistence. Sienna was illustrating that simple concept for him with every deliberate touch, every carefully chosen stroke of color she applied to the wall. How had he missed it?

"Stay awake," Tom admonished himself, feeling the dull thickness in his head as it overtook him. The place was sweltering in the late-day heat, and he dragged himself across the floor to the window, where he pulled himself up to look onto the street below. He struggled to push the sash up a few inches, so he might call down to someone, but there was no one to hear his plea. A breeze rustled through, rousting a giant dust bunny from beneath the sofa. He sat down again, exhausted and struggling to stay conscious, and watched his daughter.

"Mommy comes back," Sienna said absently, getting Tom's attention for a moment.

He awoke again sometime later. It was nearly dusk and his collarbone was throbbing, his head aching. Tom looked down at the red floor streaked with finger marks. Sienna had been using his blood for paint. She was down on her knees, working the bottom edge of her wall mural. The sight of it stunned him. She'd painted the Columbia Gorge as it had appeared every day from their motel. A vast, sweeping landscape with a vivid river at its center, gleaming like a rare gem. Mount Hood floated out to the west, muted and hazy. The river gorge transformed from right to left, the rock ridges working their way out of the westerly trees to carry the plateau evenly eastward. In the fore, thick and clumsy streaks—the grassy plain. And clouds tinged in ruby and purple amassed in a stormy sky.

"The gorge," Tom rasped, his head and body aching. "It's beautiful, Sienna."

A steady breeze was pushing through the window, and he breathed in the new air, wondering if it was real or just some cruel illusion. A windy afternoon at the end of a windless season—too late to save them.

Sienna worked without interruption, placing the finishing touches on trees and rocks along the river's edge. The breeze blew harder.

Tom dragged himself upright, knowing he had to stay awake and get help or he would die. *Justice,* he thought.

He'd come to kill them both, but instead Sienna would kill him first. He'd lived his life underestimating this child. And as he gazed at her creation, he saw what George Frazier and Charlene saw. Unlimited potential.

"Add surfers," he said, not sure why, except that the scene was somehow unfinished without them.

She looked at him, unconcerned that he was bleeding. Unaware that he was near death.

"You know, the little colored sails we see on the river."

"I know," she said with mild irritation and began to press dots into the river.

"Beautiful," he said. *You're beautiful,* he thought.

"Beautiful," she echoed.

A sudden, forceful gust howled in through the open window, scattering the empty beer cans and blowing dust against the baseboard. Tom peered up at the sky, which had abruptly gone gray and ominous. Out along the ridgeline the wind turbines made a lazy revolution with their narrow blades as if practicing a synchronized dance and not quite getting it right.

He looked back at the mural. The more surfers Sienna added, the faster the turbines seemed to move, until they struck their rhythm of one hundred and twenty revolutions per minute.

"Three hundred houses electrified," he said aloud. "Three hundred times..." He counted the turbines on the hill. "Six." He scowled, working the stupidly simple equation. "Eighteen hundred homes. Keep working, Sienna."

The wind steadied into a hard and persistent drive, pouring in through the window, bringing up a moaning whistle. It carried the cool and barely familiar scent of rain.

Sienna meticulously added sails to the river.

Pride for his daughter swelled in Tom as he looked at

her painting. And he wished he'd told someone about the art dealer. Who would make sure Sienna got to paint? Who would see to it that she was allowed to explore her talent? *I can't die,* he thought. *How will you become what you can be if I'm not here?*

Sienna paused from her work. "Mommy's here."

"No, baby."

"Let her in."

Tom listened and realized someone was pounding on the door downstairs. He laughed aloud, remembering that he had locked it. Whoever it was wouldn't get in; he'd made sure of it. He stretched his face to the window.

"Help," he called, but broke down coughing. "Help," he tried again. His voice was small and weak, and the effort caused his vision to go dark. "Sienna," he said. "Go downstairs. Open the door."

She kept on drawing.

"Sienna! Please do as Daddy asks."

Still she drew.

"Sienna, please." Tom's voice fell away. Could he burden her with this? Would she understand later, perhaps wake up and remember that her father had begged her to save his life and she hadn't responded? "Baby, Daddy needs help. Go downstairs and open the door. Please."

She kept on drawing. His heart sank. Then she sighed and trundled out of the room, leaving Tom to wonder if she would follow his instructions or get distracted in the store down there and leave him to die alone in this dusty, mouse-infested room, his blood smeared into a mural on the wall. He closed his eyes again, believing this time it was for good.

"Tom? Tom?" It was Charlene. She stood over him, shouting.

"What are you doing here?" Charlene worked with

speed and efficiency, staunching the blood flow at his shoulder with her blouse, leaving her in a skimpy tank top. "Tom—Hap went for help. Someone will be here soon."

Tom could see the fear in her face, though, and it frightened him, too. "It's a nice old building, don't you think?" he said, trying to make light.

"You goddamn son of a bitch!" she whispered.

"Listen," he gasped. "She didn't do it. Maria. Sienna didn't do it. I did."

Charlene ignored him, bent over his wound.

"It was an accident. I didn't mean to kill her. Please . . . take care of Sienna for me."

Before Tom knew what was happening, Charlene was hitting him.

He put his arm up to shield himself, but her blows came hard, catching him in his jaw and across his eye. Her fingers were already crimson and he couldn't tell if it was old blood or new.

"How could you do this to me?" she screamed.

He deserved this, and somehow knowing that he was getting what he had coming made him laugh out loud. He let her beat him, accepting each impact, but still couldn't contain his laughter. Her presence here was so sweet.

"Goddamn you," she cried, sobbing. "How could you do this to me?"

"You?" he said, his voice hoarse.

She paused in midstrike.

"You didn't want us."

Charlene crumpled against him, crying.

He struggled to put his arm around her. Tears streaked her face and he held her, listening to her sob.

"I hate you, Tom Jemmett. I fucking hate you."

"I love you," he said.

# About the Author

Heather Sharfeddin grew up in Idaho and Montana, the daughter of a forester turned cattle rancher. She currently lives near Portland, Oregon, with her husband and son. Her previous books include *Blackbelly* and *Mineral Spirits*.